## EARLY PRAISE FOR DANCE AMONG THE FLAMES BY TORI ELDRIDGE

"With *Dance Among the Flames*, Tori Eldridge gifts us with a tale as dark as the holds of the Portuguese slave ships that carried the Yoruba gods from Africa to the New World. A stunningly original novel that breaks new ground with every shocking turn."
—**F. Paul Wilson, New York Times bestselling author of** *The Keep*

"With *Dance Among the Flames*, Tori Eldridge looks for light and hope in the darkest corners of the human heart. She mixes mysticism and horror with seduction and vengeance to conjure real magic."
—**Jonathan Maberry, New York Times bestselling author of** *V-Wars* **and** *Ink*

"Tautly written, mystical, and action-packed *Dance Among the Flames* will take you on a wild, thrilling ride through centuries and continents. Eldridge is at the top of her game, delivering an irresistibly sweeping adventure that will linger long after the gripping story ends. Don't miss it!"
—**Lisa Unger, New York Times bestselling author of** *Last Girl Ghosted*

"Tori Eldridge's *Dance Among the Flames* is a mesmerizing blend of ancient dark magic and horrors both mystical and man-made. It was compelling, disturbing, beautifully crafted...in other words, I loved it!"
—**Lisa Morton, six-time Bram Stoker Award® winner**

"Eldridge wields her darkest magic yet in this sensual and richly layered novel of poverty, privilege, and power. Vibrant and brutal, *Dance Among the Flames* is a cultural triumph."
—**Lee Murray, Bram Stoker Award-winning author of** *Grotesque: Monster Stories*

"Compulsively readable, with prose so smooth and evocative the pages fly by."
—**Tim Waggoner, Bram Stoker Award-winning author of** *Writing in the Dark*

"The cost of justice is high in *Dance Among the Flames*, born in the fire of Tori Eldridge's radiant imagination. The journey begins in a Brazilian favela where characters are transformed by the need for hope. They discover power can flood through a body, allowing them to become more than human. I thoroughly enjoyed this glorious adventure!"
—**Linda D. Addison, award-winning author, HWA Lifetime Achievement Award recipient and SFPA Grand Master.**

"*Dance Among the Flames* is a fascinating page-turner of a novel, rich with details yet written with a lushly sparse elegance that manages to immerse the reader in the story, settings and characters without sacrificing pace or action. A winner!"
—**Dana Fredsti, author of *Blood Ink* and the Ashley Parker series**

"Beautiful, gripping read! The storyline of Tori Eldridge's *Dance Among the Flames* is so incredibly strong, the voice so unique and clear, the character development so rich, that I did not want to put this book down... or end. The chilling suspense of Stephen King's *Carrie* meets the near-autobiographical cultural saturation of Alex Haley's *Roots*. Powerful on so many levels."
—**Sandra Brannan, author of the Liv Bergen Mystery/Thriller Series**

"Fueled by the power of a warrior goddess, *Dance Among the Flames* is a rich story of sacrifice and strength. It's full of spirit, magic and the energy of the gods."
—**Cynthia Pelayo, Bram Stoker Award nominated poet and author of *Children of Chicago***

"*Dance Among the Flames* is an evocative, erotic, mystical deep-dive into the roiling cauldron that is race, culture and family. It transports readers to another time and pulls them back again to this one, satisfied, wiser. What a tour de force. What fun! Tori Eldridge brings the fire!"
—**Tracy Clark, winner of the 2020 Sue Grafton Memorial Award for the Cass Raines Chicago Mystery Series**

"Fascinating characters, exotic locales, and a very original plot all combine to create an enchanted reading experience. Tori Eldridge's most ambitious novel yet. You simply cannot afford to miss out on this one."
**—Thomas F. Monteleone, 5-time winner of the Bram Stoker Award**

**5-Star Review:**

"Tori Eldridge weaves an expansive, mystical tale that evokes the best of James Clavell and Alex Haley. The same tenacity and resilience we love in her Lily Wong series is here. But *Dance Among the Flames* is so much more. Tori has crafted a Homerian epic that explores every dimension of the human experience with beautifully crafted prose that often approaches poetry. A grand achievement to be savored."

# DANCE AMONG THE FLAMES

Tori Eldridge

Published in North America and Europe by Running Wild Press. Visit
Running Wild Press at www.runningwildpress.com Educators, librarians,
book clubs (as well as the eternally curious), go to
www.runningwildpress.com.

ISBN (pbk) 978-1-955062-08-4
ISBN (ebook)978-1-955062-01-5

For my husband, Tony, without whom
I might never have put words to a page.

# Prologue

## Hameau de Vieille Forêt, France 1560

Exú crouched on the rocks, his sleek skin blending with the night and his golden eyes shining like stars, while below, the young witch burned. Her screams pierced through the crackle and pop of exploding sap and the cries of indignant and horrified villagers, who only a week before, had believed Colette to be the sweetest, most beautiful girl in Hameau de Vieille Forêt.

How quickly they turned. All because of one lecherous priest.

Exú shifted on the rock so he could sit on the edge and dangle his long black legs over the side. No one would see him. Even in plain view, naked in a forest on a winter night, there was only one person in all of France who could see him uninvited. The boy. And even then, only in the form Exú had chosen to assume.

But the boy was not looking up at the rocks. He was crying at the bound feet of the witch, the person he loved more than anyone in the world. The girl who was about to die.

Révérend Père d'Amboise thumped his staff on the wooden platform, like an emperor on a stage, lording his power over his pitiful congregation. If he knew what kind of power Exú would bestow on him centuries in the future, his greedy heart would rejoice.

1

# Becoming

"If it were ever to rain soup, the poor would only have forks."
– Brazilian proverb

# Chapter One
## São Salvador - Bahia, Brazil 1974

Serafina breathed in the salty air of São Salvador as her newborn, Carlinhos, shuddered in his sleep. He had gorged himself on breast milk after humiliating her on the bus with his screams. Now, he dozed in sweat-drenched peace.

She wiped the milk drool from his jaundiced chin and smiled. How like a male to throw a fit, take his fill, then pass out, secure in the knowledge that a woman would clean up the mess.

Serafina checked for traffic then hurried away from the boats to the bustling Mercado Modelo, the famous banana-yellow market where locals hawked their arts and crafts, and tourists richer than her dined on Brazilian cuisine. Such a cheery evolution from the custom house that had stowed her ancestors as they came into port. Back then, slavers had packed her people with crates of perfume and wine. If today went as planned, Serafina would buy a bottle of each.

The narrow sidewalk opened into a plaza in front of the market and afforded Serafina her first glimpse of the sixty-three-meter elevator that connected Lower Town at sea level with Upper Town on the cliff. Long neat buildings perched along the top of an escarpment, so sheer it looked as though God had chopped the land with a giant ax. From below, faded multi-colored apartment buildings reached up from the sidewalk like the scaly fingers of an old person's hand. Even with their busted windows and fluttering laundry, any of them would have been better than the hovel where Serafina lived.

She hugged Carlinhos to her chest and darted between buses to the other side of the avenue where the Elevador Lacerda would take them to the top. Usually, she opted for the cheaper funicular or hitched a ride up the steep roads. Today, she would travel in style.

She nudged Carlinhos awake as the elevator began its climb. "Open your eyes, little one, and see what God has made."

Beyond the looping roads, docks, and boats, lay every shade of blue from the aqua ocean to the sapphire and azure sky.

"See how it shimmers, my love? Like a precious jewel, only for you."

Carlinhos was special. Serafina knew it, despite the sad resignation in the midwife's eyes as she had swaddled his protruding belly and concave chest. All babies were ugly at birth, and all mother's said things they didn't mean in the throes of unbearable pain.

"It hates me. And I hate it," Serafina had cried, as the baby refused to come out.

The midwife clutched her beads and spat on the floor. "Foolish girl. Who knows what spirits are listening? Shut your mouth before you draw their attention to you."

Serafina was not a fool, no matter what that awful midwife had said.

The shock from Serafina's dearest friend had been harder to dismiss. The older woman had nearly fallen out her window in her eagerness to hold Serafina's baby, but when she saw him, she had pulled back in alarm. The pity in Carmen's voice had been even worse.

"No worry, querida. You still young."

"What does that have to do with anything?" Serafina had said.

"You will have other children. You could save the name."

"I don't need other children."

"Não, of course not. But if you did…"

The implication had followed Serafina onto the bus, ruined her mood, and caused her baby to fuss. Everyone had stared, not from admiration for Serafina's towering height and stunning beauty, but at the squirming, screeching creature in her arms. Even the woman in the window seat beside her had turned away after begging Serafina to "feed the damn thing" and shut it up.

Serafina had never felt so embarrassed nor as determined as she did in this moment. She and Carlinhos would prove them wrong. All he needed was a strong mother to show him the way. That way began with the cobbled avenue toward Jesus Square.

As Serafina walked through the historic town, named Pelourinho for the pillories that used to lock the necks and wrists of disobedient slaves, she could almost hear the loud cries of the auctioneer and the softer cries of human chattel. The African slaves would have stood naked on the blocks, examined, degraded, bought, and sold.

What did she have to complain about? She had a house to live in, a baby to love, and a man who would soon take her out of the slums. Serafina had many blessings, but they did not stop her from wanting more. She dreamed of living here, in the Pelourinho District of Upper Town, where pastel-colored buildings lined the road like Easter candy, and happy voices shared the gossip of the day.

She fancied herself the wife of a governor—for that is surely what her lover would become—living in a great mansion that overlooked the Bay of All Saints. He would have to divorce his present wife first, but Serafina was not too worried about that. She was young and beautiful, and if she continued to do well in school, she would certainly earn a high school diploma in the next two years. Her lover's wife was a frumpy, old cow.

Serafina paused at the giant stone cross in the center of the square and gazed at the church of São Francisco. The exterior was appropriately plain while the inside held the most ornate gilding she had ever seen. The opulence would have shamed Saint Francis, but

7

Serafina loved it, just as she loved the quaint cobbled roads and pink-and mint-tinted dwellings where people lived and loved, worshipped and vexed; where housewives in flowered shifts leaned out their windows to smoke cigarettes, tattle on husbands, and shout rude remarks at younger women like her.

"Ha, look at this. The tart has a package."

"Watch it, Olivia. That might be your daughter's brother in that blanket."

"Are you joking? I wear my man out."

Serafina ignored their taunts and turned into the alley, a selling feature of Henrique's apartment that allowed them both to enter and leave from different roads, thereby maintaining his reputation. The neighbors knew, of course. There were no secrets in the Pelourinho.

As soon as she slipped inside, Serafina switched on every light. She loved the luxury of electricity. Her family bootlegged their power and only had enough to run a tiny refrigerator, a small television, and one hanging bulb. Nothing like this. Henrique's love nest had outlets and fixtures in every room, even the closet. Later, he would scold her for wasting money, but she could not resist. Everything looked so cheery in the imitation light, including Carlinhos.

"You are beautiful, meu amor. But you need to be cleaned up before you meet your papai."

She wiped the snot, changed his diaper, and had just laid him down for a nap, when keys jingled outside the front entrance. Serafina raced for the couch. Henrique was particular about his welcome. While he loved the length of her limbs as they wrapped around his hips, he did not appreciate her towering over him.

"Where is my sexy Amazon?"

His voice sent a shiver of fear and expectation up her spine. She had been without him for six months. Her body craved his touch. More importantly, her heart craved reassurance that, one day, she would become the wife of Governador Henrique Evora de Novas.

She shifted on the couch with worry. Would her heavy breasts revolt him? Would her newly rounded ass make her look like an old fat cow? Bile rose from her churning belly and stung her throat. She swallowed it down. Now was not the time for childish insecurity.

Henrique took a long look at her shapely form, strategically arranged on the couch. "Linda maravilhosa. Exactly as I want to see you."

He shrugged the linen jacket off his narrow shoulders and draped it meticulously over the back of a chair. Regardless of the season, Henrique always wore a suit. After smoothing out the wrinkles, he unknotted his tie and unbuttoned his shirt. The trousers came off as well. No matter how horny he was for her, Henrique never let his trousers pool at his ankles. He was an esteemed member of the Legislative Assembly of Bahia not a whoring João-nobody. Only when every article of clothing had been appropriately folded did he lower himself on top of her.

Serafina sighed deeply as he kissed her neck and buried his face in her swollen bosom. During their long separation, she had tried to arrange a meeting in the usual way, a coded telephone call to his secretary, and had been told to "wait until she was done."

Serafina had cried for weeks over those words. She cried louder, now, as Henrique's thrusts ripped through her newly-healed flesh.

She pressed her mouth against his chest to muffle the sound and, if not for the rules, would have clawed his back to shreds. Mercifully, it ended as abruptly as it had begun.

Henrique grinned as he brushed tears from her face. "How sweet. You are overcome with emotion."

His misinterpretation nearly brought another surge of tears, but he kissed her quivering mouth and flashed his politician's smile. "Go and freshen up. There is food in the kitchen. You can fix us something to eat."

Serafina nodded at the familiar direction and rose, but instead of heading for the kitchen, she paused. "I brought your son to meet you."

"Hmm?"

"Your son, meu amor. He's sleeping on our bed. Shall I go and get him?"

Henrique groaned with what sounded like satisfaction and rolled onto his side for his post-ravishing nap.

Deferred but not resigned, Serafina headed into the kitchen. An hour later, she stirred the pot and breathed in the perfect balance of palm oil, garlic, lime, and simmering shellfish. Fine cooking was a skill Henrique appreciated almost as much as the things she did with her tongue. Had she not been so shocked by the pain of post-birthing sex, she would have given him a lick of that skill as well.

"Is that meal of yours ready yet?" he called, from the couch.

She covered the pot of Moqueca and emerged from the kitchen, clad only in a red bib apron and flawless skin. Her encounters with Henrique always followed the same agenda: a grunting sprint, a nap while she cooked, a sensual meal, and a marathon of deviant exploration. Serafina had other plans.

She called over her shoulder as she headed for the bedroom. "Almost ready. But first, a surprise."

When she emerged, she found Henrique sitting on the couch, naked and aroused. One glance at the bundle in her arms and his happy expectation deflated.

"What the hell is that?"

"Your son, meu amor, Carlinhos Evora de Novas."

She placed the bundle in his lap. Carlinhos squirmed out of the blanket, blinking and gaping against the mucus that crusted his eyes and nose.

"He is beautiful, não? He has your mouth. And your nose too, I think."

Henrique shook his head and held his hands apart so they wouldn't touch Carlinhos.

Serafina pushed them back. "Be careful, my love. You must hold him or he will wiggle off your lap."

"No."

"But he's your son."

"I said, no." Henrique stood, forcing Serafina to grab Carlinhos before he fell. "I have three sons. Three healthy, handsome, legitimate sons. I do not want that…thing."

"But—"

"Enough." The outburst upset Carlinhos, which angered Henrique even more. "Get rid of it."

"Rid of it?"

"Throw it away." He brushed his groin as if a filthy residue remained and pulled on his pants. "I never want to see or hear of it again."

She clutched Carlinhos to her chest and ran for the bedroom before either of them could cry.

*Throw him away?*

How could Henrique say such a thing? Before she could think of an answer, Carlinhos nuzzled her breast and rooted for her nipple. The timing could not have been worse. She needed to fix herself up and soothe Henrique's fury, not nurse a baby. But when Carlinhos couldn't get past the bib of her apron, he started to fuss. Soon he would cry. Then, he would scream.

Serafina sighed and settled herself into a chair to nurse. They had only just begun to calm down when Henrique marched into the room and threw a wad of money onto the dresser.

"Be here Friday, one o'clock. Alone."

He left the room and shut the door to the bedroom, the apartment, and her heart.

Carlinhos choked on her milk and gasped for air. His jaundiced skin turned beet red as he struggled to breathe. How would he survive if he couldn't even eat? What a fool she had been. Carmen was right: She should have saved the name for a healthier baby. This one would be dead within the week.

She lay Carlinhos on the bed, put on her clothes, and stuffed the money into her bag. There was only one path for her out of the favelas. Education was great, but no one was going to hire a girl like her for a job that paid well enough to change her life unless it involved cooking or fucking. Even then, she'd be stuck in the favelas like her mother and every other woman she knew back home. Her only choice was to play the obedient slave, please her master, hoard every centavo Henrique gave her, and hope that, one day, she might be able to buy her freedom.

As she cleaned the kitchen and dumped the uneaten moqueca, she tried not to think of Carlinhos asleep on the bed.

*No*, she corrected herself, *the infant, unwanted and unnamed.*

She needed to distance herself from his—*its*—unfortunate fate. She would have other sons and give the name to one of them. No one would blame her. She was barely more than a child herself. Everyone knew the infant was doomed.

By the time she finished cleaning, Serafina's heart felt as cold and numb as her water-soaked hands. She returned to the bedroom for her things, folded the swaddling blanket to hide the infant's face as she picked it up, and headed out the back door.

Was it asleep? Was it dead? The thought did not alarm her as it would have this morning, when she still believed her future was bright.

*Throw it away.*

Henrique's words looped through her mind as she locked the door and headed to the garbage bins in the alley. She had only meant to toss in the diaper, but when she lifted the lid, she saw a perfect den for an unwanted soul. She pulled out the cardboard box of castoff clothes, carried it to a neighbor's stoop, and laid her bundle inside.

"Goodbye, little one. Someone will find you and give you the love you deserve."

She walked away and covered her ears as it mewed. So intent was she on tuning out the infant's distress that she didn't notice the danger until the man slammed her into the wall.

He bashed her head against the stone and yanked at the bag on her arm. She couldn't see. She could hardly think. She wrapped her arms around her waist and hugged it tight as he pulled. The money inside her bag was all she had left.

She screamed for help, but the sound wouldn't leave her throat. With nowhere to go, the cry grew in desperation and burst like a geyser from her mind: *Help me.*

The force of it stole her breath and weakened her knees. The day was cursed. No one would come. Nobody cared.

*Help. Me.*

A blow to the face smacked away the last of her resolve. Not only would she never be free, she wouldn't even survive. Instead of slithering to the ground, robbed and stomped to death, a powerful strength entered Serafina and turned her despair into rage.

The darkness cleared.

The pain dissolved.

Serafina's sight honed in on her attacker like a hunter to its prey as unfamiliar thoughts entered her mind and spoke from her mouth of their own accord. "You dare to touch me, you insignificant ant?"

She grabbed the man by the throat and lifted him onto his toes. "No one touches the Queen of the Wind and Rain. No one defiles Yansá and lives."

She hurled the man across the alley and screamed in fury when he only bounced against the stone. Her goddess force should have blasted him through the wall. Why was he even alive? She reached for her hunting knife and howled when she didn't find it strapped around the thigh of her jaguar-hide pants.

Serafina gripped her head and fought against the lunacy that had taken over her mind. Where were these thoughts coming from? Where had she found the strength to fight off that man? Before she could answer, her attacker crawled to his feet and fled.

The power and ferocity that had filled Serafina left her in a rush.

She crumpled to her knees, hugged the bag to her chest, and rocked it like a child. Someone had helped her. God? An angel? She tried to recall the name she had spoken, but it slipped from her mind like smoke. All she knew was that someone—or something—had cared.

Was that all it took to save a life? Show up and care?

Carlinhos wailed from the stoop. He must have been crying this whole time, yet no one had come to help. No one in the world would ever care for him.

Serafina hurried back to the stoop and lifted her baby from the box of castoff clothes.

"Hush, Carlinhos. Mamãe is here. I will protect you. I am strong enough for us both."

# Chapter Two
## Favela Tainheiros - Bahia, Brazil 1984

Serafina watched as Carlinhos dribbled the ball through his opponent's defenses. How strong he looked, dodging this way and that. As strong as any other ten-year-old boy in the favela. He darted around a girl and dribbled off the dirt road and up the refuse-ridden shore of the Mangrove swamp. As he maneuvered to score, the town bully kicked Carlinhos' legs out from under him and dropped him hard onto the gravelly beach.

Serafina wanted to run to his side and cradle him in her arms. Instead, she willed him to stand and return to the game. When he did, she sagged with relief.

Carmen chuckled and beckoned Serafina to her paneless window. "He's getting stronger, eh?"

Serafina shrugged. "Like any other boy."

It had taken years of coaching in the sport children loved most to make Carlinhos acceptable to his peers. Although he was still weaker, at least they let him play.

Carmen leaned over the rough windowsill of her brick and mortar hovel. She had moved to the Tainheiros slum about the same time as Serafina's parents. As a result, both Carmen and Serafina's family lived in sturdier dwellings built on solid ground rather than the stilt-shacks that had extended over the muddy water of the inlet.

*Had.* Not anymore.

Serafina had lost friends when some of those shacks had collapsed, taking the rickety bridges with them. That's when the government had finally torn them down and built what they had assumed to be affordable housing a few kilometers away. Of course, what the government could not seem to grasp was that when a person had nothing, even the cheapest rent was too much to pay. Instead, the homeless emigrated down the coast and rebuilt their stilts over the next swampy inlet. Now *those* shacks extended all the way to Rat Island. All the government had accomplished was to shift the suffering from one slum to another.

But who was Serafina to object? She and Carmen now had waterfront property courtesy of the government of Bahia.

"We've been lucky," Serafina said.

"You and the boy?"

"You and me."

When Serafina was little, the beach was left open for fishermen to drag in their catch, and children could run without dodging wooden posts. After Carlinhos was born, the only concession the squatters made was to dump their garbage in the swamp at the far end of the beach. Every month, more of them came, piecing together their flimsy shacks and bridges from scraps of wood, plastic, and tin. Some survived the storms. Some did not. They were gone. Serafina and Carmen remained.

Her craggy friend sucked air through the gaps in her teeth and spat "Luck got nothing to do with it. I come to Tainheiros Favela early, like your parents, before half of Bahia come to steal our jobs."

Serafina grinned. "Oh really? You helped build the railroads?"

Carmen waved her hands. "Okay, maybe not *my* job. But when I first come, the sand was white."

"White? Now I know you're exaggerating."

Carmen touched her heart and raised her hand to the sky. "Swear to God. As white as the mayor's ass." She leaned farther out her window and stared at Serafina's feet. "How you gonna run in those fancy sandals?"

"Why would I need to run?"

"Don't be stupid. A woman always needs to run."

"Is that so? Well, maybe I'm not a woman. Maybe I'm a goddess."

Carmen laughed, doubled over the window sill, and thumped the wall.

"Lean any further and you'll eat dirt."

"Ha. I'm not the dumb one who think she's a goddess. Why are you so dressed up anyway? You don't look ready to slave in a rich folk's kitchen to me."

Serafina smoothed the dress over her flat belly. "They went to the country, so I'm going to the city to surprise Henrique."

Carmen's mood pivoted as keenly as one of the futebol players. "Men don't like surprises, querida."

Serafina felt a stab in her heart as she remembered that painful surprise ten years ago. It had taken a lot to overcome her anger and resentment, but she had continued the affair to build a future for her and Carlinhos. "Não faz mal. He will like this one."

Carmen clicked her tongue and frowned. "That's what they all say."

"You're such an old goat."

"Better a goat than a lamb. You want to surprise your wolf? Go ahead. But don't come crying to me after he eat you alive."

"And how would I do that? Climb out of his belly?" Serafina turned her back and waved. "See you later, old woman. I have a man to surprise."

"Don't *old woman* me, I'm only twenty years older than you. When I was your age, boys chased me not the other way around. You hear that? And I never need no fancy sandals."

Serafina laughed and continued down the road. It took less and less to get Carmen agitated these days. At least it gave her something to do.

Serafina had never really noticed how alone a forty-six-year-old spinster could be.

Thank God for Carlinhos and for Henrique, the man who had given her son to her. Although Serafina hated her lover's cruelty and indifference, she had continued their affair and bound him to her, cock, belly, and soul. She wasn't a whore, as her father had claimed, she was a pragmatist who understood the limits of an adulterer's affection. Henrique would never divorce his wife, but he had almost given Serafina enough money to move their son out of the slums. Until that day, she would ply him with fine food and deviant delights.

Her optimism darkened as a storm brewed over the Bay of All Saints and sent a biting wind through the windows of the bus. The pregnant clouds with their bellies drooped over sediment-churned water reminded Serafina of unhappier times. The foreboding continued when she arrived in São Salvador, and the Lacerda Elevador lurched up the escarpment to Upper Town. Stones caught her sandals as she strode down the cobbled road. An emaciated dog lifted a leg and urinated in her path. A gust of wind toppled garbage into the street. Even the Pelourinho's quaint Easter egg buildings loomed over her, as if threatening to fall. As if the town itself was turning her away.

In Jesus Square, Capoeira players practiced their martial dance to the rhythmic twang of a birimbau's wire. Serafina paused to watch their languid acrobatics and smiled.

"See," she told herself. "Not everything is bad."

As if to prove the point, she turned down her usual street and was greeted by the neighborhood wives as they smoked on a stoop. "Hola, Serafina. Tudo bem?"

She was proud of the courtesy they afforded her after all these years.

Serafina unlocked the alley door and reached for the light switch. It was on. She walked cautiously into the hall. In all the years she had been meeting Henrique, he had never arrived first. Today, he had no reason to even expect her.

A low groan drew her into the apartment.

"God, you are beautiful. Yes…oh…just like that."

Serafina froze.

Henrique stood in the middle of the room wrestling with the buttons of his shirt. When freed, he let the garment fall carelessly to the floor over the trousers rumpled around his ankles—*rumpled*—while a light-skinned Brazilian girl posed on the coffee table like a stalking cat. The girl flipped the long strands of her sun bleached hair away from her face and exposed a long neck and an eager mouth.

She could not have been more than fifteen.

Henrique rocked his pelvis forward and offered his erect penis like a treat.

Although Serafina had begun her affair with Henrique at roughly the same age, she saw things differently now and could not stand by and allow him to take advantage of a child. She marched into the room and yanked him away from the table.

Henrique tripped on his rumpled pants and fell on his ass. "What are you doing here?"

"Stopping you from committing a crime."

He scrambled to his feet and pulled up his pants. "What crime? You were sucking my cock when you were younger than her."

"You bastard."

"Come on, Serafina, you know how I feel about you. This is just…" He gestured to the naked girl. "A thing."

The girl shrugged off the insult then swayed her back to show off the goods. "Forget the old lady and come back to me."

Serafina didn't wait to hear more. She stormed out of the apartment and into the alley. A moment later she heard Henrique running behind her, yelling for her to wait.

The neighborhood wives laughed and shouted.

"Better run faster than that, governor, or you'll lose your precious sweet."

"Save your legs," another said. "There's plenty of pussy right here."

"Don't get your hopes up, Olivia. He needs a pro to drown his sorry goose."

"Oh, I'll take his money. And he can drown his goose between my thighs."

The women roared their approval as Olivia raised her skirt and undulated her flab.

Serafina smiled at their support. Let Henrique have his child prostitute: She'd find another way to make money and build a better life.

# Chapter Three

Carmen placed a mug of tea on the table in front of Serafina, fetched a carton of milk from the ice chest, and poured in a generous amount. "Hot tea burns pain from the heart. Milk soothes your organs."

Serafina eyed her skeptically.

"Don't give me that look. Your mother not teach you anything?"

Serafina shrugged and drank her milky tea, comforted by its warmth. "I never should have gone. You were right. I was a fool to surprise Henrique."

Carmen grunted and motioned for her to drink more.

Serafina complied. "The girl was only a child."

"So were you."

"She called me an old lady."

"Forget about her. What you gonna do about him?"

"Do? What is there to do? I swallow my pride and find another man to please."

"Wake up, Serafina. I'm talking about punishment. Retribution. How you make that child fucker pay."

Serafina stared in shock. She had never heard Carmen speak this way.

"People do what they do, but you can't let them get away with it. If you don't punish, they steal your power."

"How can I punish a man as powerful as Henrique? Withhold sex? Big deal. He can get as much as he wants for a price."

Carmen patted Serafina's shoulder. "Go home and think. When you ready to act, come back to me."

Serafina did as she was told and found the men in her family sweating on the couch beneath the glare of a naked hanging bulb. No fancy lamps. No switches on the wall. Just an ugly bulb and string.

Pai glanced at the doorway and paused to let his gaze roam over Serafina's body in a way no father should. "About time you got home. Your mother needs help."

Her eldest brother chimed in. "Verdade, Serafina. We're starving." At twenty-five, just one year younger than her, Paulo had achieved his life's ambition of becoming an obnoxious, sexist sloth like their father.

Serafina shoved the plywood door and bounced it shut.

"Hey," said her youngest brother. "We are trying to hear."

Eduardo sat on the tattered couch, mimicking Paulo and Pai, their filthy feet on the cloth-draped crate that substituted for a coffee table. Their shirtless backs sweated into the upholstery. More disgusting was the vacancy in their eyes as they indulged in their family's sole luxury: a small black and white television, on which a rowdy game show crowd ogled a bikini-clad contestant.

Serafina looked from the grainy screen to the ugly couch. From the drooling faces of strangers to the salivating mouths of her father and brothers. From one audience of idiots to another. And seethed.

If Pai and Paulo had not stamped out every trace of sensitivity in Eduardo, her formerly sentient brother would have tuned into her rage. He would have sensed the shift inside his sister. He would have looked into Serafina's eyes and seen the darkness rising in her soul.

# Chapter Four

The next day, Carmen took Serafina to a cottage in the forest to meet Isolda, the Mother of Saints for the terreiro where Carmen worshipped. The Mãe de Santos had a bright smile and a determined nature.

"How can you know so little about your heritage?" Isolda asked. "Candomblé? Umbanda? Macumba? You must have heard at least one of these names."

"I've heard of them," Serafina said, "but my family is Catholic." She didn't add that her mother considered them to be blasphemous slave religions.

"Are you acquainted with the gods?"

"Of course. The Father who generates, the Son who is begotten, and the Holy Ghost who proceeds." Not only did Serafina attend Sunday mass, she had studied the catecismo. She might live in the slums, but she wasn't ignorant.

Isolda smiled. "My child, those are only a few of the gods, saints, and spirits here to help us." She gestured around the room at the hundreds, perhaps *thousands* of stone, metal, wood, porcelain, and clay idols that adorned her window sills, furniture, and floor. "All of these deities are available to guide us."

Serafina cringed. The idols, especially the one of Jesus, disquieted her. She wouldn't have minded if the sculptors and painters had depicted the Son of God the way she was used to seeing him—pale skin, kind eyes, shoulder length hair—but some of the artists had created renditions that were both unsettling and compelling. Priests made of onyx had sweeping white robes and tall, three tiered staves. Kings wore silver crowns and strings of white beads. Warriors wielded swords and shields.

"That is Oxalá," Isolda said. "Jesus Christ as you know him. He and Olorum—God Almighty—are but the beginning of a long list of deities we may know and honor, and in so doing, receive guidance." She took Serafina's hand and gave it a squeeze. "Forgive me for saying so, but you are in much need of guidance."

Carmen slapped Serafina's shoulder. "See? Even the Mãe de Santos agrees." She turned to the Mother of Saints. "Serafina has a rich man in the city who treats her like dirt. And what she do? Throw herself at his feet."

Isolda peered up at Serafina as if examining her for clues. "Come. It's time to learn more about you."

Serafina followed carefully as the tiny woman wove through the towers of stacked treasures and precariously placed curios. She did not fit in this toy house and had to turn sideways and cross her arms in front of her stomach to keep from toppling it all. Carmen took an easier route, wide enough for her squat figure to pass. When they made it through, Isolda placed her hand on the high back of a dark wicker chair.

"This one is for you I think, Serafina. And this, my friend," she said, gesturing for Carmen to take the unvarnished wooden chair across from her, "is for you."

Isolda chose a gracefully-carved, gold-painted chair with a rounded back, no arm rests, and a well-worn red velvet cushion. The mismatched chairs looked ridiculous around the square wooden table, yet somehow fit perfectly once Serafina, Carmen, and Isolda had taken their seats as if the chairs had been waiting for them to arrive.

Isolda unfolded a white cloth and smoothed it on the table top. "Do you know the Búzios? The oracle?"

Serafina shook her head.

"Well, no matter. They will know you soon enough."

Isolda placed a bundle on the table and peeled it open with her skinny fingers. Inside was a chrome chain, a cloth bag, and a blue glass bottle. She removed the chain and arranged it in the shape of a U with the open end facing her. She untied the bag, poured out a handful of pebbles, and used them to make a circle around the chain. Then she opened the bottle and emptied sixteen cowrie shells with the tops carefully filed and removed.

"These are the Búzios. Mine are from Angola. The cowries scattered on our Brazilian beaches are not holy. They have no power. Only the African shells speak to us and answer our questions."

Isolda closed her eyes, tilted her head to the heavens, and began to pray.

Serafina and Carmen leaned forward to hear her quiet mutterings but were abruptly repelled when Isolda slammed the table with her fist. She yelled a mysterious name, hit the table, yelled the name, and hit the table again. With her eyes still closed, she gathered up the cowries, shifted them to her right hand, and thrust them within an inch of Serafina's forehead.

Serafina tensed but did not move.

Isolda emptied the shells into the center of the U and opened her eyes. She examined the pattern, scooped the shells, and cast again. After repeating this formula several more times, she divided and counted the shells—face up to the right, face down to the left—and mumbled questions and what sounded like appeasements. Finally, she chose four of the shells, asked an inaudible question, and cast them into the U.

When all four of the cowries landed face up, she smiled with satisfaction. "There is no doubt, my child, Yansã is the master of your head, but Pomba Gira is also with you."

Carmen sucked in her breath.

Isolda smiled. "Easy, my friend. This is not a bad thing."

Serafina grabbed Carmen's hand. "What is she talking about?"

Carmen started to answer but Isolda beat her to it.

"You are the daughter of Yansá and Pomba Gira, but Yansá is your god. She will protect you and guide you, but you must take care to never offend her. Every god has their own personality, strengths, and weaknesses. Yansá is very powerful, not because she is old like Oxalá or Yemanjá, but because she is a warrior like her former husband Xangô. We associate her with Saint Barbara or Joan of Arc. She is an Amazónia, a woman of great height and strength."

"I don't understand," Serafina said. "How can you associate your pagan gods with Catholic saints?"

"How not? When the Catholic priests imposed their religion upon the slaves it was only natural that they associated these new deities and saints with the ones they already knew. Oxalá, for instance, is the son of Olorum, the oldest of the gods. Olorum is the very origin of things; the almighty. But he is too far away for his people to reach, so we seldom pray to him directly. But his son is a powerful force in our religion. He is the white dove. He is purity and charity. He is Jesus Christ."

"This is crazy."

Serafina knew bits and pieces of her country's spiritualism but, like many Brazilians, did not take it seriously. She might praise Yemanjá, the Lady of the Sea, and ask her for favors every New Year's Eve, but she never thought of that as actually praying to a god.

"Relax, my child. All will be fine. Let me tell you about Yansá, the Goddess of the River Niger, Queen of the Wind and Rain, Bringer of Change."

Serafina gasped. "What did you say? Queen of what?"

"Queen of the Wind and Rain. What's wrong? Does this bother you in some way?"

"I've heard that phrase, but I can't remember where."

"I'm sure you have. Yansá is very well known. She is a powerful and mercurial goddess, prone to fury and ready to battle injustice. She is beautiful but can appear cold and distant to those who do not know her. She prefers the clothing of men and is the only god, who dares to confront the egums, the spirits of the dead. She is very stubborn and will not give up once she has set herself to a task. She is also protective of her children and will destroy everything and anyone who threatens them. She is fierce and cold and pure as ice—and is very difficult to corrupt. This is your god, Serafina, your orixá. Praise her, honor her, and she will guide you throughout your life."

"But why is Yansã *my* god?"

"Every person is born from the spirit of an orixá. You were born from Yansã. Does she not seem familiar to you? Do you not see yourself in her description? In her characteristics?"

Serafina nodded in thought. She was very tall, especially for a Brazilian, and there was no question about her beauty. It was hard, however, to think of herself as a warrior. These days, she felt so vulnerable and victimized by life except when it concerned Carlinhos. Just thinking about her son and how she would ensure a good future for him made Serafina feel strong and invincible.

Isolda smiled. "You are beginning to understand your true nature, yes?"

Serafina shrugged. "I don't know. In some ways, I guess. But what about the men's clothing? That's definitely not me."

"There are many ways to wear men's clothing, but you have not grown into that aspect of yourself. You have been too busy being a desperate girl to become a woman of power."

Serafina bristled at the comment, although she found it hard to deny. "Are we the same then, Yansã and me?"

"Are you the same as your mother or father? Não. But you have inherited certain qualities from them whether you wish it or not. The Candomblé and Umbanda religions help us recognize the master of our head so we can live closer to our true nature. Only this will bring us true happiness."

"But what about Pomba Gira?" Carmen asked. "How can the Devil's wife make Serafina happy?"

"Don't scare your friend with that talk. Exú is not the Devil, nor is Pomba Gira his wife."

"But—"

"Acalma-te, Carmen."

Isolda patted Serafina's hand. "Exú is a powerful god to whom the seven gifts were given. With these gifts, he is able to pass through time, remember all things, and understand all creatures. Exú can mediate between space and matter, choose freely between good and evil, and change his shape. He can even multiply himself into lesser spirits. When we speak of Pomba Gira as being his wife we are referring to the female manifestation of his nature. But relax, Serafina. Although Exú is a trickster who likes to turn the world upside down and remind men of their madness, he is also the god of parties and can be bought with a strong bottle of cachaça and cigars."

Serafina whimpered. "I'm not like that, at all."

"Not in the masculine form. But from what Carmen describes, you are seductive and experienced, a combination that often leads to mischief and manipulation. You must be careful. Pomba Gira is vain and jealous. She is also the female aspect of Exú. If you offend her, you offend him. That would be a dangerous thing to do."

Serafina massaged her temples. Why had Carmen brought her to meet this awful woman? Nothing she said was comforting. Serafina felt worse now than before.

Isolda squeezed Serafina's hand. "Don't fret, my child. If you remember nothing else, remember this: Yansá is your god. Pomba Gira is your helper. Together, they will teach you who you are and how you are meant to walk in this world."

# Chapter Five

Sheets of rain pounded the night like the driving rhythms of the African drums and threatened to rip apart Serafina's family hovel, wash the scraps into the Tainheiros Inlet and out to the Bay of All Saints. She opened the front door and gazed into the storm. It called to her with promises of power and freedom. Had Isolda spoken the truth? Was the Queen of the Wind and Rain really Serafina's god?

She closed her eyes and breathed in the mingled scent of ocean and rain. The goddess' name had sounded so familiar. Serafina was certain she had heard it before, although when she tried to recall where, the memory slipped from her mind like the ping of a bell. Was this for the best? Had God taken her memory of Yansá to protect her from temptation?

Serafina was not ready to give up the Catholicism of her youth. She needed the Sacrament of Penance to absolve her sins. At twenty-six, Serafina had sinned more than most. How would she receive Almighty God's forgiveness if she took heathen gods into her heart?

Her faith was not as strong as her mother's. She went along for the ride like her brothers and father—said the prayers, crossed the heart, confessed the sins—and hoped God would stop his persecution and finally give her a better life. Her mother prayed for their souls.

Serafina held out her hand and watched as the rain washed it clean.

Was this how it was with Isolda's religion? Were Umbanda followers able to commune directly with their gods and have their sins absolved?

Did they even believe in sin? And, if not, did sin still exist?

The Mãe de Santos claimed the spiritual heart of Brazil resided in Africa and that people who knew this gathered in the terreiros where they could honor and nourish their African gods. They showered them with devotion so the gods would not abandon them and return to their home across the ocean; never to visit again. They bribed Exú with gifts and begged him to plead their case and assure the orixás of their love. Serafina had listened to all of this and more, but still wasn't ready to believe.

Yet when the storm called, she went.

Rain pelted her face and tamed her wild hair. Mud splattered up her legs and was immediately washed away. Although every muscle twitched to run back into the warm, dry house, something stronger pulled Serafina into the storm. A familiar presence shoved against her mind, like a bully knocking her from the path.

*Mine*, it cried, and shoved again.

Serafina spun in the rain and prepared to fight as her elusive memory returned. She recognized this presence. It had entered her ten years ago in the alley outside of Henrique's apartment. She had thought it was an angel sent to her by God because it had empowered her to fight off a robber and reclaim her baby. Now, she could feel its imperious rage and knew the goddess meant her harm.

A battle cry ripped through Serafina's mind, followed by triumphant laughter. Yansã had taken control. There was nothing she could do but listen to the voices as they floated in on the wind.

Saravá! Saravá!
Here comes Yansã
With her luminous crown.
Here comes Yansã
With the wind and rain.

She travels the forest,
Flying over hills.
Here comes Yansã,
Queen of the Wind and Rain.
Epazzei! Epazzei!

The god inside Serafina recognized herself in the words of her followers and rushed to greet them, but the rain and the wind made Serafina heady. She lost her direction, wanting only to dance in the storm.

She imagined herself dressed in a tunic and pants, fashioned from the hide of a beast she had killed herself. She waved what should have been her horsetail scepter to the sky and dared the lightning to strike her down. Power flooded into her body and electrified every nerve. She was Yansã, and Yansã was her.

Together, they sped across Bahia like a flash of light until they reached the great Amazon River. Their flurry disturbed the spirits of the dead. When the egums recognized Yansã—the only orixá who would dare to confront them—they fled.

Serafina threw her arms up to the sky and shouted the goddess' victory, but Yansã had left, and Serafina was alone.

"Stop fighting me," a woman said, and grabbed Serafina by the jaw. Fingers wiped the silt from her face as Carmen peered into her eyes. "Are you *you*?"

Serafina grabbed her friend. "I don't know. I think so. What am I doing in the mud?"

Serafina's mother sobbed with relief. Behind her, Carlinhos cowered as if Serafina might attack him.

"What has happened? What did I do?"

Carmen laughed. "Danced in the rain like a crazy woman. Shouted at the thunder. You make so much racket everybody come out to see.

But they say, 'Oh that just crazy Serafina. Never mind her.' They went back inside like smart people; not like us, sitting in the mud with you."

Carlinhos and her mother huddled together while Carmen pulled Serafina to her feet.

"It all seemed so real. We were flying across Bahia and running along the Amazon. We challenged the egums and made them flee."

"We who?" Carmen asked.

"Me and Yansã."

Everyone gasped, but Serafina was too overwhelmed to care. She had raced across Brazil and challenged the dead. Had any of that been real?

"I don't understand what's happening to me."

Carmen shrugged. "I don't either, but I think we know who does."

# Chapter Six

By the time Serafina and Carmen returned to Isolda's cottage, dusk had settled on a frustrating day. With employers to feed and a son to calm, Serafina hadn't been able to hop on a bus with her friend and ride into the forest, no matter how desperately she had needed answers. Now that they were on their way, she was impatient to arrive.

"That was the trail," Serafina said, as they passed the entrance to Isolda's cottage.

"I know that," Carmen said, and led Serafina farther up the road.

This time, they entered Isolda's property through a large wooden corral, empty at the moment but big enough to park dozens of vehicles. An animal trough, filled with water, stood along the fence. A man dressed in ragged shorts and a tee-shirt lit torches around the perimeter.

Carmen nodded toward the barn-like structure on the other side of the corral. "That's the terreiro where we worship." She pointed to a couple of huts sitting on the side. "Those are for spirits."

The huts were little more than sheds, the smaller one barely large enough for a child to enter. Both had torches waiting to be lit and statues sitting on the windowsill. Two of the figurines caught Serafina's eye: ceramic statues of a handsome Afro-Brazilian couple. The man wore tight black pants and a red and black cape, no shirt, and a tall black hat. His voluptuous lady wore a sexy red dress. Both of them seemed to laugh at Serafina as she passed.

"Hurry up," Carmen said. "It's almost time for Isolda to come to the kitchen."

"I'm not hungry."

"Good. We're not here for food."

Serafina followed her through a gate into a lush garden, brimming with fruit trees and brightly-colored flowers. It was lovely and unexpected.

Carmen smiled, proudly. "Is nice, no? The peji-ga takes good care of the sacred plants."

"Peji-ga?"

"Isolda will tell you. Come on. No time to smell the flowers. We have things to do."

Carmen hurried ahead and waved to an apron-clad woman drawing water from a well. "Boa tarde, Dona Maria. We are here to see the Mãe de Santos."

The woman finished drawing the water then hitched the pitcher high on her hip. "She just woke up from her nap. She won't be too long. Would you care for a cafezinho?"

"Sim, muito."

Maria led them into an enormous kitchen, larger than Serafina's entire house, where several women prepared food at separate work stations. Pots, pans, and cooking utensils hung from the ceiling like metallic fringe over bundles of dried herbs. Wood-burning stoves simmered stews and heated the room as warm as a mid-summer's day instead of a mild winter's eve. Jars, canisters, baskets, and bowls filled every inch of counter space along the walls. Like Isolda's cottage, the terreiro's kitchen was a pack rat's dream. Yet in spite of the clutter and activity, the place was spotless.

Maria led them to the table and chairs in the center of the room and brought them two demitasse cups, a small pot of coffee, a pitcher of milk, and a bowl of sugar.

"The Mãe de Santos will be here shortly. I have preparations to make for this evening's meeting."

Carmen nodded, tilting her head as if she were a grand lady. "Naturalmente. We will be fine."

Serafina coughed to keep from laughing at her friend's fine speech. Carmen didn't notice. She was too busy filling her demitasse with spoonfuls of sugar. Serafina noted her friend's blackened teeth and drank her own coffee plain.

When the Mãe de Santos finally arrived, food had been prepared and the coffee pot refilled. They rose to greet her with an exchange of kisses.

"Sit. Por favor," Isolda said, then went to the cupboard to fetch a demitasse for herself. "Between six and eight is a busy time here at the terreiro on meeting nights. The cooks need to prepare food, not only for the initiates to eat after the ceremony, but for the gods as well."

"The gods eat?" Serafina asked.

"Sim. We place a plate of their favorite foods in their peji—inner sanctum. The peji-ga takes care of this. He cares for the gods and places a lighted candle to guide their way. The gods appreciate this offering and become more receptive to our requests."

Serafina had no idea how to respond to such an outlandish explanation. She nodded as if she understood and said nothing.

Isolda patted her hand and smiled. "I am glad you have come to visit me again. You are going to stay for the meeting, yes?"

Serafina shrugged and looked to Carmen for support, but her friend was busy adding yet another spoonful of sugar to her milky coffee.

"Isolda—Mãe—" It didn't feel appropriate to call the Mother of Saints by her first name while sitting in the terreiro's kitchen. "Something happened to me last night that I don't understand."

The Mãe de Santos grinned. "Yansá made herself known to you."

"How did you know?"

"It was time." The little woman finished her cafezinho and set aside the cup. "And now it's time for you to meet the gods."

# Chapter Seven

People of all ages, shades, and status greeted each other in the corral where they parked their cars, trucks, and horses then ambled toward the open doors of the brightly lit barn. Much to Serafina's surprise, a nicely dressed gentleman greeted Carmen with genuine affection.

"Who was that?" Serafina asked, as he walked away.

"Adolpho?" Carmen waved her stubby hand as if she had been chatting with a buddy from the slums. "Just one of my rich friends."

Serafina scoffed. "Stop putting smoke inside a bag and tell me the truth. Why was that rich man talking to you like a friend?"

"Okay okay, I tell you. Everybody knows our Mãe de Santos is the best Mãe de Santos in all Bahia. So when Adolpho lose his money, he come to her."

"That doesn't make sense. The Mãe de Santos has no control over Adolpho's business. What could she do for him?"

"The gods have power. Adolpho has enemies." Carmen crooked a finger for Serafina to bend lower. "Quimbanda kill his business."

"Quimbanda?"

"Psiu." Carmen smacked Serafina's arm. "Don't invite trouble. And don't stick out that pouty lip. Who you think I am, Henrique? You think I want to kiss your sexy mouth? Ha. I know what you do with that thing. Keep it to yourself."

"Stop with the crazy talk. Tell me how a religion killed Adolpho's business."

"Okay, fine. You want to know? Pay attention. Adolpho does his work, right? But he doesn't thank the gods. He just takes and takes, and gives nothing back."

"What does that have to do with Quimbanda? What did the Mãe de Santos do for him?"

"What do you think? She took off the evil work and told him what gifts he needed to give."

"And…"

"Nossa. Why you act so thick-headed? The Mãe de Santos teach Adolpho that no man can live without the favor of the gods, no matter how important he thinks he is."

Carmen planted a hand on her hip and stared up at Serafina as if challenging her to disagree.

Serafina shook her head. "How do you know all of this? I mean, no offense, but you never even went to school. I mean, look at you."

Carmen chuckled as she smoothed her faded purple dress and raised the hem to show off her scarred dirty brown legs. "What? You no like?"

"You know what I mean. Why would someone from his world want to talk to someone from ours?"

Carmen shrugged and dropped her hem. "Umbanda is not a slave religion anymore. Umbanda is for all people. Rich, poor, black, white—no matter. The gods stay in Brazil for all of us. To them, we are the same."

Serafina marveled at Carmen's level of faith and conviction. Would she feel the same righteous fervor when she crossed the threshold of this Umbanda terreiro? Would she feel the gods entering her soul? Or would they strike her down for trespassing where she did not belong?

Serafina shivered. Nothing about this place seemed special or holy. No carvings adorned the walls, no stained glass covered the windows, no grand archway marked its entrance. It was just a simple wooden structure, painted with bubbling coats of dirty white paint. It did not even have a floor.

Serafina removed her sandals, laid them next to Carmen's, and enjoyed the hard dirt beneath her bare feet. There was energy here, and something more, something she had never felt in a church.

She wandered down the aisle, past the benches and into a spacious area, sectioned off by a railing. A floor-to-ceiling bookcase stood against the center wall, simple and unglamorous, filled to capacity with flowers, candles, statuettes, satin ribbons, flasks of perfume, chipped water glasses, boxes of cigars, and a large crucifix.

"Saravá," an attendant yelled, and dropped to the floor like a felled tree.

The Mãe de Santos helped the prostrated woman to her feet and was preparing to receive the next act of homage when a silver-haired man reached up to pat Serafina on the shoulder. He wore a loose, white shirt and pants over his bony frame.

"Peço desculpa. But the ceremony is about to begin. You must find a seat with the others."

Serafina looked back and realized her dress was the only spot of color in this reserved section of white. Carmen and the rest of the congregation had remained behind the barrier. The only people in this sectioned area were the ceremonial attendants dressed in white ruffles and lace. Embarrassed to have drawn attention to herself, she quickly crossed the open space to the sanctuary on the other side of the railing. She would have to pay more attention if she wanted to blend in.

Carmen waved Serafina over to the women's side of the aisle. "Where did you go? Sit down. It's almost time to start."

As if on cue, the silver-haired assistant stepped forward to greet the congregation with open arms. "Brothers and sisters in Oxalá, I welcome you." He bowed to Isolda. "Our Mother of Saints welcomes you." He gestured to the attendants in white. "Our Daughters of Saints welcome you." He nodded to the drummers. "Our Sons of Saints welcome you."

The energy in the room swelled with anticipation as everyone waited for the Mãe de Santos to signal her assistant to begin the ceremony. Serafina's pulse quickened. She reminded herself to keep breathing. The Mãe de Santos had said she would meet the gods and have an opportunity to petition for their help. She had not, however, explained how this supernatural interaction would occur.

Serafina wiped her sweaty hands against her skirt and took a calming breath. She was about to engage in the most blasphemous act she had ever committed. She prayed God would understand.

The silver-haired man strode to the front of the pews and opened his arms.

> Hail Umbanda, Candomblé, and Quimbanda.
> Greetings to all the spirits of the crossroads—
> The slaves of the orixás and intermediaries of men.
> Saravá, Exú, Pomba Gira, and the family of souls.
>
> I praise the orixás, the gods, and welcome them among
> us. I salute the knowledge of the Caboclos—
> The Indian spirits who hold the secrets of the plants.
> I salute the wisdom of the Pretos Velhos—
> The old black slaves who watch over us all.
>
> In the name of the god all powerful, Olorum,
> And his son, our elder father, Oxalá.
> In the name of our mother, Yemanjá—
> Queen of the seas and patron to all Brazilians.
> Bless us and guide us to harmony and prosperity.
> In the name of Jesus Christ, Amen.

The congregation answered with a resounding, "Amen."

The drummers steadied the narrow bottoms of the colorful

atabaques with the soles of their dirty feet and began beating out an intricate rhythm. With each new cadence, the assistant shouted a name, and the Sons and Daughter of Saints responded with a verse.

Carmen leaned closer to Serafina. "Gods hear the drums talk and know which song is for them. The words are for us, but maybe they like them a little bit too."

Serafina smiled. The drums were working their magic on her, as well, relaxing the tension in her shoulders and making her feel less apprehensive. "Are the Daughters of Saints also priestesses like the Mãe de Santos?"

"Não, they are mediums. The ones with blue sashes are there to assist."

The welcoming continued for some time, presumably until the Sons and Daughters of Saints had acknowledged each of the deities and spirits with their own cadence and verse. When the singers stopped, the drummers switched to a quieter vamp, and the Mãe de Santos strode into the center of the room.

She turned in place and drew a design in the air with her finger. Then she chose a stick of blue chalk from the assorted colors she held in her other hand, bent over at the waist, and drew a large circle around her on the hard packed dirt. When she was almost done, she stepped outside of it and closed the gap, exchanged the blue chalk for other colors, and filled the circle with geometric shapes, celestial swirls, and angular hieroglyphs.

"What is she doing?" Serafina asked, her voice cracking with alarm.

"Relax. She draws the ponto riscado to help spirits find their way—and for safety."

"Safety?"

"Be quiet and pay attention."

After the Mãe de Santos had completed the first ponto riscado, a blue-sashed initiate placed a lighted candle in the center, and the Mãe de Santos began the process again. In a short time, the floor flickered with tiny flames above magical drawings.

The drumbeat changed rhythm, growing louder and more intense. The initiates cleared the floor, and the mediums took the stage to dance. Serafina watched them intently, lest one of the whirling white skirts caught on fire, but somehow, the women seemed to know exactly how close they could get without disturbing the Mãe de Santos' creations. Astounding, since each of the mediums appeared to be lost in her own world.

Carmen pointed to a heavy-set woman tottering from side to side with her eyes closed and a huge smile on her face. "Look."

One after another, the mediums fell into trances and assumed peculiar positions. The spine of a nimble teenager bent and stiffened like an ancient bag of bones. A homely spinster posed as if she were a beauty. A puny woman puffed up like a giant and swiped the air with an imaginary sword. When a heavy-set matron somersaulted into the Mãe de Santos' legs, the priestess puffed a cigar and blew a cloud of smoke in the matron's face. The effect was immediate: The matron calmed down and began drawing designs in the dirt with her finger.

The drums settled into a soothing rumble, and the silver-haired assistant walked to the front of the pews. "The gods are ready to receive."

Serafina grabbed Carmen's arm as the congregation rose. "What now?"

"What do you think? We speak to the gods."

Serafina gestured to the supposedly-possessed Daughters of Saints. "You truly believe they are channeling gods?"

"I know it." Carmen clasped Serafina's hands and squeezed. "Ask for help, querida. What have you got to lose?"

Before Serafina could answer, Carmen and the rest of the believers organized into lines while initiates in blue sashes scurried among the mediums, handing them assorted props and draping strands of colored beads and crucifixes around their necks.

*Possession and crucifixes?*

Everyone in the terreiro had managed to merge Catholicism and spiritualism, and none of them looked wretched or damned. They had smiles on their faces and hope in their hearts. They greeted each other with kindness as though everyone belonged and had an equal right to seek guidance, not through the made-for-the-masses sermon of a priest, but one on one with the gods.

Carmen was right: Serafina had nothing to lose. She had tried her own methods and failed. If she wanted a better life, she needed to try a new way.

She wandered down the line, trying to decide which god to beseech. Carmen had said a bad deed should never go unpunished. Perhaps she should choose the medium wielding the cardboard sword and shield. Or did she need to strengthen her female wiles? If so, she could seek the advice of the woman holding the hand mirror and stroking her wild hair into place.

A crude laugh caught Serafina's attention. One of the mediums was pressing herself against Carmen's gentleman friend, delighting in his discomfort. When Adolpho tried to back away, the woman grabbed his ass, pulled him in for a good feel, then shoved him away.

The medium turned on Serafina with a lascivious smile. "What's the matter, girl? You never seen these before?" She squeezed her breasts together, nearly popping them out of her white peasant blouse, then sashayed across the room.

"You crave power, girl. I can smell it. It hangs on you like sweat." She ran a finger up Serafina's arm and sniffed. "Who are you, I wonder?"

"My name is—"

"I don't give a fuck what your name is," she said, with a cruel laugh. "I want to know if you know who you are." She raised up on her toes and touched her lips to Serafina's ear. "Because I do."

Serafina recoiled as if struck. Heat flushed up her neck. Sweat poured down her face. Her legs trembled, shook, then buckled, dumping her face first onto the dirt floor where she flipped and convulsed like a suffocating fish. Someone called for help. Hands pinned her arms and legs. She fought them off as blazing energy stabbed her nerves like a thousand hot needles. She had made a horrible mistake. She did have something to lose. The goddess was coming to steal her body and shove out her mind, and there was nothing Serafina could do to stop her.

*

Yansá howled in fury.

How dare this vessel resist her greatness. How dare these minions attempt to restrain her. She was the Goddess of the Wind and Rain.

Yansá leapt to her feet, thrust a fist into the air, and roared for them to stop.

The drummers ceased playing, and the mortals scurried in fear—all except for a tiny woman in a white lace dress who marched forward, took the cigar from her mouth, and shouted, "Epazzei. Epazzei."

The men and women in white clothes repeated her salute, "Epazzei."

The tiny woman bowed. "Yansá, we welcome you. This girl, whose body you borrow, welcomes you. But she is ill prepared to handle your great presence. She needs time to be purified and to learn the ways of her god. Please be patient, Yansá. I will teach her. When she is ready, she will call on you."

Before Yansá could respond, the tiny woman blew a cloud of cigar smoke in her face and flicked drops of water from a bowl carried by a silver-haired man. Yansá's anger dissipated along with her hold on the mortal she had possessed.

*

43

Carmen yanked on Serafina's arm, brought her lower, and peered into her eyes. "Are you in there, querida?"

Serafina tried to answer, then shut her mouth as the terreiro began to spin. The silver-haired assistant steadied her on her feet.

The Mãe de Santos took Serafina's hand and petted it tenderly. "Are you okay, my child?"

"What happened?"

Carmen jumped in. "You were shaking and swinging. You almost hit me."

"You were possessed by Yansã," the Mãe de Santos said.

Serafina groaned. "Why does this keep happening to me?"

"You have the gift, the calling. Now you must be taught how to safely receive your god."

"And if I don't?"

"Yansã will enter you at will. There is more to you than you know, my child. You must accept this or the conflict will become dangerous."

"How can I accept something that goes against everything I was ever taught?"

The Mãe de Santos smiled and shook her head. "Very little in life is as different as we are led to believe."

# Chapter Eight

Serafina's father slammed his palm against the wall of their living room and made the whole house shake.

"Who will take care of that boy while you are off playing with magic? Who will pay for his food, eh? Not me. I have my own to support."

Serafina clenched her fists and dug her nails into her palms. Although she had expected a certain amount of ridicule and resistance, she had not expected fury.

"It will not be for long. And I'm not asking you to pay for him. I have money saved. Tell him, Mãe."

Her mother looked away and shrugged. "Renato has a point—three months is a long time for a boy to be without his mother."

"He's ten. He'll be fine."

As soon as the words left Serafina's mouth, she questioned them. What could she do? Not leaving wasn't an option. Yánsa had invaded her twice in the last two nights, each time with far more aggression than in the alley ten years before. Serafina had to safeguard herself and learn how to control the goddess, or the next time, Yánsa might take control of her for good. Still, to abandon Carlinhos with her father and brothers?

Renato grunted in disgust. "Carlinhos is not like Paulo or Eduardo who could kick your ass if you messed with them. Your son is weak. He needs his mamãe."

Carlinhos sat in the corner of the room with his eyes fixed on the floor the way he did when he was trying not to cry. Her father's remark had wounded him deeply.

"You're the one who's weak," Serafina yelled. "Weak and stupid and—"

Renato's palm struck the side of her head and knocked her to her knees. Her temple throbbed and her vision blurred. Carlinhos yelled a warning, but she couldn't make herself react, not even when she saw her father do that familiar hitching step he always did before launching a scoring futebol kick.

Her body folded on impact as waves of pain pulsated from her ribs. She needed to run or fight, but she couldn't even suck enough breath to beg him to stop. Not that it would have mattered. Her father put years of futebol and a lifetime of resentment into every kick.

"Stop it, Renato," her mother screamed.

The kicking continued. When Renato was bored of that, he crouched on the floor and beat Serafina with his fists. Eduardo ran into the house and tackled him from the side. While smaller than their father, Eduardo was accustomed to wrestling with his older brother and soon had Renato securely restrained.

Carmen barged into the house, her gravely voice raised to a screech. "What's going on? Is Serafina okay? What is she doing on the floor?"

Serafina struggled to her knees and crawled toward Carlinhos, who was standing in the corner, frozen with shock.

He ran to her and threw his arms around her shoulders. "Why was Avô kicking you? I thought he was going to kill you."

"Shhh, meu amor. I'm okay. How are you? Did he hurt you, too?"

"He's fine," her mother said.

Serafina checked Carlinhos' face for bruises, and when she didn't see any, hugged him to her chest. "Não. He will never be fine. Not here. Not without me to protect him."

"Then don't go."

"She must go," Carmen said. "Her god is calling."

"Her god? What nonsense are you putting into my daughter's head? We're good Catholics in this house. We don't buy into that slave voodoo."

Serafina scoffed then moaned as searing pain shot through her torso. Did good Catholics beat their daughters near to death? If so, they could all rot in hell.

"If your daughter doesn't learn how to answer her god, bad things will happen."

"What kind of bad things?"

Carmen shrugged. "You want to find out?"

Mãe sobbed. "What can we do? Serafina is right; Renato will kill the boy if she leaves."

Carlinhos pulled out of Serafina's embrace. "Is that true, Mamãe?"

"Não. Of course not, meu amor." She hugged him back to her chest and winced from the pain.

"I'll take him," Carmen said. "Do you hear? Everybody stop crying." She wrapped her arms around Serafina and Carlinhos. "No worry, querida. Carlinhos can stay with me. I give him milk and cookies and keep him safe. Nothing bad will happen to him. I promise."

Serafina grabbed Carmen's arm. "Are you sure there's no other way? Maybe Yánsa will tire of me and bother someone else."

"You know that's not true."

*Mine.*

The ferocity in that word could not be denied. The goddess had marked Serafina as her own and wouldn't stop, whether it destroyed the host or not.

Serafina dug her fingers deep into Carmen's flesh. "You'll take Carlinhos home and protect him from my family? You won't let anyone hurt him?"

"Sim, querida. I will guard him with my life."

# Chapter Nine

Serafina blushed as a woman, too young to be so weathered, knelt in front of her on the rough cement floor of a large shallow trough. The attendant's spine was bent with the pained posture of hard labor. Her hands were wrinkled and stained from her task. She submerged a thick sponge in a bowl of herb-steeped water then stood up tall, stretched her arms as high as she could, and squeezed.

Serafina flinched as the cool water dribbled down her naked spine then relaxed with the soothing motion of the sponge on her shoulders. The sharp herbal fragrance cleared Serafina's sinuses and made her head spin. For the first time since last week's beating, she forgot the pain.

The attendant knelt again to soak the sponge.

This time, Serafina prepared herself as the cool liquid trickled over her collar bone and meandered around the slopes of her breasts. The caress pleased her, as did her own immodesty. She had always felt enormous pride and satisfaction in her body and saw no reason to hide that fact, even in the midst of this awkward display.

When the attendant knelt again to soak the sponge, her warm breath brushed the inside of Serafina's calf. The small gust of heat, followed by cool intakes of breath, played upon Serafina's skin and raised tiny bumps of pleasure from her flesh. She focused in rapt anticipation of the next warm gust of air. Lighter than a feather, the woman's breath traced a winding uneven path up the inside of Serafina's leg, past the crease where thigh met hip, and across the cool plane of her belly. The sponge followed, circling higher up Serafina's thigh but never quite high enough.

Again the attendant knelt, plunging the sponge in rhythmic pulses that sent lapping sounds of promise to Serafina's ears.

A shudder. A tightening. A calming breath. Then focus, surgically keen, as the sponge and breath intermingled and crept their slow, tortuous path up the slopes of Serafina's leg.

Every fiber of her being yearned to separate her bare feet further and offer a clearer, more direct path, but she feared to disturb the curious scrutiny that had obviously captivated the young attendant. Trapped between need and propriety, Serafina allowed her knees to slacken and offer whatever slight invitation might be perceived.

When the sponge crept higher and rubbed gently against the sensitive flesh between Serafina's thighs, she gasped and pressed against the pressure. The attendant responded in kind. Together, they played the tune, pushing the crescendo to the final chord when a single digit plunged deep into swollen flesh.

A low growl rumbled in Serafina's chest as the finger retreated, leaving a naked breeze where once had been such heat and texture. The absence, nearly too full to bear, betrayed itself with a single trickling drop.

Serafina followed its bold, languid progress down her inner thigh, hoping and dreading that the woman would notice. A cry caught in Serafina's throat as a touch, too wet and erotic to be anything but a tongue, intercepted the evidence of her pleasure and retraced its journey.

"Claudia," the Mãe de Santos said. "I think Serafina has been sufficiently bathed, não?"

The young attendant hurried to stand, bowed to the Mãe de Santos, and made a hasty departure.

Serafina shifted her weight into a posture she hoped would convey dignity, or as much dignity as she could manage while standing naked in a cement trough.

The Mãe de Santos smiled. "There is no doubt that you are a beautiful woman, Serafina. And it is obvious that you have a strong effect on both men and women. But while you are here, preparing yourself to become a bride to the gods, it would be inappropriate, and in fact forbidden, for you to engage in sexual relations of any kind. Is that understood?"

Serafina lifted her chest in unconscious defiance and glared.

The Mãe de Santos chuckled. "I have nothing against sex. How else can we explore the depths of who we are if not by engaging in the crudest of all human desires? But when we have sex, our bodies are turned in on ourselves, ready to give or receive the seed of life. The same is true for a woman during menstruation when her body is rejecting a part of herself. In both cases, we are closed. We are not whole. A medium must be whole and open to receive a god. Does this not make sense?"

Serafina relaxed her posture. The Mãe de Santos' explanation, while peculiar, sounded reasonable—at least enough to keep listening.

"Umbanda is not like Catholicism. We have no sexual or moral judgments, only practical rules pertaining to the medium-ness of our people. Even men, though admittedly there are fewer of them, must abstain from sex when they are preparing to receive a god." She winked. "Surely, even one so alluring as you can survive the rest of the night without seducing anyone."

Serafina nodded and smiled with embarrassment. The Mãe de Santos chuckled. Serafina did the same. Soon they laughed freely about the absurdity of it all.

The Mãe de Santos gestured for Serafina to follow.

"Let's get you out of that trough and into your new clothes. I don't want to leave you naked any longer than is absolutely necessary."

# Chapter Ten

Supper consisted of fried beef and okra, served with heavily-spiced rice. Serafina had expected a simpler meal in keeping with her bare cell and formless cotton shift. This was a pleasant surprise.

Margarita, a young blonde acolyte, watched approvingly as Serafina ate. "It is a good sign that you like Yansã's favorite dish. The food will help bind you to her as will the clothes you will be given and the rituals you will observe for the next few weeks."

The acolyte spoke with clear enunciation that, combined with her fair skin and privileged demeanor, reminded Serafina that Umbanda was no longer a slave religion. Even wealthy, highly educated Brazilians would respect what Serafina was about to become.

"Did you nap well today?" Margarita asked. "The Mãe de Santos said you would need to be well rested for this evening's ceremony."

"Not really." Serafina had dreamt of Henrique, standing beside her bed with his trousers rumpled around his ankles as he thrust his pelvis into the Pelourinho girl's face. "But the food is good."

Margarita smiled and let her finish in peace. When Serafina was done, Margarita escorted her to the same cement room where the other acolyte had bathed and serviced her. Serafina chuckled. Henrique was not the only one who could enjoy such things.

The Mãe de Santos welcomed her at the door. "You seem to be in a good mood. Did you get enough to eat?"

"I did."

"And you had sufficient time to wash up?"

"More than enough."

"Tudo bem. Then, it is time to begin."

She beckoned Serafina to the trough where a short wooden stool had been set. The room felt larger without the overhead bulb shining to define its walls. Instead, a single lamp sat on the floor, casting just enough light to see the Daughters of Saints standing in the shadows. The rest was so dark, they could have been anywhere: in a forest, on a beach, in a cave.

The Mãe de Santos motioned to the stool.

"Please sit. You have been washed with sacred herbs. You have rested. You have eaten the favored foods of Yansã. Now, it is time to bind you to your god and nourish your head."

Margarita accompanied Serafina and raised the back of her shift as she sat so her bare bottom contacted the wood. Margarita slid the garment up and over Serafina's head. Once again, Serafina found herself naked and on display. This time, she didn't like it.

The Mãe de Santos leaned in close. "The skull is the seat of the gods. It must be prepared and protected. This takes much time and much blood."

"Blood?" Serafina pulled back and clutched her hands against her chest to protect her wrists.

"Relax. It is not your blood that we need. Besides, you have shed enough."

Serafina thought of her father's beating and nodded. Her days of victimhood were over. She wanted power. If nourishing her head with blood and opening her skull to this warrior goddess would get that for her, she was ready and willing.

The Mãe de Santos took a stick of white chalk from the pocket of her dress and drew a circle around Serafina's stool. "This is for protection—for you and for us."

As she continued to fill the circle with mystical designs, the Daughters of Saints lit candles of all shapes and sizes on the cement floor, on a small altar, and in metal sconces bolted to the walls. The light should have brought comfort. Instead, the little flames increased Serafina's trepidation and the mystery of what was about to happen.

The Mãe de Santos rose and pocketed her chalk.

"Our gods are not distant and dispassionate. They are alive and vibrant. They want to be fed and honored. They want to help us. First, we must pave the way for them to walk on this earth. We soak our beads and our ceremonial tools in blood to give them power. But sacrificial blood is also needed to bind the novice to her god and strengthen her head. This is what we do here tonight."

The Mãe de Santos beckoned to a somber woman holding and petting a rooster. As she approached, the woman gripped the bird around the neck and released its body. The terrified animal flapped and clawed. No one was disturbed by this act of cruelty, least of all the Mãe de Santos.

"Listen carefully, Serafina. When Maria-Eponda pours the blood of this rooster on your head, you must not move, not even when she is done. You must remain still and awake throughout the night so a firm connection can be established between you and your god. Do you understand?"

Serafina did not understand any of this, but as she looked around the room, not a single woman appeared alarmed or surprised. Their passive expressions gave credibility to what the Mãe de Santos had said. As strange as all of this was, it seemed quite common to the Daughters of Saints.

"I understand."

"And you are ready to begin?"

Serafina took a fortifying breath and adjusted herself into a comfortable position on the stool—back straight, palms on knees, bare feet planted on the cement.

"I'm ready."

"Good."

The Mãe de Santos nodded to Maria-Eponda, who, with shocking speed and commitment, ripped off the rooster's head and poured the warm blood over Serafina, as if tipping a carafe of wine.

Serafina squelched a scream and dug her nails into her knees to keep from leaping off the stool. It had happened too fast. She had not been prepared. She was trapped on this horrible stool with blood flowing down her face and neck. Although she squeezed her eyes and held her breath, the rooster's blood seeped between her lips. She swallowed down the rising bile. The Mãe de Santos had warned her not to move. She had to remain perfectly still as the warm, sticky blood sealed her in like a coffin, covering her breasts, belly, and thighs, meandering down her back, vanishing into the secret crevasses between and under her buttocks. Only when the last few dribbles had traced their way down the backs of her calves, did Serafina remember she was not alone.

"Do not worry, my child, Yansã is with you," the Mãe de Santos said. "She rejoices in your eagerness to receive her and will protect you fiercely from harm. Spend this time binding to your god. And remember—do not move. The rooster's life force needs time to strengthen your head, and the blood must dry upon your skin to seal your pact with Yansã."

A tiny hand touched Serafina's elbow, probably the only place on her body untainted by blood. "Enjoy the night. We will return at dawn."

The hand pulled away. Fabric rustled as the Mother and Daughters of Saints left the room. The wooden door creaked and sealed with a definitive thud.

Serafina strained to hear their footsteps and bits of conversations as they departed, trying to keep track of where the women were going so she wouldn't feel so alone. She imagined them congregating in the kitchen for a cup of bedtime tea, or cleaning dishes, or sharing stories from their day. She imagined herself with them, enjoying the camaraderie.

Crusted blood sealed her eyelids and tugged at her cheeks. Her nose twitched. She yearned to scratch. Every millimeter of constricted flesh begged for release. Soon, all she could think about was clawing her skin and washing the rooster's nasty crust with her own clean blood.

Would Yansá like that? Would the goddess forgive Serafina's disobedience if she opened her veins?

Unlikely.

The Mãe de Santos had been clear: If Serafina moved, she could not be trained as a medium. Without that training, Yansá would invade her as she wished. What had Carmen said to Serafina's mother that night in the rain? *Her god is calling. If she doesn't learn how to answer, bad things will happen.*

Serafina knew what that meant: She would go mad, maybe even kill herself. Or perhaps, Yansá would do the deed, herself.

Agitation degenerated into self-pity, and when Serafina felt sufficiently disgusted with her own weakness, that pity sparked into flames of fury. Power surged through her body and fortified her resolve with indignation and rage.

How could she have allowed this to happen?

She was not a mouse to be trapped and killed. She was a hunter. Strong and fierce. The hides of her kills clothed her body. Their meat filled her belly. She rode with ease on her galloping steed with her muscular arms extended out to the night. She was spectacular. She was Yansá.

And her time had come.

# Chapter Eleven

A storm of streamers in shades of brown, gold, blood-red, and eggplant-purple fluttered from the eaves of the terreiro, from every post and rail of the corral, and from every nearby tree in the forest. These were the colors of Yansá. Today, the Queen of Wind and Rain favored Serafina with a gentle breeze, a good omen for her reentry into life as a newly initiated yão.

Many of the worshipers from this terreiro had come to celebrate with Serafina, the Mãe de Santos, and the other mediums and acolytes. Even Serafina's family and a few of her friends from favela Tainheiros had come to greet her back into the world.

Serafina smiled.

The forest clearing looked more like a rowdy block party than a religious celebration. The cachaça flowed and bodies gyrated to the energetic beat of the atabaques. People laughed and sang and were having a grand time, all for her.

She felt like a queen in her strapless white dress and multi-colored strands of Yansá-oriented beads around her neck, terracing from the base of her tight bodice to the bottom ruffle of her skirt. The Mãe de Santos had loaned her copper cuffs to wear on her arms and wrists and a crown of the same metal, Yansá's favorite, for her head. The Daughters of Saints had bound Serafina's wild ropes of thick black hair beneath a gold and brown satin scarf that trailed between her broad shoulders to the tips of the giant white bow resting at the small of her back.

Never had Serafina felt so regal. And humble.

She had learned and endured much over the last month. She had traveled through fire and blood and embraced her god, purified her head, and learned the disciplines that would allow her to channel Yansã without losing her own mind and identity. Today, she would greet the world as a fully initiated Umbanda medium.

She would also, finally, see her son.

An excited voice yelled over the commotion. Serafina turned in time to see Carmen descending on her, stubby arms and legs pinwheeling to keep up with her frantic pace.

"Serafina or Yansã? Who is this I hug? Must be a goddess. Look at you." Carmen grabbed the beaded loops that hung down the front of Serafina's dress, stroked the copper cuffs, and admired the golden crown. "You look like a goddess come alive."

Serafina chuckled. "I don't know about that. But thank you."

She gave Carmen a big hug and scanned the crowd. "I don't see Carlinhos. Is he here?"

"Of course. You think I don't bring him? Shame on you. I take good care of him. Such a good boy. I want to keep him forever."

Serafina grabbed her friend and gave her a firm shake. "Slow down, and tell me where he is."

"Oh, sorry, sorry. He's over there by the fat tree."

Serafina looked. Sure enough, Carlinhos leaned against a tree on the fringe of the celebration. He seemed so vulnerable in his solitude, so frail against the solid trunk of the monkeypod that Serafina could hardly believe he had survived the last three months without her.

"Is he okay?"

"Of course. I make him my special sugar lard cookies."

Serafina glared with impatience.

"Nobody hurt him. Like I say, I take good care."

Serafina shook her head. "Forgive me. Of course you did. I was just worried about him."

Carmen took a breath but before she could babble another word, the Mãe de Santos interrupted. "We have a problem." The Mother of Saints looked ready for battle with her fists clenched, her chin high, and her narrow shoulders spread to their maximum width.

Serafina's stomach clenched. "What is it?"

"Your father. He is unwilling to buy you back."

"Buy?" Serafina was not a slave to be bought or sold. She was a fully initiated medium empowered to channel a god. How could the Mãe de Santos speak to her in this way? "You tried to sell me to my father? How could you do such a thing? Have you forgotten the beating he gave me?"

The Mãe de Santos crossed her arms. "I remember, but that is not the point. The expense of training must be paid by the family of the newly initiated medium. It is part of the tradition."

"No one told me this."

"Even so, the bill must be paid."

Serafina and the Mãe de Santos locked eyes the way bulls locked horns, pressing and testing the other for a weakness. Finally, Serafina broke the lock, smoothed her black hand up her white dress, and patted the side of her golden crown.

"I have money. If anyone is going to 'buy' my freedom, it will be me."

Carmen tugged at the Mãe de Santos' sleeve. "Serafina save that money for years. How she get out of favela if she give it all to you?"

The Mãe de Santos shrugged. "The gods will provide."

Serafina scoffed. "How little you know of the world. And how much you are like all the others."

The Mãe de Santos was not the benevolent protector Serafina had been led to believe. She was a predator. Puny and pitiful. Another bully who abused the weak for her own self-importance. Serafina would never allow this woman to rule her life. Or her father to beat her. Or her lover to use her. She did not need any of them, any longer: She was empowered by Yansã.

"I will pay," she said. "But I am done with you."

Carmen gasped.

The Mãe de Santos sighed. "Be careful, my child."

"Of what? You? I have a goddess on my side."

"Psiu, Serafina," Carmen said, shuffling in the dirt and wringing her hands.

Serafina kept her gaze on the Mãe de Santos and grinned. "After all the training and talk of empowerment, how ironic that I will use the money I saved to escape persecution to buy my freedom from *you*." She pulled herself up to her full height and dared the tiny priestess to answer, hoping to be challenged and wanting, so much, to fight.

The Mãe de Santos took a breath then dipped her head with something akin to acceptance. "Do what you must, but be warned, the road you choose is a treacherous one."

Serafina fumed. She wanted a worthy opponent to tear and bite, not a petty woman with empty words.

Serafina smoothed the satiny scarf beneath her crown and gripped its knot—firm and soft, like smooth skin over an aroused organ—and thought of Henrique. How easy it had been to give pleasure or pain, and how intoxicating when the two could be entwined to confuse the recipient. If only she could work that magic on the Mãe de Santos, right here in the corral, in front of all these people—not because Serafina desired the woman or wished to please her but because it was time for the teacher to respect her student.

Serafina hummed a deep, guttural sound and indulged in a quick fantasy. Yes. How she would enjoy watching this pompous, tight-assed woman writhe in sexual anguish, begging for release only Serafina could give. That would be true power.

"You have an evil smile, Serafina."

"What? Am I not your *child*, any longer?"

The Mãe de Santos shook her head. "I am beginning to doubt that you ever were."

# Chapter Twelve
## Lauro de Freitas, Brazil 1994

Serafina steeled herself against the screeching as she strode down the corridor of the maternity ward. Only one woman would make such a racket. Serafina clenched her jaw and took a fortifying breath as she crossed the threshold into her daughter-in-law's room. Aside from bigotry, nothing grated on Serafina's nerves more than weakness. Her son's wife had enough of both to fill the jagged inlet of Tainheiros twice over.

"Mamãe, please, make it stop," Cesaria cried, grabbing at her mother's arm.

What a joke. Jurema da Silva couldn't help a lazy cat sleep let alone ease her daughter's pain. The cultured matron had a stick so far up her ass it should have jutted from her pursed, thin-lipped mouth. All she could do was spit venom at anyone she deemed beneath her—in this case, a wizened Afro-Brazilian nurse.

"Idiota. Get her some drugs. Can you not see my daughter is in pain?"

The nurse stumbled away from Jurema and into Serafina.

"Steady, auntie," Serafina whispered, affording the old woman the endearment to counter Jurema's disrespect. "She's nothing but a queen in the belly, full of hot air and her own self-importance. You are a nurse. Act like one."

The nurse pulled herself together, like a bag of sticks assembling itself into a rod—a very short rod—and turned on Jurema. "I'll get the doctor," she said, with fragile authority. "He will tell you what is best."

"Come back here, you insolent twit," Jurema said, grabbing for the nurse's scrubs and seizing a handful of Serafina's breast instead. She recoiled in disgust. "Put those nasty things away, Serafina. No one here wants to see your ugly flesh."

"Oh?" Serafina crossed her arms and shoved her offending breasts higher from her already low neckline. "I wouldn't be too sure about that. Your husband always takes a good, long look."

Jurema planted her fist on the pudgy ledge of her hip and arched her back to present her own sizable assets. "I doubt that very much."

"Why? Because of those saggy things?"

Carlinhos rushed into the room before Jurema could take the bait and slap Serafina with the hand she had raised. Too bad. Serafina would have enjoyed planting the pompous woman on her fat ass.

"You came," Carlinhos said, rising on his toes to blow a kiss next to her cheek.

Serafina returned the air kiss but kept her eyes focused on Jurema. "How not? You're about to become a father. That is, if your wife can manage to deliver the baby."

Carlinhos held out a calming hand to his mother-in-law before she could object. Even at twenty years of age and hours from becoming a father, Carlinhos feared confrontation. Soon life would teach him that parenthood was constant confrontation—an endless battle to protect and control, and one he was ill-equipped to win.

"My wife is suffering," he said. "Can you help her?"

Serafina softened, not because Cesaria was in pain but because, in spite of his playacting at manhood, Carlinhos still needed her.

Jurema huffed. "I forbid it."

"And what, exactly, do you forbid?" Serafina asked.

"Whatever slave nonsense you call magic. My daughter needs modern medicine and a reputable professional. Not a licentious charlatan."

Carlinhos gasped. "She didn't mean it, Mãe." He turned to his mother-in-law. "Tell her you didn't mean it."

Jurema flicked her painted nails and returned to Cesaria, who had begun her next contraction. Carlinhos grabbed Serafina's arms and rubbed them as though he could wipe away the offense.

"Stop petting me, Carlinhos. I'm not a dog. Or your wife."

The hurt in his eyes almost made her take it back. Almost. Whether he liked it or not, his wife, like her mother, was a bitch—pedigree perhaps, but still a bitch.

Cesaria hollered, sending Jurema into a flab-jiggling frenzy of ineffectual motion.

Serafina shook her head and groaned. "Enough. I can stop the pain. I can even make the child come sooner if you just stop that incessant screeching." She uncrossed her arms to show the light palms of her dark hands. "All you have to do, Jurema, is ask."

Cesaria whimpered gratefully, but Jurema was unmoved. She held her daughter's hand and jerked her head toward Carlinhos. "You have been soiled enough by this one. I won't have his mother soiling you as well."

Before Serafina could rip the lips from the nasty woman's face, the doctor approached—dignified and fair-skinned—trailed by the tiny Afro-Brazilian nurse.

Serafina stepped back and bowed. "Your doctor has arrived." Then she swept her golden skirt and strode from the room. She was half way down the corridor before Carlinhos caught up with her.

"Por favor, Mamãe, please don't leave. I'm so worried. Cesaria isn't strong like you. She's…"

"Weak?"

"I was going to say delicate."

"Of course you were. Because you don't deal with things as they are. You never have."

His eyes filled with fear as if he were five years-old again, crying in the garbage heap after getting his ass kicked by the favela boys.

Serafina sighed, her tough heart melting, as it always did when it came to him. "Is there a lounge?"

Relief spread across Carlinhos' face. "I'll show you."

The waiting area was empty except for Carlinhos' father-in-law, who sat with his legs crossed at the knee, reading a magazine. Guilherme da Silva represented everything Serafina hated: old money, inherited privilege, and a Portuguese-Brazilian ancestry that traced back to the first plantation owners. She wouldn't have been surprised if his ancestors had owned hers.

Guilherme looked up from his magazine and nodded politely. "Serafina."

"Guilherme."

"So, Carlinhos, how is she?"

"Having a hard time of it."

Guilherme shrugged. "It is this way with some women. Is that not so, Serafina?"

She smiled, cruelly. "Some more than others."

Cesaria's screech interrupted his response and caused Guilherme to cringe as if hearing something distasteful and embarrassing—which, in his social circles, perhaps it was.

A few seconds later, an orderly rolled Cesaria down the corridor on a gurney, led by the fair-haired doctor and his wizened nurse and trailed closely behind by the near hysterical Jurema.

"Are you sure this is necessary? I had hard deliveries, and they never needed to cut me open."

"Wait in the lounge," the doctor said, and hurried away to the operating room.

Carlinhos went to Jurema. "What's happening, Mãe?"

Serafina cringed to hear him carelessly bestow the title she had sacrificed so much to earn, especially when Carlinhos' wife did not do the same for her. Not only did the entitled bitch not call Serafina 'Mãe,' she wouldn't even address her as Senhora Olegario. Serafina said nothing. She was a woman of action, not complaint. When the time was right, she would make both mother and daughter pay.

Jurema passed Carlinhos without comment and threw herself into Guilherme's reluctant arms.

"Come now," he said, clearly uncomfortable with the public display. "She's not the first woman to need a Cesarean section. The doctor said she would be fine, and so she will."

Having said his piece on the matter, Guilherme returned to his chair and patted the seat beside him. "Sit. Pull yourself together."

Serafina shook her head in disgust as Jurema did as she was told. Guilherme had all the power. Without him, Jurema was nothing.

"Will Cesaria truly be okay?" Carlinhos whispered in Serafina's ear.

"I don't know, meu amor. I have no knowledge of this operation. Although I doubt it would have been necessary if your mother-in-law had let me treat your wife."

Her words stung him deeply, but she was too angry to take them back. Carlinhos had been her whole life, her one true love. To have him toss her aside in favor of a whining debutante and her haughty family galled Serafina more than she could bear.

And now, there would be a child.

Serafina turned away from Carlinhos so he wouldn't see the anger in her eyes—not directed at him but at the bad luck that had ruined his future.

How could she have let this happen? Why hadn't she forced him to give Cesaria the potion? Or better yet, dropped it in Cesaria's coffee, herself? After so many years of planning and sacrifice, she should never have let Carlinhos slip so far from her control.

Serafina closed her eyes and sighed. If not for the pregnancy, she could have pulled him away from Cesaria and steered him back on course to become an educated, powerful man. So many dreams. And none of them would come true.

An hour later, when the doctor returned, he shared the happy news—not that Cesaria had died giving birth to a still born baby as Serafina had spent the time wishing—that she had born a healthy baby girl.

Jurema hugged Guilherme. "Did you hear that? Adriana has arrived."

"Who?" Carlinhos asked.

And just like that, his fatherhood was usurped.

# Heart Ache

"He who knows nothing, doubts nothing."
– Brazilian proverb

# Chapter Thirteen

## Lauro de Freitas, Brazil 2006

Adriana tapped through the subtle resistance of the harpsichord keys with well practiced ease. Avô Guilherme had purchased the classical instrument especially for this performance, to celebrate her twelfth birthday. It had red swirls in the wood and black keys with ivory sharps, which Avô Guilherme had told her was a sign of its age. Adriana loved the sound the plucked strings made. Mostly she loved Mozart.

As she progressed from the early works of the Köchel-Verzeichnis catalog to the more mature Harpsichord Concerto No. 3 KV 107 i. Allegro in Eb Major, she grew more confident. With every trill, chord, and arpeggio, Adriana captivated the da Silva clan. But the only opinions she really cared about were those of her parents, Cesaria da Silva and Carlinhos Olegario.

For reasons Adriana could not comprehend, her mother stubbornly refused to use the Olegario name. It caused more than just confusion for Adriana, it struck at the core of her identity. At school, she was an Olegario. Among the pure-blooded Portuguese clan, she was a da Silva. Only when she played Mozart was she free to exist as herself.

Adriana's fingers flew from one end of the keyboard to the other, pouring out emotion, and racing to the finish—once, twice, and done. Her relatives leapt to their feet and applauded. Adriana stood and curtsied. Avô Guilherme joined her center stage.

He held up his hands, quieted the audience, and motioned for them to sit.

"This is a proud moment for the da Silva family. Not only are we celebrating our precious Adriana's twelfth birthday, but she has been invited to study with Jorge Ortiz Pereira in São Paulo."

Avô Guilherme paused while everyone cheered then waved his hands for silence.

"She will, of course, be escorted by her mother, who, as all of you know, was a talented pianist in her own right. Come up here, Cesaria, this is as much your accomplishment as it is Adriana's. You too, Jurema."

Adriana stared at the toes of her shiny black shoes as her mother and grandparents embraced, feeling suddenly forgotten and out of place. This often happened with music—playing made her happy, stopping made her confused.

Avô Guilherme held out his arms. "Obrigado, meu família. Jurema and I feel deeply gratified that we are able to assist our granddaughter along the path our daughter was never at liberty to pursue."

Adriana cringed. Avô Guilherme sounded angry as he delivered the happy news. Why was that? And why was Avó Jurema wiping tears from Mamãe's face? And why were the da Silvas talking amongst themselves and glancing at Papai? And why was Papai leaving the room?

None of this made any sense to Adriana, and all of it made her extremely uncomfortable. When she found an opportunity to escape, she wormed her way through hugs and well-meaning kisses, and searched for her father.

She found him on the patio beside her mother. How strikingly different they were—like the white and black keys from Avô Guilherme's harpsichord and just as discordant when played together.

"That's bullshit, Cesaria. You had no right to keep this from me."

"Keep your voice down. Not everyone in my family knows you're favela trash, and I would like to keep it that way."

"Favela trash? You mean stupid enough to do an honest day's work?"

"You don't know the meaning of honest. Your whole existence is a lie. Did you really think that you could put on my father's clothes, live in my father's house, play at my father's business, and still be your own man? I don't know what's more pathetic, the fact that you're a puppet or that you actually believe you're alive."

Adriana froze. She had known Mamãe was unhappy but not that she could be so cruel.

Papai looked devastated. He touched Mamãe's smooth hands with his rough fingers and gazed into her blue eyes. "We'll go to São Paulo together. Start over, without your father. I'll take care of us. I'll take care of you. What do you say, Cesaria? I don't want to be a puppet anymore."

Mamãe stared at him until the anger in her face melted into something bland and cold. "You don't understand anything, do you?" She removed her hands from his. "You were my adolescent rebellion, the poor boy from the favelas I could throw in Papai's face. If you hadn't gotten me pregnant, I would have tired of you before the year was out."

"You want to get rid of me? Fine. You want me out of your elitist family? Fine. But Adriana comes with me."

"Don't be ridiculous."

"I'm her papai. I decide what's best for her."

"And where will you take her? To your family in the favelas to live in one of those stilt shacks over the swamp? How will you pay for her food, her clothes, her school, her piano? Who do you think will hire you after the da Silvas turn their backs?"

Mamãe spit her words like maracujá seeds she didn't want to swallow. Papai stood there as they pelted him with hate.

Adriana balled her delicate hands into trembling fists. Her mother hated her father? How had she not known this? Even at twelve she should have seen the signs. And what was this about the favelas? Did Papai really come from the slums? How was that even possible? Avô Guilherme had always told her only thieves and murderers lived in the mangrove swamps. How could Papai have come from such a place?

And then Adriana thought of Avó Serafina, and it all seemed possible.

Papai brushed the front of his shirt as if cleaning himself from Mamãe's words. "Guilherme doesn't own the world. I can make my own way."

"Really? With or without your evil bitch of a mother?"

Adriana gasped. Could Avó Serafina hear the words floating in the night? Adriana never dared to say an unkind word about her grandmother, even when snuggled beneath the covers of her own bed. Her mother did not seem to share those fears. She didn't seem to fear anything at all.

Mamãe raised her chin and glared down her perfectly straight nose with a gaze so cold it made Adriana shiver.

"Don't be stupid, Carlinhos. You embedded a seed. So what? Adriana is a da Silva. She will never be your daughter. She never was."

# Chapter Fourteen

Adriana bolted for the stairs, pausing only to mutter a hasty response. "It's nothing, Mamãe. I just want to lie down. I have a tummy ache."

Her mother nodded. "This was a big day for you. Go and rest. We are all so proud."

Adriana forced a grin and hurried up the stairs. Her family's pride was the least of her concerns.

When she reached the safety of her bedroom, she shut the door and climbed onto her frilly pink bed, then crawled beneath a mountain of pillows and stuffed animals. She had been warned not to spy. Now she understood why. It hurt. It hurt so much her heart would explode with pain.

How could Mamãe hate Papai so much?

How could Adriana not have known?

Adriana tugged at those questions until her tears wet the nose of her beloved pink dolphin. The signs were all there, she just hadn't been looking for them. Even if she had, she would not have understood what they meant. The way Avô Guilherme scolded Papai every time he made a mistake, as if he were a child instead of a manager in Avô Guilherme's factory. The way Avó Jurema crinkled her nose whenever Papai came into the room and criticized the way he wore his clothes. Adriana had assumed her grandparents were strict with Papai because they cared; as they cared about her when they reminded her to practice the piano and do her school work. They always encouraged her and told her how smart and talented she was. Avô Guilherme and Avó Jurema never complimented Papai. Neither did Mamãe.

Adriana clutched the dolphin to her face, cried harder, then wiped her eyes with the dolphin's fin. Someone was coming up the stairs. If they saw her crying, they would know she had more than a tummy ache.

A familiar rat-a-tat-tat told her it was Papai. Adriana sunk deeper beneath her protective mountain and listened as he entered and searched the room.

"Hmm. Where could she be?"

A door opened and closed. "Not in the closet."

Knees thumped on the floor. "Not under the bed."

The mattress sank and she quickly wiped her face.

"Could the sea creatures have eaten her?"

A big brown eye peeked between the stuffed animals and looked straight at her. "There you are."

"Alô, Papai."

He brushed away the pillowy mountain and tipped her chin so he could examine her face. "Hey, what's this?"

She slid her chin out of his palm and shrugged.

"Talk to me, Adriana. Is it the concert? Because you played so good."

She shook her head.

"Then what?"

"You aren't coming with us."

"To São Paulo?" His exhale of frustration heated her forehead. "I want to, believe me, but it's not my choice."

"Because of Mamãe?"

"Why do you ask that? Have you been spying again?"

"Not on purpose. Honest." She sat up and grabbed his hand. She could not bear for him to be angry with her, not now. But he only seemed sad. She dropped her dolphin and hugged his hand. "Why does she hate you?"

"Your mamãe?" He grunted a laugh. "I wish I knew."

"Does she hate me, too?"

"No. Never think that. She loves you. Everybody loves you. Especially me."

Adriana slumped onto the pillows. What should have felt like the happiest day of her life had turned into the worst. Although she would have the opportunity to study and tour with the most famous pianist in all of Brazil, she would have to leave her father to do it. "I won't go."

"Don't be silly. Of course you'll go."

"No. I'll stay here with you. Mamãe will too. Everything will be fine. Everything will be just as it was before."

Even as she said the words, she knew they were not true.

# Chapter Fifteen
## Simões Filho, Brazil

Twenty-two years had passed since the Mãe de Santos had introduced Serafina to her gods and initiated her as an Umbanda medium. Twenty-two years had also passed since Serafina had walked away from the deceitful priestess. Serafina had seen a great deal of hardship in those years, but none of it came close to what she had suffered to become who she was today. Or more accurately, *what* she was today.

The darker side of spiritualism was not practiced in plain sight nor did its priests and priestesses advertise their whereabouts, at least not the ones Serafina had wanted to find. The Quimbandeiras she had sought did not concern themselves with spiritual evolution and do-gooding. They certainly did not soften their spells and rituals to curry favor among the Umbanda Mothers and Fathers of Saints. Those that did were frauds—like Isolda—only instead of playing at goodness, as the Mãe de Santos had done, those false Quimbandeiras cloaked themselves in sexy mystique to impress the ignorant.

Serafina wanted true power.

In order to find it, she had traveled to dangerous places, such as Bairro da Paz, ironically named since drug factions constantly warred in the Neighborhood of Peace. A gangster's bullet had narrowly missed her heart as she put herself in risky situations, as she had with the Quimbanda priest who liked to drain blood from his sleeping acolytes then serve it back to them in their coffee. In the end, she had found what she sought and had the scars and wisdom to prove it.

Serafina reached her long arms up to the night's sky beyond the canopy of trees. No church or barn for her: Serafina wanted her feet in the dirt and the stars overhead.

She had found a clearing in the forest of eastern Simões Filho, which, along with nearby Salvador where she had grown up and Lauro de Freitas where Carlinhos now lived, was one of the most violent cities in Brazil. Her forest terreiro was close enough for those in need of Quimbanda to reach her and far enough to provide absolute privacy. She practiced her magic around a tree-stump altar in a circular dirt clearing and lived alone in a cabin she had built in the trees. She answered to no one and helped those she wished, like the man standing before her inside the chalk circle she had drawn.

Jian Carlo Resende was everything Serafina wished Carlinhos had grown up to be: strong, daring, and ambitious. As with most Brazilian men, Jian Carlo was not tall, but what he lacked in height he made up for with broad shoulders, a lean stomach, and powerful thighs. He played hard, fought harder, and pursued his desires with determination and a moral dexterity she admired. The orphanage where he grew up, in the slums of Salvador, had taught him hard lessons that he used to claw his way—with her help, of course—into the lucrative business of fine wood export. He was an impressive man and an invigorating lover.

"Hold. Very. Still," she said, exhaling cigar smoke with every word.

He blinked. Other than that, he obeyed, letting the sweat drip down his face and neck and into the collar of his fine cotton shirt.

Serafina arched her back and brushed the sheer fabric of her red peasant blouse against his lips. Even then, he remained still, except for the swelling organ in his slacks that reached out of its own accord to betray his desire.

Sexual energy was the source of Serafina's power. It wasn't something she had learned or acquired. It was part of her soul, inherited from past incarnations. It had taken time to master, although at forty-eight, Serafina was no longer controlled by her desires. Instead, she funneled them into her spells and generated more power than any Quimbandeira in Bahia.

She stretched her fingers to pull energy from the heavens and kneaded the ground with her toes. Mothers of Saints—like the traitorous Isolda—could hide within their walls and roofs, but not her. There would be no obstructions between Serafina and her gods. No acolytes to channel the spirits.

She blew a final puff of smoke to the sky, laid the hand-rolled cigar on the altar along with her other offerings, and nodded for Diogo to begin beating the rhythms that would help her call the gods. He slapped the center of his weathered atabaque in a slow and measured beat, cupping and flattening his hands to change the depth and resonance of the sound, while his fingers tapped and skittered along the edges of its hide, adding a layer of intricate higher tones.

Serafina's hips and feet responded of their own accord, as they always did when Diogo made the atabaque sing. Together, they communicated their urgency and passion through sound and movement until Diogo's drumming and Serafina's dancing had synergized into a power all its own. From this power, Serafina's words of praise emerged.

"Hail, Yansã!
Queen of the Wind and Rain.
Yansã with your luminous crown.
Your child gives you respect and love.

Hail, Pomba Gira!
Queen of midnight.
Answer the call of your
Faithful daughter.

For the powers of earth,
For the presence of fire,
For the inspiration of air,
For the virtues of water,
I call to you, my queens."

She held out her hands to indicate the offerings she had left on her tree stump altar. "See the crown and knife, Yansã? See the perfume, cigar, and cachaça for you, Pomba Gira? Take them and think kindly of your daughter, for she has need of your skills."

Diogo altered his rhythm to a pulsating beat and deepened the tone of his thumps and smacks. The unfamiliar beat made Serafina's groin clench with excitement and fear. She threw Diogo a questioning glance, but he was lost in the new rhythm, head lolling and eyes glazed, as if the beating drum had taken possession of him. As it was taking possession of her.

Serafina spun like a whirlwind with her arms stretched wide and her red skirt fanning. With every rotation, she whipped her head and flung her wild hair in tight circles, propelling herself faster and faster until the stars and trees combined into rings of light and dark.

From this frenzy, a new chant emerged.

"Hail Exú!
Master of Magic,
Lord of Chaos,
King of the Seven Crossroads,
Hear my call.

Come to me, Exú.
Immortal Trickster,
Intermediary to the Gods.

Fill me with your might.

Shower me with power."

Around and around she went, whipping and chanting, over and over, until she crumpled into the dirt, mouth agape and limbs sprawled like a discarded puppet. The air thickened and obscured the trees. A throbbing pulse swallowed the sound of Diogo's drum. Serafina's heartbeat matched the pulse—answering, joining—until the two sounds became one. A flame, hotter and brighter than any bonfire she could have ignited, formed into the most magnificent male she had ever seen.

He stood at least nine feet tall, hairless skin shining like oiled night— black, mysterious, and seductive. Ropes of muscle and sinew flexed beneath his sleek skin. A blood-red cloth hung from the center of his low-slung golden waistband, like a dart to the dirt between his feet. He held a giant golden key, as a king would hold a scepter, with the teeth pointing down and the three loops of the handle pointing up like a crown. In the other hand, he held a heavy wooden club varnished to the same blood red as his loin cloth. The muscles in his arms and torso flexed with the force of his grips and displayed more cuts and bulges than Serafina had ever seen on a human body. And those legs. Meu Deus. How she wanted to run her hands up the ridges of those calves and thighs.

She forced her gaze higher, to regain her composure, and focused on the large red beads looped around his massive neck. She slid her gaze higher still, and the light from his golden almond eyes pierced directly into her soul.

"Exú?"

His chin raised in answer, sending a quiver of electricity through her body.

When preparing for battle or summoning storms, Serafina called to Yansá, the Goddess of Wind and Rain. When she needed to manipulate relationships, begin or end pregnancies, or control a person through sexual energy, she called on Exú's consort, Pomba Gira. Never, in all her years of practicing Quimbanda, had she ever dared to call on Exú of the Seven Crossroads, nor had Exú of the Seven Crossroad ever appeared to her. She knew of his reach and influence. She understood the havoc he caused, the power he wielded, and the risks she would take if she invoked him.

Or so she thought.

"Please. Please," she begged, too awestruck to articulate what she needed. She only knew she would die if she did not receive it.

Exú laughed, tossed the club and key into the dirt, and grabbed her by the hips. She arched, powerless to stop him and equally powerless to assist. Balancing her with one hand, he used the other to hike up her skirt, flung aside the flap of red cloth hanging between his legs, and plunged deep inside her.

Serafina screamed—first in pain, then in exquisite pleasure, and finally in triumph—as Exú took her for his own.

# Chapter Sixteen

Serafina groaned and rolled, stopping only when her mouth landed in dirt. She spat out the grit and smeared the mess across her face with the back of her hand. Oh, God, how she hurt.

She crawled to her hands and knees, and slowly, carefully, shook the fog from her mind. She had surrendered to a god and offered her body like a toy for him to toss, slap, and impale.

Exú—Master of Magic, Lord of Chaos, King of the Seven Crossroads, Intermediary to the Gods. Exú went by all of these names and more. Whether manipulating mortals, intimidating spirits, or entreating the gods, the Immortal Trickster inspired fear and respect. No one was safe from the trouble he instigated or the chaos he inflamed. And everyone paid the price.

Serafina scanned the ground for Exú's bare feet and strong calves then, seeing neither, raised her head for a better look. The terreiro was clear except for Jian Carlo, standing inside the chalk circle beside her tree stump altar, and Diogo gripping his drum between his thighs. They both looked terrified, jaws clenched and the whites of their eyes as round as full moons.

What had they seen? A god? A man? Whatever it was, she had to turn it to her advantage. She could not afford to look weak or her reputation would be ruined.

She stood and brushed the dirt from her skirt. "Exú has favored me. You saw this, yes?"

Jian Carlo and Diogo looked up at her and nodded.

"And you see me now, stronger than I was, infused with his power?"

"I do," said Jian Carlo.

"Sim, Quimbandeira," Diogo agreed.

She advanced toward Jian Carlo, with sultry deliberation. "And you know I can make your paltry problem disappear."

"Yes. Please—"

She held up a hand before he could beg, not wanting to remind him—or herself—of how she had pleaded with Exú. Although Jian Carlo might not have seen the god manifest in a physical form, he had undoubtedly seen her crumple to the ground. Had he also seen her float into the air, back arched and legs spread? Had he seen her body convulse with pain and pleasure? Had he seen her tossed and flipped and driven into the dirt? And if so, what had he thought was happening? Serafina could not allow any misconceptions.

"Exú has come to me. Not as one of his many Exú minions, but as his own supreme entity: Exú of the Seven Crossroads, Master of Magic, Intermediary to the Gods. He has filled me with power so that I may perform this trabalho—this work of magic—and give you what you want."

She stepped to the edge of the chalk circle, close enough for Jian Carlo to smell the scent of sex coming off her body.

"The Lord of Chaos is a brutal lover, but I am strong enough to take his might into my body. What other Quimbandeira can do this? None that you have ever heard of, I am sure."

Jian Carlo shook his head. "No one but you."

Serafina was pleased. Jian Carlo would spread the word to the Quimbanda community that Serafina Olegario was the most powerful Quimbandeira in Brazil.

She reached into the folds of her black sash and withdrew a small box of matches. As Diogo began drumming and chanting praises for Pomba Gira, she bent down to light the first candle, blew out the match, and laid it alongside the box in the dirt. She repeated the process until all seven of the red candles flickered.

Serafina had chosen red candles and worn a red dress because of the dark motive of Jian Carlo's request. Had he come to her for a love spell or to heal an illness, she would have chosen white. After Exú's manifestation, Serafina wished she had brought black candles to add to the red.

Diogo brightened his rhythm and picked up the pace, changing the energy from sultry to forceful. Serafina adjusted her movements accordingly, writhing and bucking to the beat. Erotic images of Exú flooded her mind. She shoved them down. Now was not the time to relive her experience. Now was the time to use her power.

Even as young as five, Serafina had felt empowered by sex, although she had not thought of it in that way or with those words. The feelings and effects were the same: She wanted to touch everyone she met, and everyone she met wanted to be touched by her. As she entered puberty, desire consumed her, making her easy prey for unscrupulous men like Henrique. Eventually, her impulses decreased and her effect on others intensified. The people Serafina allowed to touch her, did so often and gratefully. The people she rejected, became frustrated and angry. Overtime, she learned to manipulate people's emotions with just the force of her gaze, inciting desire or fear—or both.

Was this what drove her father so crazy around her? Did the sight of her amber eyes stir incestuous desires? Is that what he had tried, so hard and so often, to beat out of her?

The thought made her smile. With any luck, Renato Olegario was rotting in hell. Or better yet, tormented by desire and stuck with the limp dick she had inflicted on him with one of her earliest works of magic.

"Cuidado," she said to Jian Carlo, placing her hand against his chest to keep him from stepping out of the circle. Then she leaned across the barrier and brushed her lips against his ear. "Don't let desire make you foolish."

He looked from her to the chalk to the tree stump altar, as if weighing the dangers of leaving the protective circle against the pleasures he might gain.

She shook her head. "It would not be wise to test Exú's generosity: Gods do not share well with humans."

"As you say." His tone made it clear he was neither afraid nor deterred. "But tomorrow is another day."

She grinned. Bold but not reckless. This was another quality she admired about Jian Carlo—another quality Carlinhos did not possess.

She pushed the thought from her mind. She would deal with her son soon enough. Right now, she had a spell to finish.

"You have something for me?"

Jian Carlo nodded and removed a small cloth-wrapped parcel from his pocket.

Serafina took it from him and raised it to the sky. "Exú of the Seven Crossroads, Lord of Chaos, see the offerings we have brought you?" She gestured to the altar where she had laid gifts for Yansá and Pomba Gira. Since Exú had come to her, she would offer these gifts to him.

She placed Jian Carlo's parcel on the altar next to an empty wooden bowl and knelt beside an overturned basket where a rooster eyed her through the weave.

"Your time has come," she said, lifting the basket and grabbing the cock by the throat. It pecked and clawed to no avail. Using the knife she had left for Yansá, Serafina slit the rooster's throat and drained its blood into the bowl.

"See the blood we spill, Exú? It's all for you. The crown and knife, the fat cigars, strong cachaça. We even left perfume for your lady. Accept our tribute and do what this man and I ask of you."

She untied the parcel and exposed hair clippings and a photograph of a middle-aged man with a heavy beard and pockmarked skin. "This is the enemy who stands in our way, Exú. Know him and do this work."

Diogo began beating a lively rhythm as Serafina continued her animated conversation. "What? You will not? You have drunken too much cachaça and smoked too many cigars? Ha. What a trickster you are."

She glanced at Jian Carlo and nearly burst out laughing when she saw his worried expression. It would be fun to keep him in suspense. Unfortunately, the gods spoke when they spoke and did not appreciate delays. After all, they had food to eat, cigars to smoke, and thousands of eager believers to seduce. Who was she to keep the Immortal Trickster from his merriment?

"Exú has accepted our offerings. The trabalho is done."

Diogo stopped drumming, Serafina dropped her arms, and Jian Carlo held his breath. For a moment, nobody moved. Serafina brushed her foot through the chalk and created an exit for Jian Carlo to pass.

"Exit this circle backwards. Put on your shoes. Leave your donation on the stump. And walk away."

"What will happen to the inspector?"

"He'll become ill and no doctor will be able to cure him. Within a month he'll die. I expect by that time you will have secured the property?"

"I will."

"Then go."

"Sim, Quimbandeira. Thank you for your help."

Serafina nodded her approval as he backed his way out of the circle. He had addressed her by title instead of using her name. Despite their familiarity and his innate arrogance, Jian Carlo Resende would never forget who had the power and who he should fear.

# Chapter Seventeen

Serafina left the forest clearing and walked the dirt road to her rustic cottage. It wasn't much, but it was a real building with tiles on the floor and glass on the windows. Best of all, it was far away from the favelas. If it were not for the bus that came by twice a day, she would never see civilization. What had people ever done for her? The ones who needed her, or rather her services as a Quimbandeira, had no trouble finding her. And there was always someone in need.

Serafina opened the door and stepped inside. She brushed her hand along the wall, feeling for the kerosene lamp, and turned the key to ignite the flame. Long ago she had decided the luxury of electricity came at too high a price. Besides, she preferred to see her sanctuary cast in a soothing glow rather than having its flaws illuminated by harsh fluorescence.

Her kitchen had woodblock counters, a kerosene stove, and pots and cooking utensils hanging from walls. She saved the cupboard for plates, cups, and non-perishable food. Dried herbs, fruits, and vegetables hung in fishnets draped from the beams while fresh herbs sprouted in the pots on the sill beneath the open window, where they could take in the warm night air. Serafina had considered installing screens to keep out the bugs then changed her mind. If mosquitos wanted a taste of the Olegario blood, let them take it and spread her power across Bahia.

Behind the kitchen along the left side of the cottage sat a narrow bed in which Serafina did nothing but sleep. Sex generated more power outdoors, where her head could be open to the spirits and her palms, feet, knees, and—on occasion—her back grounded against the earth.

The rest of her cottage was reserved for eating, relaxing, and storing her many spiritually-charged and mystically-significant objects. Tonight, the living space with its small sofa and table, also served as a sanctuary for her troubled son.

At thirty-four, Carlinhos still slept like a child, curled on his side with his feet tucked close to his bottom as if fearing some monster might nibble on his toes. Carlinhos was the real reason Serafina had sent Jian Carlo home without a romp in the dirt: She wanted to know why, after months of absence, her son had finally come to see her.

She patted the top of his tightly curled hair and watched it spring back from her touch. The color was not as black as hers, falling closer to Henrique's shade of mahogany. Carlinhos had also inherited his father's short height but not his beautiful looks.

His lashes twitched then fluttered as he opened eyes the color and shape of a Brazil nut, the one adored by the world. Serafina sighed. Not only was Carlinhos not adored by the world, even his own wife barely tolerated him.

He sat up and rubbed his face. "Is it morning already?"

"Soon. Would you like café?"

"Não."

She sat beside him. "Why are you sleeping on my sofa instead of in your fancy bed next to your wife?"

"She's taking Adriana to São Paulo."

"On vacation without you? Is that wise?"

"It's not a vacation. Apparently, it doesn't matter what I think. Adriana has been offered an apprenticeship with Jorge Ortiz Pereira."

"The pianist. This is wonderful news, não?"

He dropped his head and gave it a shake. "It would be if the da Silvas allowed me to escort my own daughter."

"Sit up," she snapped. "You look like a beaten dog when you slump like that. Why does any of this surprise you?"

"Because I'm family."

"Wake up, Carlinhos. You're trash that seduced their princess and diluted their fine Portuguese blood. You're no more a part of that family than the dirt that clings to the soles of their fancy shoes."

"What can I do?"

"Stop whining and act like a man for once in your life. Let them go." She waved her hand to stop him from objection. "I'm serious, Carlinhos. You don't need these people. I have connections. You could start your life over, live it the way you should have done the first time if you had listened to me."

"But Adriana... I could never let her go."

Serafina rose from the sofa with a grunt of disgust. With all her power, how could she still have no influence over her son? She turned and stared down at him. "Your wife is a bitch."

"How can you say that? Cesaria is the kindest person in the world."

"To others, maybe. Not to you. Don't be stupid. Get out while you can still have a life."

"I don't know." He slumped against the cushion. "Maybe. But what about Adriana?"

Serafina moved behind him and rubbed the tension out of his shoulders. "How badly do you want her?"

"More than anything."

She smiled and dug her fingers deep into muscle as the seeds of a new plan began to form.

# Chapter Eighteen
## Lauro de Freitas, Brazil

Adriana nibbled her breakfast cake and snuck glances at Mamãe. So did Papai.

"You don't look well, meu amor," he said, between sips of cafezinho.

Mamãe stiffened and struggled to sit taller in her chair. "I'm tired from the packing. That's all."

Papai lifted the coffee pot as if to offer; and when she didn't answer, filled her cup half way to the top. He added milk without permission and dropped in a sugar cube.

Adriana frowned. Mamãe never let Papai do anything for her. Nor did she do anything for him.

"No one is forcing you to leave on Monday, Cesaria."

"We're going as planned."

Mamãe sounded angry, although Adriana couldn't imagine why— Papai was being so sweet to her. Why couldn't she be kind to him in return? If Adriana had not been taught to stay out of grownup conversations, she would have asked.

Papai shrugged, as if he had read her mind. "How about you, Adriana? How are you feeling this morning?"

"Fine, Papai."

"Are you excited about your trip?"

She glanced at Mamãe to make sure she wasn't watching then

shrugged, ever so slightly. Mamãe had been in a bad mood ever since the concert yesterday. Adriana did not want another lecture about how lucky she was supposed to feel.

Papai seemed to understand. "Try not to worry, querida. Everything will be fine."

A moment later, Mamãe fell off her chair and onto the floor.

*

Adriana did not know which was more terrifying: the mound of dirt beside the grave or the coffin shaped hole that had just swallowed her mother.

She glanced at her grandparents who stood beside her. Avô Guilherme had his arm around Avó Jurema as she cried into her tissue. Neither of them acknowledged Adriana. They had been that way all day—in the church, in the funeral home—glaring at Papai and avoiding her.

*They hate me*, she thought, *because of my Olegario blood.*

On her other side, Papai patted his forehead with the handkerchief he had taken from the pocket of his new suit. Grief had transformed him into a gentleman. Mamãe's burial had finally earned him a place in front of the da Silva clan. If only he could earn a place in their hearts.

Adriana stared at her shiny new shoes and tried not to think of what she had overheard yesterday. She had not meant to spy, but Avô Guilherme's voice had been so loud it had carried through the bedroom door and into her ear.

*Cesaria was in perfect health. She should be in São Paulo with Adriana. Instead, she's lying in a mortuary. I find that a little too convenient.*

What could be convenient about Mamãe dying?

Adriana's heart was breaking and no one cared. Not Papai. Not her grandparents. Not any of the da Silva clan who were sitting behind her with dozens of Bahia's high society guests. Adriana had never felt so alone.

The priest intoned the final blessing. Papai tugged on her hand. He had told her what to expect, but that didn't make it any easier.

She bit her lip and tried not to cry as Papai led her to the open grave. Instead of standing with their backs to everyone, as he had told her they would do, he continued walking around the pit until they were standing on the other side, facing the entire da Silva clan and all of Avô Guilherme's important friends. Everyone was watching. It took all of her willpower not to jump into the grave with Mamãe and never come out.

"Easy, querida. Just do like me."

Papai picked up a handful of dirt and held it to his heart. Adriana started to do the same when photographers crept up to the front to capture the moment. She froze, her hand above the dirt.

"Pick it up," Papai whispered.

"Não," she whispered back. If she picked up the dirt, she and Papai would be in every newspaper throughout Bahia, and everyone would know about their bad Olegario blood.

She stared at her shoes. Why was Papai doing this to her? Why hadn't they kept their backs to the people? She could have grabbed the dirt then. But like this? With everyone watching?

When Papai took her hand, she nearly cried with relief. Then he uncurled her fingers and poured his dirt into her palm.

"Wait for me," he said, as he grabbed another handful for himself.

She had no choice but to do as he did and hold the dirt over Mamãe's grave. Together, they opened their fingers and let the grains fall to the clicking of cameras.

Papai whispered. "Obrigado, Serafina. My life is yours."

Adriana glanced at him in surprise then stared at her shoes as the cameras continued to click. She thought about those words for the next hour as family and guests paid their respects and headed for their cars.

"Why did you thank Avó Serafina?"

"What?"

"At the grave. You said your life was hers. What did you mean?"

Instead of answering, he pulled her toward the car. When she whimpered in pain, he eased his grip but didn't apologize, which hurt her feelings more than his fingers had hurt her arm. She didn't mention it because he was acting strange, looking everywhere except at her. Finally, when they arrived at the car, he stooped down and stared into her teary eyes.

"You're mistaken."

She started to object.

"Get in the car, querida. We're going to a party to celebrate your mother. Try to put on a good face."

How was she supposed to do that? Nothing he said made any sense—the dirt, the party, Avó Serafina. By the time they arrived at her grandparent's Coconut Coast estate, Adriana was so confused she couldn't be certain what she had heard.

Alone and dejected, she wandered into an empty parlor and sat in the corner. An antique cabinet boxed her in, making her feel cozy and secure for the first time in days. Once again, she heard things she should not have heard.

"Disgusting." It was Avó Jurema. She sounded furious. "Did you see Carlinhos with our guests? I bet he even passed out business cards."

"It doesn't matter," answered Avô Guilherme.

"It doesn't matter? How can you say that? He turned our daughter's funeral into his coming out party."

"It doesn't matter because I'm going to cut him loose."

Adriana imagined him stroking her grandmother's shoulders as he did when she was upset.

"Don't worry. I know how he thinks. He wants to be accepted, to be part of our world, and the only way that he can do that now is through Adriana. If you noticed, he was working the São Paulo people, not those from Bahia. He intends to cut a niche for himself in São Paulo using my connections but beyond my control."

Avó Jurema mewed like a cat in distress.

"Tranquilo, meu amor. It won't happen. I did everything I could to teach him how to function in business and exist properly in our world, but he's not capable of learning. He doesn't have the foundation for business. He certainly doesn't have the foundation to raise a young woman. Not on his own. Not without Cesaria."

Adriana heard what sounded like a quick kiss. On the hand? On the forehead? She was tempted to peek around the cabinet, but Avô Guilherme was speaking again.

"We've always done what was best for Cesaria, but it wasn't enough. Carlinhos ruined her. I won't let his favela roots infect our family any more. We're going to take custody of Adriana. Then you will escort her to São Paulo and do what you can to redeem the da Silva name."

Although Adriana was upset with Papai, she didn't want to be separated from him. Could Avô Guilherme really do such a thing?

"He's her father," said Avó Jurema.

"Yes. But I know the judge."

# Chapter Nineteen
## Simões Filho, Brazil

Serafina watched Carlinhos pace the threads off her rug.

"Can you believe it?" he said. "One-hundred-thousand US. What kind of father does Guilherme think I am?" Carlinhos brushed against a table, upsetting several statuettes. "Lawyers. At my house. Interrupting my breakfast."

"Enough of this nonsense. Sit down and be still. Honestly, you move like a boar."

Carlinhos wove his way around the sofa, barely missing a vase of flowers, and sat on the cushions like a petulant child. "You need a bigger house. This one is built for pygmies."

"I don't need a bigger house. I need a more careful son."

He pouted and huffed. "You should have come and lived with us when we first got married, like I asked you to, instead of moving out here into the jungle. It's not civilized."

"And losing your job, your house, and your daughter at the whim of a rich man is civilized? No, thank you, I've already tried that route. I'm much happier out here in the jungle where I can tell the animals from the people."

She sat on the coffee table, facing him, and placed her hands on his knees. "Speaking of moving... Now that Cesaria is dead, it's time to move Adriana out of Guilherme's reach."

"You're sure about this?"

"Stick to the plan. Once Guilherme and his fat wife believe Adriana is dead, she'll be yours. No custody battle. No interference. Raise her however you like, wherever you wish."

Carlinhos gazed up at her with hope and need. "No one has ever believed in me like you do."

Serafina hid her triumph behind a humble nod. "And no one ever will."

# Chapter Twenty

Adriana lay as still as the dead on the hard floor. The blanket around her was scratchy, not at all like the soft comforter on her bed. Giant crystals and statues of devil people crowded the floor around her.

She blinked to clear the grogginess in her head. Where was she?

Beyond the frayed woven rug and the stubby legs of the coffee table, a red skirt cascaded onto a pair of large, dark feet.

"Come and sit, Carlinhos," Avó Serafina said, in that familiar growling voice that always made Adriana tremble.

Is that where she was, Avó Serafina's cabin in the woods?

"Sit? Are you joking?" answered Papai. "Do you have any idea how traumatizing it was to look down the ravine and see that burning car? Even knowing it wasn't her…" He exhaled forcefully. "Who was that in the car with my maid?"

The red skirt swished as Avó Serafina moved her feet to the side. "Do you really want to know?"

"Never. I want to forget all about it."

Papai's words troubled Adriana. Forget about what? Had something happened to Lina and her car? Before Adriana had a chance to figure it out, Avó Serafina chuckled, low and harsh.

"It's time to grow up, Carlinhos, and live the life you were always meant to live."

Adriana closed her eyes as her father came around the sofa toward her.

"How is she?" he asked.

"Still asleep. I thought it best to keep her knocked out until you returned."

Adriana stayed perfectly still as Papai's breath heated her face.

"She looks like a princess."

Avó Serafina snorted. "If you believe in that sort of thing."

He kissed Adriana's cheek. "Always."

His feet shuffled near her head as he turned. "Tell me we did the right thing."

"Of course we did. The da Silvas are bigots. They've never accepted you, and I doubt they have ever truly accepted Adriana. How could they? Her skin and eyes are nearly as dark as yours. All the piano lessons and pretty dresses in the world won't change that. To them, she will always be the daughter of a trash town rat. We did her a favor by taking her from them before they could throw her out."

Adriana bit her lips to keep from whimpering. Could Avó Serafina be right? If so, it would all make sense—the judge, the trip to São Paulo, Mamãe's cruel remarks before she died. Avô Guilherme and Avó Jurema weren't trying to do what was best for her; they were trying to send her away so she wouldn't taint the da Silva family's reputation.

She hugged the blanket and peered over the top as Papai walked toward Avó Serafina and sank onto the sofa like a stone into water.

"I had hoped to take Adriana to São Paulo where she could pursue her music. I can't do that, can I? They'll find her and take her away from me."

"What do you want most, querido?"

"I want to be a good father. I want to do what's best for Adriana. I want us to be together."

"Ah, well there's the problem. No one gets everything they want, especially not parents."

Avó Serafina rose from the sofa, pulled Papai to his feet, and kissed his forehead with such tenderness that Adriana questioned why she had ever been afraid of her. Had Adriana been influenced by her mother and relatives into believing that black was scary and white was pure?

Avó Serafina hugged him tightly then looked deeply into his eyes. "Sacrifice and suffering. This is what it means to be a parent. To do things you do not want to do and tolerate things you cannot bear."

# Chapter Twenty-One
## Rio de Janeiro, Brazil 2010

Adriana had no idea her childhood in Bahia was so glamorous until she began sharing her tales with the scholarship girls at the boarding school in Rio de Janeiro. They gathered around her on the campus lawn, eager for the next fairytale about a half-black girl in a rich white family whose father had clawed his way from the slums to marry a queen. Her stories made them feel as if they all had a princess hiding within them waiting to break free. All they needed was a bit of luck.

The Escola de Edução Sustentável was a government funded and philanthropically supported school, specializing in sustainable studies. It followed the American school system from sixth to twelfth grades and took great care to attract students from Brazil's largest sector—the poor.

The founders of the school understood that to effect real change in the future, they needed to invest in Brazil's underprivileged youth. To this end, they gathered their board of directors from the most influential minds in science, education, and sociology, as well as the deepest pockets of Brazil's most globally conscious philanthropists.

The students were selected from a broader pool.

Adriana had been fortunate enough to receive one of the fifty full scholarships when the school had opened four years ago. Another fifty students were awarded partial scholarships. The rest paid full tuition, which helped offset the astounding costs and ensured that Brazil's wealthiest, most globally-aware families had a vested interest in the school's future.

Although the favela girls surrounding Adriana bullied the rich girls, they treated Adriana kindly and accepted her as their own. She was Adriana Olegario from a slum, just like them, but with a cultured air they could pretend they also possessed.

"Did the princess ever get to São Paulo?" asked the youngest of the girls, who Adriana had secretly nicknamed Number Five. "You know, to study with the famous violinist?"

Adriana looked away without answering. She had divided her life into two sections: her childhood, which ended with the harpsichord concert in Lauro de Freitas, and her teenage years, which began after moving to Rio de Janeiro. The eleven-month gap in between was a time she tried hard to forget and never discussed, not even in make believe. Especially not today.

Adriana tossed her head to one side in a half-hearted shrug, to let the favela girls know story time was done, and spotted the one cheery person in an otherwise dreary day. Without thinking, she caught Isabel's attention.

"Why are you waving to her?" asked Number Two, whose height and size made her second in command.

"Shit. Look what you did. She's coming over," said Number Three.

"Do we have to stay?" asked Number Five.

"Não. We go," said Number One, an intelligent yet aggressive leader whose alienation and defamation tactics had caused three girls to change schools. One was rumored to have tried to kill herself, although no one would confirm this.

Adriana sighed with relief as the girls walked away. From her first week at school when Number One had approached her after history class, Adriana had known she would have to forge a friendship or become a target. The choice was easy. As individuals, the favela girls were misguided and ignorant. Together, they were dangerous. Under the leadership of Number One, they were vicious.

Isabel Rosario was none of those things, which was why Adriana loved her, and why she needed Adriana's protection.

Isabel had grown up in a loving family who had sheltered her from cruelty and ugliness. She went out of her way to help any creature in need and had soft, round features that made her look years younger than she was. All of this kept her sweetly naïve. If these qualities had not been enough to make her a target for the pack, the fact that her rich parents served on the board of directors for A Esocla de Eduçāo Sustentável had clinched the deal. Isabel Rosario was doomed.

Adriana stood and greeted her friend with a cheerful voice loud enough to carry to the departing girls. "Where have you been? I'm in desperate need of conversation."

"You shouldn't have done that," Isabel whispered, hiding her smile behind her hand.

Adriana feigned innocence. "Done what?"

They giggled and hugged. Behind them, a spout of recycled water shot up and rained down in the center of the lake, emitting a soothing sound and a refreshingly cool mist. It was one of many landscape inspirations designed by Isabel's father.

Adriana had no idea what her own father might be doing because she hadn't seen him since he and Avó Serafina had put her on a bus for Rio de Janeiro. Four years and not a single call. Not even a postcard. He had assured her he would visit as soon as he got his business up and running, but still no word from him or Avó Serafina.

Adriana shivered. Just the thought of her grandmother's name brought up memories of that dark cabin in the scary woods and the clearing where Avó Serafina worked her Quimbanda magic. Adriana wasn't supposed to go to that clearing and yet, one night, she had and saw her grandmother dancing naked in the moonlight, drenched in the blood of a slain lamb.

Isabel poked her arm. "Hey. Don't be sad. How does it feel to be sixteen? Did you have cake for breakfast?"

Adriana laughed and shook her head. "No cake."

"Any presents?"

Adriana shrugged.

"How about a card?"

"What do you think?"

"I think you need a new family."

Adriana coughed out a laugh and wondered if that would help. Did she really want a new family or just to be loved and accepted by the family she had?

She still remembered the pain in her heart when Papai had explained why they were hiding in the woods.

"The da Silvas are not like you and me, Adriana. They come from a different world. A whiter world. I wish things could be different, but the truth is, they never wanted us in their family. Now that your mamãe is dead and buried, they don't have to tolerate us."

"What do you mean?" Adriana had asked. "I thought you and Avó Serafina took me away from them."

Papai nodded. "A preemptive act. Your grandfather had plans to put you in an orphanage in São Paulo after I had signed away my paternal rights. I refused the money, and your grandmother and I made our own plans. If not for Avó Serafina, you'd be living in a Sâo Paulo orphanage, and I'd be fighting stray dogs for food."

"But they love me."

"Não, querida. They loved your mother, not us."

Adriana shook the hurtful thoughts from her mind. Isabel was right, she needed a new family. "Can I borrow yours?"

"Are you kidding? They would trade me for you in a heartbeat."

The girls laughed. Both of them knew that wasn't true. While Isabel's parents were fond of Adriana, they loved their daughter more than anything in the world.

Isabel frowned.

Adriana turned to see who had cast the shadow across her friend's face and saw a vagrant with stained clothes, sunken cheeks, and dark skin crusted and wrinkled from the sun. If he hadn't been staring at her with such hope and adoration, Adriana never would have recognized him.

"Papai?"

His eyes filled with tears.

"Happy birthday, querida."

# Chapter Twenty-Two

That night, Adriana sat at the Rosario's dining table with everyone she loved in the world: Isabel, Isabel's parents, and Papai. All of them had cheery expressions, except for her father, whose face furrowed as he chewed, as though he had never eaten in front of fine people before; as if those twelve years of living with the da Silvas in posh Lauro de Freitas had never happened.

"Tell us, Carlinhos, what do you do for work?" Papá João asked. "Because you look like a man who does an honest day's labor."

Papai nodded and took a careful sip of wine. He covered his scabbed fingers with his other hand, saw it was just as battered, and set down the glass.

Papá João adjusted his spectacles and smoothed the wisps of hair on his balding head. "Nothing wrong with that. Without dependable labor, my designs would remain scribbles on a page. Ana can tell you. Nothing gets built without skill and hard work."

Mamã Ana gave Papai a conspiratorial wink. "They are messy scribbles, I assure you."

Mamã Ana had the same cherubic features as Isabel, except on her, the soft lines appeared elegant and motherly instead of childish and naive. Her eyes sparkled with merriment, and her cheeks balled into apples when she smiled, which was often. She wore her toffee-brown hair swept up in a twist and fastened with a silver filigree comb. Her navy dress showed just enough cleavage to appear womanly without the slightest hint of impropriety. Although her waist was a bit thicker than Isabel's, she still retained a youthful voluptuousness. Isabel would be lucky to look like her mother when she grew older.

Sadness flooded Adriana. She would never look like *her* mother. The Olegario genes would see to that.

"We're so glad to finally meet you," Mamã Ana said, passing the platter of sliced steak to her husband. "Adriana is dear to us and has been a good friend to our daughter."

Papá João snorted in agreement. "With the way those girls pick on Isabel that's no small thing."

"They aren't that bad," Isabel said.

Papá João took several slices and passed the plate to Papai. "She's making light of a bad situation. We know how cruel kids can be, right Carlinhos?"

The corners of Papai's mouth dropped into a frown, making Adriana wonder just how well he knew. He had never spoken of his childhood, but from the way the da Silvas had bullied him, Adriana could guess. Was that why he was so dependent on his mother? Had she protected Papai the way Adriana tried to protect Isabel? The possibility stirred up uncomfortable thoughts.

Adriana had always admired the da Silvas and feared the Olegarios. What if her fear of Avó Serafina stemmed from the same bigotry she had experienced from Avô Guilherme and Avó Jurema? What did that say about Adriana as a person?

Papai took her hand, as if he could read her mind, and squeezed it reassuringly. Then he cleared his throat and spoke for the first time. "My Adriana..." He cleared his throat again. "She's a good girl." He took a sip of water, paused, then drank the rest, his hand trembling so much he had to steady the glass with the other to keep it from knocking against his teeth.

Was he ill? Or just uncomfortable? Adriana had never seen him this uncertain and downtrodden. Even when Avô Guilherme and Avó Jurema were at their worst, Papai had always been able to talk and hold himself with dignity. What had happened to him over the last four years?

He set down the glass and clasped his hands. When he spoke again, he did so with fluidity, like the father she remembered. "It makes me proud to hear how she protects her friend. I'm grateful for the kindness you have shown her. All of you. Your generosity..." He shook his head. "It means more than you know."

Mamã Ana waved away his concerns. "She's like a daughter to us."

"Absolutely," Papá João agreed.

While they said this with easy smiles and lighthearted voices, Papai responded with surprising seriousness. "Do you mean this? Can I count on you?"

The Rosarios exchanged puzzled looks, shrugged, then nodded— first to each other and then to him. "Of course." Their unity lent conviction to their words.

"Obrigado. Then I can rest easy."

Adriana replayed her father's words during the rest of dinner and dessert. When the Rosarios departed to attend to the dishes, she leaned in close. "What did you mean, Papai?"

"About what, querida?"

"When you said you could 'rest easy.' It was an odd thing to say."

He shrugged. "I'm not used to speaking with such grand people."

"Yes, you are. The Rosarios are no grander than Mamãe's family."

"I'm out of practice."

"I don't believe you. Tell me the truth. What have you been doing all these years? Why haven't you called or written? Why did you send me away?"

Papai wiped her tears but did not hug her as she hoped. "I wanted us to be together, forever. Your mother... you and me..." He shook his head. "Sometimes parents must do things they don't want to do."

"Like what?"

Papai shook his head. "It's not important. All that matters is that I wanted you to have a better chance in life."

"I didn't need a better chance. I needed you."

He shook his head. "I'm nothing, Adriana. I work in the fields and live with my mother. I have nothing to offer a daughter as fine as you."

"Why are you here?" The words came out harsh, but she didn't take them back. Four years was a long time to be alone.

He took a deep breath and squeezed her hand. "I had to raise enough money to buy a car and pay for the gas that would bring me to Rio, but every day, I thought of you. I couldn't let your sixteenth birthday pass without seeing for myself the good life you are living."

"But—"

"Enough," he said, in the same abrupt tone Avô Guilherme had often used with Avó Jurema. "You wanted the truth. I'm giving it to you." He gestured around the room. "This is where you belong, in a beautiful house, with kind and educated people who love you. This is what you have always deserved."

He raised her hand and kissed it tenderly.

"I love you, Adriana. Now dry your eyes and walk me to the door."

# Chapter Twenty-Three
## Simões Filho, Brazil

Serafina entered the general store feeling more optimistic than she had since Carlinhos wasted his money on a car and disobeyed her wishes. Done was done. She would use the expensive trip as motivation for him to finally accept her help and stop slaving the fields. Then, she saw the store clerk's expression and froze.

"What's wrong?"

He reached beneath the counter and brought out a folded piece of paper, turned it around, and slid it in front of her. "I'm so sorry, Senhora. The police called late last night. I was going to send someone to you if you didn't come in today."

Serafina closed her eyes and prayed, *Please, God, not Carlinhos.* When she opened them, the message was still there. It was such a small piece of paper. Could she throw it away unread? Go on with her life as though whatever it said had never happened?

"Senhora? Are you okay?"

She nodded, afraid to take her eyes from the paper. What if her son was in pain? What if he needed her? Ignorance never solved anything. It only made her vulnerable and weak.

She unfolded the message.

*Notification from the police:*
*Carlinhos Olegario was found dead...*

Serafina cried out and squeezed her eyes shut. Dear, God, it couldn't be. He couldn't be dead. She stared at the paper, now crumpled in her hands. It would tell her what had happened, how he had died, where he was now. She needed to know. But how would she bear it?

She uncrumpled the paper.

*Carlinhos Olegario was found dead in his car at the bottom of a ravine off the Rodovia Washington Luís highway in Petrópolis. Time of death: 18, March, 11:30 pm. Body has been sent to Petrópolis city mortuary in Rio de Janeiro.*

She smoothed the paper on the counter and read it again. Nothing had changed. Her baby was dead.

Her baby was *dead*.

She wailed like a wounded animal as grief tore at her gut. When a hand touched her shoulder, she smacked it away. The only touch she wanted was from Carlinhos—her baby, her love. She hugged her chest. The chasm in her heart would never be filled.

"Senhora?"

People were staring. She had to get herself under control, but how could she when Carlinhos was… *Stop it, Serafina.* She sniffed and wiped and gasped until her tears stopped and her breathing calmed. "It's okay. I'm okay. Go about your business."

She folded the paper, slowly, carefully, and brought it to her lips for a kiss. Then she slipped it into her pocket.

The store clerk came up beside her. "I'm so sorry. I've driven that highway before. It's very dangerous. The curves. The cliffs."

Serafina nodded and sucked back another wave of sobs. "Why didn't he take the other highway? It would have been faster. He would have been home." She turned to the clerk. "There was no mention of how this happened?"

He shook his head.

"I see." She took a breath and smoothed her skirt. "I'm going to leave now."

"Do you need any help? A ride, perhaps?"

"Não, obrigada. You've been very kind."

She took a fortifying breath and walked out the door with her head held high.

The bus stop was empty. Thank God. She leaned against the post before her trembling legs buckled. Carlinhos was gone. She had to accept it. There was nothing more she could do for him.

"Meu amor," she whimpered. "Was Henrique right? Should I have thrown you away?"

A cry burst from her mouth. "I'm sorry. I didn't mean it. You were pure and gentle. It was the rest of the world that was dirty and cruel. If anyone should have been dumped in the garbage it was Henrique—and Renato, Cesaria, Guilherme, Jurema. All the boys who ever knocked you down. All the girls who ever stood you up. All the adults who treated you like trash. I hate them all. Every one of them."

She wiped her face and gazed up the street where the store clerk jogged towards her.

He panted to a stop. "My apologies. There's another message from the police. They believe your son drove off the cliff on purpose. There were no skid marks or signs of a collision at the scene. A witness was found to confirm this. I'm so sorry."

He ran back toward the store before she could respond.

*On purpose?*

Serafina clenched her hands. He killed himself on purpose?

She looked at the sky and shook her fist at Yansá. "Why did you make me save him if you weren't going to give him the courage to live?"

Yansá didn't answer.

Serafina knew why. Carlinhos had courage. What he lacked was love.

She stared to the south where she imagined Rio de Janeiro to be. Where Adriana would be.

"What did you say to him, you miserable girl? Did you shun him at your fancy school? Did you blame him for your lost piano career? Did you throw him away, like every other cruel person in this world?" She fell to her knees and sobbed.

When grief had finally drenched her anger, she whispered, "Your father loved you more than anyone in the world. He loved you more than he loved me."

# Chapter Twenty-Four
## Rio de Janeiro, Brazil 2012

The condominium door opened mere seconds after Jian Carlo sounded the chime, as if someone had been expecting his arrival. *As well they should*, he thought. He had made much of himself since his lowly beginnings in the jungle with Serafina.

João Rosario smiled and held out his arms in welcome. "Jian Carlo. Glad you could make it. Please. They are just now cutting the cake. Would you care for a drink?" He spoke with bursts of energy and what sounded like genuine affection.

Although João was only a few years older than Jian Carlo, his portly belly and receding hairline made him appear older—so unlike Jian Carlo's trim physique and full head of hair. That said, João carried his age with the comfort of a man well established in life. A quality Jian Carlo intended to emulate.

"Sim, obrigado." Jian Carlo's voice was as deep and fluid as aged whiskey, cultivated from a lifetime of careful observation and mimicry. No one in Rio would ever guess he had started life as an orphan in the slums of São Salvador.

Not like the men and women in this condominium.

The families attending this celebration formed the cream of Escola de Edução Sustentável on whose board of directors João and his wife, Ana, served. The young women lined up at the far end of the living room were daughters of judges, politicians, land developers, art collectors, capitalists, and philanthropists. Marry any of them and he'd be set for life.

"Would you care for a cocktail?" João gestured to an adjoining bar room where a dozen-or-so men in their forties to early seventies conversed and drank. "Or would you rather join the ladies?" he added, with a wink.

Jian Carlo glanced at the women seated on couches and standing on the edges of the parlor. Some were homely, a few beautiful, all wore tasteful dresses and expensive jewelry. Each chattered with excitement as Ana Rosario cut a gloriously pink three-tiered cake.

João nodded toward a couple of boys and a girl who sat in the hallway playing cinco marias, a game similar to the American game of jacks. "I know you don't want to sit with the children."

Jian Carlo grinned. "The men will be fine."

João patted Jian Carlo's back and laughed as if he had made a grand joke. "I will fix you one of my famous caipirinhas. I learned the recipe from the original bartender at Melt. He liked to use vodka, but I prefer the authentic sweetness of cachaça. I guarantee you won't have tasted better."

"I'm sure not," Jian Carlo said, although he would have preferred a shot of the Glendronach he saw displayed on the glass shelf behind the bar.

"Listen up, my friends. This is Jian Carlo Resende. We're doing a bit of business together." He smiled broadly, signaling to the other men that Jian Carlo was a man of wealth and influence who was clearly important to him. They leaned in to learn more, but were interrupted by a burst of applause.

"Ah, look." João opened his hands toward the young women entering the parlor, receiving plates of cake. "Are they not beautiful? Like presents in their pretty dresses. The one in the lavender gown is my daughter, Isabel."

Jian Carlo saw the resemblance instantly. Isabel had João's cheery smile and her mother's cherubic face and full-bodied curves. With her tawny hair swept up in the same elaborate twist, Isabel and her mother could have been the same person in different stages of life.

"Enchanting," said Jian Carlo, but it was the beauty standing next to Isabel, sneaking a fingerful of icing, who caught his eye. "Who is the young woman hanging on your daughter's arm? They seem as close as sisters."

"Indeed they are. Foster sisters, in fact. We took in Adriana after her father died a few years back. Tragic, really. He drove off the Rodovia Washington Luís on his way back to Bahia."

"A dangerous road."

"Yes, well…"

Jian Carlo raised a brow. "Is there something more?"

João shrugged and walked behind the bar. "We had him to dinner before he left. He was a very sad man. He asked if he could count on us to look after his daughter. Of course, we said yes, never imagining that he might…" João picked up a knife and began slicing limes. "Adriana took it hard, as you can imagine."

João dropped two lime quarters in each of the two crystal old fashioned glasses, added a tablespoon of sugar, and muddled the combination. Jian Carlo grimaced. Although he enjoyed sweet foods and drinks as much as the rest of his countrymen, adding sugar to cachaça was as redundant as sprinkling chili on chili peppers. João pulverized the limes so the sugar could bind to the pulp and oil, filled the glasses with ice, poured in two shots of cane liquor, and continued his story.

"The father was the only family Adriana had besides that awful grandmother of hers, a witch of the highest degree."

Jian Carlo tensed. Had Serafina's reputation as a Quimbandeira traveled all the way to Rio de Janeiro? "By witch you mean—"

"A despicable woman. She called me soon after her son's death, demanding to know what Adriana had done to make him take his own life. Can you imagine? A girl as sweet as Adriana? I still kick myself for letting that witch speak to her. Poor girl was so overwhelmed. She never defended herself or denied any of her grandmother's accusations. She just kept apologizing, saying it was all her fault that her father had killed himself. When Ana and I heard about the funeral, we thought it best that Adriana not attend. We didn't want her to have anything more to do with that witch of a grandmother."

Jian Carlo relaxed. Clearly, João did not realize the accuracy of his description, which also meant he didn't know that Serafina was the reason Jian Carlo was in João's condominium on the night of Adriana's graduation party.

A week had passed before Jian Carlo had heard the news about Carlinhos' death. Knowing that Serafina would be devastated, he had gone to visit her. Instead of finding a grieving mother, he had found an enraged Quimbandeira. Broken statues and a shredded blanket lay outside her cabin beneath an open window where shards of the broken glass he had installed still clung to the frame. At first, Jian Carlo had feared that Serafina had been attacked. Then he heard her shout and knew that anyone foolish enough to trespass would be long gone from this world.

Jian Carlo had risked his life that day when he entered her cabin, but that risk had brought him great rewards. After she had exhausted her fury at neglectful gods, deteriorating highways, bigoted rich people, ungrateful children, and even Carlinhos for the countless ways he had disappointed her, Serafina had focused her anger onto only one person—Adriana.

Not only did Serafina blame Adriana for Carlinhos' suicide, she was convinced that Adriana's birth had cursed her son and derailed all of Serafina's careful plans. She even accused Adriana of being a vengeful spirit sent by an enemy to ruin Serafina's life. How else could the girl have had such a mystical hold over Carlinhos?

Since a smart man did not make himself a target for witchcraft, Jian Carlo had wisely agreed. When Serafina's tirade had run its course through all of Adriana's imagined offenses, Jian Carlo had comforted Serafina in the only way he knew how. Sex that night had been a brutal, demeaning, and erotic experience.

The next morning, Serafina had told him of her plan.

João Rosario swirled the caipirinhas and handed a glass to Jian Carlo. "To friendship."

Jian Carlo smiled. "The best tonic to a bad family."

They clinked their glasses and drank with the other men in the bar while, in the parlor, the ladies laughed and ate cake.

João glanced at Adriana and Isabel, feeding each other pink frosting. "We offered to send Adriana to university with Isabel, but she felt strongly about supporting herself. She's taken a job as an assistant teacher at A Esocla de Edução Sustentável."

"Where she and Isabel went to school?"

"Sim. Isabel was not a boarding student, you understand, she lived here with us. Adriana came from Bahia on a full scholarship. Her mother had died. So much tragedy. And to have no one visit her in four years?" João shook his head as a dog shook water from his coat. "Forgive me, my friend, I get too worked up about such things. Ana tells me it will give me a heart attack one day. Says I should learn to meditate or some nonsense. Can you imagine? Me sitting on some cushion, humming to myself? There's too much work to be done. Am I right? Like this development you and I will work on together."

The development would involve the construction of a dozen more condominiums, each as luxurious as the one where the Rosarios lived. Península Barra would become the finest example of eco-urbanization in the country. João Rosario—renowned for his ability to integrate art, natural resources, and urban living—was the project's landscape designer and had just contracted Jian Carlo's company to provide the rare Brazilian wood required for art, gazebos, and outdoor furniture.

João held out his glass to offer another toast. "To Resende Fine Woods and Export and João Rosario Eco-Urban Landscaping. May we enjoy decades of profitable business."

"Saude," they said in unison, then downed the rest of their drinks.

# Chapter Twenty-Five

Adriana was in Heaven.

She had never spent time alone with a man before, let alone one as handsome and charming as Senhor Jian Carlo Resende. His tailored suit, his proud posture, his impeccable grooming, even the tone and cadence of his speech all flowed together with the polish of a cultured man. She had to make a good impression, not just for A Esocla de Edução Sustentável but for herself.

As an orphan, with no savings or inheritance, Adriana's opportunities were limited. The Rosarios treated her like their own daughter, but potential suitors were well aware of the difference. All of the social invitations during the last two years had come through Isabel. No one had ever called Adriana directly. Not once.

She smiled and tried to relax. This was the first time she had given a school tour. Senhor Resende must have sensed her nervousness because he had guided her with basic questions: How did the school teach sustainable ecology? How did they integrate the wealthy and the poor? Did the campus have separate facilities for boys and girls?

With each new question, Adriana became more at ease until what had begun as a factual exchange evolved into an intimate disclosure of her own experiences; one she did not want to end.

"Will you send your niece here?" she asked, hoping she might see more of him. A silly thought. After all, he was a sophisticated man of the world, and she was just an eighteen-year-old assistant teacher.

He checked their surroundings then leaned closer. "I have a confession to make. I don't have a niece."

"But I thought—"

He held up a hand. "She's the daughter of a dear friend of mine who's very ill. He has no family, and if he dies, I'll be the closest person she has."

Adriana stared at her feet. Should she tell him about her own father's passing and the way her best friend's family had taken her in?

Senhor Resende smiled. "I've occupied enough of your time. Surely you have classes to teach?"

"No," Adriana blurted. "I mean, I'm still in training. My employment doesn't officially begin until the fall."

"Oh? In that case, perhaps you'd join me for lunch."

Adriana's heart fluttered. "I'd love to. I mean—if that's what you really want. I don't want you to feel obligated to take me to lunch just because I gave you a tour of the school."

"Is that what you think?" He chuckled. "How charming."

Jian Carlo—as Senhor Resende insisted she call him the instant they stepped off school property—led her to a lovely French bistro, where he ordered a bottle of Meursault and a plate of pâté de foie gras.

"Tell me more about your piano playing. You must have been very good to attract the attention of Jorge Ortiz Pereira."

Adriana's face flushed with heat, though whether from his compliment or the wine she couldn't say. "I was. But sometimes good isn't enough. Life interferes. Plans change." She shrugged. "What can you do?"

She spread pâté on her bread in the same slow rhythm as Mozart's Adagio in E Major. It was her favorite piece to play and the one that haunted her mind whenever she remembered those sad days. "It's still in my soul. I don't think it will ever go away."

"Do you want it to?"

"Sometimes. I don't know."

Jian Carlo nodded. "I understand. How about we order more of this delicious food and talk about happier things?"

Adriana sighed with relief. How could someone she had just met understand her moods so well? It was almost as if he already knew her and they were meeting again after a long separation. Nonsensical, of course, yet that was exactly how it felt.

By the time they had finished the escargot and duck à l'orange, Adriana felt comfortable enough to talk about Mamãe and the way her sudden death had affected her father, changing him from a rough favela man into a confident gentleman into a frightened son who did whatever Avó Serafina told him to do.

"Your grandmother sounds like a formidable woman."

Adriana laughed. "You have no idea."

He grinned. "I can imagine." He took her hand and kissed it. "Especially when you're such a good storyteller."

Adriana trembled. Was it wrong to wish he had kissed her lips, instead?

"What's going on in that beautiful head of yours?"

"Nothing. I was just remembering a birthday wish I made a long time ago."

"Oh?"

She rolled her eyes. "You know, the usual…handsome prince, true love, being understood. Being seen."

"Don't belittle something so important as being seen. We all yearn for the same things."

He took both of her hands and gazed into her eyes. "I see you, Adriana. And I know exactly who you are."

# Chapter Twenty-Six
## Simões Filho, Brazil

Serafina crumpled the wedding announcement.

How dare he betray her?

She had sent Jian Carlo to Rio de Janeiro to ruin Adriana not marry her. What was he thinking? That Serafina wouldn't notice? That she wouldn't care? Did he honestly believe a couple thousand kilometers could protect him from her?

Fool.

How quickly he had forgotten their final midnight encounter on her forest altar, under the searing gaze of Exú of the Seven Crossroads. Before that night, Jian Carlo had been too naive and ambitious to fully appreciate the danger. Serafina, empowered by Exú, had taught him the fragility of life and the enslaving power of desire.

When she sent him into the Amazon to despoil the forest, he went.

When she used her magic to help him dominate the rare-wood industry, he accepted.

When she ordered him to Rio de Janeiro to spy on Adriana and later worm his way into the Rosario's good graces so he could seduce, disgrace, and destroy, he had obeyed.

Why was he challenging her now?

Serafina kicked dirt onto the ponto riscado she had drawn the night before. The warrior goddess Yansá couldn't help her today, not with this, and seductive Pomba Gira had already failed. How else could Jian Carlo have fallen for a chaste teenager in a city known for its lustful women?

What was it about Adriana that men found so appealing? Guilherme da Silva had doted on her. Carlinhos had wasted his life for her. And now Jian Carlo? Serafina had thought him too pragmatic to fall for a pretty face. And what about João Rosario? What would a man as accomplished as him, with a daughter of his own and a high society wife, want with Adriana?

Sex.

It had to be. No matter how innocent Adriana appeared to be, men could smell the scent as surely as a Pampas stag in mating season. From the moment of her ill-gotten conception, Adriana had seduced every man she ever met.

Serafina tossed the newspaper into the fire and watched as Adriana's pretty face burned. From the moment she had learned Carlinhos had driven off that cliff, all Serafina could think about was making Adriana pay. She spat into the fire. Luck rained on the girl like a winter storm, drenching her in good fortune and happiness while Carlinhos lay rotting in the ground.

Why couldn't a drop of that good fortune have fallen on him?

Serafina had done everything in her power to give Carlinhos a chance. She had even used sex and magic to get Adriana that scholarship to the fancy boarding school in Rio de Janeiro so Carlinhos could focus on himself without distraction. Instead, he sank into depression, turned away all of the job opportunities she arranged, and worked in the fields like a slave. And why? Because she had sent away the daughter he should never have had.

No more.

Carlinhos was gone and the cause of his downfall remained.

Serafina took a piece of chalk from her tree stump altar and drew a new ponto riscado in the dirt—not for Yansá or Pomba Gira but to summon Exú.

Excitement tingled her nerves. And fear. Although the immortal trickster had visited her several times over the last six years, she had never attempted to summon him. Serafina had no idea how he would react.

She took a hefty swig of cachaça, sprinkled a little in the fire, and poured the remainder in the dirt. She lit her candles. No drums tonight. Only her and her god—Exú of the Seven Crossroads, Master of Magic, Lord of Chaos. She breathed in the heady smoke of herb-scented firewood and peeled the clothing from her body until her dark skin blended with the night. Then she danced—spine supple, hips loose, arms raised to the stars.

"Come to me, Exú. I'm ready. Come inside."

Her head grew heavy, swinging and flopping as she twirled around the fire. She was losing control of her mind and body, and she welcomed the loss.

"Come to me, Exú. Show me the way."

Her legs buckled. She collapsed, limbs splayed, back pressed against the ground. She couldn't move. Fear coursed through her veins. What if Exú didn't come? What if she laid in the dirt until she died, unable to feed or defend herself? What if—

The fire flared and her magnificent lord appeared, shining skin, taunt muscles, gleaming almond eyes.

Serafina reached for his calf, wanting to pull him near, but her hand flopped to the ground. She tried again. Failed. Why was this happening? Exú had always greeted her eagerly, filling her with power and knowledge. Now, he squatted beside her and watched with amused fascination, as a boy might ponder a captured bug.

Then the stars shifted into a new formation and Exú waved goodbye.

# Chapter Twenty-Seven
## Hameau de Vieille Forêt, France 1560

Révérend Père d'Amboise dug his staff into the hillside and took another step, dragging the hem of his dingy white cassock across the dirt. Not only did the sturdy wood support his aging spine, it acted as a scepter of his command lest the parishioners who followed behind him forgot who was in charge. The French priest would allow no rebellion during this tumultuous time of Protestant corruption and witchcraft, no matter how difficult the task or how beautiful the witch.

D'Amboise grunted with disgust, which startled the peasant leading the way and made his arm shake. The firelight of his torch flickered against the trees like dancing demons.

"Hold steady, you fool."

"Sorry, father."

D'Amboise dug in the staff and quickened his step. Just the thought of what was to come made him feel young again. Why should he chase pleasures of the flesh when righteous execution could provide the same excitement and satisfaction?

When they crested the hill, d'Amboise continued to his platform without so much as a glance at the girl staked to the pyre.

"You can't do this to me," Colette cried to the villagers. "I'm innocent. The reverend is not a man of God. He's a monster. Please listen to me. Someone help me. Please."

A child screamed and a woman cried, but d'Amboise refused to look. He knew who they were just as he knew they could do nothing to stop what was about to happen. The villagers feared witchcraft almost as much as they feared him. Colette Richard would burn.

D'Amboise thumped his staff against the wooden platform and waited for silence. "We gather tonight to execute the will of God."

"Blasphemer," cried Colette, causing the crowd to grumble.

"Gag the witch," a man yelled, followed by numerous cries of agreement.

D'Amboise nodded his approval. "Yes. Gag the witch. Evil has walked among us disguised as beauty long enough, speaking lies and tainting every woman, child, and man in Hameau de Vieille Forêt."

Women moaned. Children whimpered. Angry men, who had probably lusted after Colette for years, shouted for her death.

D'Amboise breathed in the glory of the moment. "Take heart, my children. There is nothing to fear. The witch has made herself known to me."

He gestured to the pyre and gasped.

Colette had never looked more alluring than she did in that moment, with her lovely face tipped back by the tightly knotted gag and her long, creamy neck exposed as if for a lover's kiss. Her auburn hair draped like silk down the sleeves of her white gown while the coarse fiber of the ropes dug into her slender form and accentuated every youthful curve.

D'Amboise exhaled slowly, taking care to keep his expression neutral. He couldn't risk having anyone other than Colette and her family know the truth behind his actions.

He signaled to the peasant who had guided his way up the trail to light the pyre. When others advanced to do the same, a boy screamed and attacked the man nearest to him.

D'Amboise smiled. It pleased him to see Philippe suffer. Almost as much as it would please him to watch Colette burn.

# Chapter Twenty-Eight
## Simões Filho, Brazil 2012

"Did you enjoy your trip?" Exú asked, as Serafina opened her eyes.

The Lord of Chaos was seated on the edge of her tree stump altar, legs spread and smoking a cigar. As before, he was naked except for the red cloth that flowed from his golden waistband, over the bulge of his groin, and fell between his powerful thighs, like a waterfall of blood.

She sat up and brushed the rocks from her bare back. "Why did you send me to that place, into the body of that priest? Who were those other people—the witch and the boy?"

"Patience, Quimbandeira. You'll know when you are meant to know. For now, you must leave this forest."

She crawled to her knees. "I don't understand. Am I not safe here?"

Exú's laughter shook the ground and planted Serafina on her face. She took it as a warning and extended her arms in full prostration. When his laughter subsided, he whispered in her ear.

"An American is coming. Find him before he finds you."

# Obsession

"You can only take out of a bag what was already in it."
— Brazilian Proverb

# Chapter Twenty-Nine
## Rio de Janeiro – Present Day

Michael Cross stood on the sidelines of the art gallery, observing the intricate dance of Rio's high society. His one-man show had attracted an international crowd of residents and visitors who dressed to impress and spoke to be heard. He closed his eyes and let the cacophony of language wash over him.

"Hoping it will all just go away?" a woman asked.

Michael opened his eyes to a flock of multicolored macaws flying across a bright cerulean silk caftan. He followed their flight up to Jackson's pudgy, carefully made-up face and stepped back to take in the full effect. A less confident woman would have looked ludicrous. His agent looked resplendent.

"Making a statement?" he asked.

"Oh, for Christ's sake, Cross, loosen up." She swayed her hips to the bossa nova performed by a trio of musicians and their lusty songstress. The movement sent her macaws fluttering on the blue background. "Would it have killed you to wear something more festive?"

Michael looked down at his own white T-shirt and tan suit and shrugged. "I didn't want to compete with my art."

Jackson laughed and patted his cheek. "Honey, nothing could compete with those paintings, not even you. You're a goddamn artistic genius."

She grabbed an appetizer from a passing waiter and popped it into Michael's mouth. "Have a shrimp ball." She turned him towards the crowded gallery. "It's time to work."

He coughed as he swallowed. "Where are you going?"

"To mingle, darling. One of us has to." She gave him a wink and headed boldly across the room to do battle.

Thank God someone was up to the task. Five years in the public's eye had done nothing to enamor Michael to it, which was why he stood on the sidelines of his own show, trying not to be noticed. Fat chance of that. At six-foot-one with sun-streaked blond hair and blue eyes, Michael stood out in this mostly Brazilian crowd like a lighthouse beacon.

Jackson White powered her way into every situation with unabashed command. Even back in Los Angeles, where women were measured, consciously or not, by beach-girl movie-star beauty, Jackson's audacious and ferocious determination dominated the scene. Which was exactly what made her LA's premier fine arts agent. And why Michael praised the day she had discovered him painting a mural on Yoshimura-san's corner market wall.

Although supported by a sizable trust fund, Michael had taken the grocery clerk job after he had burned every one of his charcoal sketches mere days before what would have been his gallery debut. Lost and devastated, he had found solace in menial labor and Yoshimura-san's quiet presence. He had learned a great deal from the octogenarian about dignity and humility and had thought himself at peace in his colorless world, until the day Yoshimura-san had asked him to paint the exterior wall.

Michael cringed as he remembered the storeroom filled with cans of mix-matched paint. If Yoshimura-san had known about Michael's mother-induced guilt and spirit-inflicted fear concerning such un-Godly color, he never would have made the request.

Michael scanned the vibrant abstract paintings displayed on the Ipanema gallery's white walls. Who would have thought all this could come from him?

A pair of blue-haired Brits glanced his way then giggled to each other.

He should have followed Jackson's advice and brought Panchali on this trip. His loft-mate could have provided the illusion of mingling, but she also would have added complications. Michael liked to keep his relationships simple and compartmentalized. He had the guys on the basketball court, his agent in the field, the women he dated, friends at social gatherings, and a psychic loft-mate he struggled to keep out of his head. He didn't want to blur the lines.

The Brits glanced again, this time catching his eye and waving their fingers. The ladies had an air of history about them, a story to be shared. Michael loved stories, providing they weren't about him.

He wiggled his fingers in return and gave them his best charming-young-man smile. If there was work to be done, he would do it on his own terms, which meant having a conversation about something more meaningful than the musings of an artist. He swallowed the last of the shrimp ball and went to greet his guests.

It took finesse and clever redirection, but Michael managed to keep the British dames talking about themselves. He did the same with the Brazilian restaurateur and his wife, the mayor of Rio de Janeiro and his entourage, and the Argentinean diplomat who had just purchased a thirty-thousand-dollar painting.

Now, he was done.

"If you'll excuse me," Michael said. "I need to check in with the gallery owner."

The diplomat nodded. "Of course, Mr. Cross. I have taken up too much of your time. Good luck with the rest of your show. I'm sure your paintings will find many appreciative buyers here in Rio."

"Thanks. And I hope you enjoy *Euphoria*."

Michael had almost reached the balcony and fresh air when the gallery owner, Sebastião Nunes, caught his arm. "Senhor Cross. You must meet Uxía Moreno, one of Rio's prominent art collectors."

Michael forced a smile. He was one prying-question away from bolting, but he also had a career to protect. Instead of running away, he allowed Sebastião to lead him into yet another conversation.

"How marvelous to meet you," Uxía said, grasped his hands, and buried them between her inflated breasts. She licked her collagen-filled lips and winked at Sebastião, as if to warn him of her impending brilliance. "I must know what lurks behind these glorious paintings of yours? Tormento, não?"

"I'm sorry—what?"

"Torment. Agony." She gestured to an abstract with a swirling red vortex. "Do you suffer? Or are you searching for truth?"

Michael stared at her wrinkle-free face, stretched beyond any possibility of expression. What could a woman like her possibly know about the truth?

"I'm sorry but..." He searched for a worthy excuse and came up empty. "I have to go."

His agent was going to kill him when she heard about this, and Jackson would definitely hear about it, but if he had stayed a moment longer he would have blurted something irretrievable.

Sebastião's voice carried across the room as Michael made his escape. "You know how artists are, Uxía darling. Eccentrics, all of them."

Michael knew he should go back and apologize, but he couldn't make himself do it. His need for air outweighed any sale he might lose.

He glanced behind him to make sure no one was following and bumped into someone. He didn't know who, but since any interaction was bound to lead to another soul-testing conversation, he didn't look. He just rolled off the person's back and continued on his way to the balcony. Or he would have, if not for the wall of fire.

# Chapter Thirty

Serafina snorted with disgust. How dare this privileged American ram into the coach of Brazil's national futebol team and push himself away without a word of apology. What appalling arrogance. She should have stayed at home and saved herself the trip.

And yet, she could not ignore Exú's warning.

*An American is coming. Find him before he finds you.*

Exú had delivered this warning six years ago, after sending her back in time into the body of a French priest. Instead of explaining why he had done this or why the priest had burned the young witch, Exú had commanded Serafina to leave her beloved forest. At first, she had resisted, attempting to lure Exú back to her with the finest cachaça and most expensive cigars. He had not come. After months, she feared he would never visit her again.

She packed her treasures, chalked the ground of her property with warnings—only a desperate or ignorant person would be stupid enough to invade a Quimbandeira's cabin—and moved to São Salvador, where American tourists were more likely to visit.

Still, the Lord of Chaos did not come.

Knowing in her heart that Exú would not visit her until she had obeyed his command, she devoted all of her time to hunting down the American by whatever means, magical and mundane. After two years, she gave up on São Salvador and moved again.

*Find him before he finds you.*

This time, she chose the most famous city in all of Brazil—because where else would an American go? Four years later, she had a new terreiro in a new forest with new followers. But still, no American.

Although Exú had warned her that she would not be happy with the results if she failed, he had not told her what form this unhappiness might take or whether it would be inflicted upon her by this unknown American or by Exú himself.

Big difference.

Serafina could handle the abuse from a man, but from a god? Even Exú's favors were excruciating to bear. If the Lord of Chaos ever intended to truly torture her, Serafina had no doubt the anguish would last an eternity.

She turned her attention to Michael Cross.

Although she could not investigate every American who entered her city, Serafina kept her mystic senses attuned for anyone out of the ordinary. Those senses had erupted when she had opened the newspaper to one of Michael Cross' paintings.

Something about the swirling colors had dragged her to this pretentious Ipanema event.

The paintings were even more vivid in person. She could not say the same about the man. He was as bland as his sun-bleached hair and tanned Caucasian skin. In fact, of the two Americans in the gallery— Michael Cross and Jackson White—his obese art agent was by far the more impressive of the two. Jackson White exuded confidence and took charge of the room in a way Serafina could respect. Michael Cross faded into the background. The artist exuded so little energy it had taken Serafina thirty minutes just to find him at his own art show.

She snorted. The man looked as though he had seen a ghost. Perhaps, he was a crazy savant who could only function when he was doing what the gods had blessed him to do; assuming gods blessed Americans. Her cackle drew disapproving looks from a pompous man and his ugly wife.

"What?" Serafina asked, tossing her wild black hair and raising her breasts toward the flat-chested sow. "Did I disturb your fragile sensibilities? How about you, papi?" She ran her hands down the sides of her tight green bodice and over the waist and hips of her black flare-leg slacks. "See anything you like?"

The husband scoffed and turned his wife away from Serafina, muttering about cheap whores and favela trash. Serafina didn't care: People who mattered more had called her worse.

A waiter paused to offer her a choice of wine from his tray.

"Do you have anything stronger than this?"

When he shrugged, she took two glasses of red, guzzled them down in quick succession, then replaced the empty glasses on the tray. She flicked her fingers at the stunned waiter and gave him a wicked smile.

"Go away, boy, before I drink you, too."

She was done with Ipanema and its weak, bland people. Time to return to Rio Comprido, where the surrounding favelas added color and the nearby forest provided cover for more interesting endeavors.

She took a step and was stopped by a whimper.

Michael Cross was frozen, mid-stride, as though he had surprised a wild boar in the woods. His eyes were huge, as blue and gray as the Bay of all Saints before a breaking storm, a portent of something ominous.

It made no sense. He had everything a man should have—a powerful body, good looks, talent, fame, wealth. What could have terrified him in this ritzy gallery with all these soft and privileged people?

# Chapter Thirty-One

Michael tried to run, but his feet were fixed. He tried to find Jackson, but his head wouldn't turn. All he could do was stare into the inferno while his paintings melted on the walls, until nothing remained except the voice.

"Michael," it whispered, growing louder and more insistent with each repetition.

Beams fell. Clothing caught fire. Bodies were burned and trampled. All he heard was his name repeated with increasing urgency by a heavily accented and disturbingly familiar male voice. Then, as suddenly as it had appeared, the blazing infernal condensed to a single flame and vanished with a click.

Michael stared at the lighter. The tiny gold box was all that remained of the fire he had just seen.

"Fascinating work," the man said, then palmed the lighter and pulled a fat cigar from lips the color of dried blood.

Michael gasped. Julius Amodei? It couldn't be.

The Brazilian smiled and flashed his gold-capped incisor.

"So different from your earlier work," he said, then raised the top of his ivory snake cane to the rim of his white Panama hat. The snake's head paused, ivory eyes watching, ivory tongue distended as if tasting Michael's scent on the air. "I approve."

The tiny man blew a puff of smoke into Michael's eyes, making them water and sting. By the time Michael had rubbed away the discomfort, Julius Amodei was gone.

"You okay, Cross?" Jackson asked, causing Michael to jump. "Hey. What's wrong?"

Instead of answering, he scanned the room. It looked the same as it had before with paintings on the wall, people drinking and chatting, and Julius Amodei nowhere to be seen.

Jackson locked her arm in his. "You're not going to lose it on me, are you Cross? Because I just sold another painting, and I don't want the mayor of Rio thinking you're some kind of nutcase."

"No. I'm okay."

"You sure? Because you don't look okay."

"I'm fine, honest. I just thought I saw someone I knew." He wasn't about to mention the blazing inferno.

Jackson peered up at Michael, as if deciding whether or not she should believe him. When he looked away, he spotted another woman doing the same. She was easily six feet tall with wild black hair and startlingly amber eyes that bored into his own.

Jackson tapped his shoulder. "Hello? What's wrong with you? Who was this person you thought you recognized?"

Michael pried his gaze from the amber-eyed woman and turned his attention back to Jackson. "I don't know. I mean, we're in Rio. It's not like I know anyone here."

She shrugged. "Why not? Your patrons are rich enough to travel. Why wouldn't one of them be here?"

She had a point. Julius Amodei was from Brazil. Sebastião might have invited him.

"Have you seen the guest list?" he asked.

Jackson frowned. "What do you think?"

Of course she had. Not that she would have needed it. Aside from her astounding mental catalogue of names, Jackson made a point to shake every hand at every one of his events.

"His name is Julius Amodei."

She pursed her lips. "Doesn't sound familiar. How do you know him?"

Michael thought about the mysterious influence the man had exerted on his life; inspiring, motivating, destroying. How could he explain any of that to Jackson? It barely made sense to him. Better not to try.

"He once told me my work was shit."

Jackson's laughter bounced off the walls and drew inquiring glances from every person in the gallery. She laughed again and dismissed them all with a shooing motion of her brightly-painted fingernails before returning her focus to Michael.

"Well it's not shit now, Cross. Definitely. Not. Shit." She patted his shoulder. "Go outside and get some air. You're scaring the guests." She caught his chin before he could look. "I was kidding." She pinched his cheeks. "Seriously, go get some air. I've got this."

He nodded. If she wanted him to get some air, he'd happily comply, especially since it was what he had wanted to do in the first place. Lucky for her, they were on the second floor of the gallery and his only escape was a balcony that ran the length of the building. If they had been on the ground floor, he would have hit the streets running and not stopped until dawn.

The night air felt uncomfortably warm after the air conditioning, but at least it was fresh. He breathed it in and smiled. Freedom. He shrugged off his jacket and draped it on the railing, leaned his forearms on either side, and admired the Ipanema lights.

It felt good to be alone with no one to impress, no one to study his every expression, no one to analyze his motivations or dissect his artistic mind. Just him, the lights, and his scar. He wasn't obsessed about the patterned flesh that covered the back of his knuckles and extended up to the elbow of his right arm, but after the hallucination he had just seen and the blue balcony light shining down, it was hard not to look. Harder still not to remember.

The burn scar had faded over the years. His fear and confusion about the incident had not.

"You're the artist, aren't you?" a man asked, tapping a crinkled pack of Lucky Strikes against his palm. A tan and green bowling shirt hung over his equally crinkled slacks. "Tom Kerrigan, art critic for the Rio Times."

Michael looked up the shirt to a scruffy face. "You sound American."

Kerrigan nodded. "Expat. The Rio Times is an English language paper."

"Ah."

Michael considered walking away but didn't want to be rude, especially to a critic. "How do you like living here?"

Kerrigan shrugged. "It's got its obvious pluses—women, beaches, food. Humidity's a bitch, but you get used to it. Carnaval is like nothing you've ever experienced. Events like this?" He glanced back through the glass doors and shrugged. "It's a bit much for my taste."

Michael laughed. "A bit."

"I find a smoke and fresh air helps. Yes, I'm aware of the irony."

He flipped the top of the pack, shook out a few cigarettes, and offered one to Michael.

"No thanks."

"Yeah, I probably don't need another one." He patted the cigarettes back into the pack and flipped the lid shut. "I'm guessing you're more of a solitary person, huh? Makes sense, being an artist. You probably need space to create."

Michael sighed; so much for turning the conversation away from himself.

He stared at the view, hoping the critic would take the hint and leave. He didn't, although he did refrain from asking any more questions. After a few minutes, Michael decided to reward his courtesy. "It's all about the art, either you respond to it or you don't."

"Is that a statement or a question?"

"Statement, I guess."

"Is there a question?"

Michael thought for a moment. "Why do they need to know me? Why is everyone so interested in the inner workings of my mind?"

Kerrigan chuckled. "Haven't you ever read a poem or listened to the lyrics of a song and wondered what had inspired it or the stories behind the metaphors? And if you ever had the opportunity to meet the artist, wouldn't you want to ask?"

"No. I've always been satisfied with my own interpretations. I mean, isn't that what really matters? How the art affects us, personally? How it makes us feel when we read, listen, or look at it? Art is meant to evoke emotion and thought, to expand our perspective with new ideas and questions we never thought to ask. How can we expect it to do any of that if we don't take the time to digest what we find? It's not a Big Mac. It shouldn't be handed to us in some neat little wrapper that tells us what it is."

Michael stopped, shocked by all that had tumbled from his mouth. It wasn't like him to disclose personal thoughts to a stranger, let alone a journalist. Kerrigan had caught him at a weak moment with too many thoughts begging to be spoken. Now, he'd probably read the regurgitated mess in tomorrow's paper.

"You know what bugs me the most?" Michael said, ignoring the voice in his head telling him to shut up and run. "That there has to be some deep, dramatic meaning in every work of art. What's wrong with the mundane? That's where the magic is. That is, if people have the eyes to see it—which, by the way, most do not."

Kerrigan didn't react, giving Michael every opportunity to hang himself.

"I think I've said enough for one night."

The critic nodded. "Maybe so."

Michael wanted to walk away, he really did. But for some reason, he needed this man to understand.

"When I'm experiencing someone else's art, I don't want to know what was going on in their head. That's their experience. I want my own. Does that make any sense to you?"

Kerrigan shrugged. "It might make sense to my readers."

Michael sighed. He should have shut up and run.

# Chapter Thirty-Two

The balcony ran the length of the building and connected the main gallery to the adjoining showroom where Sebastião had displayed Michael's smaller paintings; canvases that measured less than five feet in length. Some of Michael's favorite pieces hung in that room. He looked through the glass doors and was pleased to see so many guests until he realized that they weren't admiring the paintings; they were gossiping.

What could be more important than the art? Wasn't that what they had come here to see?

He slipped on his jacket, came inside, and leaned against a stone pillar the same shade of bland as his clothes. No one would notice him, not with the way they sloshed their Chardonnay and flashed their shiny watches and sparkly rings. Some shared pretentious thoughts about his paintings. Most of them just bragged about their lives, so intent upon projecting their own fabulousness they set the room buzzing with sound and motion.

That's when he saw her. As still as a statue in a garden of bees.

She examined the painting with intense concentration, so still she might have stopped breathing. She tipped her head in thought, moved closer to inspect a detail, then stepped back to take in the whole. Deliberate. Focused. Oblivious of the buzzing around her.

She was beautiful, painfully so, and his heart ached just to look at her. The dark sable hair. The honey pecan skin. The pearlescent sheath that draped from one shoulder, across her breasts, and fell to the floor like the gown of a Grecian goddess.

Everything about her called to him.

He moved closer, taking care to project as little presence as possible. He didn't want to disrupt her focus or attract the bees.

She moved on, examining one painting after another with studied care. Each one seemed to evoke a different emotional reaction. He had never seen anyone this engaged for so long. It was as if she were locked in the midst of a meaningful conversation that only she could hear.

He cringed at the thought. Disturbing memories of his own secret conversations with non-existent beings shoved their way to the front of his mind. He shoved them back. They didn't belong in this magical moment. Besides, the beauty had settled in front of his favorite painting.

Slashes of crimson, peacock, and cadmium orange. Swirls of emerald. A zigzag of magenta. All intermingled with the deepest bittersweet chocolate, dancing around a molten amber smudge.

Could she feel the same heat and movement he had felt while painting it? He smiled at the irony. After lecturing the art critic about how art should be experienced independently from the artist, here he was hoping this lovely stranger would intuit his intent.

Hypocrisy? Ego? Desperation? He didn't know what flaw had led to his lapse in artistic morality, but he couldn't deny it. For some inexplicable reason, he needed this woman to understand.

"Voce gosta?" he asked.

She answered without taking her eyes from the painting. "Sim. Gosto muito."

She liked it, but that wasn't enough. What he hungered to know required more than Rosetta Stone basics. He abandoned his rudimentary Portuguese, switched to English, and hoped she would understand. "How does it make you feel?"

Her lips parted with a sigh and her chest collapsed. The change was so startling it made him wish he could take back the question. He was just about to tell her to forget it, when she surprised him with an answer. "It makes me want to be inside of it."

He held his breath and willed her to say more.

"They call this abstract art," she said, with a shrug of uncertainty. "But these paintings feel very real to me. Can you not feel the dance?"

Of course he did. He would have told her so if she hadn't continued.

"It feels tribal to me. Do you think that was intended?" She laughed and shook her head. "Maybe I'm seeing what I want to see."

*Don't say it, Cross. Just this once, keep your mouth shut.*

"Does it matter?" he asked, disregarding his good sense.

She thought for a moment then shook her head. "Não. It only matters how the art makes *me* feel."

Michael gaped, shocked to hear his innermost thoughts spoken by her lips.

She waved a graceful hand. "Don't mind me. I'm just thinking aloud. His art speaks to me of my life, that's all." Reluctantly, she turned away from the painting and looked at him. "How about you?"

He laughed. "Oh, yes. It speaks to me all the time." He offered her his hand. "Michael Cross."

Her warm brown eyes widened with surprise as her face flushed to an appealing shade of lovely. "I'm so embarrassed."

"Don't be." Her hand felt soft and warm in his. "I loved hearing your impressions. I can't believe I just said that. Never mind. I mean, not never mind that I loved your impressions. Never mind that I can't believe... You know what? Just—never mind."

*Pull it together, Cross.*

He was still holding her hand. He knew he should let it go, but he couldn't bring himself to do it.

"You know," he said, dragging out the moment. "You still haven't told me your name."

She took a breath and released it with a glorious sound. "Adriana."
He repeated it in his mind like a sigh. Ah-dree-AHH-nah.
Those four syllables struck his heart like a perfect chord.

# Chapter Thirty-Three

Michael Cross was a sociopath. Serafina felt certain of it. Her fleeting contact with his emotionless blue-gray eyes had unnerved her. It was as if the man hadn't noticed her, or worse, dismissed her as unworthy of his attention.

*He* dismissed *her.*

Serafina found the notion so infuriating that she considered stealing a strand of his hair or a drop of his spit to work a magic so powerful he would scream her name as he died. But that would have meant wasting her time on yet another weak man. Serafina was done with weak men.

She stormed from the main gallery and marched down the corridor when the left side of her face grew hot. She covered her cheek with her palm and turned, expecting to see a spotlight pointed at her. Instead, she gazed through the open door into another gallery. Curious as to why the flash of heat had come from there, she entered.

The scene inside this gallery appeared much like the other, only smaller in scale and without musicians. Why would her magical senses have called her in here?

And then she saw her.

Serafina had spied on her granddaughter many times since coming to Rio, which hadn't been easy because Jian Carlo usually kept his wife sequestered in his estate. Yet here she was, alone and vulnerable.

Serafina watched from behind a cluster of people, considering how to capitalize on this opportunity, when Michael Cross came up to

Adriana. Was he as smitten with her as he appeared to be or simply charming a potential buyer? It was hard to tell. Unlike Adriana, who advertised her adulterous desires like a billboard, Michael Cross kept a tighter rein on his expressions. Still, with a little mystical manipulation, Serafina could make sure Adriana not only got what she wanted but what she deserved.

What both she and Jian Carlo deserved.

Michael Cross may or may not be the American Exú had commanded Serafina to find, but she could definitely use him to inflict her revenge on Adriana and Jian Carlo.

Serafina had seen enough. She left the gallery and found a dark alley in which to wait. Twenty minutes later, Adriana emerged and hailed a taxi. Serafina let her go. There was no reason to risk recognition just for a snip of hair or dress, not when she could walk up to Michael Cross and stab him with a knife. Blood strengthened spells, especially blood from a target's own body.

Serafina grinned. She would enjoy causing him pain.

The anticipation sustained her for the ninety-minutes it took for the gallery event to end and the last of the guests to finally leave. During that time, Serafina ran through possible methods of attack and enjoyed the excitement building in her loins.

That's where it always began. Not in the head, as Isolda had tried to make her believe when she drenched Serafina in rooster blood and left her in that cement trough overnight to bind with Yansã. Ordinary mediums, like Isolda, felt the seat of power in their head. Serafina drew power from her sex.

The heat between her thighs radiated up and down. Whether Michael Cross left the gallery alone or with his agent, Serafina would be ready. A quick nick of the knife as they entered a taxi or, if he was alone, a whore's seduction where she could take her time in the shadows, strip away his arrogance, and reduce him to a quivering mass of need and desperation. Give his cock a taste. Then stab him with the knife and leave.

The gallery door opened and Michael Cross emerged.

Serafina advanced.

His agent called down from the balcony. "Sebastião has a car for us."

"I'm going to walk. Probably beat you there."

She laughed and waved, flapping her arms like a giant blue bird in that ridiculous caftan. "Breakfast tomorrow?"

He flashed a thumbs up and walked away.

Why would a successful woman like Jackson White waste her time on an arrogant, talentless client? Children finger-painted with more artistry than Michael Cross. Yet, if not for the bright colors of his painting against newsprint, Serafina would never have looked twice at his work. Never come to this event. Never seen him with Adriana.

Oh yes, it would please her greatly to stick him with her knife.

He tossed his jacket over his shoulder and turned down a one-way street that led to the shore. He seemed in no hurry as he paused to stare at an intersection paved with red and blue geometric patterns. When he crossed the street, he ran up and down a flight of steps for no apparent reason.

Perhaps he was crazier than she thought.

A bicyclist whizzed by and clipped his arm. Instead of yelling at the boy or chasing after him, the crazy American bolted up the street in a different direction. Horns blared as he charged between cars. Serafina had no choice but to chase after him.

He ran effortlessly, as if his body were made for speed, and although her legs were long and strong, she couldn't match his pace. He leapt over cement posts, bicycle racks, and a dog scrounging for food. He darted through parked cars and strolling tourists.

Why was he running?

Serafina jogged to a stop and clung to a corner lamppost, panting with exhaustion. As much as she wanted to pursue, she could not.

He shouted from somewhere not too far away. "Why are you following me? Get out. What do you want?"

His words made no sense. No one was following him except for her, and she had yet to catch up with him. Who was he yelling at? If she wanted answers, she had to keep moving.

When she rounded the corner, Michael Cross was running beside a taxi, shaking the door handle and screaming. "What do you want from me? Get out and face me, you coward."

He slapped the trunk.

"Amodei. Do you hear me? I'll find you."

As the taxi passed Serafina, the rear window rolled down and the head of a white snake emerged—the top of an ivory cane—followed by the face of a very black man wearing a very white hat. His laughter carried through the night, as did his words.

"I'm counting on it."

# Chapter Thirty-Four

Adriana closed the book with a sigh. She envied the fictional heroes. No matter how hard and dangerous their lives, they still persevered. No matter what the challenge, they faced it with resolute spirit and clear purpose.

Her spirit and purpose had fled when she married Jian Carlo; when she had chosen to live his life instead of hers.

She could still see the sterile room in the civil registry offices where the officiate had pronounced them man and wife. Despite her devout Catholic upbringing and the Catholic beliefs of her foster parents, Jian Carlo had convinced them all that a church wedding without family would stir up too many painful memories for Adriana. She had agreed, feeling grateful for her future husband's sensitivity. Now, she was not so sure.

She closed her eyes and tried to picture the vibrant paintings she had seen this evening. Michael Cross had purpose; or he wouldn't have touched her soul with mere canvas and paint.

How would it feel to wake up each morning knowing exactly what she needed to do?

She opened her eyes. Even the sight of the rosewood piano, standing meters from her chair, could not resurrect that kind of passion and purpose.

Jian Carlo had given her the piano as a wedding gift to make her feel comfortable in his house. At first, she had marveled at the instrument's warm beauty, resonant sound, the gentle resistance of its keys…and the gorgeous wood. Every piece of furniture, floor, banister, and door in Jian Carlo's house had been crafted from the trees in his company's forest. All the more reason to appreciate his thoughtful gift. Or so he had said.

During their courtship, Jian Carlo had visited her every day and every night—a freedom he attributed to owning his own business. After the wedding, his workdays grew progressively longer.

She had not minded, at first, since there was much to be done to settle into her new home. However, as the workdays bled into night, Adriana grew lonely. She missed Mamã Ana and Papá João. When she told Jian Carlo about this, he asked how she could feel lonely when she had such a beautiful piano? She filled her emptiness with Mozart and Bach, but while the music kept her company, it also brought memories. Betrayal. Loss. Depression. The notes pulled Adriana back to her final concert when her life had been perfect, before she had destroyed everything by spying on her parents. One bad decision had ruined it all.

If Adriana had not spied on her parents, she would never have discovered her mother's animosity for her father. She would not have worried about leaving him behind to study with Jorge Ortiz Pereira. Without that worry, she would not have guilted Papai into confronting Mamãe. If not for that confrontation, Mamãe would have been happy and healthy in São Paulo. She wouldn't have caught pneumonia or whatever it was that killed her. The da Silvas would still be family. And Adriana and Papai would not have gone to live with Avó Serafina in her scary cabin in the woods.

Mamãe was dead because Adriana had spied.

She realized all of this during her years at A Escola de Eduçáo Sustentável, before her father finally came to visit. Now, years later, she still felt the same. What a selfish and ungrateful child she had been, buried in her stuffed animals and sniveling to Papai as if her world were coming to an end. Had she really believed she would die of heartache without him? She had never been that lucky. She would have survived whether she wished it or not.

She hugged her book and nestled deeper into the armchair that should have been comfortable but was not. Like all the gorgeous furniture in Jian Carlo's house, the warm wood left her cold. These days, everything about Jian Carlo felt cold.

Adriana stood, her book and chair no longer a comfort. She was done wallowing in self-pity. It was time to take responsibility and change the conditions of her life. Be brave like the heroes in her books.

She left the parlor and headed for the stairs, taking care to admire the polished tigerwood balustrade. From now on, she would feed the positive and starve the negative by focusing on her blessings, like the rhythmic chirps of bats and frogs coming from the adjacent park. How beautiful they sounded.

Adriana smiled, pleased with how quickly the blessings appeared. It proved what Mamã Ana had always promised: If Adriana looked for the good, she would find it.

Her husband was not neglectful. He was responsible.

She was not directionless. She was discovering herself.

Her home was not isolating. It was...what?

Adriana stopped at the base of the staircase, not wanting to carry her negative feelings to the next floor. She missed the familiarity of Rio's West Zone, where Mamã Ana and Papá João lived and where she and Isabel had gone to school; but that did not mean the South Zone was bad. Jian Carlo's estate was within an hour's walk of both Ipanema and Copacabana, something Adriana appreciated since she did not have a car of her own. When Jian Carlo allowed it, as he had tonight, she could attend exciting events. Like gallery shows for handsome American artists.

Just thinking about Michael Cross made her flush in places a married woman should not flush, except with her husband. It had been years since Jian Carlo had done anything to pleasure her.

"Stop it," she scolded herself, determined not to dwell on the negative. Like how she had begged Jian Carlo to let her attend the art show. Adriana did not want to dwell on that, either.

"Then you will think of nothing," she said, and headed up the stairs.

When she neared the top of the curve, she heard Jian Carlo speaking on the phone in Spanish, probably to his client in Mexico City. She stifled a bitter laugh. How like him to conduct business after midnight.

She approached the doorway and stopped. Like any predator, Jian Carlo made his boundaries clear. The office was his lair. While she could not see or smell the territorial markings, the feel of them prickled her skin.

Jian Carlo sat in profile, reclined on a tilting chair with his bare feet dangling over the corner of his massive bloodwood desk. He seemed relaxed and confident. She waited, hoping to get his attention for the first time since breakfast.

His easy smile tightened into a grimace of impatience as he covered the mouthpiece of the phone. "What now?"

Adriana stepped back. She had no idea how to respond when he treated her like a pestering child. Her indignation was muddled by doubt. She had been caught spying. Of course he was annoyed.

Jian Carlo opened his hand as if to invite an explanation he clearly did not want to hear then took his feet off the desk and swiveled his chair away from her.

Adriana stood there a moment longer, stared at the back of his head, and listened to his ramblings in Spanish. Once upon a time, he had courted her with respect and passion. Once upon a time, she had friends and family to support her.

Once upon a time belonged in storybooks.

When she reached the doorway to her bedroom, she paused. Across the hall, Jian Carlo's open bedroom door gave her a clear view of his massive four-poster bed. Five years had not dampened the memory of their passionate honeymoon, nor had the years dampened her desire to repeat them. But that was silly. Marriage could not be an endless honeymoon. He had told her this many times, especially during those nights when he had barged into her bedroom, drunk and mean. Perhaps romance could not be sustained, but did sex have to be so harsh?

Adriana sighed.

Jian Carlo was not harsh. He was pragmatic.

Their marriage was not loveless. It was adult.

She was not forgotten. She was…

How could she feel forgotten when he depended on her to run the household and make a good impression on the philanthropic society wives?

She turned away from his bedroom and the bloodwood bed she had not laid on in years. It was dark and red and imposing. A perfect match to his desk. How appropriate. A bully in business and a bully in bed.

Jian Carlo had decorated Adriana's bedroom quite differently, with furniture made from a lighter, more feminine wood. Never mind that the wood's nickname, stone tree, was used in vulgar slang, or that he had not consulted her before making the choice.

Adriana replaced her novel in the shelved headboard, which held everything from texts on religion and ecology, to adventure-fantasy and literary-fiction. She loved her books and the ingenious headboard that allowed them to watch over her dreams. Jian Carlo had commissioned the shelved headboard for her as a wedding present—a deeply romantic gesture.

Wasn't that a sign of love?

Adriana crawled into bed and smiled at the photo on her dressing table of a person she loved above all. The two of them were hovering over a pink cake, eyes sparkling, as they dipped their fingers into the frosting—Isabel excited about college, Adriana eager to become an assistant teacher. Both of them had promised to always be sisters and friends.

"Sweet dreams, Isabel, wherever you are."

Adriana shut out the light. Perhaps, they should have just promised to stay in each other's lives.

# Chapter Thirty-Five
## Hameau de Vieille Forêt, France 1560

Philippe groaned as all around him villagers marched up the hill, lighting the night with fire. He clawed at their arms, trying to knock the torches from their hands, when a farmer grabbed him by the hair and threw him to the ground.

"Stay, you dog."

Philippe dug his fingers in the dirt and growled. During times of stress, he always resorted to his animal ways. Simple-minded they called him. Everyone except Colette.

At the top of the hill, Révérend Père d'Amboise stepped onto a crude wooden platform. Philippe wanted to tear out the man's throat, but he was only a child. He did the only thing he *could* do—he crawled up the hill to watch his only friend die.

"Don't let him do this to me," Colette yelled to the crowd, bucking against the ropes that bound her to the stake. "I'm innocent. D'Amboise is not a man of God. He's a monster. Please listen to me. Someone help me. Please."

No one listened.

Philippe barked.

No one listened to him, either.

Révérend Père thumped his staff on the platform and waited for silence. "We gather tonight to execute the will of God."

"Blasphemer," Colette shouted, making the villagers grumble and

Philippe swell with pride. Colette was the bravest person on Earth. Even now, about to face a horrible death, she would protect Philippe as she always had, no matter the cost, even when he had begged her not to.

"Gag the witch."

The man who yelled these words lived across the creek from Philippe and Colette. He was an ugly man, mean as a badger, who had sniffed around their cottage many times trying to entice Colette with biscuits baked by his wife. As the badger-man gagged Colette, Philippe hugged Maman—the mother lent to him by Colette since he didn't have one of his own—and snarled at Révérend Père.

The priest smirked at Philippe then turned to the rest of the villagers. "Take heart, my children, there's nothing to fear. The witch has made herself known."

Révérend Père gestured to the baker, standing beside him with a torch, to move forward and light the pyre.

"Let those who embrace the darkness burn in the righteous flames of purity."

The baker ignited the grass stuffed beneath the kindling. The blacksmith and weaver advanced to do the same. Philippe screamed and lunged at a farmer boy barely older than him, but the teen just swatted him away. The wood caught fire, the thinner branches first and then the logs, until the entire pyre was ablaze.

Colette screamed through the gag as flames caught on her gown and climbed her legs.

Philippe screamed as well.

He screamed as the fire ate Colette's flesh. He screamed as the villagers went back to their homes. He screamed as Révérend Père faded into the night. He screamed away the last sounds he would ever utter.

Colette was gone. Philippe was to blame.

He picked up a polished tin, left behind by one of the villagers, and studied his reflection as ash and hair blew across his miserable face.

# Chapter Thirty-Six
## Rio de Janeiro – Present Day

Michael cried and thrashed against the sheets that bound him like a burial shroud. He had to get free, but the more he jerked and kicked, the tighter the sheets became. He needed to calm down and stop moving. He needed to get a hold of this panic and think clearly.

He took a deep breath and stared at the ceiling; not a night sky. A ceiling, in a room, in a hotel, in Ipanema; not a hillside in some God forsaken village in France. When he had stared long enough to distinguish molding from walls in the dim evening light, he calmly unwrapped himself from the sheet and sat up.

A gentle glow from the moon and the street lamps below bled through the gossamer curtains and provided enough light to see. If he had pulled the blackout drapes, the room would have been dark as the country night of his dream. Thank God he had left them open. Though after witnessing that priest's cruelty, Michael wasn't so sure God was keeping watch.

He shoved away the Egyptian cotton and the goose-down pillow, swung his feet off the bed, and planted them firmly on the hardwood floor. The breeze felt good on his sweat-dampened skin. He enjoyed it a moment, slipped on a pair of drawstring pants, and walked out to the balcony.

Ipanema Beach stretched below, beyond that, the Atlantic Ocean, and off to the right, the twin peaks of Dois Irmãos. Two Brothers Mountain looked darker this wee-morning hour when most of the residents had gone to bed. Only a few dozen lights of diehard partiers or insomniacs remained lit to define the mountain's shape.

Michael breathed in the salty air, hoping to cleanse the nightmare from his mind. The scent was tainted with smoke. Smoke and heat and screams. Even freed of the dream, he could still feel the remnants of the horror. He could still feel the ash dusting his forehead and the wisps of hair blowing across his face.

Michael gasped.

*It couldn't be the same boy. Could it?*

He hurried back into the suite, this time through the living room door, and tangled himself in another set of gossamer curtains. The damn place was full of them. He shook himself free, switched on a light, and scanned the room. The tree trunk slices that served as coffee tables were bare, except for flowers and tourist guides. The small dining table and the glass desk behind the couch were scattered with an assortment of travel crap. He checked the floors and the chairs and the couch.

He had to find it. He had to see that face.

His heart raced and his torso sweat when he finally found the object of his search exactly where it should be—on the nightstand beside his bed.

He picked up the sketchbook and stroked the soft leather cover, afraid of what he'd find inside. It was a stupid fear. His childhood sketch was either tucked in the rear pocket or it wasn't. It either showed what he remembered or it didn't. Not looking wouldn't change a thing.

He unwound the leather strap, opened the cover, and fanned the pages, letting the penciled images flash by in disjointed animation, until he reached the back of the book. A flat pocket had been sewn into the leather with just enough room for a folded piece of art paper. With trembling hands, he unfolded the paper and held it under the light.

There, in shades of gray and black, was the grief-stricken boy from Michael's dream. He was sure of it. He knew Philippe's face as well as if he had stared at it for years in still-water reflections and shiny metal pans. The ash-dusted hair swept across the boy's face exactly as Michael had watched it blow in his dream.

"It's not possible," he muttered, as he stared at the face he had drawn twenty-three years ago while lying on a bearskin rug in his family's Lake Tahoe Estate. Michael had been seven at the time—a boy haunted by the face of another boy he wouldn't see again until now.

But why?

Michael stroked the patterned skin on his scarred arm, a memento from that horrible night. The sketch. The boy. The fire. His previous encounter with Philippe had not ended well.

# Chapter Thirty-Seven

When Adriana found Jian Carlo sitting at the breakfast table, sipping café com leite and reading O Globo, she flashed back to her grandfather, Avô Guilherme—elegant, aloof, and powerful. The similarities were uncanny. And here she was, just like Avó Jurema, waiting on the sidelines, hoping to be thrown a bit of affection.

"You slept in," he said.

"A little."

Adriana nodded for Irma to fill her china cup with sweetened milk-coffee. "Obrigada."

The maid smiled politely, brought over a basket of hard-crusted bread and a terrine of dark yellow butter, and she returned to her corner post.

Irma had worked for Jian Carlo since before the marriage. Adriana often wondered what secrets the maid knew about her husband that she did not. Although, if there were any tales to be told, Adriana doubted Irma would be the one to tell them. The rustic woman was as stiff as the starched gray uniform she was forced to wear.

Adriana buttered a thick chunk of bread and browsed through the discarded portion of the newspaper. She didn't care how the politicians, celebrities, and other prominent Cariocas would ring in the new year. It gave her something to do while she waited for Jian Carlo to ask about the art show.

She never went anywhere alone at night. He should have been dying to hear about it. But there he sat, reading, as he did every morning. If his dismissive behavior were not so typical, it would have infuriated her. This morning, it only made her impatient.

"I saw some beautiful paintings last night," she ventured. "Perhaps, we could buy one." When he did not respond, she continued. "We could put it in the entryway. Or maybe, here, in the breakfast room?" His silence was unbearable. "I think the colors would be stimulating."

Jian Carlo folded the section he was reading and exchanged it for another. "I like the art we have. I chose it with great care."

"I just thought—"

"Don't."

"What?"

"Think."

Jian Carlo lowered the paper a few inches and fixed her with a stern gaze. "Look. It was sweet when you tried to educate yourself about my business, memorizing the names of the trees and so forth. But you remember how that turned out, right? You got it in your head that you could somehow work for me, as if that would be acceptable on any level."

"This isn't the same thing."

"Of course it is. It is exactly the same." He looked back down at his paper. "Leave the art to me, Adriana. Go find yourself another hobby."

Sweet? *Memorized?* She had done more than that. She had spent days in the library, researching everything there was to know about the exotic woods of Brazil and the various forestry projects throughout the country. And not just the trees, she had also researched the artists that he employed. She had evaluated their public reach, mission statements, and style. She had even written up a proposal describing who she thought would be best for upcoming projects. Hobby? Meu Deus.

He turned another page. "What do you have planned for today?"

"It's New Year's Eve. I thought we'd spend it together."

He peeked over his paper. "I have work to do. You can't expect me to cater to you all day."

She bit the insides of her cheeks to keep her smile frozen in place. Nothing she did pleased him. Not sexy lingerie and candle-lit dinners. Not doting on him or learning his business. Not philanthropy or self-improvement. When she had asked to go to college, he had said, "Married women don't run off to play with their friends." And a year later, "I won't have my wife assisting teachers at a government-run school."

Nothing she did made him happy.

"Oh. I forgot to tell you," he said, folding his paper neatly and setting it on the table. "I have to entertain distributors this evening." He held up his hands before she could respond. "I know, but they're leaving tomorrow. It's important I spend as much time with them as possible."

"I could come with you."

The words fell from her lips before she could stop them. She shut her eyes against the ridicule that would surely follow. When none came, she felt encouraged. Maybe he'd let her join him for once.

She took a breath and opened her eyes, just in time to watch him leave.

# Chapter Thirty-Eight

Michael had rechecked the charcoal image so many times in the last five hours that the creased fibers of the paper had finally disintegrated. He stacked the pieces carefully and returned them to the secret pocket of his leather-bound book. After all these years the boy had returned.

Why?

Michael closed the sketchbook and slid it to the side of the desk. Better to spend his time on questions that could be answered.

Where could he find Julius Amodei?

Michael scrolled down the web list displayed on the hotel's computer screen, hoping a different internet access from a computer with a different search history would provide different results. Unfortunately, this computer brought up the same hits he had seen on his laptop back home.

How could a prominent Brazilian art collector be so hard to find in his own country?

The door to the business center opened, admitting the ambient noise from the lobby and his exuberant agent.

"I looked for you in the restaurant. You missed one helluva breakfast."

Michael nodded toward a cloth napkin, loosely wrapped around half-dozen balls of pão de queijo. "Got some."

"Ooh, cheesy bread. May I?"

She stuffed an entire ball into her mouth and squeezed herself into the chair at the adjoining computer station.

"I love Brazil." She licked the butter from her fingers. "What're you doing?"

"Checking my emails."

"What's wrong with your laptop?"

"Didn't bring it."

"Your phone?"

"Charging."

"Tablet?"

"You're nosy this morning."

"*This* morning?" Jackson chuckled and snagged Michael's leather-bound book with one of her long, pink nails. "What's this?"

Michael clasped his hands to keep from snatching back the book. If she thought he didn't want her to look inside, she'd never let it go.

"These are incredible. How did I not know you did this?"

She settled on a sketch he had done the previous day of a lone sunbather reclining in the shallows of the rooftop pool, back arched, face to the sun, knee bent to repeat the shape of the Twin Brothers Mountain behind her. Unlike his abstract paintings, Michael penciled with realistic detail, from the grains of wood on the privacy walls to the steel bolts fastening the glass railings. If Jackson looked closely enough, she might even see Michael's reflection drawn into the wood-framed ear-shaped mirrors that hung on the wall behind the lounge chairs.

Michael gave her a satisfied smirk. "Unobservant?"

"Amusing. But seriously." She thumbed back through the other sketches. "I don't even know what to say. These are phenomenal."

"They're just snapshots—places I've been, things I've seen. They're not show-worthy."

"Excuse me? You're just the artist. I decide what is or is not show-worthy."

She fanned back to a drawing of an animated couple sipping cappuccinos at a Venice Beach sidewalk café while a sparrow stole crumbs off the edge of their table. Jackson shook her head then peered at Michael as if she had never truly seen him before.

"Have you always done this?"

"What?"

"Recorded life with such painstaking detail."

He shrugged. "Pretty much."

"I've always thought of you as a grand conceptualist—huge canvases, vibrant colors, evocative themes. But these intricate little drawings?" She shook her head in wonder. "I have to admit, I'm surprised you can even see in black and white. I mean, come on. Michael Stark without color?"

Michael stiffened, remembering that awful day when Julius Amodei had appeared on his doorstep weeks before Michael's professional debut.

*You draw with charcoal because you are handicapped, Senhor Cross. This is not art. This is weakness.*

Even now, ten years later, his mentor's words stung.

"It was a simple question, Cross."

"Sorry. I just spaced out. What did you want to know?"

"Have you ever tried using charcoals?" When he didn't immediately answer, she touched her pink nail to the bottom of his chin and lifted his jaw. "Don't gape, darling. You're not a fish."

He closed his mouth and shook his head, at an utter loss as to how he was supposed to answer such a loaded question. Should he tell her how deeply Amodei had betrayed him, showing up at Michael's college art event, convincing him to move to Venice Beach, setting him up with a gallery, then telling him his work was shit? Or should he tell her what he had done to those charcoals after Amodei had left?

He shuddered.

How could he explain the fury he had felt alone in his apartment? Or the hysteria that had arisen as he ran through the alleys of Venice

Beach hunting for Amodei? Or the disgust he had felt upon returning home and having all those accusing eyes watching him from the walls? He had let them down, every one of them. His subjects had opened their souls, trusted him to tell their stories with skill and empathy, and he had made a mockery of their suffering or so he had felt at the time after hearing his mentor's cruel denouncement.

He shouldn't have been surprised. His mother had done the same, and his father, and his college girlfriend. Everyone who ever supported Michael had turned against him when he didn't fulfill their dreams and agendas. Even his guardian spirits—who had always been there to comfort and guide him—had abandoned him when he had needed them most. Why should Julius Amodei have been any different? Why should Jackson?

He closed his sketchbook, slid it out of her hands, and bound it with its leather strap.

Maybe one day he'd trust her enough to tell her why he had torn down every charcoal portrait in the apartment, piled them in the fireplace, and burned them all to ash.

# Chapter Thirty-Nine

Serafina glared at the librarian who had shown her the way to the computer lab then lurked in the corridor to spy. Did she think Serafina was too stupid to know how to use technology or that she would vandalize the equipment? Either possibility made Serafina itch to cast a work of Quimbanda.

She flicked her fingers in dismissal and turned her attention to the screen. The librarian could stay or go, Serafina had more important work to do. Like track down information about Michael Cross.

The "About" page of his website had a large smiling photo and a miniscule biography.

*Michael Cross is a California artist who paints vivid abstracts that evoke powerful emotions and stimulate the imagination. He lives in Venice Beach, California where he paints in his loft, plays basketball at the beach, and runs every day.*

What kind of biography was that?

Wikipedia told her a little more: Michael Cross was from Atherton, California, a town outside San Francisco that his ancestors helped to establish. He had captained his high school basketball team, broken state records for cross country running, and won numerous scholastic awards. Although his father was a professor of Early Modern European History at Stanford University, Michael had attended art school, where he won more prestigious awards. After that, he did nothing noteworthy until five years ago when he painted a mural on the wall of a Japanese market in Venice Beach, became an instant local celebrity, and snagged the most powerful art agent in Los Angeles.

Serafina grunted in disgust. Another rich kid stealing luck from the poor. The more she read about Michael's privileged life, the more she resented him. When she came across a news article about him burning his arm in a fireplace when he was a child, she was glad.

No one deserved that much luck.

# Chapter Forty

Michael did a final sweep of the gallery to check the status of his work. Five of the larger paintings and six of the smaller had discreet placards beneath them, marking them as sold. A lucrative night's work.

He paused in front of the vibrant dance of swirls and slashes that had so captivated Adriana. The piece was called *Abandon*. Michael straightened the placard beneath it until it felt just right. Private Collection. Jackson would be baffled when she learned of this sudden change of heart, but he couldn't sell it. Not after last night.

"Is there anything else I can do for you?" the gallery assistant asked.

The young woman had been exceedingly helpful. Just the fact that she was here, fifteen minutes after the four o'clock closing, instead of preparing for the evening's festivities, was a miracle: Brazilians did not mess around with New Year's Eve.

"No, but thanks. Obrigado. You've been a big help."

Did she give this level of attention to all of their visiting artists? If so, she was a valuable asset to the gallery.

As he started to leave, she strolled along beside him, forcing him to slow his pace.

"You're fortunate your hotel is here in Ipanema. Traffic is terrible during Réveillon, especially in and out of the South Zone. Are you going to one of the private parties?"

He shrugged. "Nathan Borges, I think."

The assistant lit up. "Oh, how very fortunate for you. The Borgeses have a penthouse apartment facing Pedra do Arpoador. Do you know of this? They light it up at night for surfing. Tonight, everyone will be watching the sky. From their penthouse, you'll be able to see the fireworks in Copacabana and Ipanema. Or at least, that's what I've been told. I've never been invited myself. I've always wanted to go."

And there it was, the reason behind her admirable work ethic.

Michael sped up his pace. The last thing he needed around him on New Year's Eve was a woman with an agenda, no matter how alluring she might be.

"Thanks again for staying late." He ignored her slump of disappointment and walked out the door toward a magical view. Twilight had transformed an ordinary street into a transient state of perfection, as though the world were suspended between what was done and what could be. If he had brought his sketchbook, he would have recorded this moment.

"What do you see?" a woman asked. Although her voice was infinitely more appealing than the gallery assistant's, the soothing texture of it did not pry his attention from the evanescent light.

What did he see? How could he possibly explain? More importantly, how could he imprint this image in his mind without the benefit of paper and pencil?

He pressed his hand against the empty pocket where his sketchbook should have been. With that fleeting gesture, the magical light dissolved into dusk. He sighed then turned to apologize to the woman he had so rudely ignored.

It was her. As still as a statue in a garden of bees.

His heart quickened. As with the night before, she was clad in white. This time, instead of sheathed like a Grecian goddess, she had attired herself more casually in a spaghetti-strapped sundress that hugged her breasts and flowed freely over her thighs, stopping at the knees to display shapely calves and graceful ankles. No makeup hid the glow of her skin or lessened the impact of her eyes. Her lips had no need of color or gloss to enhance their fullness. Her face was so perfect Michael couldn't see any way to improve on it.

"Adriana." He whispered it again so he could enjoy the feel of her name in his mouth.

"You remembered." She smiled then flushed. "I didn't mean to intrude."

"Right…I mean, no. You're not. Intruding, that is. Why are you here?" He shut his mouth to stop his rambling.

"I wanted to see your paintings."

"Oh." He shrugged. "The gallery's closed."

"Of course."

She stared at the sidewalk and twirled her finger around a long strand of azure beads, winding them up to her throat and down to her waist. He looked away before she could notice him staring at her breasts, not exactly *at* her breasts but in the general vicinity *of* her breasts. "Shit."

"Excuse me?"

He forced his grimacing face into a show of pleasant civility, and undoubtedly failed. What was wrong with him? He had spoken freely and politely to the gallery assistant, and yet he couldn't string together a coherent sentence for Adriana. Perhaps it was better to cut and run.

"Thanks for dropping by," he said, and turned away.

He felt as awkward as he had when inviting Cindy Clark to the seventh-grade dance. He never did get those words out, and she went with someone else. He stopped on the sidewalk and turned back to face Adriana.

"I'm going for a walk. Would you like to join me?"

He waited for the polite decline. Instead, she smiled and bashfully agreed.

They ambled in companionable silence for several blocks, leaving the awkwardness of their initial encounter behind.

"I'm glad you came," he said.

"Me, too."

This section of Ipanema was quiet, but when they turned a corner, they ran into a crowd of party goers in skimpy clothes, crazy hats, and loud horns blown between gulps of beer. Tourists and locals alike danced in the streets and shouted for women to bare their breasts. Many did. And it wasn't just them. The closer Michael and Adriana got to Copacabana the rowdier the crowd became.

"This is crazier than Venice Beach."

"Italy?"

"California."

"I'd like to go there some time. Are your beaches anything like this?"

Michael looked from the high rise buildings across the broad avenue, to the gray and white paved boardwalk where they stood, to the seemingly-endless beach swarming with humanity. No tiny streets and funky buildings lined the strand. No potheads toked outside seedy motels. No yuppies drank micro-brews on the balconies of their five-million-dollar condos, wedged incongruously between taco stands and tattoo parlors. There were no suntanned weightlifters, break-dancing street performers, or homeless encampments that sprouted after sunset and vanished at dawn. Copacabana was ritzy, expansive, and exotic.

"No," he laughed. "Venice Beach is nothing like this."

He stared into the crowd where congas, steel drums, and guitars competed with recorded music and the deafening live percussion of the samba schools, and shook his head in wonder. "I'm not sure anywhere is like this."

Adriana laughed. "Copacabana is the only place to spend Réveillon."

"What?"

"New Year's Eve."

"Right. Well, I can see why."

Her eyes sparkled with excitement or reminiscence—Michael

couldn't tell which—but both were appealing. He even liked the way her nose twitched as she scrutinized his chest.

"This is not a good shirt," she said.

"What's wrong with it?"

Her fashion statement annoyed him. He had planned to change into nicer clothes before he went to the Borges party, but that wasn't the point: He had expected something deeper from the woman he had seen focused on his art with such intensity. Had he made a mistake?

"Look around you," she said. "What do you see?"

Although people were dressed in all sorts of clothing, most of the locals seemed to be wearing white.

"Did I miss the memo?"

"Excuse me?"

"What's with all the white?"

She shrugged, as if the question were too broad or too obvious to answer.

"Never mind. If it's that important, let's find me another shirt."

"Yes, please. How about over there? I'm sure they'll have something to fit you."

It seemed an odd thing to say until he realized that none of the men around him were taller than five-eight or nine—finding a shirt that fit might not be as easy as he had assumed. Why did it even matter? Adriana hadn't seemed embarrassed by what he wore back at the gallery in Ipanema. Why should she care how he looked now that they were in Copacabana?

He reconsidered his New Year's Eve plans. If Brazilians were this concerned with fashion, he'd rather hole up in his hotel room. But if he bailed on the Borges' party, Jackson would kill him. Nathan Borges had purchased three big-ticket paintings. Although he had to make an appearance, he didn't have to take Adriana.

Before he could come up with a plausible exit plan, she pointed to a white, button-down shirt in a store window. Michael sighed. Even in Rio, the Hawaiian shirt was king.

He gave her a reluctant thumbs up and within a minute, had the shirt bought, tags clipped, and buttons done up to his chest—still exposing the top of his russet tee. If that bothered her fashion sense, too bad. He'd placate her for thirty minutes or so, make his excuses, and leave.

She studied the bit of color at his neck then shrugged. "I guess it'll do. Although I don't know what kind of luck that bit of brown will bring you."

"Luck?"

"Of course. Why else would we be doing this?"

He shook his head. Which was worse: romanticizing her as a goddess or reducing her to a shallow fashionista? Neither were fair, and both made him feel like an ass.

# Chapter Forty-One

Michael's tension faded as he and Adriana joined the tide of excited people on the boardwalk. Normally, the only times he felt this relaxed were when he was painting, running, or deep into a game of basketball. He certainly never felt this way around women. Yet here he was buying flowers from a traveling vendor, kicking off his slippers, and wandering onto the sand as though he and Adriana had done this together all their lives. It felt strange and enjoyable, lulling and exhilarating.

Behind them, strings of Christmas lights draped from balconies, hung from trees, and wound around pillars and poles. The windows from the hotels and condos shone like a thousand eyes peering over the river of red taillights and white headlights flowing along Avenida Atlântica. Farther down the beach, colorful spotlights and neon flashed from the frames of four giant stages and illuminated audiences who jumped and gyrated to the music. Deeper into the beach, the brightness dimmed to the muted glow of firelight.

They wandered near a tight gathering of men and women dressed in loose white clothing who had etched out a small section of sand for themselves. Some, mostly the women, danced in the center. Others clapped and sang. Half-a-dozen men gripped brightly painted drums between their legs and slapped rhythms against the hides.

Michael stepped up to the circle and listened to the man singing beside him. His voice was rough and the tune hardly traceable, but he sang with passion in perfect time with the rhythm. Michael strained to

178

find the meter of the intricate pattern. "I can't follow this beat."

Adriana laid a comforting hand on his shoulder. "You're trying too hard. You must listen but not listen." She removed her hand. "Understand?"

Michael nodded, although he had no idea what she meant. How could someone listen without listening? How could he concentrate when his shoulder still felt the lingering warmth of her touch?

He shrugged away the feeling and focused on the task, ignoring the impulse to group the musical measures into mathematical equations, and let the song wash over him. Every time his logical mind tried to take control, he shoved it aside and envisioned the music as waves, crashing and receding of their own accord. After a while, a rhythm emerged. Not one that he could count but one that his hips and feet seemed to understand.

"You feel it, sim?"

He did. And he liked it.

Inside the ring of swirling white skirts and next to the small bonfire, he glimpsed a statue of an aquamarine mermaid lounging on a square of cyan-blue cloth. "What's with the mermaid?"

Adriana smiled. "That is Yemanjá, the mother of all spirits. Back when our African ancestors were sold to the Portuguese traders and brought across an endless and violent ocean, they prayed to Yemanjá, the goddess of the sea, to preserve them. She answered by delivering them to Brazil. On Réveillon we honor her."

Michael looked at Adriana in surprise: This was the most she had said in one burst since they'd met.

She shrugged. "I spend a lot of time in the library."

"It's interesting. I'd like to hear more."

"Really?"

He couldn't imagine why this would surprise her, but before he could ask, the drummers changed their rhythm. The dancers restrained their movements and the crowd chanted with subdued intensity. Michael struggled to decipher the words, but his rudimentary Portuguese wasn't up to the task. All he could tell from words like Deus and the singular focus of the group, was that the music had become less of a song and more of a vehicle for divine communication.

He stopped swaying. "Should we go?" He didn't want his awkward movement to diminish the ceremony.

Once again, they ambled in silence, letting the crowd carry them where it willed through cigarette-smoking teens, boozing adults, and joyful children. Everyone was having a great time. Drum circles gave way to cheap champagne, flowers, and little toy boats. People laughed and danced and drank.

Michael thumbed to the group behind them. "That felt like a religious rite, but this?" He gestured to the craziness in front of them. "This is a party."

Adriana laughed and danced with the nearest tune. "It's like Christmas. Nearly the whole population celebrates, but only a fraction actually worships."

The energy had animated her in a most appealing way.

"Most Brazilians don't really believe in the goddess Yemanjá, but they still seek her favor. And why not?"

She spun in the sand, propelling her white sundress dangerously high up her shapely tanned thighs.

"We may be a Catholic country, but Umbanda is in our blood."

Her shoulders rolled to the beat of a nearby samba, making it hard for Michael to concentrate.

"What was that?" he asked.

"Umbanda, Macumba Candomblé."

She accentuated each word with a tight rotation of her hips. As the figure eight evolved into a hula-like sway, she beckoned for him to join her, but he was too stunned by her sudden sensuality to do anything but gape, which didn't slow her in the least.

"The Yoruba-based religion has many names in Brazil. Anyone can participate. It's like superstition—even those who don't believe, follow it for luck. Who couldn't use good luck?" she added, with a wink. "We wear white to bring in peace, jump the waves seven times to make our wishes come true, and give offerings the way Americans drop coins in wishing wells."

She took his hands, pushed and pulled to get him to dance.

"Do you see?"

He did. Adriana was more than just a beautiful woman: she was intelligent, perceptive, and passionate.

"Do you believe?" he asked.

She gave him a sly smile. "I do not disbelieve."

He chuckled. And evasive. Adriana was the perfect blend of comfort and mystery. The longer he spent with her, the longer he wanted to stay.

# Chapter Forty-Two

The sky was black when Serafina lit the fire at Devil's Beach, the tiny cove tucked into the rocks of the Arpoador peninsula. This beach did not draw the New Year's Eve crowds like its neighbors, Ipanema and Copacabana. Even the young people who liked to party at Praia Diabo on weekends chose more exciting locations for Réveillon.

Serafina cupped her hands around the flame and encouraged it with her breath until the fire spread from brush to twigs to sticks. She added another log from the pile. There was much work to be done.

She had not brought offerings for Yemanjá as the revelers at Copacabana and Ipanema had undoubtedly done. What was the point? No amount of blue beads or candle-lit boats bearing trinkets and fruit would get Serafina the answers she needed or the power she craved.

Danger had come.

She had dreamt of it last night and could still smell the stink of it on the ocean breeze—an entity determined to seek, save, and destroy. Like a vision glimpsed in dissipating smoke, the unknown entity called to her even as it repelled. Should she answer or flee? Attack or welcome? Her mystic senses tingled with dread and excitement. So much magical potential. But what did it mean? How could she turn it to her advantage?

If she rode the energy like a beast, she could take control of its power and direct it where she wished. If she contained the energy and released it later to do her bidding, she'd have to generate that power herself. Both options required skill. Both, if applied incorrectly, could get her killed.

Serafina needed Exú. If anyone could answer these questions it would be the Master of Magic. If the danger could be turned to her advantage, only he could augment her power and guarantee success.

Serafina shrugged her boat-necked blouse off one shoulder and the next, taking her time as if undressing for a lover, until the garment hung from her breasts. There was power to be had in the suspension before unveiling one's nakedness, especially on a public beach for a god. It was as if she were shouting to the spirit world, "Here I am, a force in my own right, ready and worthy for the challenge."

Six years had passed since Exú's last visit. Six years since he had put her in the body of the French priest. Six years since he had commanded her to search for a mysterious American who might in some way do her harm. After six years of waiting, Serafina was done.

No more chasing her tail. No more pleading for Exú like a heartsick teenager crushing on a samba star. No more guesswork. She would force the Master of Magic to appear if she had to bleed her body dry to do it. One way or another, Exú would come—if not to provide answers then to carry her to Hell.

She yanked down her blouse and skirt and kicked them away, planting herself on the edge of the firelight, legs spread and arms stretched to the night.

"Hail Exú!
Master of Magic,
Lord of Chaos,
Intermediary to the Gods,
Your daughter is here, open and ready to receive you.
Keep me waiting no longer.
I command your presence
And invoke the powers of the Seven Crossroads."

She stalked the rim of the firelight with a jaguar's predatory grace. She crouched and spun and leapt to a music all her own. She ignored the cacophony of drums, tunes, and voices that drifted to the promontory from Copacabana and Ipanema.

"Come to me, Exú,
Immortal Trickster,
Lord of Chaos,
King of the Seven Crossroads.
Your daughter awaits.
Fill me with your power."

Serafina stepped into the firelight so she could be seen. "I am here, Exú. Come inside."

"Why should I?" he asked. "The view is nice from here."

Serafina whirled toward the sound and found Exú lounging on a rock beyond the fire's reach. His posture was as cocky as his expression—one leg bent, the other draped down the front of the rock to expose the bulge beneath the strip of blood-red cloth.

"You have come," she whispered. Just gazing at his magnificence was almost too much to bear. It took every bit of willpower not to spread her legs and beg.

Exú chuckled, making his muscles roll in serpentine waves and his cock twitch beneath his loincloth.

Serafina pried her eyes from the growing shaft. She had to stay focused. God or not, Exú had tossed her aside like all the men in her life. Let him strike her down. She would die as defiantly as she had lived.

"I followed your commands. I shed blood in your honor. And you abandoned me."

Exú glared but Serafina held firm. What did she hope to gain by challenging him in this way? Self respect? A small prize for the risk she was taking. If Exú sent her to Hell, his torment could last forever.

He burst out laughing. "Alcalme-te, Serafina. You are too much fun to kill."

He sat up straight and spread his knees wide, the tented loincloth stood as a clear message between them. He growled, and the vibration of it traveled through the rocks, into the sand, and up Serafina's legs. She flexed her knees to keep from falling and rode the undulating beach. Exú growled louder and deeper until her womb gripped and her vagina ached. She clenched her groin against the assault, but there was nothing she could do to stop the torment of ecstasy he had forced upon her.

What a fool she had been to think she could withstand his punishment. How grossly she had underestimated his creativity. He hadn't even moved from the rock and yet his growl had stimulated her nerves into a frenzy of need. Every twitch shocked her with excruciating pain.

Then he laughed, and she learned the true meaning of torture.

After what felt like an eternity, the laughter stopped, the rumbling receded, and Serafina collapsed. "Forgive me, lord. Forgive me." She pried her face from the sand and braced herself on trembling forearms.

Exú jumped from his perch and kicked the sand like a playful boy. "Why so serious? Get up. Dust yourself off. We have exciting things to discuss."

Serafina elbowed herself up higher. "We do?"

Exú peered back in fascination, making him appear more like a curious child than an immortal god. Even his laughter had changed, tickling her with glee rather than penetrating her with lust. An innocent boy in a fearsome body.

Serafina crawled to her knees, brushed the sand from her face and breasts and belly, then rose to face him with as much dignity as she could manage.

"Is it about the entity or the American?"

Exú flashed his bright teeth. "Both. Neither. You tell me."

"How? I have no knowledge of these things. All I feel is dread."

His eyes gleamed with mischief. "Dread or promise?"

Serafina thought about the climax she had just endured. Now that her suffering had ended, she craved and feared more in equal measure. Pleasure and pain. Had her lord been teaching her a lesson?

There was no Heaven and Hell, righteous and evil, good or bad. Not really. These labels described opposing forces that could, at any moment, be altered or reversed. Even the benevolent forms of her mystic Brazilian religion explained the fluid relationship between good and evil. Exú and his consort, Pomba Gira, were prime examples of this—both erroneously portrayed as devils yet beseeched for favors and protection the way Catholics prayed to saints.

Dread or promise?

"Both?" she asked.

Exú leaped into the air and landed in a wide stance, arms extended and tongue wagging like a crazed Fijian warrior. As he did this, his skin lightened to expose swirling blue tattoos. He changed into a frolicking devil with curved horns and a whipping tail. Again, into a Balinese demon with a shaggy wig, painted mask, and a ribbon-like tongue that draped over the front of his red, black, and white zigzag-printed pajamas.

Exú changed his form and attitude with increasing speed—ugly, comical, handsome, seductive—until the images blurred back to his former glistening onyx skin and powerfully sculpted body.

He held out his arms and smiled.

"What do you think? Are you ready to learn real magic?"

# Chapter Forty-Three

Adriana had not talked, danced, or laughed this much in years. Just the feel of Michael's hands in hers sent tingles of excitement up her arms and into her neck. How could this be happening? She was married. Before Jian Carlo she had never even kissed a boy, let alone...

She let go of his hands and twirled, trying to rub away the tingles.

"Are you cold?" he asked.

"What? Não. Of course not."

*It had to be eighty degrees. Why was she shivering?*

"Yes, you are. Come here."

He wrapped his arms around her and rubbed her back, creating shocks of pleasure. The silky rayon of his shirt against her skin, the hardness of his chest, the tiniest adjustments of flesh against flesh stimulated her beyond sanity.

*Breathe, Adriana. Breathe.*

Michael stopped rubbing and gave her arms a comforting squeeze. "There. You're all warmed up. Isn't that better?"

She suppressed a laugh. Better than what? He had stopped rubbing and pressing, but now she had to look at those kissable lips.

She forced a smile and nodded, not trusting what her rebellious mouth might do if she opened it to speak, then pried away her gaze and looked up into his blue-gray eyes. Big mistake. Their intensity made her lips quiver. She leaned forward for a kiss then pulled back a moment before their lips met. No matter how much her body objected, her mind was still in command. Married women did not kiss men who were not their husbands; no matter how enticing they might be.

"The fireworks will start soon," she said. "We should head for the water and find a good place to watch."

She headed for the shore, emboldened by her practical words and shaken by romantic notions of Michael sweeping her into his arms and forcing her into a kiss. She walked faster. Just because Jian Carlo had ditched her on New Year's Eve did not give her the right to break their marriage vows. He was not kissing another woman; he was entertaining distributors. Isn't that what he had told her this morning?

And the morning before?

# Chapter Forty-Four

Michael's chest felt cold without Adriana pressed against him, as if suddenly deprived of something dear. It made no sense. He had only embraced her so he could rub the warmth back into her body, and yet here he was shivering in her stead.

Logical people did not obsess about illogical things, no matter how their bodies felt.

The woman had caught a chill. He had warmed her up. End of story. So what if his palms could still feel the silkiness of her skin, made abundantly available thanks to the low back of her spaghetti strap dress? So what if he kept sniffing the air for traces of her intoxicating shampoo? Sensations were fleeting gifts to appreciate and release.

Gifts.

Michael was wary of gifts. Too often they came with unexpected price tags.

*Keep it light, keep it fun.*

A giggling brown-eyed girl tugged on his shirt and handed him a flower. She smiled, exposing a gap in the center of her tiny upper teeth, then darted back to her friends, who congratulated her with pats and laughter. Michael stuck his nose in the well of the bright pink blossom and made a huge show of inhaling its sweet fragrance, extracting squeals of delight from the girls. He dipped a gallant bow in thanks and tucked the wilting flower behind his ear.

Rio was a wicked tease sending adorable children to lower his defenses, but if she wanted to play, he would.

He ate the raisins given to him by a wrinkled granny and followed her instructions to spit the seeds in his wallet to attract money. He drank the shockingly sweet cane alcohol, sweetened even further with condensed milk, offered to him by a couple of drunken husbands, and washed it down with the coconut water provided by their wives. He ate homemade empanadas at one campsite and greasy pork on a stick at another—but avoided the shrimp because Adriana warned it had a tendency to go bad in the heat. He bounced and gyrated to a frenzy of samba, disco, hiphop, and jazz, blasting from each of the four gigantic stages, and even joined a conga line to the craziest rendition of "Ticket to Ride" he had ever heard, complete with whistles, tambourines, and enough cowbells to make Christopher Walken proud. He accepted every gift the night had to offer. And he did it all with Adriana by his side.

"Look," she exclaimed, pointing to the ocean. "Are they not beautiful?"

Michael pried his eyes from her lovely profile and looked beyond the shore-break where hundreds of miniature candlelit boats bobbed in the water. Beyond those, a dozen fully-lighted barges followed the wide curve of the coastline like a grin.

"Gorgeous," he said, but what he really meant was her. Adriana's face had relaxed into an expression that was both melancholy and hopeful as she watched people wade into the water to release their boats, toss their beads and trinkets into the surf.

"Those are for the mermaid, right? What was her name?"

"Yemanjá." Adriana twirled her finger around her own strand of azure beads. "The offerings are to thank the goddess for her blessings and protection, and to make our requests for the New Year. If it suits her, she will accept our gifts."

Adriana pulled the beads over her head, cupped them in her hands, and gave them a kiss.

"How can you tell if she accepts?"

"She keeps them. Otherwise, she sends them back."

Adriana cocked her arm and launched the beads far out to sea.

Michael laughed. "She won't be sending back those beads."

"I hope not."

The sadness in her voice gripped his heart. "I just meant it was a helluva throw. Are you okay? What's wrong?"

For a moment, it looked as though she might tell him, but then she shook it off. "Just Réveillon regret. That's all." She gave him a false smile. "Each New Year brings hope. Isn't that true?"

He traced the scar that ran from his knuckles to elbow. The physical effects of sticking his arm into a fire had been relatively easy to heal. The mental anguish that had followed? Not so much. Despite it all, here he stood on a beach in Rio the day after a tremendously successful gallery opening with the most enchanting woman imaginable.

"There's always hope."

She smiled. "Thank you for that." She pointed excitedly to the sea. "It's starting."

The barges had gone dark, leaving only the distant yachts and cruise ships to sparkle in the black sea. The music stopped. Movement stilled. People held their breaths in anticipation.

A voice, amplified by a loudspeaker, led the crowd in counting down the final seconds to the New Year. "*Quatro, três, dois, um—Feliz Ano Novo!*"

The crowd cheered as sparks shot from the barges and created giant fans of white light. Rockets soared and exploded into a riot of color. Thunderous booms shook the beach. Constellations of fireworks died and re-birthed at a frantic pace.

Michael had seen astounding fireworks displays, but none of them came close to this.

Canon after canon shot new miracles into the sky while corks popped and sprayed champagne. People oohed and aahed and gasped and cheered, clapped their hands, and held up cellphones to capture a brilliant story told with dramatic pauses and hurried phrases. The sky erupted with fiery passion, blinding Michael's eyes with explosions of white from one end of the coast to the other.

\*

Adriana had not witnessed this spectacle from the shore since her days at A Escola, when she and Isabel had taken the subway to Copa with their friends. That had been a great time, but not nearly as awe inspiring as tonight. Her body thrummed with so much excitement she thought she might burst into a thousand bits of glorious light. After years of sipping expensive champagne with Jian Carlo's friends and watching pyrotechnics through walls of condominium glass, she was here—in the sand, soaked with cheap wine, beside the most beautiful man she had ever seen.

She ran into the surf and jumped the waves. With each leap over the frothy water, she made a wish—for peace, for joy, for purpose. A wave caught her by surprise and splashed full force in her face. She squealed with delight. Beside her, others jumped and squealed as they made their own seven wishes for the new year.

She glanced back at Michael.

*Please, Yemanjá, make him follow.*

And then she dove.

\*

Michael gasped. What was Adriana doing? What if someone accidentally elbowed her in the head? Or her dress got tangled? Or a riptide swept her out to sea?

He ran and dove through a wave, surfacing on the other side with a forceful sweep of his hair. Water sprayed around him. Brazilians laughed and splashed back at him. It was all in good fun, but until he found Adriana, he couldn't share it. He scanned the darker water searching for signs of her bobbing head or worse, the skirt of her white dress floating on the surface.

"Adriana."

He lunged forward, dodging human obstacles and the occasional candle-lit toy boat, into slightly deeper water where he was only just tall enough to stand. When he didn't find her above the water line, he dove into it, searching, panicking. When he ran out of air, he shoved off the ocean floor and broke the surface like a missile, ready to shout her name, and found her treading water a yard away.

He sighed with relief. Why had he freaked out over losing sight of her? They were surrounded by people. She obviously knew how to swim. She lived next to the most famous beach in the world. There was absolutely no reason for him to panic.

*Get a grip, Cross. Pull it together.*

And then she kissed him.

Michael had never felt such delicious agony. No matter how firmly he held her or how hard she gripped him with her thighs, he couldn't feel enough of her. He needed to be inside of her and to have her inside of him in a way that felt humanly impossible yet undeniably correct. So powerful was this feeling that when her lips broke from his, he expected blood to flow from the wound.

"Please," she whispered.

He heard the word clearly. And when she slid down his body and locked her legs around his hips, he felt it as well. Together, they moved the obstacles between them and danced to the most intimate of songs, crumbling decades of emotional brick and mortar.

His mind screamed for him to stop, pull away before it was too late, but he was too far gone to care.

# Deceived

"In the house of a blacksmith the ornaments are made of wood."
– Brazilian proverb

# Chapter Forty-Five

Adriana stood before her open refrigerator and hoped the cold would clear her mind. How could she explain her absence to Jian Carlo? She had never gone out by herself after dark until the gallery show, let alone stayed out all night. Jian Carlo would demand an explanation. She'd better make it good.

The truth, or as close to the truth as she could come, would be best.

*I went to Copacabana for guidance, and Yemanjá told me it's time for me to leave our marriage.*

She repeated the words in her head until they flowed with confidence. She would not tell Jian Carlo about the joyous freedom and profound connection she had felt with Michael and how this had led her to do the unthinkable. Nor would she tell him how she yearned to do it again. But if she did not share these truths, how could she make him understand? How could she convince him to let her go?

Adriana was under no illusions that she could simply file for divorce—she had already tried that and failed. It had only infuriated Jian Carlo and caused him to tighten his control. Although he obviously didn't want her, he wouldn't let her go. He wore her on his arm like an ornament, put her on a shelf, and took her down again when he needed a target on which to vent. She had no money of her own and had lost all contact with her family and friends. Meanwhile, Jian Carlo had wealth, power, and vindictiveness.

Adriana shuddered as she remembered the things he had done.

"You're up early," he said, jolting the refrigerator door out of her hand.

She yelped in surprise and braced herself for the inquisition.

"Move over. I'm thirsty."

He brought out a bottle of soursop juice and set it on the counter.

"We have to fend for ourselves today."

He retrieved a glass from the cupboard.

"Irma will be back by evening. I think she left pão de queijo somewhere around here. Find it, will you? And fix us some cafezinho."

She stared at him, dumbfounded.

"Adriana? Coffee? You do know how to make it?"

"Sim. Of course."

*Was it possible that he didn't know?*

She found the puffs of cheesy bread in a bakery bag on the counter and poured them onto a plate while Jian Carlo settled himself on a counter stool. Then she set about making the coffee.

"Why is there sand on the floor?" he said. "I can feel it stuck to my feet."

"Really?" She examined the area and surreptitiously checked her sandals. They were clean, but a few grains of sand still clung to her ankle. She rubbed the top of her foot down her calf to shed the damning evidence.

Jian Carlo frowned. "I give Irma the night off and this is how she thanks me? By tracking sand into my kitchen? If I had known, I would have made her stay and clean it up."

He stuffed a hunk of bread into his mouth and chewed.

"It's just a few grains," she said. "I'll clean it up."

Jian Carlo grunted his approval and turned his attention to the newspaper. With luck, the sand would be forgotten before Irma returned. If not, Adriana would take the blame. In the meantime, she waited for Jian Carlo to say something—anything—about her absence.

Finally, after finishing the last bit of bread and coffee, he folded the paper and shoved himself away from the counter.

"I'm going to lay by the pool and enjoy the morning sun, maybe even take a nap."

She stared in bafflement. That was it? Nothing else? They had spent the second most important Brazilian holiday apart from each other for the first time in their marriage and he was going to the pool? Did their failing relationship not at least deserve an honest discussion or, failing that, a show of interest?

"How was your evening with the distributors?" she asked, acutely aware that her inquiry would likely invite one of his own.

Jian Carlo hummed in thought, a smug expression on his face.

This was what he had been waiting for. She should have kept her mouth shut and let him go. There were quite a few things she should have done—chief among them not marrying Jian Carlo.

She braced herself for the inevitable castigation.

Instead he chuckled. "It was a profitable and enjoyable evening," and wandered out to the pool.

# Chapter Forty-Six

Jian Carlo stretched out on a chaise lounge and turned his face toward the morning sun. He had steamed away his fatigue in a long shower, changed out of his stained club clothes, and soaked up the remaining alcohol with pão de queijo. Now, the caffeine was kicking in to revive him from his cocaine crash, making him feel both energized and relaxed.

He slipped his hands behind his head and smiled. His New Year's Eve had gone precisely as planned.

His client had been extremely impressed with the glamorous nightclub and the gorgeous party girls Jian Carlo had attracted to their table with good looks and an open wallet. He had shown the girls a good time, and they had shown the men their appreciation in many innovative ways—in the shadows of the club, in the back seat of the limo, and in the hotel suite he had procured. He and his client had indulged in every vice and used the beauties in every way imaginable until neither man had the strength for more. Then they signed a multi-million-dollar contract and finalized it with long snorts of cocaine down the belly of the blonde and up the thigh of the brunette.

Jian Carlo brought his hand down to stroke his swelling erection. What better way to bring in the New Year?

# Chapter Forty-Seven

"Are you ready to learn real magic?" Exú had asked.

Serafina had foolishly agreed.

Was it too late to change her mind?

Serafina had never heard of the spells Exú had taught her the night before; had not even thought them possible. Capture demons? Lock them in a hell of her own making? Why would she ever be so foolish? When she asked, Exú had laughed so hard her cries of apology had morphed into screams of yet another excruciating climax.

She did not ask again.

Serafina picked up her cafezinho and steadied the trembling cup with her other hand. When the coffee still sloshed, she set it on the table. A Quimbandeira did not greet the New Year shaking with fear.

She grabbed the cup, guzzled the hot coffee, and winced as it burned her throat.

Exú had taught her those spells for a reason. Her only safeguard was to learn them well.

# Chapter Forty-Eight

Michael gaped at the touristy T-shirt in Adriana hands, neon green parrots stretched in flight beneath a glittery magenta-scripted Brazil. She couldn't be serious.

Adriana jiggled the shirt. "Well?"

*Keep it light. Keep it fun,* he reminded himself and pushed the image of Jackson's electric blue caftan out of his mind. "It's nice."

"Good." She tossed the shirt to him. "Then all your friends will be jealous."

"Wait. This is for me?" He was never going to hear the end of it if Jackson saw him wearing this garish shirt.

"Of course." She paid the street vendor a couple of bills. "Who else?"

Michael could think of a few thousand people he would rather see wearing it but wisely kept his thoughts to himself. He rolled up the shirt and tucked one end in the back of his waistband. If she didn't see him holding it, she wouldn't ask him to put it on. Heck, if he was lucky, someone might even steal it.

"What's so funny?" she asked.

"Nothing." He offered an innocent smile and changed the subject. "Are there always this many vendors on the street, or is it because of the holiday?"

She shrugged. "Always. You can find anything here."

They browsed through tables that displayed electronics, underwear, incense. He picked up a stick and smelled it. "I have this growing in my yard."

"Incense?"

He laughed. "Jasmine."

They had been trying to share pieces of their lives—nothing too involved, disjointed bits of history—which, as it turned out, was not as easy as it seemed. Every time Michael began down a path, he found himself at a gate through which he dared not go. Art, childhood, family, school...every topic of conversation trailed back to his mental illness. Better to leave her in doubt than share the truth.

He wasn't like other people and he never would be. He might as well suck it up and put on a good face because no matter how much he wanted to let himself go, he had to stay in control. He couldn't leave an opening for the spirits to enter or whatever his damaged mind imagined had happened. He still wasn't sure. It had all seemed so real, yet utterly impossible. The imagination of a child? The ravings of a lunatic? Neither were topics he wanted to discuss.

"Hey, wait up." He hurried to catch Adriana.

She waited at the street corner beside what appeared to be a candle-lit dinner laid out on the sidewalk on a bright blue cloth. Flies buzzed around a piece of cooked meat and a congealed mess that vaguely resembled vegetables and rice. A bottle of red wine sat uncorked next to a cheap-looking glass, like the kind Michael could have bought at a ninety-nine-cent store back home. A candle sat in the center. While the flame had blown-out, a trail of wax had hardened around the sides. Next to the candle, a mason jar filled with water held a bouquet of bright flowers.

Michael bent down to take one of the blooms.

Adriana grabbed his arm. "You can't touch that. It has been left for espíritos."

"Espíritos? You mean spirits?" he asked, with alarm.

"Com Certeza. It is a despacho, an offering. Even the poor and starving won't touch these."

Michael chuckled with relief. "You're kidding, right?"

She gave him a stern look. "Even stray dogs won't come near them."

"Even stray dogs, huh?" He could feel his face contorting as he fought the urge to smile. "People just leave these despachos lying on street corners?"

"Oh, no," she said, gravely. "Not just any street corner, only the ones that form a cross."

Michael choked back a laugh then wrestled his face into a pseudo-serious expression. "Do you do this, too?"

She raised her chin. "I have."

In spite of his best efforts, the laughter fell out and kept rolling.

"It's not wise to laugh at what you don't understand."

He tried to pull it together, but she was so darn serious. And that pouty lip? The more annoyed she became the more adorable she looked.

"You're hopeless." She turned her back and crossed the street.

"You're right. I'm sorry."

He snuck another peek behind him and saw people skirting the cloth as casually as if it were a hole in the sidewalk instead of a fly-ridden candlelit dinner. He knew he shouldn't make fun of this, but between the New Year's Eve euphoria, this morning's insecurity, and the caffeine-sugar jitters from the potent Brazilian coffee, he couldn't keep it together.

He trailed behind her until the giggles had finally run their course then eased up beside her. As uncomfortable as this morning had become, Michael still felt inexplicably drawn to Adriana. Everything about her called to him. It wasn't just her sensual, exotic beauty; it was her mystery and depth and poignant melancholy, broken by sudden bursts of childlike joy. And what had he done? Doused it with a fire hose of insensitivity.

*Way to go, Cross.*

# Chapter Forty-Nine

*Why am I acting like such a child?*

Adriana wanted to scream. First, she had forced that stupid shirt on Michael, which he obviously did not want, and now, she made a fool of herself over someone else's offering. What was wrong with her?

Jian Carlo.

As cold and dismissive as he had been this morning, he was still her husband. And here she was with another man.

"I'm a bad person, Michael."

"What? Don't be ridiculous."

He touched her arm and turned her face. "It's my fault. I shouldn't have laughed. I get giddy when I don't get enough sleep, that's all. I want to know more about you, your culture, your traditions." He looked around and pointed to a local art gallery across the street. "Teach me."

Adriana stared at Michael, incredulously.

*Teach me?*

Jian Carlo never would have said such a thing. To him, Adriana was a prize to be won and forgotten, not an intelligent woman capable of teaching. Was Michael sincere? Or was this courtship flattery? Before she could decide, he took her hand and led her through a gap in the traffic to a tiny gallery wedged between a liquor store and a dress shop.

He pointed to the tribal painting displayed in the storefront window. "That's Yemanjá, right? The mermaid goddess? Right there in the middle of all those..." He swirled his fingers at the assortment of characters surrounding Yemanjá and shrugged. "I have no idea." He laughed. "Which is why I need you to explain it to me."

He pulled her inside and looked around in delight at the colorful folk art. There was a raw energy to the stylized crudeness that, apparently, appealed to him. Images of dancers, drummers, and fire gave way to mighty warriors, fanciful gods, and African slaves—all depicted in vibrant colors.

Michael stopped in front of a painting that depicted Yemanjá as a disconsolate mermaid, suspended in a sky ablaze with color.

"She reminds me of you."

"Me?"

"Sure. Gorgeous wavy hair, warm sensitive eyes, sensual lips. She even has the same high cheekbones. Aside from that iridescent tail, she could be you."

Adriana stared at him in shock.

"What's the matter? Did I say something wrong?"

"Uh, no. It's just—"

She shook her head. How was she supposed to explain the outrageousness of his comparison? She was nowhere near as beautiful as the mermaid the artist had painted. And she certainly was not as courageous, wise, and forgiving as Yemanjá had been in this scene. Fortunately, Adriana did not have to explain because Michael had gone back to studying the painting.

"Who are all these exotic costumed beings floating beneath her, and what's with the water spouting from her breasts into these lakes? There are seven. The Seven Seas? Is this an origin story?"

Adriana sighed. "You're very perceptive."

He shrugged and studied the images. "Not really. I just know art. This is definitely a story. Do you know it?"

He stepped back and stared at her with those startling blue-gray eyes. She had never seen anyone else with eyes that color. They were like a stormy sea or a forbidding sky, with an intensity that made her feel utterly exposed. Their intensity demanded an answer.

"It shows the creation of the fourteen orixás, the children of Yemanjá."

"Pretty wild bunch." He moved his attention from the child-sized adult figures to the face of Yemanjá. "Why is she so sad?"

Adriana took a breath and decided to keep her answer short and direct. "She was raped by her son and fled in shame."

"By her son?"

"Sim."

"Wow. That's a pretty harsh story."

Adriana shrugged. "We can't question the ways of gods."

"I guess." Michael peered back at the painting. "This god looks a little like Jesus Christ."

"It is. Actually his name is Oxalá. He is the god of purity and goodness, so it was quite natural to associate him with Jesus. Most of the Umbanda gods and spirits have a Christian counterpart. It made it easier for the slaves to assimilate the teachings of the Catholic priests, and since Rome was not particularly concerned with Brazil at the time, the priests chose not to make an issue of it."

She gestured to the next painting, a European knight on horseback lowering his lance at a fire-breathing dragon. "Do you know Saint George?"

Michael scoffed. "Yeah. Him and every other saint." He shook his head and wiped his hand in the air as if erasing a bad memory. "Don't mind me. Why is Saint George in a gallery with Brazilian gods?"

"Here in Rio, we associate him with Ogúm, one of our most powerful orixás, the warrior god of metal work and protector from negative forces. This painting tells the story of Saint George and the Dragon from the Golden Legend, a Medieval text containing stories about Catholic saints. Do you know the story?"

"I don't." He sounded surprised. "Tell me."

"Are you sure?"

"Absolutely, I want to know."

"Okay," she said, and hoped he wouldn't be bored.

"Once upon a time, there was a town on a lake inhabited by a fearsome dragon. To placate the beast and keep it from destroying the land, the townsfolk fed it two sheep every day. As you can imagine, the sheep ran out rather quickly. So the townsfolk were forced to start feeding the dragon their children."

Michael winced. "Are you sure this is a Catholic legend?"

"Oh, yes. It's from the time of the Crusades. Religion has always been a bloody affair. Anyway, the townsfolk sacrificed their children, one by one, and appeased the dragon until, one day, the lottery system they used to choose the children named the king's daughter. The king begged his subjects to exempt the princess and spare her life. When they refused, he was forced to send his beloved daughter to the lake where the dragon lived."

"Is that when Saint George arrived to rescue the princess?"

Adriana smiled. "He tried, but the noble princess refused to leave the lake. Saint George waited beside her until the dragon appeared. He charged the beast on horseback, wounded it with his lance, used the princess' chain-belt girdle to harness the dragon's neck, and forced it to follow the princess back to town. The king was overjoyed, but the townsfolk were terrified. Saint George promised to kill the dragon on one condition—that the king and all the townsfolk convert to Catholicism. When they agreed, Saint George slew the dragon and freed the town."

Michael smiled at her, like a kid at story time. "How does this relate to your Brazilian deity?"

"Ogúm is not only Brazilian; he comes to us and other Latin American countries by way of Africa. Umbanda, Macumba, and Candomblé are all variations of the Yoruba religion brought across the sea in the hearts of African slaves. Even Quimbanda, which some people think of as black magic, originated from the same ancient source."

He shook his head. "Still doesn't explain the connection."

"It does if you keep in mind that Brazil was colonized by the Portuguese."

"You're going to have to connect a few more dots than that."

"Dots?"

Michael laughed. "Never mind. Just keep going."

"Well, I don't know about any dots, but Portugal is a Catholic country. The slaves had no choice but to embrace the religion of their masters. So they did it in a way that made sense to them, preserved their traditions, and kept their gods alive by matching key traits, powers, or sometimes just general appearance between their deities and the Catholic saints. Saint George slaying the dragon probably reminded the African slaves of Ogúm, the warrior god of metal work and protector from negative forces."

"I get it now."

"But that's not all." Adriana gestured to other paintings with excitement, thrilled to finally have an outlet for all the knowledge she had accumulated. "The ancient Brazilians worshiped their own deities, ancestors, and mystical beings. These Caboclos, for example, are the spirits of our indigenous people as is that warrior over there, Indian Seven Arrows, and those Crianças, the happy spirits of children, the most sacred of which are the Ibeji Twins, who remind us to laugh and share their wisdom so we can evolve into better incarnations. Brazil's spiritualistic religions—Umbanda, Macumba, Candomblé, even Quimbanda—are amalgamations of Catholicism, Yoruba, and Brazil's indigenous heritage."

She sucked in a deep breath and spun back to Michael, feeling invigorated. When she saw him staring at her with his mouth hanging open, she backed away in embarrassment.

"I didn't mean to get so carried away. You must be bored."

"Not even close. You're amazing. I can't believe how much you know. And the passion. Jeez. Are you a teacher? If so, I wish I had one like you when I was in school. I might have given up art and gone to Stanford after all." He laughed. "Then again, it's a good thing I didn't have a teacher like you or how would we have met?"

Adriana didn't know what to say. It had been years since someone had considered her knowledgeable about anything—and yet, there he was, waiting for an answer to what was clearly a serious question.

She stared at the floor. "Não. I'm not a teacher…but I want to be."

She held her breath to see if he would scoff, or worse, laugh. Instead, he nodded, as though what she had said made perfect sense. His reaction made her feel bold and reckless.

"Would you like to see where?"

He laughed. "You mean you've already picked out the place?"

His was not the mocking laughter she had dreaded, but one that sounded spontaneous and joyful. It emboldened her.

"It's where I went to school, not too far from here."

"Then what are we waiting for? Let's go."

Her relief was so strong she nearly cried. Later—as they strolled past the outdoor amphitheater of A Escola de Eduçăo Sustentável, with the fountains spouting a fan of water in the lagoon—she did.

# Chapter Fifty

Jian Carlo's maid trembled before him. She, more than anyone, knew how little he cared for fairness. The only reason Irma was even alive at this point, unlike the rest of her stinking village, was because Jian Carlo had needed someone to work in his household who he could control. If that changed, he could always find a new maid.

"Forgive me, Senhor Resende, about the sand. I will clean."

Jian Carlo let her apology hang without response, knowing she would not dare to move without it. That would require a level of volition Irma no longer possessed. Or did she? He stared into her timid eyes, searching for a glimmer of defiance or a hint of self-worth. He found neither. Only anxiety, and anxiety could be used.

"It has already been taken care of," he said, in a tone that was both dismissive and disapproving. "What I want to know is how the sand got on the kitchen floor in the first place."

He gave her a hard look and watched the sweat pool in the valley beneath her nose. She blotted it by rolling her lips. It seemed to be a nervous habit, like the nail she dug into the web of her thumb. She'd drawn blood on several occasions over the years.

"Well?"

She began to cry. "Forgive me, but I have never even seen a beach. Never."

He started to argue but realized the answer was not as ridiculous as it sounded. It cost money to travel to the coast. Even the inland favela dwellers of Rio de Janeiro State might not be able to afford a trip to the beach. Irma's village had been deep in the bowels of Brazil on the banks of one of the many tributaries of the Amazon River. It would have taken her weeks to reach the ocean, and that was assuming she would have had the courage and curiosity for such an expedition, which he knew she did not.

Irma, while physically strong, was emotionally weak. The big city terrified her. On the rare times he had given her a day off, she usually chose to remain in her room, hidden from sight. When she did venture outside, she rarely went beyond the neighborhood markets where she shopped for household necessities. Although she had become familiar with several of the other maids, she had made only one friend, a woman from a tenement in Taquara. If Irma had gone there for Réveillon, she would not have been near a beach.

That left only one possibility.

# Chapter Fifty-One

Adriana laughed as Michael leaped onto the amphitheater stage. "You should have been an actor."

He stretched out his arms. "Why's that, milady?"

"Oh, no." She headed across the lawn for the lagoon. She wasn't about to tell him how gorgeous and charismatic he was or how her bones vibrated like a tuning fork whenever she saw him. Or how adorable he looked jumping over benches and rebounding off boulders. "You're like a giant puppy."

"First an actor, now a dog? I'm not sure how to take this."

Adriana laughed again and looked at her beautiful school.

Isabel's father had done a remarkable job integrating nature, architecture, and ecology. It showed in the pebbled swales that led excess rainwater to the school's lagoon, and in the gentle bowl of the stone amphitheater, naturally shaded by towering jacarandas.

Michael jumped onto the base of a lamppost and hung out from the pole. "This place is amazing. Is this why you're pursuing a master's degree, so you can teach here?"

*A master's degree?*

Adriana walked faster, so he wouldn't see the surprise etched on her face. Where had he gotten that idea? How could she answer a question based on such an astounding misconception?

"Did you say this school is run by the government? That's hard to believe."

"Government funded." Adriana jumped on the opportunity to direct the conversation away from herself and back to the school. "It's run by a board of directors. Half of the students are on full or partial scholarship."

"Really? Half the students?" He jumped off the lamppost, picked up a rock, and skipped it across the lagoon. "That's impressive."

"It is. Without a full scholarship, I would never have been able to attend."

"Really?"

"Does this surprise you?"

"A little. You seem so refined."

The tone of his voice carried disappointment. Did he want her to be more like him?

"Actually, my mother's family was quite prominent in Bahia. It was my father who was poor. My grandfather made him a manager for one of his many factories and bought us a house down the street from his Coconut Coast estate. My grandfather paid for my piano lessons, bought me fancy clothes, and made sure my mother and grandmother taught me how to live in polite society. We were close. And then my mother died."

Michael touched her arm. "I'm sorry."

She waved off his concern. "It was a long time ago. But I learned that my mother's family did not love me as much as I thought they did."

"What do you mean?"

"They rejected me."

"Rejected? What, like disowned you?"

She felt her mouth crease in what must have been an ugly grin. "I wasn't told the details. I only know that my father and I had to leave."

"Why?"

"He was from the slums. I guess my skin was a little too much like his."

Michael looked both astonished and disgusted. With her? With her family? Adriana couldn't tell.

"Where did you go?"

"Into the forest to my grandmother's cabin. This school had just opened up, and they were searching for impoverished students with potential." She laughed and held out her arms. "That was me— impoverished with potential."

Her bitter attempt at humor fell flat.

"How old were you?"

"Twelve."

"That must have been hard."

"It was very hard. Even with the scholarship, it cost my father so much to move me here he wasn't able to visit for four years." She took a breath. "Then he died."

"And you just stayed in Rio? Alone?"

She shook her head. "I was taken in by my best friend's family."

"Oh, thank God. I'm so glad you found a happy ending. This story was killing me."

Adriana closed her mouth. She had almost told him of the animosity that had developed between Papá João and Jian Carlo, but that would have meant admitting that she was married. Michael's caring reaction had stopped her from telling him the whole truth. Now the moment was gone and she was relieved.

She forced a smile and infused her voice with happiness. "Would you like to see the Cristo Redentor? No trip to Rio is complete without visiting our famous statue. And you must see the view from Corcovado."

She tried to make it sound casual, but the truth was that she was in desperate need of forgiveness. Perhaps the giant arms of Christ Redeemer could comfort her soul.

# Chapter Fifty-Two

"You were right." Michael stared down at the city from the Corcovado summit. "This is incredible."

The Art Deco statue of Jesus Christ towered behind him with its arms spread wide. In front and below, the lush mountain gave way to a meandering cityscape of white buildings, forest-green hills, and azure bays, lagoons, and ocean. Now that Michael was above the pockets of shocking poverty and clouds of unchecked exhaust, he could honestly say that Rio de Janeiro deserved to be called The Marvelous City.

Adriana tugged the hem of his shorts. "Are you ready to come down?"

He jumped from the rock wall and scooped her in his arms. "Was I making you nervous?"

"A little."

He kissed her nose. "You're adorable. And smart. And…" He ended the sentence with a slow, deep kiss. "Why has it taken me so long to find you?"

"Because I've been in Brazil?"

He laughed. "A sorry excuse."

He kissed her again and wouldn't have stopped if she hadn't slipped her fingers between their lips and gently pushed him away.

"There's somewhere else I want to take you," she whispered.

"Any place. Any time."

It was a funny thing to say, and yet, it felt absolutely correct. Time felt differently when he was with Adriana, as if past and future had joined in the present.

When they reached the rental car and he began driving down the winding road, that present felt damn treacherous. "Doesn't anyone stay in their lane?"

She pointed to the other side of the road. "Park over there. Hurry, before you miss it."

He cut across the road, seconds before the next car rounded the bend, and pulled up against the mountain side. Once safely moored, he shut off the engine and exhaled with relief. After a day of eating bus exhaust and dodging locals who seemed to think the tiny size of their cars gave them license to invent lanes, slam breaks, or thread through any space wider than a chair, Michael was ready to turn the keys over to someone else.

"Why did you want to come here?" he asked, over the rumble of a passing bus.

Not only could he not hear her answer, she had already left the car. He hurried to follow. By the time he had extricated his legs from the tiny Fiat, Adriana had disappeared into the jungle.

He hopped the eroding wall onto an overgrown trail.

The dense rainforest reminded him of a Hawaiian vacation he had taken with his parents when he was six, before the fire incident had stolen his childhood and warped his relationship with his mother. His parents had seemed fun and adventurous back then, Mom thirty, the same age Michael was now, and Dad four years older than her. To them, hiking to the Seven Sacred Pools with only a tourist pamphlet as a guide had been akin to a trek through the Amazon jungle. What would they think of this?

He yanked at one of the aerial roots and dislodged a shower of sticky leaves, bark bits, and ants. He smacked them away and shook himself like a dog. Served him right for letting those memories invade.

Where was Adriana?

Monkeys chattered as they scurried up the trees.

He was about to backtrack and check for a fork in the trail she might have taken when he heard the sound of a waterfall. A short jog later, he found her sitting on the ledge of a pond behind a veil of water. She reached her hand through the falls and beckoned for him to join her.

Off went the shirt, shorts, sandals, and briefs and into the water he waded. He would have dived straight across the pond if he had been familiar with the depth and rocks, but he wasn't about to botch up this island fantasy by cracking open his skull. Besides, now that he had her in sight, he was more than happy to prolong the anticipation.

He sank below the surface and enjoyed a gentle massage on his head and shoulders as he passed beneath the falls. When he resurfaced on the other side, he found Adriana sitting on the edge of a smooth rock as naked and beautiful as God had intended.

He lost himself in the silkiness of her skin and the tensing of her thighs. Every gasp and quiver he drew from her tortured him with his own rising need.

Something powerful was building, and although he could not have explained what it was or what it meant, he knew enough to surrender.

# Chapter Fifty-Three

Serafina cast the cowrie shells on the square white cloth and counted. Half of the sixteen had landed cut-side up and half cut-side down. She had cast the Búzios seven times and, still, no definitive answer.

"Já chega."

She was done with these stupid shells. They might speak to an Umbanda Mother of Saints like Isolda, but they had never spoken to her. It was a mark of her desperation that she had even dug them out of hiding.

She covered the shells with the cloth, stuffed the bundle into a plastic bag, and threw it out the window and onto the street. Maybe a child would pick them up and add them to a shell collection, or a car's tire would crush them, or a superstitious neighbor would take them to the local Mãe de Santos. Serafina didn't care. It was time to rid her life of false oracles.

Forty-four years was a long time to cling to old illusions.

Back when Serafina had been a frightened teenage mother and Carmen had taken her to meet the Mãe de Santos of her terreiro, Serafina had been duly impressed. When Isolda had given Serafina her own set of Búzios—not holy ones from Angola like Isolda's but special, none the less—Serafina had treasured them among her most prized possessions. Even when Isolda had offended Serafina by demanding she pay for her freedom from the months-long initiation process, Serafina had kept the mementos.

Why? In the hopes that one day she might become pure enough to use them?

"Basta."

Purity was a lie made up by weak people without the guts to face the truth. There was no good or evil, only context and conditions. View something as bad and it was. View someone as evil and they were. Spend your life bemoaning your fate and you suffered. Treat every hardship as another step toward power, and you became invincible.

Let the sheep of this world baa for God's stingy approval. Serafina sought a more attentive ally. If that ally turned out to be the Devil, so what? She would happily accept Exú's friendship over God's indifference.

But had she actually befriended Exú or made herself his pawn?

"Enough."

She did not have time for this nonsense: She was a powerful Quimbandeira, perhaps the most powerful in all of Brazil. What did it matter if Exú used her to further his own agenda? She was doing the same thing with him.

Theirs was the perfect partnership. Serafina performed the magic in this world, and Exú carried it to the next. Without her, he could not effect material change. Without him, she could not summon and control the demons of the afterworld. Both of them needed the other to do what they could not, and neither of them trusted the other enough to explain exactly why they wanted to do it.

Which was why Serafina had dug out the Búzios from the bottom of her keepsake chest and cast them on the table.

She shook her head as she thought about her dream of dread and promise. The Búzios hadn't told her what entity was bringing it to her shores. Back in the forest, Exú had told her to watch out for an American, but she didn't think the presence she felt now was Michael Cross. This was something grander than a California painter; something Exú believed would require stronger magic to combat. Why else had he shared those secrets and given her those instructions? Clearly, she needed more power than she currently possessed.

It was time to take her first step on the path to "real magic." As always, that step began with blood.

# Chapter Fifty-Four

Adriana traced the scar that ran from the back of Michael's fingers up to his elbow. "How did you get this?"

He tensed. Sooner or later, they always asked.

He sat up, no longer able to enjoy the after-glow of their lovemaking. Scar or art—it never mattered which topic piqued someone's interest, their curiosity always led to the same place.

Usually, he deflected his secrets with a curt "childhood accident," or a skillful redirection of the conversation. When that didn't work, he sicced Jackson White on them. If that failed, he ran. Only once in his career had he completely lost his cool, and even then, Jackson had managed to convince the L.A. Times reviewer that "none of your goddamn business" made Michael Cross "California's most intriguing new talent in modern art."

None of these tactics would work with Adriana. She meant too much to him not to share the truth. The only question was: How much of it should he share?

With Jackson, he had gotten away with the bare minimum, "I was sketching too close to a fireplace and caught my arm in the fire." Not the whole truth by any means, but not exactly a lie. He had required deeper disclosure with the psychic potter who shared his loft back in Venice Beach.

He and Panchali had bonded the instant she had crossed the track of his rolling metal gate and stepped foot inside his two-story atrium carport. Something about her bright smile, flaming red hair, and the turquoise turban she had wound around it had instantly attracted him to her; not in a sexual way but in a way that was familiar and comforting. After using his trust fund money to convert the old Venice Beach textile factory into what Jackson liked to call his "impenetrable fortress," Michael offered Panchali an affordable lease. It turned out to be a perfect living situation until he made the mistake of telling her about the voices in the banyan tree. After that, the rest of his secrets bubbled out of his mouth: the malevolent presence at the lake, sticking his arm in the fire when he was seven, and how fascinated he had been by the firebirds pecking at his sleeve.

"Michael? Did you hear what I said?"

He shook away the image of those hungry little birds to find Adriana watching him with concern.

"I burned myself as a child."

"How awful." She reached for his shoulder, but stopped when he flinched. "I'm sorry. I didn't mean to pry."

He shook his head. "I want to tell you. It's just that this isn't something I usually talk about. Ever." He laughed. "What am I worried about? You live in a place where people leave sidewalk dinners for spirits. You shouldn't have any trouble with the ones that have plagued me."

Adriana blinked in surprise. "You believe in spirits? But I thought—"

"Yeah, I know. I'm sorry I made fun of you. Defense mechanism."

He waved a hand to dispel the bad energy and caught sight of the scar. It had faded over the decades, but the memories of what had caused it remained.

# Chapter Fifty-Five
## Lake Tahoe, CA 1995

Michael crossed and uncrossed his ankles, enjoying the rough feel of the bear's fur on his tummy. Although the pelt wasn't much bigger than him, he liked to imagine it had belonged to a giant grizzly, terrorizing the Tahoe mountains before his great-great-somebody had hunted it down and saved the day. As long as he kept his knees bent and his toes from touching the polished wooden floor, he could pretend he was riding the beast through the forest or sleeping on its back in a secret cave. Anywhere besides a boring old living room in his parents' lakeside estate.

He patted the head and winked at the bear's empty eyehole. It used to have a marble eye like the other side, but one of his dad's friends had crushed it with a chair.

It was a sorry way to lose an eye.

Michael had invented a more exciting story and drew the whole thing out in a series of pictures: The ferocious grizzly patrols his forest and awakens a fire breathing dragon. Claws and teeth rip into flesh as the grizzly and dragon do battle. A knight on horseback charges with his lance to kill the dragon and stabs the grizzly through the eye, killing him by mistake.

*Much* better story.

Dad called it fantasy. Mom called it terrible. Neither of them understood.

The grizzly was the hero. And although Michael was only seven, he knew that, sometimes, heroes had to die.

On this night, Michael drew a different story. Well, not a story exactly. A boy. A sad peasant boy who kept showing up in Michael's dreams and appearing in sketches where he didn't belong.

The boy was seven, like Michael, but different in every other way. He had dark wispy hair and smudges of dirt on his pale face, so unlike Michael's thick sandy hair and tanned skin. He wore ragged clothes Michael's mom would never have let Michael wear in a gazillion years. The boy was shorter—not surprising since Michael was the tallest boy in his class—and way skinnier, so skinny that the tips of his shoulders stuck out through the holes in his shirt. But the biggest difference was in the eyes: Michael's were blue metal, and the boy's were grizzly black.

Michael covered the drawing with his arm and listened for footsteps, then peaked around the legs of the heavy wooden chair. Everything in the lake house was ginormous—high ceilings, big steps, huge furniture. Even the counters were taller than normal, making it a pain in the butt for Michael to brush his teeth or grab a plate. His parents didn't care. They were too into their boring stuff to notice.

Like this music.

The lady singer had a growly voice and a funny name that reminded him of rice.

*"Her name isn't Pilaf, Michael. It's Piaf—Edith Piaf."*

He liked the rice name better.

At least she wasn't an opera singer. They were the worst, screeching and wailing. Pilaf's voice was low and trembling, like a hummingbird's wings, and her songs were like marches to war. Mom wouldn't like that comparison. She sat on the couch reading her book while Dad read his paper at the giant dining table and nibbled on a Christmas cookie. Neither paid any attention to him.

Michael nestled back into position, face rested on the grizzly's head, and stared at his drawing.

The boy's hair needed a softer look, as if a breeze blew it around his face. That was the way it should be—breezy hair and sad eyes, sadder than any eyes Michael had ever seen.

He smudged the pencil-marks with his pinky. The boy's hair gave him a hard time. Well, not the hair—the fire *in* the hair.

Flames emerged, threaded through the strands, peeked around the boy's neck, tickled his nose. Yet still, the boy would not respond. Michael made the flames bigger and meaner until they popped out of the boy's ragged shirt and crawled up his throat. There was no way the boy couldn't be terrified now. And yet, he wasn't. What was wrong with this kid?

When a log popped in the fireplace, Michael put down the pencil and crawled off the bear.

The fire wasn't real enough. He needed to see it up close. He needed to understand what made it alive.

He army crawled across the floor and up the stone step to the hearth, where logs popped in a steady beat, and the fire heated his face. It had secrets to share. Secrets that would make Michael's picture come to life. Secrets the boy in the picture would understand.

Moving slowly, so he wouldn't alert his parents or scare the fire, Michael eased open the safety curtain. He ignored the heat stinging his eyes and held out his hand to make friends with the fire. But the fire didn't shake. It didn't do anything. He tried again. This time, he offered his arm to the flame like a perch to a bird.

On they hopped; the little flames bobbed and flapped. Happy to see him. Happy to be on his arm. Happy to peck at the sleeve of his sweatshirt. Happy little fire birds, hungry and loud. As loud as drums in a marching band.

Michael was afraid.

He wanted the birds off his arm, but he didn't know how to make them go. They pecked and ate. Pecked and ate. Until a bright red blanket dropped on their heads and buried them all.

*Take that, you lousy birds.*

"Michael. Can you hear me, son? Emily, call 911. It's going to be alright, Michael. Can you hear me? You're going to be okay."

Michael did hear. But he could also feel—pain worse than a thousand scraped knees. Pain so bad he wanted to die.

# Chapter Fifty-Six
## Rio de Janeiro - Present Day

Adriana stared at Michael, dumbfounded by his courage and her own shame. He had bared his soul while she skated across her past and avoided her present. She owed him the truth.

"Michael, there's something I—"

He grabbed his clothes and began getting dressed. "I have to meet Jackson at the gallery in a couple hours. We should go."

He sounded angry. And why not? He was an intuitive person. He would have sensed her many omissions.

When he smacked the leaves from his shorts, she jumped like a frightened child.

What was wrong with her? Michael wasn't like Jian Carlo or her grandmother who would lash out at her whenever they pleased. He was kind and thoughtful and brave. Thank goodness he had already headed up the trail so she could follow in silence and hide. She was good at hiding. She had had years of practice, not just in her marriage but with Avó Serafina.

Adriana shivered as the memories flooded in—scared and isolated, ripped from her family, trapped with a father she didn't understand and a grandmother she feared.

As she and Michael walked, drove, and parked, the silence became so unbearable that Adriana jumped from the car the moment it stopped in front of her house.

"Hold up." Michael scrambled out of the car to catch her. "Please wait. I have something for you."

She nodded, too flustered to argue. The sooner he gave her whatever it was, the sooner she could run away and abandon this doomed romance.

He hurried to the trunk and withdrew a canvas the length of his arm, wrapped in translucent paper. When he reached her, he turned it around so she could see the front.

"I took it off the market the morning after I met you. I didn't know why at the time. I just knew I couldn't part with it." He held it out to her. "I want you to have it."

Adriana stared at the painting and fell in love with the piece all over again. Slashes of vibrant orange and peacock-blue, magenta bolts of lightning, green as brilliant as emeralds whirling around streaks of bittersweet chocolate beneath a molten amber moon.

"You seemed to like this one best," Michael said. "As if you could feel the movement. As if you understood what I had been feeling when I created it. That's not something that ever mattered to me before."

Adriana blinked back tears. "I don't know what to say."

Michael laughed. "Say you'll take it."

"Are you sure?"

"Absolutely. In fact, I think I may have painted it for you. God that sounds lame. What I mean is—I think it's meant for you. It's called *Abandon*."

"Of course it is," she whispered.

"What was that?"

"I said, of course. I'll treasure it always." She accepted the painting and turned away before he could see her cry.

"Wait. What about tomorrow? I'll take you to lunch. Pick you up here?"

She punched in the code for the gate, desperate to get away. "Não. That's not possible."

"Okay then. We'll meet at the gallery. Eleven sound good?"

Tears rolled down her face. Why was he torturing her like this? He had to know she was a fraud. He had to know it was over.

"Sure."

As soon as the gates began to swing, she dashed onto her driveway.

Tomorrow she would be brave. Tomorrow, she would tell him the truth.

# Chapter Fifty-Seven

Serafina whipped her head, around and around, as she spun in the dirt, arms wide, hair fanned like a helicopter's propeller. The long panels of her white skirt flared and rose to expose her bare legs and feet. She gave herself to the beat of the atabaque drums, the chant of her followers, and the moon that shone overhead. She had put aside her habitual brazen-red attire and donned the white blouse and skirt of a supplicant. Tonight, in her jungle terreiro, Serafina would play sorceress and sacrifice, mistress and slave.

When the dizziness became too much, she stopped spinning and began to sway, arching her back so her dark nipples might protrude against the sheer fabric of her blouse as she swished the panels of her skirt between her legs. She had not hid her body beneath puffy lace or constrained her hair the way Isolda's Daughters of Saints had done. Although Serafina didn't know what kind of entity would answer her called, she knew sex would play a part. It always did.

Sex and blood.

Serafina thrust out her hand, and a female acolyte hurried to fill it with a large fixed blade. The hunting knife was the favored weapon of Yansá, Queen of the Wind and Rain, and, as Isolda had informed her decades ago, the master of Serafina's head. No matter how thoroughly Serafina had dedicated herself to Exú, she could not deny the god from whom she drew her personality, physical traits, and warrior nature. For this reason, Serafina thought it only fitting to draw the blood sacrifice with Yansá's blade.

Serafina swept her gaze around the ring of acolytes, supplicants, and drummers. "Come, my people, my followers, my lambs. Give yourself to Yansá's blade, without question, without pause."

The acolyte who had given Serafina the knife stepped forward.

Serafina had found the teenager scrounging through the garbage of a fancy condominium and known, in an instant, the girl was meant for her. Her name was Laís, and she lived in a brick cubical shuttered by rotted planks and roofed by sheets of corrugated tin. Laís had an unfortunate face, short crimped hair, and blotchy skin. She also had a fierce heart and a strong stomach for survival; valuable qualities for a Quimbandeira's acolyte.

Serafina took Laís under her protection. In exchange, Laís did whatever Serafina needed her to do, without question and without pause.

Laís stepped before Serafina, eyes lowered and wrists presented for cutting. Behind her, the local Quimbandistas—most from Favela Paula Ramos but a few from posher sections of Rio Comprido—lined up, uncertainly. While all of them attended Serafina's terreiro for worship and to communicate with the spirits, none of them had ever been asked to contribute blood. Serafina had cages of roosters for that. And yet, they all respected her and were quick to brag that their Quimbandeira was the most powerful in Rio. None of them would shame themselves in front of the others.

Serafina whirled with the knife high in the air, planted her free hand on the top of Laís' head, and shouted, "Epazzei!"

A woman at the back of the line shrieked and was hushed, but Laís did not even flinch. Serafina had trained her well. Even when the blade touched the inside of the girl's wrist, Laís remained calm and steadfast.

Serafina closed her eyes and opened herself to her gods, allowing their will to guide her hand. When the knife did not move, she opened her eyes, and pushed Laís to the side.

"Keep your blood, my daughter. The Lord of Chaos has no need of it tonight."

Serafina went through the same process with each of her fourteen followers. With every one of them—even the shrieking woman, who shook so badly she nearly cut herself—Serafina's hand did not move. The Lord of Chaos had made his will known.

Serafina swept her hands, herded her followers back into a circle, then nodded to her drummers to accelerate the beat. When the tempo felt right, Serafina pulled her blouse off her shoulders and bared herself to the night sky. The breeze piqued her nipples and rustled the leaves. The spirits were coming, flying on the wind, galloping over land, swimming down the creeks. She welcomed them all: the egums (spirits of the dead), the caboclos (spirits of Indigenous Americans), the Pretos Velhos (the old black slaves), the Crianças (children), the Boiadeiros (gauchos), and any other native spirit that might wish to attend or brush against her as they flew by.

She also welcomed the orixás who deigned to visit, although most would not. Yemanjá and Oxúm had not appeared to Serafina since she had trained to become a medium in Isolda's terreiro, nor had any of the Catholic saints—George, Sebastian, Lazarus, and Jerome, known by their Afro-Brazilian names as Ogúm, Oxóssi, Omulu, and Xangô. Only mighty Yansá, the warrior goddess who syncretized with Saint Barbara, still empowered and protected Serafina with her light and favor.

As Serafina opened herself to the spirits, she felt a profound sense of wellbeing. This was not an emotion she associated with the Lord of Chaos. Fear. Exhilaration. Ecstasy. These emotions she understood. Peace and hope? Never. And yet, surrounded by her followers and energized by the drums, a divine presence had settled upon her.

Serafina shook away the spirit's feathery touch. She could not afford to have its peaceful countenance weaken her, not when she needed force and power.

She thrust her knife to the sky and yelled.

"Hail Exú!
Master of Magic,
Lord of Chaos,
King of the Seven Crossroads,
I am ready and willing to serve.
What would you have me do?"

When the moonlight glinted off Yansã's blade, Serafina received her answer.

She beckoned to her acolyte. "The bowl, Laís. Bring it here."

This sacrifice could not be spilled on the ground. It needed to be kept for a future time and a grander spell. Although the nature and purpose of this spell remained hidden, it would bring Serafina everything she craved and everything she feared.

All that was needed was her blood.

# Chapter Fifty-Eight

A surge of energy knocked Michael against the shower wall, like a giant swatting a bug. He slid down the granite and crumpled onto the floor. *What the hell?*

He grabbed his head and waited for the throbbing vertigo to stop. When the dizziness receded, he crawled onto the shower bench and sat. Hot water stung his chest, but he didn't trust himself to stand and turn it off.

Something had shot through him, bounced in a thousand directions, and exited before he hit the ground. But what? He'd never felt energy like that before.

He hung his head and waited for the nausea to pass. He hadn't felt this queasy since he was a kid, riding in the back seat of Dad's Bentley—which was why he always opened a window. And why Mom had always scolded him.

Why was he thinking about them?

Ever since he arrived in Rio, his mind kept returning to home. Returning to the past.

He pressed his temples and stared at the shower floor. Instead of wet granite he saw dry cement, as dry and clean as Dad's garage, with perfect squares like the French doors in Mom's living room.

He shook his head and sprayed water from his wet hair against the shower glass. Or was it the glass of the French doors? It didn't matter. Glass was glass, right? Like the crystal vases perched on skinny tables, waiting for seven-year-old Michael to bump. What had Dad said?

*Your mother's house makes men take notice, women swoon with envy, and little boys dream of mud puddles.*

\*

Michael didn't care about puddles. He cared about the banyan tree.

Great-great-grandpa had brought it back from a place called India, before Atherton was even Atherton. It had a fat trunk made up of skinnier ones, standing side by side or winding around each other like a nest of climbing snakes. Some of the branches went up, but most of them went straight out to the side with roots that hung from their arms all the way to the ground. The banyan was the most awesome climbing tree in all of Atherton, in all of California, probably in the whole world.

Michael leaned against the tree and hugged his arm. Running had made his burned flesh sting. He needed a moment to catch his breath. He wasn't supposed to climb until his arm had healed, but he didn't care. Just because his skin had melted off didn't mean he had to stop doing everything. It wasn't like they had to sew pieces of his butt onto his arm the way the doctor had said they might. He didn't even have a cast. The nurse just smeared on some ointment and wrapped his arm like a mummy. No big deal.

"Is it painful?" The Lady asked, from inside his head.

Usually, Michael liked when she visited. Today he itched for a fight.

"We've been very concerned about you, Mikey."

"Oh yeah?" He spoke out loud even though he didn't have to. "Where were you when I needed you? And don't call me Mikey."

"I thought you liked it."

"Not anymore."

He reached for the trunk with his good hand, wedged his shoe onto the first twisted knot, and began to climb. It wasn't easy climbing with one hand, but after a few sketchy moments, he got the hang of it. Before he knew it, he had made it to the lowest horizontal branch. After that, he walked using his uninjured hand to exchange one hanging root for another until he had made it to his second favorite spot in the tree. His first favorite was ten feet higher and a whole lot harder to reach.

He squatted down on the branch and nestled himself into the giant knot in the wood.

When they were at home, Michael climbed the banyan almost every day. It was a secret clubhouse where he came to talk—or rather thought—to the voices. He had grown to depend on their friendship and their guidance. He loved them dearly, but not today. Today, he kept his mouth shut and let his mind do the talking.

"Why didn't you stop me?"

"We can't interfere, Mikey."

Her tone implied that he should already know this. Which he did. And which made him even more irritated.

"Oh yeah? Well, real friends help each other. They don't let each other walk into fires."

Another voice entered the conversation, one whose thoughts rumbled in Michael's mind like a steady train and whose voice felt as kind and wise as the grandfather Michael always wished he had.

"Why the gloomy face?"

Michael shrugged.

"He thinks we should have stopped him," The Lady explained. "He feels we've let him down."

"Yeah, that's exactly what you did."

The Grandfather hummed. "I see. Because of Brother Fire?"

"He's not my brother."

"And yet, you reached out to embrace him."

"It wasn't my idea to stick my arm in the fire."

"Not consciously, perhaps. There are many sides to you beyond what you can see. Each has its own agenda. Each has its own need that must be fulfilled."

Michael didn't understand what The Grandfather was saying, and The Grandfather obviously didn't understand what Michael was feeling. Why wouldn't he stop talking and wrap Michael in one of those yummy thinking hugs? That would be a lot more helpful. Instead, he pelted Michael with confusing words.

"Holy wisdom confounds wickedness, but it takes a pure heart to hear it. Someday you will, and it is for that day that we are here. Trust me. Any decisions you make have been, and will always be, your own."

Although Michael didn't understand, The Grandfather's words caressed him with reassurance and sprinkled him with hope and peace.

Like a gentle shower.

A very cold shower.

\*

Michael spit out the water and hugged his shivering chest. He slumped on the shower bench, pelted by a frigid spray. His fingers had wrinkled and his teeth chattered.

*What the hell just happened?*

# Chapter Fifty-Nine

Steam rose from the asphalt. Exhaust puffed from tailpipes. Traffic inched forward despite the noisy relays of horns and curses. The city had turned hostile overnight, and tempers, like the climate, ran hot.

Michael pushed the overcooked shrimp from one side of his plate to the other and wondered how he could possibly turn his day around.

Across from him, Adriana picked at her salad with equal disinterest. She seemed oblivious to the angry commotion outside the restaurant window. She probably wondered how a New Year's fling could turn into such a major pain in the ass.

Michael stabbed one of the shrimps then lowered the fork. No way was he going to let his disturbing morning, lousy traffic, and overcooked crustaceans ruin his chance with Adriana.

"Let's go somewhere."

She looked up from her salad. "Where?"

"Fortaleza."

"*Fortaleza?*"

"Sure. We could spend a few days bumming on the beach, maybe even a week. It doesn't have to be Fortaleza. We could go anywhere you like, just the two of us. What do you say?"

She stared at him with a blank expression. "I can't."

"You can't or you won't?" Then he realized the problem. "Oh. I'm such an idiot. You're worried about college. Do you have exams? Wait. You're on vacation, aren't you? You must have a little more time before school starts. Are you afraid your friend's family won't approve? That's who you live with, right?"

Her forehead wrinkled and her eyes narrowed with what appeared to be consternation. Not exactly the emotion he hoped to elicit.

"Look. I'm really sorry about yesterday, okay? I tried. It's just..." He shook his head in frustration. "I'm not the most open person, I know that, but I want to be."

"It's not that."

"Then what? Please, just say it."

She looked up at the ceiling, blinked to stop the tears that had clouded her eyes, and whispered something he couldn't understand.

"What was that? Please, Adriana, your silence is killing me."

"I said...I'm married."

Confusion struck him dumb. He couldn't have heard... She couldn't have said...

"Married?"

She wiped her tears. "I'm so sorry, Michael. I didn't—"

"No." He held up a hand and turned to the window. "I don't want to hear it."

She might have reached for him. She might have mouthed words of parting. She might have brushed her glorious hair from her lovely brown eyes. She might have done any number of things, but Michael would never know because he never looked away from the window.

How could she have lied to him? How could she have led him on as if they had something special, as if they had a chance?

He clenched down on his churning gut to keep from spewing hateful words.

He didn't know what Adriana did or didn't do as he stared at the ugly, exhaust-filled street. When he had finally swallowed his rage and raised his walls, higher and more impenetrable than before, she was gone.

# Chapter Sixty

Serafina waved the exhaust from her face as it floated in through the open window. She hated sitting in the back of the bus. At least the woman next to her was skinny and minded her own business. Nosy bus riders raised Serafina's hackles and reminded her of Carlinhos.

She hated missing him. It made her feel vulnerable in a way she had not felt since that bus ride to São Salvador forty-four years ago. Now he was gone, and her heart had a hole she would never be able to fill.

"Já chega," she muttered. Nothing good ever came from pining for what she could not have. Better to let anger burn away the hurt and focus on what she *could* do.

Serafina opened the newspaper and stared down at a picture of Michael Cross and Sebastião Nunes shaking hands in front of a colorful painting. The art show had been a big success, and the article encouraged people to visit the gallery before the rest of the paintings were sold or shipped back to America.

Exú had not confirmed whether Michael Cross was the American he had commanded her to find, although the immortal trickster's gleeful attitude whenever she had mentioned the artist's name suggested that he was.

But why?

It had to do with Adriana, Serafina was certain. But how? Would Adriana's fling with the American cause trouble for Serafina? Or was it an opportunity for Serafina to cause trouble for Adriana and Jian Carlo?

241

Outside, on the street corner, a dark man in a white leisure suit caught her eye, tipped his Panama hat, and pointed his ivory snake cane farther up the road.

Julius Amodei.

Why was the man that Michael Cross had chased through Ipanema tipping his hat at her?

Serafina pressed her cheek to the glass so she could get another look at him before the bus crept too far away then turned her face to see what lay ahead.

At that moment, Adriana rushed out of a restaurant, upset, crying, and waved for a taxi. Inside the restaurant, Michael Cross sat at a window table and glared out toward the traffic.

A lover's spat? Or the end of a romance?

Which would be better for Serafina, and why had Julius Amodei been there to point the way?

# Chapter Sixty-One

Jian Carlo answered his driver's call on the first ring. "Well?"

"She has left the American."

"How do you know?"

"She's hailing a taxi. In tears."

"And the American?"

"In the restaurant. Looking ready to kill."

"Good. Stay with him."

"Sim, chefe."

"And, Roga…"

"Yes, boss."

"Keep him away from her."

# Chapter Sixty-Two

Adriana closed the heavy door and leaned her weight against it. She had cried so many tears in the taxi that the driver had offered to take her to the police station or a church, as if either could ease her misery. She sniffed back another onslaught of tears and pulled the hair away from her puffy face. It would not do for Irma to see her in this state.

Quietly, she made her way up the stairs, keeping to the hallway runners to avoid the clacking of her sandals against the polished wood. Not quietly enough. When she arrived at the top, Jian Carlo's voice greeted her from his office. "Is that you, Adriana?"

Her heart lurched. Why was he home?

She continued across the landing to his office and stopped outside of his door. He sat behind the bloodwood desk—not working, not talking on the phone—sitting, waiting.

"You look nervous," he said. "Is everything okay?"

"You startled me. That's all." She pulled her lips into what she hoped was a smile. "I didn't expect you to be home."

"Nor I you."

He looked like an emperor on a throne, all powerful, all knowing.

She crumbled. "I'm sorry."

She had not planned to apologize, and having done so, her mind scrambled for a way to undo it. Could she pretend it was a reflexive phrase, a casual regret for a minor inconvenience? Or did her false apology sound like the deeper confession it really was?

Every tendon in her body felt coiled to bolt, yet Adriana stood fast. Jian Carlo was a predator and predators loved to chase. The only body parts that refused to hold still were her fingers, which folded and unfolded at a compulsive pace. She squeezed them together and hoped he would not notice.

A moment later, his chest was inches from hers, separated only by those feeble fingers, which she had clenched into a single fist.

He leaned into her hands, pressed her thumb knuckle into the hollow spot between her ribs, while his hands slid around her back in a restrictive embrace. The pressure of her fist against her diaphragm made it hard to breathe.

"Of course you are sorry," he whispered. He caressed her back in slow, deliberate circles.

Her jaw slackened. Her lungs strained as she inhaled a sliver of Jian Carlo's scotch-infused breath. She tried to turn her face, but one of his palms had slid up to cradle her cheek. She was trapped. No hands. No air. Just the heat of his breath and the pain in her gut.

Ever so gently, he kissed her lips.

The act caught her completely by surprise. It had been more than a month since she had felt his lips on hers, and even then, it had not been a caring gesture. He had not kissed her this intimately since their courtship, when everything he had said and done had made her head spin and her heart flutter. Back then, she had wished his kisses would never end. This time, she wished they had never begun.

She pushed with all her might, moving her trapped fist away from her and into him so she could breath. "Please, Jian. I'm so tired."

"Of course you are, meu amor." He offered an indulgent smile, but he didn't let her go.

# Chapter Sixty-Three

Jian Carlo eased his embrace enough for Adriana to move but not escape.

Maintaining absolute power while giving the illusion of choice and control was a tactic he had used many times in the past, not only with Adriana but in business. By letting his opponent win a small advantage, he gave the illusion of power, which lowered his enemy's defenses and made them less resistant.

Adriana's panic eased. Soon, the fear would fade until she would not be able to pinpoint what had made her feel so threatened.

He slid his palm from her cheek to her back and closed the circle of his arms. He would confine Adriana in this way until the struggle left both her body and her mind—another tactic, this one learned from a Fila dog breeder. Before Jian Carlo had met Adriana, he had coveted those aggressive beasts, but she was a far greater challenge than any mastiff and a much more satisfying conquest.

He petted and cooed until her muscles slacken and the resistance evaporated. Soon, she would surrender herself entirely.

"Of course you are tired, meu amor. How could you not be?"

When her fingers unclasped and her arms fell limp to her sides, he knew the moment had come. Just like the squirming Fila pup, Adriana had given herself over to the alpha dog.

"Are you tired, querida?"

"Sim. I think I'll go lie down."

"Okay. Whatever you want," he said, reinforcing the illusion of choice.

As Adriana went to her room, Jian Carlo returned to his office where he sank into his leather chair and tapped a key on his sleeping computer. The smiling face of Michael Cross appeared—handsome, young, talented, wealthy, and, worst of all, American.

Jian Carlo noted the steel in Cross's blue eyes. The man might be angry with Adriana, but that didn't mean he would stay angry with her. Even if he didn't welcome her back into his bed, he might be inclined to help if he thought she was trapped in a bad marriage. American's were meddlesome in that way. The only way to guarantee Adriana never saw or spoke to the man again was to eliminate her desire to do so.

Jian Carlo opened the bottom drawer of his desk and removed a small, faded leather book—one he had not touched in four years. One that contained a phone number he swore he would never call again.

# Old Friends

"God writes straight even on wavy lines."
— Brazilian proverb

# Chapter Sixty-Four
## Venice Beach, California

Michael dropped his bags in the entryway of his loft, shut the door, and muted the squawking parrots outside in his carport atrium. If he could get rid of the scent of jasmine, he'd be golden. The tropical paradise he had designed with such care was a taunting reminder of things he'd rather forget.

The inside of his loft wasn't any better. The Travertine stone, white leather, and dark wood reminded him too much of the Hotel Fasano in Rio. It even had a similar free-standing staircase with glass railings. The only things missing were the gossamer curtains and the hotel's trademark wooden-framed, ear-shaped mirrors.

Michael charged up the stairs toward a place and person with no connection to Rio. Unfortunately, the only way to his loft-mate's second-story suite was via an outdoor balcony that overlooked the atrium. He had no choice but to go back to the tropics to get to her, which pissed him off all over again.

He glared at the parrots squawking in the jacaranda. "Fly away if you want. No one's stopping you."

When he had first bought them three years ago, Jackson had admonished him for wasting money on exotic birds that would escape through the atrium's open ceiling at the first opportunity, which they had, but they had also returned. At the time, Michael had felt vindicated that his parrots had chosen his trees over all others. Now he wondered if they were just too afraid to leave.

Like Adriana?

He shrugged away the thought. It didn't matter why she stayed with her husband, only that she had one.

He glanced into Panchali's art studio and caught a whiff of musty clay and acidic glaze through the open window. Ceramics in various stages of completion sat along the counters, but no potter. He followed the jingling of Tibetan chimes down the balcony corridor to Panchali's living space. Although her second-story suite had the same footprint as his own, it couldn't have looked more different. His was stark and angular. Hers was billowy and soft. His reflected a love of sports and an appreciation of Japanese simplicity. Hers indulged in supernatural excess.

Michael ran his fingers over the points of a giant crystal. Panchali claimed the rock gave off energy, and while he didn't buy into that, he figured it couldn't hurt to check. He closed his eyes and cupped the crystal, searching for signs of heat or tingling. Nothing.

He was about to give up when his shoulders relaxed and jaw unclenched. A sense of calm permeated through his body and mind. A low-pitched drone resonated pleasantly in his head. He didn't question it. He accepted its presence and enjoyed the peace. It felt so good to just be. He yanked his hands from the crystal. He didn't want to accept, and he damn sure did not want to surrender. Not after the voices. Not after Rio.

He moved away from the rock, but everywhere he turned he ran into some sort of New Age symbol or decoration promising peace of mind or a path to some higher power. The worst were the alien-like angels with their bald heads and astral halos. Pale eyes followed his movements, ghostly fingers reached out to touch him. When he backed away, billowing wings prevented his retreat. He swatted at the hanging fabric.

The low-pitched drone continued, coming from the back of the suite. He followed the sound to Panchali, who sat with crossed legs on a meditation cushion amid curls of incense smoke. He wasn't losing his mind. The voices hadn't returned. He had lost his cool over a red-headed potter.

He plopped down on a spare cushion and did his best to ignore the candles flickering on the altar beside him. Even twenty-three years later, Michael was uncomfortable near fire. He focused on his loft-mate's freckled face and Irish features that belied her exotic name. She'd chosen "Panchali" as her yoga name and refused to be called anything else. He thought the reason was silly, but the name suited her. Sitting serenely on her cushion, she looked every bit the princess.

He watched her breathe and waited for her to surface from the meditation. No matter how "out there" she went, Panchali returned to Earth and grounded Michael with the facts. He trusted her, and she always told him the truth.

# Chapter Sixty-Five

Panchali slid off her cushion and moved closer to Michael's, eager to be near him after his seemingly endless absence. Then she noticed his frown.

"What's the matter? Didn't your show go well?"

He shrugged. "I sold nine paintings."

He looked so sad. She yearned to take his hand, brush the hair from his face, and hold him in her arms. She did none of those things because that wasn't what he wanted from her. "What's going on?"

"You're the psychic. You tell me."

"Okay." She assumed her best gypsy demeanor. "You've fallen in love with a gorgeous Brazilian maiden."

He snorted.

"You've fallen in love with a gorgeous Brazilian man?"

He sighed. "She's married."

The words smacked the joy out of her heart.

"You look shocked. Didn't you think I was capable of falling in love?"

She shook her head and stalled for time. She had been out of her meditative state for all of thirty seconds and already her serenity was shot to hell. She needed a moment to calm her mind. This was dangerous territory. One careless word could undo three years of careful avoidance.

She and Michael shared an artist's perspective, an introvert's need for seclusion, and a history of spirit intervention—although Michael wouldn't have described it this way. There was so much she loved about him aside from being ridiculously handsome. Why wouldn't she be attracted to him? At first, she had hoped he might feel the same about her. Stories had been shared, hearts opened, and a kiss nearly exchanged before she ruined it by offering to channel her spirits to reconnect Michael to his own. After an hour spent telling her about his fears, she had volunteered to awaken them.

"Of course I think you're capable of love. But in the three years I've been living here, you've gone on what…half dozen dates? I just didn't expect it."

It was more than that: As long as Michael remained emotionally immune to the effects of all women, Panchali didn't have to take his rejection personally. Now that another woman had broken through his barriers, she'd have to face the truth.

Michael groaned. "It happened at the gallery show. I had spent the whole evening trying to get away from people, but when I saw her, standing in front of my painting like she was a part of it, all I wanted to do was crawl inside of her, feel her heart beating against mine. Does that sound crazy?"

"No." It was exactly how Panchali had felt when she had first walked into the atrium and met Michael. The sense of familiarity had been so clear she had almost told him how good it was to see him again, but she couldn't afford to lose an awesome rental by implying she had known her landlord in another life. On that day, she kept her reincarnation ideas to herself. On this day, she felt secure enough in their friendship to risk it. "She might be a soul mate."

"Then how could I have lost her?"

Panchali shrugged. "We don't always get to be with the ones we love. Soul mates can make appearances in our lives to fulfill roles and lead us to lessons. They don't necessarily stay. Sometimes other karmic issues are more important."

Was she speaking for his benefit or hers?

She shook her head. "Don't worry. Soul mates find us again, eventually. A past lover becomes a mentor. An enemy becomes a family member. Who knows? Maybe some connections are too significant to be confined to one lifetime or one relationship. Or maybe we just need a lot of lives to learn what we need to learn."

Michael grimaced. "I know you believe in all this past life stuff, but all I know is that I met a gorgeous woman who touched my heart and turned my life upside down. Now she's gone, and I have to fill a hole I never even knew existed."

Panchali nodded. They both had work to do, but not now. Now, they needed camaraderie and comfort food.

She stood up and offered him her hand. "Come on, Romeo, I'll fix you a nice lentil loaf."

When Michael placed his hand in hers, she smiled and reminded herself not to cling.

# Chapter Sixty-Six
## Rio de Janeiro

Serafina stared at Jian Carlo, her face impassive. Her fingers clutched the door's edge as she fought the urge to slam it in his face. She had deliberated for three days before she agreed to meet with him.

Their reunion wasn't supposed to be like this. She had planned to choose her own time on her own terms, where she could creep into his subconscious with insidious spells and fleeting appearances, to invade his dreams and instill him with lust. Instead, he had called and begged her to cast a spell on Adriana.

"Are you going to stand out there all day?" When she stepped back and gave him room to enter her home, he didn't move. "It's a little late for fear, Jian Carlo. Either get in or leave me alone."

Jian Carlo raised his chin. "Who says I'm afraid?"

Serafina laughed. "Close the door."

She strode into her kitchen as Jian Carlo meandered through her living room and looked at pictures while he touched her statues. She poured herself a cup of tea but didn't offer any to him.

"You're having trouble with your wife. Why should I care?"

"You sent me to her."

"To ruin, not to marry."

He twirled a fragile statue in his fingers, reset it on the table, and winked. "Who says one won't lead to the other?"

Who did he think he was coming to her like this, a rich man in his fine clothes, disrespecting her treasures? Was he trying to intimidate her? She sauntered over to him and stopped, close enough to make him crane his neck to look up at her.

"Don't be stupid, Jian Carlo." She traced his lips with her fingernail, scratched the corner, and made him yelp. She licked the blood and smiled. "What do you want from me?"

Jian Carlo feigned indifference, but the bulge in his pants told a different story. Adriana might be young and beautiful, but no other woman could take him to the edge of sanity and drive him wild enough to give up his very soul. Serafina leaned her breasts closer to his face. If he begged nicely enough, maybe she'd give him another taste.

He backed away. "Adriana cheated on me. I took care of it."

"Then why are you here?"

"He's an American. You know how they are. I need to make sure he minds his own business and stays out of her life."

Serafina had watched Adriana flee from Michael Cross at the restaurant and read that he had returned to America, but she had not realized that Jian Carlo had known about the affair. This might be the perfect opportunity to reestablish control over both him and Adriana. No matter how much Jian Carlo had—money, women, power—it would never be enough. That was his fatal weakness, which Serafina would happily exploit.

"The only way to keep him out of her life is to make sure she won't let him back in," she said.

"That's exactly what I thought. Can you do this?"

"Have you brought me anything of hers to use?"

He pulled out a tortoise shell comb, the kind used to fasten hair in a bun, and handed it to Serafina. "Will this do? It has a few strands of her hair tangled in the teeth."

"Perfect. When I'm done, she won't even remember who Michael Cross is."

Jian Carlo's eyes narrowed. "How did you know his name?"

Serafina ran her nails up his bare arm and watched his skin prickle beneath her touch. "I know everything there is to know about you; even the secrets you hide from yourself."

# Chapter Sixty-Seven
## Venice Beach, California

Panchali had waited a month before she invaded Michael's inner sanctum under the ruse of bringing him lunch. After seeing the disastrous state of his studio, she wished she had let him starve. Michael needed order and silence to paint. Why was he playing this loud music? And why Edith Piaf? Panchali could have handled the passionate romance of "La Vie en Rose," but "Je Ne Regrette Rien?" Piaf's pounding march against regret made Panchali's head throb.

"Can you turn that down? Michael? For the love of…"

She set the kale salad on a table between two weirdly tribal images, neither of which fit with Michael's vibrant abstracts or even the detailed snapshots he penciled in his leather journal. The new paintings were raw and pagan and decidedly unnerving.

The studio was worse. Broken pastels and spilled paint had mixed with crumpled sheets of used drawing paper to form a papier-mâché crust over the exquisitely polished wood floor. Soggy art paper stuck to the tops and sides of cabinets. Canvases of varying sizes were stacked along the wall, one against the other, with no concern for the wetness of the oils. The Michael she knew would have freaked if his work space had been so defiled.

She pried apart two of the canvases to see what he had painted. It was as if his abstracts had come to life: swirling skirts, swinging beads, glistening limbs, and faces caught in the throes of erotic passion. Both paintings contained startling images of dancing women, wild animals, and bare-chested men in grimy white pants who gripped the barrels of African drums between their legs. It was both disturbing and compelling.

She glanced around at the other paintings. They all featured a blazing bonfire and at least one apparition observing the scene. Neither of these elements should have appeared in the work of a pyro-phobic supernatural cynic.

She cut off the music, took a moment to savor the silence, then went to Michael. Since he never allowed her to see a painting in progress, she fought a pang of guilt as she positioned herself behind him. The sour odor of his sweat made her eyes water. When she brushed away the tears, she saw his wretched creation.

The painting was of him; not the Michael she knew, full of strength and vitality, but a hunched and ragged abomination. Stringy hair hung in clumps over hooded eyes that stared out in anguish. The image frightened her.

She took a calming breath and cleared her throat, not only to draw his attention, but to find her voice. "You trying a new style?"

Michael groaned and leaned in closer with the brush.

"What do you call it? Neo-Voodoo-Realism?"

She waited for one of his habitual quips. None came, as if he didn't know she was there. The more she watched him, the more certain she became that he didn't know *he* was there. He seemed completely immersed in what he was painting—a tiny figure beyond a wall of flames, kneeling on a four poster bed.

Panchali gasped. "Is that her?"

With a few quick strokes from his brush, her dark hair sprang to life, thick and heavy.

"Michael?"

He dipped his brush in an ugly shade of gloom and deepened the torment of his own image.

She snatched the brush from his hand, grabbed his arm, and yanked. "Hey. Look at me." She clapped her hands in front of his face. "Can you see me? Say something."

After a long frozen moment, Michael's eyes widened in surprise. "Panchali?"

"Oh, thank God."

"What are you doing here?" He looked around in shock. "What the hell happened to my studio?" He picked his foot off the sticky, paint-covered floor. "What's that smell?" He sniffed around and finally checked his own armpits. "Is that me?" He pulled his shirt closer to his nose, took a whiff, then cringed. "What's going on?"

She nodded toward the easel. "You tell me."

He looked, shuddered, and began to sway.

Panchali steadied him. "You okay?"

"This is…disturbing."

Demented would have been closer to the truth.

She tried not to look at the horror he had made of his own face and pointed to the woman in the background. "Is that her? The woman from Brazil?"

He nodded without looking.

She pointed to the other paintings. "What's up with these?"

He scanned the room and shook his head, slowly at first then progressively faster as he grew more agitated.

She touched his arm. "It's time, Michael."

"For what?"

"You know what."

He looked away. "I can't."

"It's not like you haven't done it before."

"That's not the same thing."

"Yes, it is. And it won't be the first time."

He sagged onto a stool. "I can't believe you're going there."

She knelt in front of him. "You've avoided this long enough. You have a gift. Why are you so afraid to use it?"

He ground his thumbs into his temples. "It's not a gift, Panchali, it's a curse. I'm not afraid. I'm terrified."

"Of what? Your parents' disapproval? You're a grown man, not a frightened little boy."

"It's not that." He looked as if he might scream. Instead, he clenched his teeth and growled. "I'm not what you think."

"What could you possibly think you are that's so horrible you couldn't tell *me*?"

He opened his mouth to answer then snapped it shut.

It broke her heart to see him this distressed, but he needed to face the truth.

"I know you don't want to admit it, but you've channeled spirits since you were a child. You can't block them out any longer. They've taken over your art. If you don't listen to them, they'll take over your life."

# Chapter Sixty-Eight
## Hameau de Vieille Forêt, France 1560

A torch tumbled through the country night sky, end over end, while peasants watched and trembled. A haggard farmer clutched his son, unable to look away as the torch landed onto a mound of tinder and ignited the dried grass. Flames grew and ate, catching onto branches and logs, climbing the barrel in the center of the pyre. When they crested the top, the fiery tendrils ignited the coarse cloth of Colette's gown. She bucked against the ropes that bound her to the stake.

## Venice Beach, Present Day

Michael screamed.

His skin was on fire—feet, legs, torso, arms. He was burning alive, and there was nothing he could do to stop it. The nightmare had followed him into his bedroom, but instead of Philippe, he had become Colette. He could see it all: the shuddering peasants, the cruel priest, the horrified farmer and son, sharing the same space as his bedspread, chest of drawers, and Lakers' memorabilia.

His door flew open and Panchali ran into the fiery mix, yelling something he couldn't hear above the wails of women and the explosions of sap-drenched logs. She jumped onto his bed and grabbed his shoulders. He screamed as her fingers dug into his scorched flesh, but she didn't care. She shook him hard, as if to shake his bones clean.

"Wake up," she yelled, and somehow he heard the words. "It's a dream, Michael. Whatever you're seeing, it's not real."

The fire receded into the country night and took with it the pyre and the people and the pain; and just like that, it was gone.

Her green eyes glistened from tears as she searched his face. "Are you all right?" When he didn't answer, she crushed him in a hug.

"I couldn't get out," he said. "I couldn't get out of the dream."

"Shhh. It's okay. It's going to be okay."

He shook his head and wiped his tears on her shoulder. "You don't understand. It followed me into my room. Into my life."

He pulled away and grabbed her shoulders. "It's finally happened. I'm going insane."

# Chapter Sixty-Nine

Michael shifted uncomfortably on the cushion. He looked nervously from one flickering candle to the next. He had worked up the courage to extinguish a few of the offending flames when Panchali adjusted from her cross-legged meditative posture into a daintier position, legs tucked to one side, hand perched on the cushion. Michael had never seen her sit like this nor had he ever heard her speak in such a deliberately gentle tone, like a certain lady he had tried hard to forget.

"It's nice to see you again," she said, with eyes still closed.

Michael didn't answer.

"Don't be afraid."

"I'm not." It was a reflexive response and one that was not entirely true. Michael's current level of discomfort had yet to reach fear status, but it was headed in that direction. The crystals, the candles, the trance, he found the whole charade unnerving. Why couldn't Panchali just say what she needed to say? He had told her he was ready to listen. He had warned her that this whole trance thing was going to make it harder for him to take her seriously, but she had insisted that channeling spirits was the only way to access "higher wisdom."

Her eyes were closed, body poised, and a syrupy expression on her face. "We've missed you."

"Oh, yeah?" Michael lifted his chin in that rebellious way he had as a child. "We who?" Her fake caring annoyed him. "Forget it. I thought we were friends. I thought you could be trusted." He felt more childish by the second, but he didn't care. "You know what? I'm out of here."

"Mikey, we did not set you on fire."

He froze, triceps tense, hips hovered over the cushion in mid-escape. "What did you say?"

"We would never—"

"No." He lowered himself back down and leaned right in front of Panchali's face. If her eyes had been opened she would have seen one very pissed off man glare at her. "What did you call me?"

She sighed. "That's what you're afraid of, isn't it, Mikey? That we'll lead you into the fire? That we'll make you burn?"

He shook his head. This couldn't be happening.

"Are you worried that your mother was right? That you deserve to burn? That you're evil?"

The blow hurt more than an elbow strike to the gut. Unlike a basketball skirmish, Michael couldn't just brush it off and keep playing. This bitch had struck him at his core.

"We've always known, Mikey. Or rather, we've always known that you believed it. It was the only answer your logical brain could accept. But logic won't be enough this time. This time, you're going to need faith. It's the only way."

"Faith? Faith turned my mother into a demon-exorcising evangelist. You were there. You saw what she did to me. All those nights kneeling on the floor, praying for salvation, tripping over words too advanced for a child to recite? Artwork torn, paints dumped in the trash, and why? Because her faith told her I was unclean. You know where you can put your faith?"

"I'm sorry, Mikey. I know it hurt, and we did everything we could to help you. But faith is not the enemy. On the contrary; it will protect you."

"Against what?"

"When you make friends with the Devil."

He never should have asked. He never should have opened his big, stupid mouth. His mother was right: The demons were coming to finish the job.

"Be calm. It's going to be okay."

"You don't know that." He coughed out a bitter laugh. "You don't know anything."

"I do. Trust me, Mikey. You'll find the courage, I promise. But you have to go back to Brazil. She's waiting. And when the time comes, you'll face your fears and find absolution, I promise."

A gentle mist of lavender and pink swirled around Panchali's face. At first, Michael thought he imagined it. Then her flaming red hair paled into the whitest blonde, and the freckles faded from her face. She opened her hazel eyes, and they were crystal blue.

"We still believe in you," The Lady said. "We always will."

The pastel mist swirled, collected The Lady's image like leaves in a whirlwind, and vanished.

# Blood

"God is big, but the forest is bigger."
– Brazilian proverb

# Chapter Seventy
## Rio de Janeiro

Serafina had drained a month's worth of blood from her veins and still had no idea how she was supposed to use it. Exú had not visited, tormented, or pleasured her since Devil's Beach. Aside from sending the moonlight to glint against Yansã's blade, the Immortal Trickster had not communicated with her in any way. To make matters even more annoying, she had not heard back from Jian Carlo since she had cast the spell that would make Adriana fall madly in love with him and forget all about Michael Cross.

"Anything else, senhora?" The merchant slid over a pink bag of popped rice and a freshly blended avocado smoothie.

Serafina shook her head. "Não, obrigada." She tore open the bag and gobbled a handful of rice, as she had done as a child. "See you tomorrow, Matheus."

"Com certeza, senhora."

Ever since she had moved to Rio Comprido, Serafina began each morning by strolling down the narrow cement road to the corner market. She liked the character of her street, with its overgrown rock retaining wall and modest dwellings in various states of disrepair. She also liked the Easter egg condominiums across the street, trimmed in pink and yellow like the apartments in the Pelourinho District back in Upper Salvador. If it weren't for her frustration, she would be living her dream.

Serafina ate another handful of popped rice then washed it down with more of the smoothie. How dare Jian Carlo call her out of the blue then vanish like a wraith. She should have dusted his drink with her essence. He would have returned for sure, clawed on her door, panted at her feet, ready and eager to please. Instead, she had been overconfident and proud. She never imagined that, after seeing her in the flesh, her former lover would be able to resist coming back. What bothered her most was that it bothered her at all.

She had spent the last four years tracking Jian Carlo's achievements, saving photos of him from the newspaper and spying on him at events like a lovesick teenager, all under the guise of preparing for revenge. As much as it galled her to admit, Jian Carlo was the perfect man. He was handsome, strong, smart, ambitious, and had the balls to take what he wanted out of life. Like her, he ate his bitter past and spat the seeds of abuse and deprivation like bullets at those who would keep him down.

Compared to Exú, Jian Carlo was small pickings. Why did his indifference bother her? She didn't need the attention. She certainly didn't need the sex. Yesterday, every man and several of the women in her terreiro had eagerly volunteered their bodies for her use. She was only obsessed with the man because she could do to him what the god had done to her.

Just thinking about Jian Carlo groveling before her, stripped of dignity, driven mad by desire made Serafina wet. Nothing satisfied her like breaking a powerful man. It filled her soul and fed her starved heart in a way love never had. It reminded her that she was the most powerful Quimbandeira in Brazil, which was why it galled her that Jian Carlo had not crawled back to her the next day. Instead, he remained bewitched by Adriana.

Witchery would explain the trouble the girl had caused. Even before her birth, Adriana had hooked Carlinhos away from Serafina and yanked him on her line like a flopping fish too stupid to know it was already dead. If Adriana was a witch, perhaps Serafina should deal with her as the French priest had dealt with his. How satisfying it had felt to be inside Révérend Père d'Amboise as the one who had wronged him thrashed and screamed on the pyre. If only Exú had left Serafina in that lifetime a little longer, she could have fully enjoyed the vengeance instead of coming home hungry for more. Serafina would not be cheated with Adriana.

"You have no power, witch."

Her shout startled a dog who barked and jumped at the fence. She snarled back. The dog yelped and ran into the house. It felt good to be feared. She should do it more often.

She guzzled the smoothie and tossed her trash onto an overflowing garbage bin and was met with an unwelcome image. At six or seven, she and her friends had found a dead baby in the garbage heap along the mangrove swamp. The memory unnerved her. Serafina crossed her heart then stopped. It had been a long time since she had done that. Not since Carlinhos was a baby and she had abandoned him on a stoop. Not since Serafina had given up the Catholic religion and dropped out of high school to protect him. Not since Yansá had possessed Serafina for the third time and Isolda had convinced her to join the Umbandistas.

"Basta, Serafina. Stop acting like a child and remember who you are."

But the image of that baby, eyes bulging like a dead fish, skin pale as a ghost, arms extended as if reaching for help, haunted her. That could have been Carlinhos. That could have been her. That could have been any unlucky, unwanted soul in Brazil.

# Chapter Seventy-One

Jian Carlo looked up from his newspaper as Adriana entered the solarium, dressed to perfection and only for him, just as she had every day since Serafina had cast the spell. When his wife stopped at her chair, he held out his hands. "What? No kiss?"

She paused, as if confused, then tossed her hair and came around the table to him.

He pulled her into his lap and buried his face in her cleavage. When she struggled, he held her in place until she surrendered, then pushed her from his lap, and smacked her on the rump. "Go have your cafezinho. I'm trying to read."

Serafina had instructed him to switch his moods abruptly to keep Adriana off balance so her subconscious would cling to the Quimbanda spell. It seemed to be working. Adriana was pliable and adoring, yet oddly vacant. No matter. Once again, he had the perfect wife.

"I'll be home for dinner tonight."

Adriana perked up as expected. "We must have feijoada and quindim. Irma, will you see to that?"

"Sim, senhora."

Irma poured sweetened milk coffee into Adriana's cup and brought the silver coffee carafe to Jian Carlo. He smiled, well pleased with his women. Hot coffee in the morning and black bean stew and coconut custard for the night. He was about to praise Adriana for her thoughtfulness when Irma over-poured his cup.

"Idiota!"

She jumped and sloshed the scalding coffee onto his arm.

Jian Carlo cried out and knocked the carafe from her hands and onto the Oaxacan rug, an expensive gift from his Mexican client. "You clumsy ass. Clean that up."

Irma dropped to her knees and pulled a rag from her pocket.

Jian Carlo wrung out his napkin and wiped the coffee from his arm. "I should have let you wander the forest with the rest of your stinking village." He raised the tablecloth flap to blot the mess around his cup. "You don't know how lucky you are. I've given you everything—a job, a place to live, food to eat." He grabbed Adriana's napkin and threw it at Irma. "Hurry up, before that stains."

Irma's tears soothed Jian Carlo's anger as did the hatred that simmered beneath her fear. Seeing the forest woman each day, slaving for the man who had destroyed her village, reminded him of the power he wielded and the heights to which he had risen.

When he felt settled, he took a careful sip from his brimming cup, replaced it in the messy saucer, and turned to Adriana as though nothing upsetting had happened. "So, querida, what will you do today?"

Adriana looked from him to the sobbing maid, then shook off her confusion. "I'm going to shop for my Carnaval dress."

Jian Carlo smiled. Serafina's spell was as powerful as ever. "Oh? I assumed you had already bought one."

"I looked, but I need something special for the Magic Ball."

"Ah, the Magic Ball. That is special. Will you be shopping in the usual stores or will you need to borrow my credit card?"

From the beginning of their marriage, Jian Carlo had arranged for Adriana to have near unlimited funds but only at select stores. Anywhere else she wanted to shop, she had to borrow his card. He also gave her a small weekly allowance for taxis and threw in a little extra cash for those cheap incidentals young women always seemed to need.

He did this under the pretense of making her life easier. In reality, it kept her under his control.

"The usual shops," she said.

"Excellent. Then you'll be set."

He rose and guided her to her feet. "I'm sure you'll be the most enchanting creature at the ball in whatever dress you find." He pulled her in for a kiss and waited for that delicious moment when acceptance turned to passion. Just knowing she would permit him to do whatever he wanted, whenever he wanted to do it, made his cock stiffen like a metal rod. "I have to go to work, but we will continue this tonight, yes?"

"Mm-hm." She tipped back her head and bared her neck for his kisses.

He traced his tongue down her neck and grazed her skin with his teeth. He could take her, right now, on the table, and she would spread her legs willingly. Instead, he smiled and pushed her away. Better to let the anticipation sweeten his work day. Besides, he did not need to fuck his wife in front of his maid to exert his control. He had already made his point with both of them.

# Chapter Seventy-Two

Horns blared as Michael dodged a mini-coupe, narrowly missed a weaving motorcycle, and swerved into a new lane where he sandwiched himself between a bus and a garbage truck. He gripped the steering wheel tighter. Rio driving was the worst. No wonder there had been cars available at the airport during Carnaval: No one else had been stupid enough to rent them.

He cranked down his window to alleviate his motion sickness and came to a full stop behind the bus as it screeched and farted a black cloud of stinking exhaust. Reluctantly, he cranked up the window and turned the pitiful air conditioner to high. He didn't know where Adriana was going in that taxi, but he hoped she would get there soon.

According to the travel board video on the airplane, the festivities would begin later this afternoon when the mayor of Rio de Janeiro handed over his mayoral duties in the form of a giant key to this year's King Momo, a three-hundred-pound bank teller, thus kicking off five fun-filled-days of excess before the abstinence of Lent.

Michael's timing could not have been worse.

Once The Lady, or whoever the hell that had been speaking through Panchali, had told him to go back to Rio, he couldn't wait a moment longer. He spent a ridiculous amount of money for a back-row seat on a three-stop flight on an airline he had never heard of, spent five times that amount to book a closet-sized hotel room he was only able to get because Jackson White had once done a favor for the owner's second cousin, and rented this piece of shit rental car so he could suck exhaust out of a bus' ass. If all of that hadn't been enough, he had driven up to Adriana's estate just in time to watch her rubbing against her husband like a bitch in heat before getting into a waiting taxi.

He couldn't believe it.

The woman he had seen in that driveway had been nothing like the thoughtful, intelligent, and sensual person who had captured his heart.

He needed an explanation. He needed to vent. He needed to get the hell out of Rio.

If Adriana didn't get out of that taxi soon, he was going to explode.

At last, the driver pulled to the right and dropped her in front of an expensive-looking dress shop. Michael forced his way behind the garbage truck in the next lane, earned a screaming objection from the woman driving behind it, and squeezed into a spot intended for motorcycles. By the time he barged into the store, he heard Adriana call out from the dressing room.

"É perfeita, Leandro."

The store clerk, who had been heading over to greet Michael, shrugged in apology. Both men turned as Adriana emerged from the dressing room sheathed like a goddess in shimmering gold. Michael's anger vanished with his breath.

"Que bela, senhora," the store clerk said.

Adriana beamed. "I think I'll take it."

"You must. No question." The clerk turned to Michael for approval. "Don't you agree?"

Time stopped as Adriana looked at Michael for the first time. She smiled and waited patiently for his response. When he didn't speak, she returned to the dressing room without a word of greeting or an expression of surprise.

Michael was stunned. It had only been five weeks. How could Adriana not recognize him?

He left the store and wandered onto the sidewalk, utterly deflated. Of all the possible scenarios, he had never imagined her complete disregard. Was he that forgettable? Did their time together mean so little? The more he thought about it, the angrier he became. If she wanted to brush him off, fine, but not without acknowledging what she was doing.

He leaned against his car and waited for her to leave the shop. Once again, her gaze drifted by him without recognition.

"Hey," he said. "You don't get to do that."

"Excuse me?"

"You don't get to treat me like a stranger."

Adriana hugged the garment bag as though afraid he might steal it. "I think you're mistaken." She hurried away as if he might harass her.

"Wait."

She quickened her pace.

"Adriana, wait."

She stopped.

"Please. Look at me."

She turned around and looked, really looked, as if seeing him for the first time. The garment bag fell to the ground. A second later, so did she.

# Chapter Seventy-Three

Adriana nestled her cheek against the warmth and sighed. The touch felt so right and the caress so comforting.

"Come back to me. Please?" a voice said, full of love.

She leaned into the sound and tried not to mind the hot seat against her legs or the stuffy scent of plastic and exhaust. She was uncomfortable, but the warm hand against her cheek felt so nice.

"Adriana. Are you awake?"

She opened her eyes. A man knelt on the sidewalk outside the car where she sat. The fog clouding her mind cleared.

"Michael?" She touched his face. "Is this really you?"

He chuckled with relief. "Last I checked."

A sob escaped, catching her by surprise. "I can't believe it."

She spread her fingers across his brows, cheeks, and jaw, verifying the contours of his face then pulled him in for a kiss. Like cool water down a parched throat, she drank him in.

"Adriana," he whispered and pulled away.

"Hmm?"

"What's going on?"

She shook her head and pulled him in for another kiss.

He stopped her with his hand. "I'm serious. I saw how you were with your husband. And how you were with me in the store, treating me like a stranger, as if nothing…" He shook his head in frustration. "And now this? Help me understand, Adriana. Tell me what the hell is going on."

She recoiled, shaken by his vehemence.

He took a steadying breath. "I'm sorry. I didn't mean to scare you, but I really need to know."

She fought back the tears. Of course he needed to know, so did she, but Adriana had no idea what was going on. She looked around the strange little car and back out the open door to Michael.

"It's like a dream. Or a nightmare. I'm not sure which. But it hasn't felt real, you know?" She squeezed his hand. "Not like this."

"I don't understand."

"I know. I'm not making sense." Did she really have to say the words? "I forgot." She kissed his hand. "I don't know how, but I forgot all about you."

She held her breath and waited for him to forgive her, to say he understood, that everything would be okay.

He pulled his hand out of hers. "So that's it then."

"No. That's not what I meant. I love you, more than I can even explain."

He stood. "You're killing me."

She got up out of the car. "Michael, please."

"What, Adriana? What do you want from me? You think I didn't try to forget you too? Because I did. Believe me, I tried. And guess what? It didn't work."

"But you were home, not here in Brazil."

"What difference does that make?"

"Things happen here." She cupped his face in her hands. "I don't know why I forgot you. But I know, with all my heart, I didn't want to."

He slid her fingers off his face, clasped her hands together, and let them go. "I'm sorry, Adriana. That's not good enough for me."

He handed her the garment bag and closed the passenger side door. Then he walked into the street, slid into his car, and drove away.

# Chapter Seventy-Four

The hot bath eased the tension from Adriana's muscles but did little to soothe her agitated psyche. Too much had happened. Too much she did not understand. How could she have forgotten Michael? Unless Avó Serafina had been right when she had yelled at Adriana on the phone after Papai's death and told her she was a fickle, selfish person.

Adriana sank deeper into the bath until the water tickled the base of her nostrils with promises of sweet relief. Could it be that simple? Sink beneath the water, wash away her sins, and find peace? When she tried, all she found were thoughts of Jian Carlo.

He had seemed so genuine when she first met him, caring and accomplished, before she had learned his true nature. Before she learned the meaning of despair.

She submerged herself fully. The heat stung her face, but she made no move to assuage the discomfort. Everything seemed quiet and peaceful under the water. Painless.

She let the air escape, watched the bubbles, and ignored her need to breathe.

She heard Yemanjá call her name, over and over. A silly notion. Yemanjá was the goddess of the sea not the bath. The lack of air must have affected her mind.

As the need for air constricted her chest and befuddled her thoughts, Adriana braced her arms against the tub. Did a person have the strength of will to refuse to breathe? Did she? As she stubbornly refused to rise, a dangerous thought emerged: What if Jian Carlo had kept her down like this? Under the water. Under his control.

She bolted up and sucked in wheezing gasps of air. It couldn't be. That would make everything she had ever felt for him and everything he had ever said to her a lie. The horrible emptiness she had suffered throughout their marriage could not have come from him. No person had the power to do that to another. No one kept her down except herself.

"Adriana."

Jian Carlo's voice startled her out of her reverie. He sounded impatient and angry, as though this had not been the first time he had called her name.

She threw on her nightgown and opened the door, realized too late how it clung to her wet skin.

"I was wondering what was keeping you, but now I see."

Why hadn't she dried off? Why had she opened the door?

# Chapter Seventy-Five

Never in all their years of marriage had Adriana said no to him. Now she was sobbing like a child.

How dare she make him feel this way? Fury he understood, but this? He had destroyed villages and never once questioned his right to do it. He had stolen clients, bribed officials, and ruined careers. He had done what was necessary to achieve success. He had evoked terrible power, over and over, and he had won. People had died. Why should he feel guilt over a few tears?

He marched into his office and slammed the door behind him.

It was not the tears that bothered him but his failure. He had taken by force that which he had always been able to coerce with skill. He, who prided himself on his powers of manipulation and who could afford to buy any piece of ass on the planet, had behaved like a common thug.

He sat behind his bloodwood desk and picked up the telephone, ready to call Serafina and yell at her for casting such a lousy spell. And say what? That he couldn't arouse his wife without witchcraft? He slammed down the receiver. He would not allow himself to be undone by one undisciplined act.

It had been a mistake to go to Serafina for help, he saw that now, but the damage had been done, and he needed it fixed—not on the phone, in person.

The scales of power had shifted since their time together in the forest. Jian Carlo was no longer the pliable youth he had been. Those images of Serafina dancing naked in a cloud of cigar smoke, head thrown back as she guzzled cachaça, as she guzzled *him,* were woefully outdated. He did not need to fear the grip of her thighs or the intoxicating scent of her lust. These and the other memories that plagued him were only that, memories.

# Chapter Seventy-Six

Serafina chuckled when she saw him. "You return, even though you swore you would not."

Jian Carlo shifted from foot to foot on the other side of her threshold, lips pinched, cheeks puffed, like a greedy squirrel. *Good,* she thought. Animals reacted from their gut not their head, especially hungry ones.

"Come in."

She remained in the doorway and arched her back to make sure he got a good feel as his face brushed against her breasts. Time had favored her. She wanted him to know and remember the way he had crawled in the dirt and climbed up her legs. How he had begged to touch and lick and please. Remember the way she had spread him on the altar of her forest terreiro, his mouth wet with her juices and his cock throbbing with need, as her followers pinned his arms and legs to the wooden stump. Remember the way he had moaned and had pleaded as she straddled over him, undulating her lips a hair's breadth from touching. And the way he had screamed as she had impaled herself on him, again and again, through one climax and another, until he had begged her to stop.

Jian Carlo shoved past her through the doorway. "I didn't come for that."

"Are you sure? Because your cock says otherwise."

"Knock it off, Serafina. I came because your spell was weak."

She fought the urge to curse him on the spot. Later, she would take great pleasure in reminding him who was boss. For now, she would play.

"The spell stopped working? Too bad. I warned you what might happen without your semen to strengthen the bond, but you were too scared to give it to me."

Not only had he refused her request at their last meeting, he had fallen on his ass trying to keep her from taking it. What had he thought she was going to do? Tie him to a chair and suck it out of him? As much fun as that would have been, she preferred willing donations, like the one he had given her back in Simões Filho. Jian Carlo had nearly lost his soul to the decadence of that night. He took her like an animal in the forest. He had feasted on her flesh and begged to be enslaved. He would have slit his own throat and fucked her until he dropped if she had asked it of him. Lucky for him she had not. All the while, Exú of the Seven Crossroads had watched from his perch like a glistening black raptor of doom.

She had left Jian Carlo sprawled in the dirt, drenched in sweat and rooster blood, and used his semen to cast an obsession spell on the daughter of a politician who had been obstructing a business deal. Under Serafina's spell, the girl had thrown away her virginity and integrity in a spectacularly deviant manner, which Jian Carlo had recorded from several key angles and shared with the girl's devastated father. The politician stepped aside and Jian Carlo completed his business deal. The girl's obsession escalated until she lost her mind and took her own life. This unexpected event caused the father to give up politics; a shame since he would have made a useful pawn.

Serafina watched as Jian Carlo wandered through her living room. Now he was the pawn. He was just too prideful to realize it.

# Chapter Seventy-Seven

Jian Carlo hurried deeper into Serafina's apartment, desperate to escape the scent of her musk and the heat of her flesh. He had to take back control and find a vantage point from which to defend, or if necessary, to attack.

He tossed an envelope onto her dining table. "Here. Get it right, this time." It was a bold move, but he had to exert a semblance of authority while he still had the chance.

Serafina raised her brows and approached with predatory grace. Instead of touching him, she moved the mystic paraphernalia from a chair and laid it on the floor next to a giant crystal. She seated herself at the head of the table and indicated for him to sit.

"Let's see what you've brought." When he remained standing, she shrugged. "Suit yourself."

She opened the envelope, poured the contents onto a square of white fabric, and separated the colored flakes with her fingernail.

"Paint? From Michael Cross?"

Jian Carlo nodded. "I took it from the painting he gave to Adriana. You said he wouldn't come back."

"No. I said she would not think of him *unless* he came back."

"Whatever. Just tell me if this will work."

"It depends on what you want to accomplish."

He thought of the photos Roga had taken of the smug American, dining alone in the hotel restaurant, no doubt after a day spent fucking

Jian Carlo's wife. Why else would Adriana have resisted him?

"I want what belongs to me, on my arm, in my bed, and I want her to like it."

Serafina laughed. "Of course you do."

Jian Carlo turned away before she saw his indignation and belittled that as well. Humiliation made him angry, and anger made him careless. He couldn't afford to lose control in front of her.

He walked away, giving her space to work and time for himself to cool down. He perused the religious artifacts that crowded each surface and every wall.

Her glass cabinet contained multiple representations of Exú. Some were fierce, others dashing or comical. Jian Carlo had seen one of these versions on that fateful night in Serafina's forest—powerfully-built, glistening black skin, feet spread wide ready for battle, and his blood-red loincloth blowing in the breeze. This was how Exú had looked before taking Serafina in the dirt and making her scream in the way Jian Carlo had always wished he could.

He turned away. He did not need another reminder of how insignificant he was. Serafina could do that all by herself. Besides, it was time to see what she had done with the paint.

He returned to the table where she had lit a candle and was picking up the corners of what appeared to be a handkerchief. She molded it into a pouch and held it over the flame, high enough to heat the contents without catching fire to the material. Paint melted and turned the white cloth into a muddied shade of violet.

"Will that make her mine again?"

She shook her head. "Without your essence there's nothing strong enough to bind her to you, not while the American is here in Rio." She gave him a lascivious smile. "Unless, of course, you've changed your mind?"

Jian Carlo's groin tensed with desire. "No."

She shrugged, as though his rejection were of no consequence. "Then what *do* you want?"

He thought more carefully, this time, before answering. "I want him to leave, for good."

She clicked her tongue, regretfully. "Americans are unpredictable."

"Why are you giving me such a hard time? I want him dead, okay? Is that what you wanted to hear—me speak the words? Well, consider them spoken."

Serafina chuckled, low and rumbling. "Such passion. Just like the old times, eh Jian Carlo? Before you became such a fine gentleman? It's good to remember your roots. It keeps you humble."

"What would you know about humility?"

She grabbed his cock through his trousers and squeezed until he screeched in pain.

"Okay, *okay*." He pried off her hand, cursed and moaned until the throbbing subsided.

"Disrespect me again, and it won't be my hand that teaches you manners."

He nodded and shifted his balls to a more comfortable position in his pants. This pain was nothing compared to the damage she could cause with her magic. He remembered a man back in Simões Filho whose face had fallen off in chunks, and that was just physical. She could ruin everything Jian Carlo had built, drive him back to the slums, revert him to a life of poverty and crime.

"Forgive me, Quimbandeira. My anger with this American has clouded my judgment."

Serafina grinned. "I'll think about it." She folded the stained cloth and slid it into the envelope. "How soon do you want this done?"

Jian Carlo placed a stack of hundred-real banknotes on the table. "Before the end of Carnaval."

"Two days is not much time."

"Can you do it or not?"

She raised a warning brow.

"I meant, will it be possible?"

She flipped through the stack of bills. "Anything is possible with enough money and blood."

# Chapter Seventy-Eight

Jian Carlo's fury had grown steadily as he and Roga followed Adriana's hired town car to the Sheraton where it picked up Michael Cross and continued through the congested traffic to the glamorous Copacabana Palace. Although he had expected Adriana to sneak out with her lover after he had pretended to be stuck with clients, it still galled him that she would bring him here.

"Be quick," Jian Carlo said, as Roga drove onto the center divider and parked between the trees. "And wear this." He handed over a full-face party mask. "It would be disastrous if she recognized you."

Roga would not be permitted onto the red carpet walkway of the Copacabana Palace without a ticket, but dressed in a black suit and party mask, he would blend in with the fancy crowd well enough to get close to Michael Cross as he exited the car; provided he could squeeze through the spectators.

A mission like this should be easy for Roga, who had dodged the ROTA special police force and the PPC gang of São Paulo before Jian Carlo had inadvertently rescued him from a street war. Dragging the bullet-riddled gangbanger into his car had been one of the best decisions Jian Carlo had ever made, although, to this day, he could not say why he had done it.

Jian Carlo watched as his chauffeur moved through the traffic like a phantom, lit from behind by the aqua-marine lights shining on the face of the Art Deco hotel. He jumped a traffic barrier, bypassed the spectators on the sidewalk, and continued down the line of limousines toward Adriana's town car. It had stopped behind a stretch Hummer, delivering a crew of privileged party boys. Cameras flashed. Spectators cheered. Roga wove through the commotion as Michael emerged, annoyingly tall and handsome in a tailored tuxedo. As he walked around the back to assist Adriana out of the car, Roga fell in behind him.

The rest of what happened played out in glimpses between passing vehicles, like crude animation: a gruesome mask, a golden dress, a tailored tux, and the flash of steel. Then a bus pulled forward and blocked Jian Carlo's view.

He scanned the crowd for signs that someone had noticed what Roga had done, but everyone behaved normally. And why not? It's not as if he had killed Michael Cross on the sidewalk. Jian Carlo was impatient but not stupid.

He jumped in his seat as Roga knocked on the passenger window then motioned for him to hurry up and get in the car.

"Did you get it?"

Roga handed Jian Carlo a knife tipped with a drop of blood.

"He didn't even notice."

# Chapter Seventy-Nine

Michael gaped at the sparkling butterflies hovered overhead, caught in the trees like kites. Resin drops clung to their feet, as if carried from puddles of dew left on giant ceramic leaves. In the trees, pythons wrapped around the branches, monkeys hung, and wild cats appeared to swipe their claws at the costumed people below, gorgeous beyond belief.

A trio of feathered beauties sambaed through the Magic Ball, flapped their sequined arms and proudly presented their down-covered breasts. Stunning drag queens teetered on towering glittered heels. Elegant women and dapper men pranced in couture gowns and black coats and tails.

Michael shook his head. "This is amazing." He handed Adriana a flute of champagne and followed it in for a kiss. "You're amazing."

After their heartbreaking reunion outside of the dress shop, Michael had returned to the hotel with every intention of booking a flight home, but he couldn't do it. Although Adriana's reaction and incomprehensible explanation of why she had forgotten him had hurt him deeply, he couldn't bring himself to leave. He was relieved when she had tracked him down, told him she was leaving her husband, and invited him to the Magic Ball. If this spectacle was any indication, she had been right about Brazil: Things happened here in ways he would never fully comprehend.

"I love you," he said.

"And I love you."

They clinked their glasses and sipped, eyes locked on one another in promise and hope.

"Are you hungry?" she asked.

"Starved. But I'm way too excited to eat."

She laughed. "You haven't seen the buffet."

She wasn't kidding. One glimpse of the spread and Michael's stomach growled to be fed. Sea bass ceviche, garlic prawns the size of small lobsters, seafood stew loaded with every shellfish imaginable.

"That's mariscada. And this is coxinha." Before he could ask what it was, she popped a fried bit of chicken-filled heaven into his mouth.

"Oh my God."

"What did I tell you? And over there—pasta, pastries, vegetables, fruit. Or we could visit the churrasco station if you're feeling carnivorous." Her lips curled into a mischievous grin.

He pulled her against him and ran his hands down her back. "I don't need a carving station for that." He kissed her neck and cheek and mouth, deeply enough to make her sigh, then glanced longingly at the spits of beef and lamb. "Although it does look pretty damn awesome."

She laughed and slapped his chest. "You're so bad."

"Me? What about you, tempting me with your evil ways."

His stomach growled.

"Come on," she said. "Let's eat."

"Okay. Just so you know, we're not done here. I intend to spend all night worshipping you."

He was only partially kidding. She looked like a goddess, but that was only a small part of what bound him to her. He pulled her to a stop. Despite the horns and percussion blasting the room, he had something important to discuss. It wasn't the time, but something told him there wouldn't be another chance.

"Do you ever feel like there's more to us than us?"

She pointed to her ear. "I can't hear you."

He guided her away from the speakers, but the drums and horns still blared.

"This connection between us," he yelled. "Is it fate? Because I feel like I know you. Like I've been trying to find you. Does that make any sense? Do you feel it too?"

She smiled and nodded.

"Thank God, I thought I was making a total ass out of myself."

She laughed and shook her head. She hadn't heard anything he had said, and he had a horrible feeling she never would.

# Chapter Eighty

Jian Carlo cursed as a crowd of costumed locals swarmed down the steep, cobbled road and surrounded his Mercedes. Their ragged costumes and drunken behavior disgusted him, as did the ugly whores who yanked open their tops and pressed their saggy breasts against his windows.

"Run them over if you have to, just get us out of here."

"Sim, chefe."

Roga jolted the car forward, which caused the bare-breasted women to shout and the indignant drunks to pound on the car as it drove past.

"Keep the pace. I don't want any more delays." If he missed this opportunity with Serafina, he would not get another chance.

He braced himself in his seat as Roga sped over the rutted asphalt between leprous buildings and graffiti-tagged retaining walls. With every turn, the streets grew more treacherous and crowded, forcing Roga to slow lest he plow into a person or a shack. Soon, the slum ended and the forest began.

Roga snapped on the high beams and slowed the Mercedes to a crawl. Aside from the headlamps, the forest was black without so much as a glimmer of moon or starlight to penetrate the dense canopy.

"Where does she find these places?"

"Que, chefe?"

"Não importa. Just drive."

Roga negotiated their way over and around whatever he could see and stomped on the brakes when he could not. It would not do to bust an axel or puncture a tire in the middle of a jungle with God knew who or what waiting to attack. A sudden stop threw Jian Carlo forward into the back of the front seat.

"Sorry, boss." Roga shifted into reverse, backed down the rocky road, then turned onto even rougher terrain.

Jian Carlo gripped the door handle and the seat back until the jarring lessened and the trail flattened. Between the trees and the night, they could be headed for a cliff. Hopefully, Roga's eyesight was keener than his own.

When the road widened, they passed a pickup truck parked along the berm, motorcycles wedged between the trees, and cars slanted against the slope. Off to the side, a cabin sat in a clearing, reminiscent of another cabin in another forest.

Jian Carlo shook away the memory and pointed over the front seat. "Park over there by the trail."

Roga did as he was asked then cut the engine and lights. A distant bonfire shone through the trees. Jian Carlo opened the door to the sound of atabaque drums and animal hoots, trills, and caws.

He got out of the car and tapped on the driver-side window. "Let's go."

Roga shook his head.

"What? You can't be serious. After all we have been through, *this* is where you draw the line?" He smacked his palm on the glass. "Come on."

Roga turned the ignition enough to lower the window a few centimeters then shut it off. "Sorry, chefe. I would do anything for you, you know that. But not this. Not Quimbanda."

Jian Carlo slammed his palm on the roof. "You fucking coward."

He stomped away from the car but slowed as he approached the narrow trail. Was Roga right? The former gangbanger had faced death more times than Jian Carlo. If he was afraid, maybe the trail led to something truly evil.

Jian Carlo gripped the bloodied knife and headed toward the drums.

# Chapter Eighty-One

Adriana's face ached from smiling and laughing. Michael had turned every familiarity into something fresh and exciting.

"Do you want to see a samba contest?" she asked, eager to watch his reaction.

"What, and leave here? No way."

"It's next door in the Golden Salon. You'll love it."

A cacophony of steel, wood, and whistles exploded as they stepped into the lobby. People cheered and leapt from their lily pad seats to race toward the music.

Adriana grabbed Michael's hand and pulled him into another outrageously decorated salon. Stuffed jaguars crouched on buffet tables while flamingos hovered, mid-flight, in a crystal forest. The stage at the far end of the room was framed by snakes and billowing clouds that rained tinsel over the sparkling headdresses of seven pulsating dancers. Behind them, musicians wore silver and blue uniforms as they pounded on percussion instruments and sang.

Michael's jaw hung in amazement.

Adriana laughed. "I told you. Isn't it marvelous?"

The Master of Ceremonies emerged from the wings. "Boa noite, Rio de Janeiro."

The crowd screamed and whistled. Contestants hurried to form a line. Skin glistened with sweat, breasts heaved as they sucked in air through their frozen smiles. The MC stepped beside the first contestant, and the music hushed to a rhythmic drone.

"Estais preparado?" he yelled to the audience.

"Sim!"

"Quereis ver a samba?"

"Ja. Ja. Ja. Ja."

"What's going on?" Michael yelled.

"You'll see."

The MC shot his hand into the air and the drummers jumped into overdrive. The first contestant gyrated in a frenzy of motion. The crowd whistled and shouted their approval as dancers took their turns in a dazzling display of footwork and jiggling flesh.

Michael's jaw dropped and his face flushed. Adriana laughed again.

"Beijo. Beijo," a man shouted beside her. The chant was picked up by his friends and their friends until everyone, including the MC, chanted for Adriana and Michael to kiss.

What could she do? She loved this man with all her heart, as if he was a part of her, as if they had been together since the beginning of time. She didn't care if someone recognized her. She didn't care if Jian Carlo learned she and Michael were together before she had petitioned for a divorce. The only thing that mattered was this moment, this man, and this kiss.

# Chapter Eighty-Two

Jian Carlo cringed as Serafina's followers twirled, crouched, and leapt in the firelight, casting demonic shadows on the surrounding trees. Their animal costumes captured the essence of the spirits they imitated but were nowhere near as flamboyant as the ones adorning the guests at the Magic Ball, nor were their bodies as beautiful.

Puckered skin, flabby bellies, sagging breasts. These were not the tight, young bodies of the club girls Jian Carlo was accustomed to screwing or the muscled athletes who frequented his gym. Serafina's followers came from the favelas of Rio Comprido and danced with grotesque abandon.

Sinewy men beat on the atabaques, invigorated the misshapen acolytes to greater feats of repugnance, then smacked the hides and changed the rhythm. The acolytes stopped their gyrations and separated to reveal a spray of red plumes emerging from behind the bonfire.

As if born of flames, Serafina rose, clad in red, over nine feet tall from the top of her headdress to the bottom of her feet. Her wild hair was bound and her breasts secured by a red leather brassiere. Matching strips of leather swung from the bands around her outstretched arms and swaying hips.

She grabbed a cat o' nine tails from the tree stump altar and sauntered toward him. He couldn't move. Every stride opened her paneled skirt and gave him glimpses of the darkness between her thighs.

She flicked her wrist and snapped the tails of her red leather whip. He knew that ecstasy and pain. And God help him, he wanted to know it again.

# Chapter Eighty-Three

Serafina laughed as her whip grazed the front of Jian Carlo's pants and gave him a taste of what would come. She would treat him to a longer meal once she had fed and honored her gods. For now, she would return to the circle created by her followers.

She tossed red dust over her shoulder and into Jian Carlo's face. The effects of the drug would take place soon.

Beside the bonfire was a tree stump she had sawed and sanded into an altar. It was smaller than her altar in Simões Filho but equally useful and gave her a place for the gifts and tools she would need.

She exchanged the red-leather whip for a brick of limestone chalk and a metal cheese grater. As her followers danced and her drummers played, Serafina grated the chalk onto the dirt. The hieroglyphs she created focused her intent and communicated her will to the spirits. Once completed, she exchanged the chalk and grater for seven cigars and fourteen candles—half red, half black—which she planted, wick-up, around the magical designs. She raised her arms to the sky, and the red fringe dripped from her armbands like blood.

"Hail, Exú, King of the Seven Crossroads and Master of Magic.
Hail, Pomba Gira, Consort to Exú and Mistress of Witchcraft.
I invite you to visit and honor you with gifts."

Serafina knelt in the dirt, lit the fourteen candles and seven cigars, then opened seven small bottles of cachaça, brought to her by a man who wore a furry brown coat. She took a long swig from each of the bottles and arranged them in front of the other offerings.

"See the gifts I have brought for you?"

The bear-man returned, gripping the neck of a terrified rooster. It flapped its wings against the man's coat and emitted a cloud of dust and feathers. As the creature clawed for escape, Serafina tied a length of twine around its neck with quick precision. She handed the leash to the man and nodded toward a stake impaled in the ground a few meters away.

While the bear-man tied the cock's leash to the stake, Serafina took the cloth she had stained with Michael Cross' paint from the waistband of her skirt. She would use this and the blood-tipped knife Jian Carlo would provide to direct her magic to the American and close the paths of life that traveled from the Universe to his body.

All she needed to generate the necessary power for her spell was a worthy steed for the journey and enough blood to soak the trail.

# Chapter Eighty-Four

Jian Carlo cringed as the man in the shaggy bear coat lumbered through the circle of grotesque dancers as they leapt and twirled to the pounding beat of the atabaque drums. On any other night, Jian Carlo would have made fun of the skinny street man as he growled and pawed the air. Not tonight. Not with Serafina cracking her whip above the bear-man's head and egging him on. Not when Jian Carlo's hallucinating mind made the bear-man seem real.

Jian Carlo felt his bladder loosen and clenched his stomach to keep the urine in place. He could not afford to embarrass himself in front of these scraggly people or to show weakness in front of Serafina. He had power. He was in control. He had the knife she needed to complete the spell he had hired her to do. And yet, when the bear-man grabbed his arm, Jian Carlo yelped like a frightened child.

He shook off the bear-man's grip and staggered, on his own power, through the ring of dancers. If he hadn't known better, he would have sworn he was drugged. When he reached Serafina, she towered over him like an angry god with flames shooting from her crown and blood-red leather dripping down her arms and legs. Raw power radiated from her glistening skin, and the scent of her musk choked him with desire.

She snatched the blood-tipped knife from Jian Carlo's grasp and shoved him to the ground like a schoolyard bully. Blood lust shone in her eyes. Despite all he knew, he crawled to meet her, climbed her legs, pulled the panels of her skirt, and clawed at the band that held them to her hips. He had to have her. Now. In the dirt. In the jungle. Surrounded by animals.

She stomped on his chest and splayed him on his back. When he wiped the sweat from his face, his hands came away coated in red dust. He licked it from his fingers and moaned.

He tore off his clothes, threw every piece into the fire, and recoiled when Serafina snapped him with the whip. She planted her foot on his chest and drove him onto his back. She walked up the sides of his hips and straddled him.

He gazed up the muscular length of her body to her slack mouth and hungry eyes, and nearly blacked out from desire. He bent his knees, thighs tense, cock ready, and reached for her calves to pull her down. She kicked away his hands. Then, with erotic deliberation, she lowered herself into a deep, undulating squat.

Jian Carlo raised his hips to meet her, but she hovered teasingly out of reach. Finally, when he thought he would die from need, she lowered.

Her body muddled his mind into a drunken stupor of erotic sensation while the atabaques beat and the animals danced and the surrounding jungle grew bigger and bigger until it swallowed the world. She could fuck him to death if she wanted, and he would meet her thrust for thrust.

His muscles tensed into excruciating knots as she pounded him toward the climax he craved yet fought. Through the tears of ecstasy that clouded his vision, he saw the gleam of firelight on steel.

He tried to scream. He tried to shove Serafina off his body and run, but he could not move. The climax had begun and his traitorous body convulsed in rapture as Serafina plunged her knife not into him but into the rooster tied beside his face.

# Chapter Eighty-Five

Michael cried out as if stabbed with a bolt of power so shocking it dropped him to the floor. His body convulsed, his limbs and head smacked against the hardwood, his teeth bit into his tongue. Shards of pain cut into his heart and ripped through his organs.

Someone screamed. Man? Woman? He didn't care. Hands pinned his flailing arms and legs to the ground. Another caught his head. A woman shouted his name. Eyes stared into his, dropping tears onto his face. He stared into those eyes as the pain strangled his body, cut off his breath, and constricted his heart.

She was his lifeline. His hope. The goddess who would stop the pain. Then the blackness swallowed her from view.

# Cursed

"As long as I am running, my father will still have a son."
– Brazilian proverb

# Chapter Eighty-Six

"Senhora Resende?"

Adriana lifted her head from the hospital bed and tried to orient herself. Her hand rested on Michael's, which had a tube taped to the back, delivering fluids that hung from a metal stand. Wires emerged from the sleeves of his gown and connected to monitors that beeped and hummed with assuring regularity. What was not reassuring was Michael. His lungs rasped as they struggled for breath, and his tanned skin had taken on a sickly pallor.

"Senhora?" A diminutive woman in a pale blue coat waited patiently in the doorway. "I am Doctor Ramirez."

Adriana nodded and blinked the weariness from her eyes. "How is he?"

"Stable, for now."

"What's wrong with him?"

The doctor shrugged. "The test results will give us a better idea. Right now, all we know is that he is failing. I wish there was something more I could tell you. You probably saved his life. Are you a nurse or a lifeguard?"

"What?"

"The CPR."

"Oh. I read."

The doctor seemed puzzled, but Adriana did not have the energy nor inclination to explain how she gained most of her knowledge through books.

"Perhaps, you should go home for a while, senhora. Get some rest. Change?"

Adriana looked down at her evening gown. The doctor was right: She needed sturdier clothes to face this challenge.

After catching a taxi home and changing into jeans and a black shirt, Adriana froze at the threshold of Jian Carlo's office. Irma had told her he had not come home last night, yet Adriana hesitated. It would anger him to catch her in his office, but she needed money to survive the day.

She slid behind the bloodwood desk and searched through the drawers. She did not expect to find any credit cards, nor would she have dared to use them if she had. She searched for the box where he kept the cash and found it in the back of the bottom drawer. It contained a stack of one-hundred-real banknotes. She took three bills, the equivalent of about one hundred forty dollars, and was about to close the drawer when she noticed an old leather book.

Unlike the rest of the orderly contents of the drawer, the book sat askew, as if tossed in hastily. She picked it up, thumbed through the pages, and stopped at a spot bookmarked by a folded piece of printing paper. The name at the top of the address book page was "Serafina."

Adriana sucked in her breath. Even alone in this office, she feared to move.

Serafina was a common name. There was no reason to think that this Serafina was her own witch of a grandmother. Brazil was a big country, and the state of Bahia was far away. The odds that Jian Carlo would know the same Serafina were next to nothing.

Still…

"Be brave. Take risks," Paulo Coelho had written. "Nothing can substitute experience." Adriana hoped her favorite author was right because once she moved the folded paper and saw what was hidden beneath it, she would have to deal with the truth.

She braced herself, lowered the paper, and checked the municipality of the address.

Simões Filho.

She cried out loud then covered her mouth, not wanting Irma to catch her rifling through Jian Carlo's private things. She looked more closely. The Bahia address had been crossed out with ink and replaced with an address in Rio de Janeiro. The evil witch lived two small neighborhoods away from Adriana's precious library sanctuary. Tears streamed down her face. Nowhere was safe anymore.

Beneath the address was a notation written in capital letters. *QUIMBANDEIRA.*

Adriana's darkest suspicions were true. The cabin in the woods, the chalk-marked clearing, the empty bottles of cachaça, her father's fear— Avó Serafina was a Quimbanda priestess.

Adriana shut her eyes and clenched the folded paper as ugly thoughts assaulted her mind. Had Mamãe *really* died from natural causes? It had all been so sudden, so "convenient," as Avô Guilherme had said. What about Papai? Had Serafina killed him too? How much of Adriana's family tragedies had been caused by her grandmother's magic?

Now there was Jian Carlo. Adriana knew so little about her husband's history. If he'd known Serafina back in Simões Filho, then meeting Adriana might not have been the accident she and Papá João had assumed. Jian Carlo had controlled her from the start, Adriana understood that now, but what if Serafina controlled him? It was all too horrible to contemplate. Better to shove the book into the drawer and never see it again.

Adriana returned the bookmark paper, but she had crumpled it in her fist. When she tried to flatten it, she caught sight of the word California. She unfolded the sheet and was greeted by Michael's smiling face. Jian Carlo had printed out the biography from Michael's website and stuck it in front of the page with Serafina's address.

# Chapter Eighty-Seven

Serafina led a naked, sexed-up Jian Carlo past his driver and opened her arms to show the man her own naked body in the pre-dawn glow. She even waved an invitation for him to join in the fun, but the big man sank down into his car seat to wait. She hoped he was comfortable because she planned to keep his boss for a very long time.

Inside the cabin, Jian Carlo fell onto the sofa and into a deep sleep. She had ridden him hard. He deserved a few hours to recover but no more than that. She had waited a long time to break him and was not about to grant him any more freedom than he absolutely needed to function at peak sexual performance.

In the meantime, Serafina fixed herself a plate of bread and cheese. She didn't need to rest. The power she drained from Jian Carlo had replenished her. She could not survive forever in this way, but the jolt of energy she gained from dominating his spirit would invigorate her for days. The stronger the spirit the greater the boost.

Serafina's magic and Jian Carlo's childhood hardships had forged him into the strongest man she had ever known, the man her son should have become. Serafina would never forgive him for marrying Adriana and defying her will. She would tear him down and drink him up.

The day had hardly begun, and before the night was over, Jian Carlo would beg to be enslaved. Then the real fun would begin.

# Chapter Eighty-Eight
## Hameau de Vieille Forêt, France 1560

Philippe saw into people's souls. Sometimes, what he saw reminded him of animals, the way they strutted or pecked or snarled. Other times, he caught glimpses of their future or past. No matter how the images came to him, Philippe always saw something, but he did not always share what he saw.

Philippe's favorite place to sit was on a crude wooden stool, where he could mend his shirt at the edge of the stone hearth and swirl his toes in the fire's warm ashes. When Maman was not watching, Philippe would sneak across the stones and snatch a small loaf of bread baking on a brick or a ladle of soup from the pot that always hung above the flames.

Every night after supper, Colette filled the pot with new water to steep in old remains so their family might have something more filling than tea and less satisfying than stew in the morning. If they were lucky, she would add roots and beans. If they were very lucky, she added bits of meat gifted to her from a neighbor or from a rabbit caught in one of her snares.

Colette was the prettiest girl in Hameau de Vieille Forêt and the most beautiful person Philippe had ever met, not just on the outside with her milky skin and long coppery-brown hair but on the inside where only he could see. Why else would she have saved him from starvation and brought him into her home?

Maman slammed her palms on the table. "What do you expect me to do, Colette? The man is a priest."

"I expect you to protect me." Colette leapt from the bed she and Philippe shared.

Maman grabbed a clay bowl and tipped it so Colette could see the roasted potatoes inside. "Protect you from what? From this?" She set it down hard, picked up a chicken leg, and waved it at Colette. "Or how about this? Because we would not have any of it without Révérend Père d'Amboise."

Colette shook her hair and made it fly around her head like fire in a wind. She was a force of nature, fierce and passionate and wild. Maman was wrong to contain her, and the reverend father even more foolish to try and buy her.

Colette snarled at Maman. "I know how to snare and forage as well as any man in the hamlet. I'll keep food in the pot. Me. Not him. We can't afford his charity."

Maman growled back and threw up her hands in disgust. "How did I raise such a stupid girl? Can you not see what a dangerous position you have put us in? Do you not understand how bad our lives can get? No. And do you know why? Because you are a selfish child."

She pointed at Philippe. "What do you think will happen to him if you insult the most powerful man in our hamlet? The fool can barely mend his shirts. How do you expect Philippe to survive without the charity you are too proud to accept?"

Philippe did not like it when Maman spoke about him in this way. He was not as simple-minded as she thought, as everyone in the hamlet thought. Everyone except Colette.

"Philippe is holier than that wicked priest. We should all be praising him."

Maman gasped. Colette glared.

Philippe leaned forward, eager to see what would happen next, when someone rapped at the door. For a long moment, nobody moved. Three more raps, hard and sharp, made Philippe's teeth hurt. Three more, even louder, could not be ignored.

Maman smoothed her hair and went to open the door. "Révérend Père." She bowed her head. "Please, come in. We were just about to eat this bounty you have so generously provided. Would you like to join us?"

As she stepped aside, Philippe saw the reverend father as he always did: as a tall, gnarled, mangy white wolf who stood on hind legs and balanced his crooked body with a tall crooked staff.

"Merci, madame. But no, I will not be staying. I only came to inform you of my intention to marry Colette."

"No," Colette yelled, but Maman shushed her and apologized to the wolf.

He received it with a nod. "Two weeks should suffice for the preparations. I will, of course, provide you with whatever you require. Does this satisfy you, madame?"

Philippe stood, abruptly and without volition. "You can't marry Colette. You'll be dead."

It happened like this, sometimes. A message would spurt from him without any warning or foreknowledge; like a rooster at dawn's break, he simply felt compelled to crow. Maman and Colette gasped and clutched their throats.

Révérend Père d'Amboise drove his staff into the floor and advanced, menacingly. "What did you say?"

Colette rushed to Philippe's defense. "He's a fool. Everyone knows this. He says crazy things, all the time. Or just repeats what other people say, like a mockingbird, repeating anything he hears, never singing his own tune."

Philippe knew he should keep quiet, but another message blurted out of his mouth. "Horses will come for you when it rains. You'll die in the mud, trampled beneath their hooves. It will be a painful death."

Révérend Père slammed the bottom of his staff against the floor with enough force to crack the clay. He thrust the top of it at Philippe. "Satan."

Colette shoved aside the staff and stood in front of Philippe. "Those were my words. He's just repeating what he heard me say."

Maman shrieked, "She's lying. She makes up stories all the time. But she'll make a good wife for you. I promise."

Révérend Père pried Maman from his arm and his waist and shoved her to the floor. "This boy is an idiot and your daughter is a witch."

# Chapter Eighty-Nine
## Rio de Janeiro - Present Day

Michael stroked the head that rested on his chest. He didn't know who she was or why she was so sad, but her hair felt silky, and her sorrow hurt his soul. "Don't cry. Please, don't cry." He tried to focus, but disjointed images swirled in the fog: a snarling wolf, a shrieking woman, a stunned boy, a sobbing girl. "I won't let him do it," Michael whispered, although he didn't know why he said that or how he could prevent "him" from doing "it" when his body felt so heavy he could hardly move.

"I'm so sorry," the woman said. "This is all my fault. I should have known this could happen. I should have seen the signs. He does not lose. Not ever."

Michael recognized her voice, but her name drifted out of reach.

"They used black magic on you, Michael. Quimbanda. They called on the Devil."

Her words didn't make any sense. Magic? Devil?

"You're dying."

That he understood. He could feel his body giving up. The fog weighing him down.

"Michael."

He needed to sleep. Why wouldn't she let him sleep?

"They can't help you here. Do you understand? I have to take you away."

"Sure," he muttered, and closed his eyes.

# Chapter Ninety

Adriana watched the hovels go by as the taxi driver sped through the hilly streets of Favela Morro da Coroa. The shacks were built from scraps of wood, tin, glass, and brick, jammed together like an organized trash heap rather than an actual neighborhood. The residents looked equally shabby. The driver did not stop or even dare to slow as he passed them celebrating in the streets.

Adriana had heard rumors as a child that her father had grown up in such a place. It had seemed ridiculous to consider while they lived in their fancy house in Lauro de Freitas. After moving to the woods in Simões Filho, she could easily imagine him, torn shirt and dirty face, in the doorway of one of those hovels.

A scraggly old man shook his gnarled fist at the speeding taxi while urchins threw clumps of dirt and rock. If only Papai was here. Rich, poor, clean, dirty, she'd love and cherish him no matter what.

The terreiro lay outside Morro da Coroa on the other side of the Santa Bárbara tunnel. An eclectic mix of people parked their cars and motorbikes—some cheap, some expensive—in sight of grubby teenage hoodlums and drug addicts, then crossed the street to the shabby terreiro without the slightest sign of unease. Despite their class distinctions, the people greeted each other cheerfully and without prejudice. Some carried flowers or food. An old man led a goat. Two favela girls in short skirts and colorful strands of tinfoil beads paused to dance in the lot.

The driver pulled up to the curb. "You are lucky this Mãe de Santos is so dedicated. Most terreiros close down for Carnaval."

"Aren't you going to drive us to the entrance?"

"No time. Lots of money for me today."

"Well, can you at least help me get him out of the car?"

"Ask one of them."

She paid the driver, less than she would have if he had helped, and hurried around to Michael's side of the car. He was more lucid now that the pain medication had worn off, but he still did not have the strength to walk across the lot on his own. She grabbed the drawstring bag with Michael's Carnaval clothing, slipped it over her shoulder along with her purse, and struggled for leverage.

"Fine," said the driver. "I'll help. But only to get him out of my taxi." He waved at a couple of men who approached from the sidewalk. "Hey, this man wants to meet your Mãe de Santos."

The men helped Michael out of the car and slipped their arms under his for support.

"What's wrong with him?" the younger man asked.

Adriana shrugged. How could she possibly explain?

The older man nodded as if he understood. "You have come to the right place."

"Obrigada. But wait a moment. Please?"

Adriana removed the strap from her purse and used it to wrap his gown and close the opening in the back. "Better?"

Michael grimaced. "Like Caesar. And you know how that ended."

"No jokes, okay? People are waiting to help you."

She followed the men through the lot and past a miniature house the size of a small tool shed. A chained dog lay in the doorway between statues of Exú and Pomba Gira, costumed in matching red and black capes. More statues lined the window sill. Most followed the red and black theme and ranged from comical to sexy to scary.

Adriana had read that terreiros put these spirit houses in front to attract mischievous entities that might otherwise disrupt the ceremonies. She had no reason to feel threatened, yet she could not shake the feeling that the statues laughed at her, especially the one with the sly smile dressed all in white. She turned away from the dolls and nearly crashed into a tiny old woman, who wrinkled her nose and cursed.

Adriana shrank with embarrassment. She had not even entered the terreiro and had already drawn negative attention from both humans and spirits. She had to be more careful. This was an Umbanda place of worship, not a Catholic church. She needed to show respect to every member of this terreiro and open herself to every god and spirit they were able to call.

Up ahead, the men picked up Michael's legs and carried him across the threshold.

Resisting the urge to cross herself, Adriana hurried to join them.

# Chapter Ninety-One

The men carried Michael to a bench on the right side of the aisle. Adriana was forced to sit on the left. Although she had not read anything about the segregation of men and women, apparently it was a custom in this terreiro. Not wanting to draw ill will, she did as she was told.

Across the aisle, Michael slumped on the bench and closed his eyes. He looked so frail. She could hardly believe he was the same man who had lifted her in the air at the Magic Ball and spun her around the dance floor. If she had left him at the hospital, he would have died. She prayed to God and Jesus and Mary, to Olorum and Oxalá and Oxúm, to all the orixás, the Catholic saints, and the indigenous spirits of her land. Adriana prayed to them all that Michael would live.

The main room of the terreiro had clean lines and white walls, with none of the ornate moldings and carvings of a church. The benches, which occupied the back half of the room, were equally plain, some with backs and others without, as if they had been scavenged from old churches or built from cheap materials before being painted white. The gleaming white tiles of the dance floor in front reflected light from a mishmash of wall fixtures that were also painted white. The only items of color, aside from the clothing worn by the congregation and the gifts they had brought, were the preset atabaque drums, the statues displayed in the white bookcases along the front wall, and a painting of Jesus.

Conversations quieted to a murmur as three men in white shirts and pants walked past Adriana down the aisle. When they reached the front of the terreiro, they sat on stools and pulled the colorful drums between their knees.

The leader set the rhythm with thumping palms and tapping fingers, a solo voice sung to the gods. Another drummer added depth and strength to the beat. Another brought vitality. Together, the three drummers energized the terreiro and called for the ceremony to begin.

A white door opened on the women's side of the altar to admit an enormous Afro-Brazilian woman garbed in layers of shining white satin and handmade lace. Her triple chin rested on an enormous bosom.

She spread her fleshy arms out to the congregation. "Welcome my sisters and my brothers."

She nodded at the drummers. "My Sons of Saints."

She gestured up the aisle. "My Daughters of Saints."

A procession of women entered through the front door and everyone turned to watch.

The Daughters of Saints ranged in height, weight, age, and skin tone, but none were as impressive as the Mãe de Santos. Like her, they were dressed in white, with peasant-style tops and full cotton skirts that stopped at the ankles to show their bare feet. Instead of the lace headband that restrained the Mãe de Santos' unruly hair, the mediums had topped their heads with white lace caps. Long ropes of colored beads hung from their necks. Barefoot female attendants followed in white blouses over light blue skirts, no caps or beads.

The Mãe de Santos gestured behind her to a painting of Jesus Christ with his arms outstretched in love. "We welcome you to the House of Oxalá, the god of purity and goodness, where you will be blessed and comforted, and where we may beseech and appease the gods. Welcome."

The Mãe de Santos gestured for blue-skirted attendants to light the tall standing-candles then signaled the drummers to change the beat. The congregation clapped to the new rhythm, lending their hands to the talking drums. The mediums formed a circle and began to dance. The blue-skirted attendants sang.

> "Saravá! Saravá! We are waiting.
> Praise to the Orixás.
> Praise to Exú and Pomba Gira.
> Praise to Olorum, Oxalá, Yemanjá.
> Join us, your faithful.
> Find us, we are here.
> Saravá! Saravá! Saravá!"

Adriana clapped as though her life depended on it. On the other side of the aisle, Michael trembled and twitched as he struggled to fight whatever demons were trying to kill him. How could Quimbanda do so much harm so quickly?

The drums and the voices grew more fervent, fueling the movements of the mediums until they seemed to lose themselves in the sound. One of the mediums stopped, arms spread, fingers tense, head thrown back, and shook as though electrified. Her arms dropped, her shoulders slumped, and her spine bent and twisted into the posture of someone very old.

Adriana gasped. There was a big difference between expecting something to happen and actually witnessing it.

An attendant came forward to support the medium by the arm and handed her a pipe.

On the other side of the dance floor, two other mediums fell to their knees, giggling like children. One tickled while the other squealed and slapped. Two attendants hurried over to break them apart.

One after another, the mediums shed their worldly personas and took on the characteristics of the spirits who seemed to possess them. Attendants rushed forward with props suited to the new personalities—

toy bow and arrow, cardboard lance and shield, tunics, pipe, sea shell, horse-tail whisk—and guided the women to form a line across the center of the dance floor. The congregation murmured with excitement and rose, eager to visit whichever god or spirit they wished to engage, then sat when one of the mediums broke rank and strode up the aisle.

Adriana stiffened. The woman had sucked in her childbearing flab and held herself like a warrior. What if she shot that toy arrow into Adriana's heart? It was ridiculous, and yet...

"Please help us." Adriana glanced across the aisle at Michael. "He's dying."

The medium considered her request then slowly turned to face Michael, now fully conscious and alarmed.

# Chapter Ninety-Two

Michael grabbed the pew in front of him for support and stared at the savage Indian warrior standing in the aisle, bare chested, bow and arrow in hand, hunting knife strapped to his thigh. Where had he come from? Moments ago, women in white dresses had danced to the beat of the drums. Now they were gone, and this Indian warrior was here.

Michael tensed, ready for fight or flight, then sagged. If the warrior wanted to slit his throat or shoot him with an arrow, all Michael could do about it was die. At least it would be quicker than whatever was killing him now.

He took a breath and straightened as best he could to meet the threat.

The warrior had a broad and angry face, accentuated by a mask of red war paint around the eyes and a wide black line across his nose and mouth. He wore a peaked headdress of tall blue feathers and a string of crude wooden beads that dangled over his intricately tattooed chest. Although not a large man, he had a commanding stature with deeply cut muscles, a testament to lean years and a hard life. He wore no clothing other than a belt of thick woven cloth tied around his hips and knotted to hang in front of his genitals. He had wrapped strips of the same cloth around his knees.

The warrior probably came from an Amazon Indian tribe although Michael could not imagine how or why the man was here, standing way too close to Adriana.

"Get away from her," Michael said, then coughed from the effort.

Adriana shook her head. "Tranquilo, meu amor. She is here to help."

She? What was Adriana talking about? The warrior was clearly a man and a dangerous one at that. Michael didn't want him anywhere near her. He looked around the room for support, and found insanity instead.

On the dance floor where the women in white had been, a white stallion adorned with full medieval regalia reared up on its hind legs to strike at a fire-breathing dragon. When its hooves smashed to the ground, an armored knight lowered his lance, raised his shield, kicked the steed, and charged.

Michael screamed. He couldn't help it. The dragon was huge, terrifying, and utterly impossible. When the lance pierced its throat, the dragon disintegrated into colored dust.

"Michael? Are you all right?"

He glanced at Adriana who clung to the Indian warrior's arm as if seeking his support or protection. Her pretty face was marred by worry.

*This isn't happening.*

He dug his fingers into his temples to stop the throbbing. The pain hurt so bad he could hardly breathe. No wonder she looked worried: she was watching him die, and all these hallucinations—the warrior, the knight, the dragon—were part of the process. He took a breath and struggled for calm.

The dragon and stallion were gone, but other strange beings had taken their places. Beside the knight, stooped an old black man with snow-white whiskers dressed in the tattered clothes of a slave. He sucked on a wooden pipe and blew the smoke at a pair of twin boys who wrestled on the white-tiled floor. They stopped, jumped to their feet, and smoothed their matching Spanish-styled tunics.

Michael blinked hard to dispel the vision, but it remained.

A goddess in a sea-blue dress, scaled like a mermaid's tale, stepped

DANCE AMONG THE FLAMES

onto the stage with a fierce-looking woman in rawhide riding clothes who held a machete in one hand and a horse-tail whip in the other. Her chestnut hair blew around her shoulders even though there was no wind.

Michael grabbed the pew in front of him and rose onto wobbling legs. He'd be damned if he'd allow these delusions to steal his dignity. He looked each of the six beings squarely in the eyes and gave them all a curt nod. It boosted his confidence to acknowledge their presence. At least it did until they parted and revealed the most astounding hallucination of all.

Jesus walked forward to greet Michael, arms extended in welcome. "You are among friends."

The sea goddess stepped to his side. "We will help you."

The horse woman nodded. "We can protect you."

The ancient slave stepped forward. "Tell us, den, who put this hex on you." His sing-song cadence added to Michael's confusion.

The knight pointed his lance. "He does not want to hear."

The twins piped in, "Or see. Or speak."

The Amazon Indian sneered. "He is afraid."

Michael stumbled out of the aisle and fell.

# Chapter Ninety-Three

Adriana rushed to Michael as he convulsed on the floor. "Somebody help him. Please."

One of the mediums, whose spine was bent from the spirit she channeled, sucked on her pipe and shook her head sadly. "Dis one close himself from us."

Adriana wrapped her arms around Michael, tried to stop the spasms, while the other mediums watched from the dance floor with maddening detachment. She should never have brought Michael to this horrible place. These superstitious people, with their silly props and amateur theatrics, would not save his life.

She craned her neck and searched for the Mãe de Santos. Surely, the Mother of Saints would do something to help, give him a potion, say a prayer, call for an ambulance. But the white-clad priestess she had expected to see had changed into a garish red dress and crown. She shoved her way through the mediums and swaggered up the aisle, sucking on a fat cigar. She waved a bottle of cachaça at her stunned audience and cackled with glee.

"Is this all the welcome I get?" she asked with a laugh. "You should be celebrating. It's not every day Exú of the Crossroads comes to visit."

The congregation muttered nervously. Adriana hugged Michael tighter, no longer wanting the Umbanda priestess anywhere near him.

"Silly girl. You think you can stop me? After you bring him into my house?" The Mãe de Santos waved Adriana off the floor. "Out of my way. I need room to move." She rolled her flab in an obscene belly dance that bounced and swished the layers of her red dress.

Adriana froze. Had Exú of the Crossroads possessed the Mãe de Santos? If so, Michael was in even more danger than she had imagined.

She hugged his shaking body and cried. She couldn't move him if she tried, and she doubted anyone here would help.

*Please, don't let this be a mistake.*

She kissed Michael's head and obeyed.

# Chapter Ninety-Four

"What's the matter, my friend? Not feeling so well?" The voice mocked Michael with digging familiarity.

He clenched his jaw and waited for the convulsions to subside. When he felt more in control, he opened his eyes. "Oh my God."

Julius Amodei raised the brim of his white Panama hat with his ivory snake cane and grinned. "Close. But not quite."

He puffed on his cigar, took a swig from the liquor bottle he held in the same hand, then bent at the waist and poked Michael with his cane. "You don't look so good, my friend. Would you like me to get rid of your pain?"

Michael coughed out a laugh. "Sure. Why not."

Amodei swept his cane toward the congregation. "See why I like this guy so much? He's always ready for a good time." He hooked the snake's head under Michael's chin. "Get up and give me a hug." He yanked Michael to his feet, stuffed him under his arm, and shook him back and forth like a rag doll instead of a man twice Amodei's size. "Look at you, so happy to see me you cannot hold still." He planted his cane, stuck the end of his cigar in his teeth, and brought the bottle of liquor to Michael's mouth. "You want a drink?"

Michael grabbed the cane for support and heaved.

"Easy, my friend. You don't want to mess up my nice white suit." Amodei used the bottle to turn Michael's face and forced him to look into his cruel black eyes. "You might make me angry." Then he threw back his head and laughed.

"What do you want, Amodei?"

"Amodei? No, no, no, Michael. I know you are not well, but you really have to keep up." He leaned in and whispered, "There is no Julius Amodei. There is only me."

He shoved Michael against a pew and began to transform: first, into a bare-chested man with a red satin cape, tight black pants, and a black stovepipe hat; next, into a hulking beast with a shaggy coat, black and red pajama pants, long tusks, and Medusa-like hair; and again, into a towering blue demon with black horns and fire in its eyes. He changed his size, color, and features, faster and faster, until he was a blur of strange and formidable entities. All of them at once and none of them at all.

"Who are you?" Michael cried.

"Me?" He whirled into a massive figure, dark as night, sleek as a seal, and shimmered with sweat. Huge red beads encircled his neck and a red loincloth hung between his legs to the floor. He flexed his arms and raised a golden scepter and a wooden club. "I'm Exú of the Seven Crossroads, Lord of Chaos, Intermediary to the Gods." He whirled again and transformed back into the familiar little man in the white suit, Panama hat, and ivory snake cane.

He gave Michael a sly grin and shrugged. "Just a few of my many titles, but you get the idea. The point is, my friend, that you are in— How do they say it in your country? —deep shit."

"Oh God."

"There you go, again. Did I not tell you to pay attention? I am *a* god, not *the* God. Get it? Master of Magic, Immortal Trickster, Julius Amodei—call me whatever you want, but call me, eh?" He slapped his knee and laughed. "Or how am I going to get this hex off of you?"

Adriana gasped, as did quite a few people in the room.

Michael ignored them all and focused on the little man in the white suit who was, apparently, a freaking Brazilian god.

"What the hell is going on?"

Exú grabbed Michael around the neck and tapped his cane against Michael's forehead. "Now you understand."

Michael trembled with anger and humiliation.

*This can't be happening. I won't believe it. I won't.*

"Acalma-te, Michael, your thoughts are deafening. All this agitation is not good for your health. Besides, I have to talk to my other friends. Stop hogging my attention."

Exú turned full circle, Michael still locked under his arm, and addressed the crowd. "So… Who has cursed my dear friend Michael Cross?"

# Chapter Ninety-Five

The Mãe de Santos' gaze stopped on Adriana. "How about you, little girl? I bet you know who did this work of Quimbanda. Tell me. Who closed the paths of health from this man?"

Adriana wiped the tears from her face.

"Pay attention, girl. Can't you see my friend is running out time?"

She could. Michael looked so pale and weak hanging over the big woman's arm. Adriana had to do something. She sniffed back the tears and blurted, "Jian Carlo."

The Mãe de Santos glanced down at Michael, braced against her flabby hip, and frowned. "He has come all the way from California, and that is the best you can offer?"

Adriana shook her head. There was no way out, she had to say it. "My husband hired a Quimbandeira to kill him."

The congregation gasped. A few twittered. Adriana wanted to sink in a hole and die.

# Chapter Ninety-Six

Michael didn't understand or care why Adriana looked so upset, he just wanted his pain to end. "You're the Devil."

Exú chuckled. "Me? Não. I'm a messenger, a trickster—and a teacher, I like to think, although the living have rarely enjoyed my lessons. Romans, Mayans, Mesopotamians, they all lacked a sense of humor. Like your girl. So serious. And after you came all this way and played your part so magnificently."

Michael wheezed and coughed. "Is this...a game to you?" He had more to ask, but he could hardly breathe.

Exú propped up Michael so he could face Adriana. "Tell us, girl. Who's the Quimbandeira who cursed your lover?"

"I'm sorry, Michael. I never meant to bring this on you."

"Tell us."

She sighed in resignation. "My grandmother."

Michael coughed out a bitter laugh. Adriana had lied about being married, and now her husband *and* grandmother were trying to kill him? To hell with her. To hell with all of them.

He glared at Exú, his coughing fit squelched by rage. "You did this. I never would have come to Rio if I hadn't been chasing you."

Exú clapped him on the shoulders as though he had won a great prize. "You are so smart. Come, my friend. We have much to do."

He swept Michael into his arms and carried him down the aisle to the front of the hall where Saint George, the old black slave, the twin boys, the sea goddess, and the horse woman with the wind in her hair waited in a semi-circle. The fierce Amazon Indian followed behind and joined the others.

Exú looked down at Michael. "You see them, yes? In their true forms?"

Michael nodded.

Exú whirled him around then set him on his feet. "See? I knew it. You're the one. This is why you are here. But first, I must get rid of your pain, or how will you be able to finish the job?"

Exú released Michael to stand on his own and signaled the drummers to play.

Michael swayed, reached for Saint George and the old black slave to help, then slumped to the floor. Drums pounded into his brain. The room spun. Spirits and saints blurred until Michael couldn't tell one from the other. This was it. This was the end. Then water drenched his head.

Michael sputtered and coughed. Above him, Exú held two pitchers, one empty, the other full. "With this water, I cleanse your spirit and open your paths."

Michael yelled as Exú drenched him again. "Cut that out." He shook his hair and flung a spray of water around the dance floor.

People cheered from the benches and pews. Dancers in white dresses and women in blue skirts clapped their hands. Drummers stopped playing. An enormous woman in a hideous red satin dress waved empty pitchers in the air.

Michael crawled to his feet, yanked the tangled hospital gown out of the way, and exposed his ass. Laughter erupted throughout the room. He was about to yell and curse when he realized that the pain was gone, not even a twinge remained. The people laughed and cheered because they had witnessed a miracle. Michael jumped and spun and laughed along with everyone else. He didn't know why or how, but he was going to live.

The woman in the red satin dress scooped him up in her flabby arms and squashed him against her bosom in a suffocating hug. He hugged her back with all his might. If this devil-woman had anything to do with how he felt, he was thankful to be her friend.

# Demons

"Where blood has been shed, the tree of forgiveness cannot grow."
– Brazilian proverb

# Chapter Ninety-Seven

Adriana stuffed the remaining clothes into a roller-suitcase, already heavy with books. The shoes and other unbreakables had gone into assorted totes. The rest of her belongings would have to stay. She could survive without them.

"Would you like some food, senhora?" Irma asked. "It's almost morning. I could make you breakfast."

She had become agitated when Adriana had started to pack, no doubt worried Jian Carlo would blame her if Adriana disappeared. Perhaps he would, but Adriana couldn't worry about that, she had a slim window for escape and she intended to take it.

"Não, obrigada. Go to bed, Irma. I'll be fine."

According to Irma, Jian Carlo had not come home after his supposed meeting the night before, and if he had gone to watch the samba parades while she had been moving Michael from the hospital to the terreiro, he had not come home to get her. Adriana had no idea where he might be, but she planned to be gone before he returned.

She closed the suitcase and went to the closet for her most precious possession. *Abandon*. Perhaps in time, Michael's painting would inspire her to find that same sense of glorious freedom. It seemed hard to imagine, but she could hope.

"Hello, my dear," a familiar voice said.

Adriana froze.

"What? No hug for Grandma?"

After all the years, the wicked witch had finally returned. Adriana turned around. Serafina filled the doorway with her towering height, her wild hair, and her layered blood-red skirt. Her presence made Adriana feel small and confined.

"What are you doing here?"

Serafina stepped aside and Jian Carlo joined her in the doorway.

Adriana gasped. His tailored clothes were dirty and torn, hanging from a body that looked kilos lighter than the last time she had seen him. His well-groomed hair spiked in unruly directions above twitching bloodshot eyes. His mouth hung slack like a salivating dog as he stroked Serafina's arm. He looked as desperate as the drug addicts hunched on the sidewalk across from the Umbanda terreiro.

Serafina placed a finger beneath Jian Carlo's chin and lifted his gaze. "My pet, your wife asked me a question. She wants to know why we are here."

Jian Carlo's face twitched as he pried his gaze away from Serafina, as though he couldn't bear to break the connection. However, once broken, the tension in his face eased and his mouth curved into a haughty grin. "I thought the two of you should be reunited."

Whatever pity Adriana might have felt for him vanished. "You thought wrong."

She tucked Michael's painting under her arm, pulled the suitcase off the bed, and started for the door. She could do without the rest of her belongings. What mattered most was getting out of this house and leaving Jian Carlo for good.

Serafina stepped in her path and laughed.

# Chapter Ninety-Eight

Michael stretched out his arms as far as he could reach and filled his lungs with life. He had faced his fears in the Umbanda house of worship, made the Devil his friend, and survived, just as The Lady had said.

The truck hit a bump and landed him on his ass. The men in the back of the pickup laughed. Michael flashed them the double thumbs-up. He had been amusing his new Brazilian buddies ever since they had whisked him away from the terreiro to celebrate. Together, they had torn up the town: danced in the streets, banged on drums, celebrated life.

The truck pulled in front of the hotel and Michael hopped out. If the doorman noticed his bare chest and disheveled appearance, he didn't show it: No doubt he had seen stranger sights than Michael rolling in this morning.

Michael waved to the driver and the rest of his buddies. "Obrigado, meus amigos." He kicked off his borrowed slippers and tossed them into the cargo bed, earning a final round of laughter from the men as the truck drove out of sight.

When Michael entered his hotel room, he fell onto the bed and lay like the dead for several minutes, then gave up, too wired for sleep. He switched on the television, ordered breakfast, and took a shower. By the time he had dried, dressed, and answered the door for room service, he had become engrossed in a news special on CNN.

The host was an attractive blonde with heavy makeup. The guest was a no-nonsense woman of authority. Michael was more impressed with the guest, who, according to the caption at the bottom of the screen, was a psychiatrist and human rights activist.

"Human trafficking is slavery," she said. "And it's happening where you live."

The two-shot of the interview switched to a photograph of an Asian maid peering through the iron gate of a western-style mansion.

"It's happening to people like you."

A well-dressed Caucasian woman stared into the camera as though harboring a tremendous secret from which she would never escape.

"It's happening around the world."

Mexican prostitutes posed on a street corner under the watchful eye of a pimp. East Indian children labored in a garment sweatshop. A Scandinavian teen stared out of a car window, her terrified face framed by her fingers splayed on the glass like the toes of a tree frog.

The room service waiter paused as he set Michael's breakfast on the table and watched the television. The photos of women had switched to a pre-recorded interview with a Brazilian laborer. The man spoke Portuguese, but Michael learned his story through the English subtitles.

The impoverished man had been lured to a remote cattle pasture under the promise of employment. Once there, he had been forced to drink the same water as the cattle, had barely been fed, and had been threatened by armed guards into working eleven-hour days. When he finally received a paycheck, his salary had been docked for the purchases he had made from the price-inflated company store. Two years passed before he had managed to escape.

Michael looked at the waiter and his somber expression. "You know someone like this?"

The man shrugged and slipped quietly out the door.

Michael picked at his food as the conversation between the host and her special-guest-authority evolved into the subject of coercion.

"So, you're saying that the most secure captive is the one who will not leave even when the door is open?"

The psychiatrist nodded. "A sophisticated manipulator understands how to use his victim's strengths against her."

"How so?"

"The mind has a natural inclination to seek truth and order. The choices we make help us define that order. The more choices we have, the more in control we feel, and the greater our sense of freedom becomes. This autonomy gives us a sense of dignity and identity. When someone is enslaved, all of that is taken away. Information is controlled, choices are manipulated, identity is altered, dignity is undermined."

The host frowned. "How are choices manipulated?"

The psychiatrist spread her hands. "It's surprisingly easy. The victim is only offered options that either further the predetermined agenda or that make no difference in the outcome. For example, if I were going to limit your food, I might ask if you would prefer a potato or a bowl of rice. If I was dictating your destination, I might ask who you wanted to drive you there: me or the chauffeur. The choice that you make is irrelevant. You are still going to eat less and go where I want you to go."

"But why bother?"

"Because choice gives the captive the illusion of freedom. Choice makes us an active participant in the conditions of our lives. It's hard to blame someone else for something that we have helped to create."

"That's very subtle."

"Yes it is, but it's also very effective. And insidious. Someone skilled in coercion could use a victim's own pride and sense of responsibility against her and alter her perception of identity and reality without her realizing it. And if she ever did notice the change, she would probably believe she had done it to herself."

The host paused as she considered the full implications of what her guest was saying. "We're not just talking about human trafficking any more, are we?"

The psychiatrist shrugged. "There are many forms of enslavement."

Michael shut off the television.

Adriana fit the psychiatrist's profile: She wanted to work, but she didn't have a job. She adored learning, but she wasn't in college. She dreamed of becoming a teacher, but she wasn't doing anything to make that happen. A woman like Adriana should have known her worth. She shouldn't be trapped in a stifling marriage.

*Trapped.*

Is that what she was?

Michael thought of the parrots, nesting in his jacaranda trees back in Venice Beach. Although he left the skylights open most of the time, they never flew away. Was Adriana like them? Did she truly want to stay in her marriage? Or had the captive grown so accustomed to the prison she was afraid to escape? Michael didn't know, but he wasn't about to leave Rio until he heard the answer from her lips.

# Chapter Ninety-Nine

Michael pulled himself over the wooden gates of Adriana's estate and dropped onto her driveway. Although no one had answered the gate buzzer, it didn't mean no one was home. After what he had learned about coercion and enslavement, he needed to know for sure.

He raised his fist and knocked loudly on the wood. He knocked again, and the door opened to reveal a rustic-looking woman in a gray maid's uniform. She had a stocky build, weathered skin, and a nervous demeanor. Her eyes darted between Michael and the closed gate, probably wondering how he had entered the estate.

"Adriana, por favor?" He kept his voice soft and his expression pleasant.

The maid shook her head, ready to bolt.

Michael clasped his hands together. "Please? É importante."

The maid replied with a flurry of words he couldn't follow then stepped back and shut the door in his face.

He stopped it with his shoe. "Sorry, but I really do have to see her."

Without waiting for an invitation, he pushed his way inside. The maid followed, jabbering a stream of incomprehensible Portuguese, while he checked the first floor of the house. When he didn't find anyone, he headed up the stairs.

"Adriana?"

The first room was an imposing office, obviously her husband's. The second had the neat appearance of a guest room. The third made Michael gasp.

The bedroom, too small and too feminine to be the master suite, looked as if a cyclone had hit it. Clothes, shoes, books, toiletries spilled from the suitcase and the bags on the floor. Trinkets lay scattered on her dressing table and chair. The bedding had been pulled onto the floor and toward the door. Across the room, the painting he had gifted her was ripped, and the frame broken.

He grabbed the maid before she could run away. "Where's Adriana?"

"Não sei."

He marched the struggling woman to the last room at the end of the hall and stopped. The door was closed. It looked ordinary enough. There was no reason to be afraid. No reason why he shouldn't open it and enter. Yet something menacing about the door froze him in his tracks.

He shook off the premonition and opened it. A thousand votive candles flickered on the floor.

The maid yelped and backed against the wall, away from the dark room and the flickering lights. Michael ignored her and focused on what lay beyond the candles: an enormous canopy bed that must have weighed as much as a small car. It had four thick posts, heavy boards at the foot and head, and a monstrous roof that made the bed look like an ornately carved cage, all in the same blood-red wood as the furniture in the office. In the center of this repulsive cage, behind the barrier of fire, knelt Adriana, with her dress fanned around her knees and her eyes glazed with despair, exactly as Michael had painted her in his studio back home.

He turned to question the maid, but she had run away. If only Michael could have done the same. No matter how far or how fast he ran, he would always return here. He knew this in his bones.

# Chapter One Hundred

Serafina watched from the doorway as Michael tried to cross the barrier she had erected around the bed, and grinned as it shoved him back. He tried again with more commitment, and the barrier repelled him with equal force, tossing him in the air, limbs flexed like a frightened cat. He shook off his surprise and crept forward with his hand extended to test what he could not see. Meeting with resistance, he backed away, stooped forward like a runner on the block, and charged. The barrier received his momentum and flung him across the room like a slingshot into the doorframe with a loud and satisfying smack.

Serafina burst into laughter. "I wouldn't try that again if I were you."

Michael jumped to his feet and scrambled away. "Who are you?"

He puffed himself up big, as if trying to intimidate her with his size. She saw his fear. A man like him—tall, handsome, rich, white—would be accustomed to having the advantage, to being in control. Too bad for him.

"You're the grandmother, aren't you? The witch who tried to kill me."

She inclined her head.

"Well, I'm still here."

"I see that."

"Does it disappoint you?"

She shrugged. "I'll get over it."

She walked to the edge of the candles and looked over at Adriana, who seemed unaware of anything happening in front of her.

"Such a beauty, eh? Locked away in a castle like Rapunzel. You know this fairytale? Because you may be a prince back where you come from, but not here. Not in Brazil. Here, I am queen."

When Michael scoffed, she beckoned for Jian Carlo, who appeared in the hallway behind her and waited like an obedient dog. The American needed a lesson in respect and nothing showed power like a broken man groveling at her feet.

"Have you met Adriana's husband?"

Jian Carlo knelt beside Serafina and rubbed his cheek against her leg.

"Like you, he was an arrogant fool. But look at him now?" She hooked her finger under his chin, raised him to his feet, and kissed the top of his head. "Who am I, Jian Carlo?"

He gazed at her adoringly. "My queen."

"That's right." She turned his face toward Adriana, sitting on the bed with her dress fanned around her knees. "And who is that?"

He wrinkled his nose. "The whore."

Serafina smirked at Michael. "You see? Adriana is not the angel you think she is, so pretty, so sweet. When I'm done with her, you'll see her for the way she truly is—a selfish, conniving whore."

Michael lunged at her. Jian Carlo shoved him back, growling like a dog. Serafina stroked his back.

"Go back to America, Mr. Cross. This is not your concern."

"Like hell it isn't. What's wrong with you people? She's your granddaughter."

"She is nothing to me. Just a cancer my son was too stupid to let me kill."

They glared at one another; him at a loss for words and her with too many to utter.

"Get out," she said.

"Not until you drop this voodoo bullshit."

She pushed Jian Carlo aside and stepped up to Michael, eye to eye, the slight heel of her sandals putting them at equal height. "You ignorant little gnat. You think you know how things work here? You know nothing. You think because you have a piece of meat dangling between your legs that you have power? I've been dealing with men like you my whole life and have paid them all back in full. No one interferes with Quimbanda. No one dares."

His hot breath smacked her face, as he exhaled in frustration. Then he smiled, turned his back on her, and charged for the bed.

# Chapter One Hundred One

Michael woke in space or a lava lamp, he wasn't sure which. Either way, it was the most beautiful sight he could ever have imagined, a pulsating nebula of color, texture, and depth.

Was this Heaven? If so, there was enough artistic inspiration to last an eternity—or would be if he had any paint. He grunted. More like an artist's Hell.

There had been some kind of explosion, so he must be dead. But since he felt no pain, he sat up and focused on the tunnel of light up ahead.

Maybe he was in Heaven after all.

In the distance, stood a lone figure with a friar's tonsure, trimmed with hair the same dull color as his robe. His feet were bare and his countenance humble. Sparrows fluttered around his head. He reached his hand down the tunnel of light. The instant Michael extended his own, he was transported through the tunnel and onto a cloud in the heavens.

"Welcome."

The words rumbled from every direction, making the friar's body seem unsubstantial and his voice all-knowing. And yet, familiar. A voice from the past, from the banyan tree where Michael used to play as a child, from his place of safety and comfort.

He peered more closely. "Grandfather?"

The friar smiled. "I've never had that pleasure, but I've always liked that you thought of me so." He opened his arms. "It's good to have you back."

Michael took in the friar's tonsure, robe, and the chirping birds that fluttered around him. Was the spirit guardian of his youth really who he appeared to be? "Saint Francis?"

The friar shrugged. "Call me Francesco. It is a name for which I have great fondness, as it was given to me by my father in a moment of playful affection. Or you can call me The Grandfather, as you did when you were a boy. All that matters is that you have returned."

"But you're the one who left—after Mom made me recite that prayer."

"Ah, yes...the exorcism."

"She thought you and The Lady were demons."

"So did you."

"I was angry."

"You were scared. But we understood."

"Then why did you leave?"

Francesco smiled. "Who do you think shoved you out of your daze when you set fire to your artwork and nearly burned down your first Venice Beach apartment?"

"That was you?"

He nodded.

"But you said you couldn't interfere. That's what you told me when I was a kid after I stuck my hand in the fireplace and burned my arm. You made it seem like I had done it on purpose. Like part of me had some secret agenda."

"I also told you that you would always have a choice."

"Really? Because it didn't feel like it then. Or now." He looked down the tunnel of light into the darkness from where he had come.

Inside the darkness was a bedroom. In the bedroom, was a wooden canopy bed where Adriana waited, alone and scared. In front of her, beyond the ring of fire, Jian Carlo and Serafina were frozen—one shocked, the other satisfied—staring at Michael's body, crumpled against the wall.

"Am I dead?"

"You'll survive. It's Adriana who needs our help."

"Our?"

"You cannot pass through the barrier alone, and I cannot carry her out."

Michael shook his head in frustration. "I don't know what you're talking about. What's happening to her?"

"The sorceress has trapped Adriana in her fears, twisting every noble and courageous virtue into self-serving cowardice and corruption. Serafina is breaking her granddaughter of everything she is in order to transform her into what Serafina perceives her to be."

"It won't happen. Adriana's stronger than that."

"Is she? Is anyone?" Francesco grew thoughtful, as though reflecting on his own past frailties. "Few things in human life are as dangerous as doubt or the loss of faith. And then, there is the trickster to consider."

"Who?"

"Exú. But he's had many names through the eons. I think you know him as Julius Amodei."

Michael grunted out a harsh laugh. "I can't get rid of him, can I?"

"Unfortunately, no. He's been waiting for centuries for you, Serafina, and Adriana to be born again in the same lifetime. The boy, the priest, and the witch—together again to right a terrible wrong."

Michael gazed off into the nebula as the mysteries of his life came together like swirling stardust. The sketch. The vision. The fire. His obsession with Adriana.

"I'm Philippe? No wonder I keep trying to burn myself. Colette's death was my fault."

"That's not what I meant."

"Why does Exú care? It was one death, four hundred years ago. Why isn't he tormenting warlords or serial killers? He must have bigger offenders to punish than me."

"Exú doesn't punish; he manipulates. And for some reason, he believes that bringing the three of you together will generate enough power to throw the world into chaos."

"That's ridiculous."

"Only because you don't understand what he has enabled Serafina to do. And why we have to get Adriana out of there before it's too late."

Michael looked down at Adriana, caught in a prison he couldn't see and didn't understand. "You're telling me that whatever is going on with Adriana, her grandmother, and me can affect the whole world?" He shook his head. "I'm sorry. I just don't buy it. I'm not that important. None of us are."

"The monk in me would like to disagree and tell you that all of God's children are precious and important in his eyes. However, you are right. Separately, and perhaps even together, none of you has the power to create world chaos."

"But it's not just us, is it?"

"No. The Lord of Chaos plays a subtle game, one that crosses eons and serves a purpose known only by him and, I assume, God."

"What can I do?"

Francesco looked down at Adriana. "Save her."

"Then let's go. You said it takes both of us, right? What are we waiting for?"

When Francesco didn't answer, a worrisome thought wiggled into Michael's mind. All his life, he feared one thing even more than fire. He had avoided it with his mother, women, art critics, fans...basically everyone he had ever met. Ever since a spirit had taken over his body and forced him to stick his hand in the fire, he had fought to keep everyone and every *thing* out of his head.

"No."

"I need an invitation."

"No."

"It's the only way."

"*No*. Why can't you understand? You were there. You saw what I went through—the skin grafts, the isolation, the exorcisms. You knew a spirit had taken possession of me and you did nothing to stop it. And now you want to do it yourself? No one controls me but *me*."

Francesco waited for Michael to cool off then glanced down at Adriana.

Michael cringed.

*It's not fair.*

"I know it's not," Francesco said, reading Michael's mind. "But it's only for a moment. I don't want to take over your life. I want to give it back to you. You just need to have a little faith."

That's what The Lady had said or Panchali or whoever that was back in his loft. She had told him to make friends with the Devil. That last bit of advice had saved his life when Exú, in the guise of that enormous woman in the red devil dress, had broken Serafina's curse. Would faith help him now?

"You can help me reach Adriana?"

"I can."

"And you'll leave when I tell you to?"

Francesco nodded. "Free will, Michael. Everyone has a choice."

# Chapter One Hundred Two

Serafina looked down at Michael's broken, bleeding body and smiled. Her barrier had taken the arrogant, privileged American and smashed him against the wall like a bug on a windshield.

Stupid man.

She turned to Jian Carlo. "You see? No one can reach her."

"Not even me?"

Serafina snaked a fingernail down Jian Carlo's chest. "Do you still want to?"

He frowned, as if confused by the question. After all the abuse she had inflicted upon him in the last twenty hours—sexual, psychological, and magical—she was amazed he could think, let alone converse. But then, she had been careful. It would not have served her purposes to have him self-destruct too soon.

She dragged her fingernail down his stomach and slipped it between the buttons of his shirt. He shuddered as the meat between his thighs rose in answer. She drove the nail deeper into him. "Not yet. You have work to do." She had more to say, but the words caught in her throat as Michael Cross rose from the floor.

He stood tall and strong, seemingly unbothered by the external wounds or internal trauma he must be suffering. Gone was the arrogance that had so annoyed her, replaced by a disturbing aura of serenity. Without so much as a glance in her direction, he walked to the edge of the candles and stepped across.

# Chapter One Hundred Three

Wailing cries and foul accusations thundered in the darkness as Michael's consciousness slammed back into his body. The noise hurt. The vitriol was worse. All of it was aimed at Adriana, who still cowered on the bed.

He closed his eyes and squeezed his head with his palms, trying to force his senses into submission. Where was Francesco? The monk had been in control as they crossed the barrier. Why had he vanished once Michael crossed into this hell? The irony was rich. Now more than ever, he needed the monk in control.

Michael opened his eyes to darkness. No wall, no sky, no floor. He had nothing on which to orient, just the unbearable noise and the floating bed. He windmilled his arms to keep from falling, first in one direction and then in the other, then stopped. There was no place to fall from or to.

Adriana screamed and scrambled back against the headboard. She pulled up her knees and arms. He had to get to her, but how could he propel himself forward when there was no floor beneath his feet?

*Faith.*

He would have preferred logic, but there didn't seem to be much of that around.

He took a step. When that worked, he put one foot in front of the other and kept going, picking up speed, nearly tripping from nothing more than uncertainty.

Adriana cowered behind her arms. "Stay away. Don't touch me. The filth. Stay away from me."

When he crawled onto the bed, she kicked him in the head.

"Adriana, stop. It's me, Michael."

She battered him with wild kicks. "You'll die. Stay away. I'll corrupt you. You'll die. You'll die."

He grabbed her arms and pinned them to her side. "I'm not going to die." He hugged her in a fierce embrace. "You're okay. It's going to be okay."

But how could it be when vile accusations spewed at Adriana from every direction? They were lies, of course, but they were hard to ignore.

"We have to get out here." He pushed her away so she could look in his eyes. "Do you understand? We have to go."

She touched the gashes on his face and sobbed. "I've hurt you. You see? You have to stay away."

He grabbed her arms. "You didn't do this. We have to get out of here. Now."

He turned around, expecting to find the line of candles that separated Adriana's mystic prison from the rest of the bedroom. Instead, he saw a wall of fire.

Francesco appeared beside him and whispered into his ear. "It's not real."

Michael didn't respond. He couldn't even move. The inferno popped like gunfire and buffeted him with heat. How could it *not* be real?

Francesco touched Michael's face and whisked him away from the fiery scene to a place of soothing colors and light. "Nothing can harm you if you trust in me."

Michael gazed through the swirling nebula. From this height, the fire below looked insignificant, hardly bigger than Michael's catatonic body, poised on the bed beside Adriana.

"I'm going to burn, aren't I? Why do I always have to burn?"

Francesco turned Michael's face toward his. "You don't. Trust me, Michael."

"I can't. It's too much."

"That's exactly why you must. Faith only counts when it's challenged."

# Chapter One Hundred Four

Adriana shook Michael's shoulders. "Come back. Please. I can't bear it."

*Whore. Liar. Murderer. Filth.*

A thousand voices screamed, and all of them sounded like her voice, her doubts, her truths. The images were worse. Her face in the throes of ecstasy. Her body performing deeds so vulgar they made her want to vomit. Her soul withering in corruption.

She covered her eyes and ears and screamed.

The torment quieted. Fingers pried hers away from her face. Michael's voice whispered in her ear. "All will be well."

She opened her eyes. His face seemed different somehow—gentler, older, wiser—as if he was not Michael, at all. And yet, she trusted him just as much.

He stepped off the bed onto the darkness and opened his arms as, beyond him, the walls of her prison blazed. "Trust me."

How could she possibly climb into his arms and allow him to carry her into an inferno and certain death?

"I'll keep you safe. I promise."

She didn't believe him, not because he would lie to her but because what he promised wasn't possible. As the vile accusations grew louder and the damning images multiplied, Adriana climbed into Michael's arms: Better to burn with him and be done, than to suffer this slow corruption. She buried her face in his chest and sighed with relief as he covered her ear with his hand. The warmth and smell of him made the growing sounds bearable.

"I love you, Michael."

Would God bring them together in Heaven? Would they be reborn together in another life the way the Umbandistas believed? Or were these precious seconds all they had? As the heat stung her arms and the wind from the inferno buffeted her hair, she hugged him tight. If there was a journey to take, in this life or the next, she would take it with him.

She took one last look at Michael then closed her eyes as he stepped into the flames.

The heat vanished. The wind stopped. The accusations silenced.

Adriana opened her eyes and slid out of Michael's embrace onto the bedroom floor. Behind her, a thousand votive candles formed a line in front of Jian Carlo's massive bloodwood bed. In front of her, Jian Carlo shook his fists at Serafina, like a child throwing a fit.

"You said this couldn't happen."

Serafina grabbed Jian Carlo's face. "Be careful, my pet. Be very, very careful." Then she shoved him away.

Adriana gasped. Who was this sniveling creature? Certainly not her husband, the man who had stolen her youth, isolated her from family and friends, controlled every aspect of her life. Who had raped her. "Who *are* you?"

Jian Carlo seemed puzzled, but Serafina just smiled in that reptilian way that had always terrified Adriana as a child.

"He is mine. And you need to be taught to respect what is mine."

"What are you talking about? I've never taken anything from you."

Serafina let her hand fly, but her slap never landed: The old Michael was back, full of righteous fury.

He gripped Serafina's wrist and glared in her face. "Don't you fucking dare." He shoved her into Jian Carlo and reached back for

Adriana. "Come on. We're out of here."

Serafina pushed Jian Carlo forward. "Stop him."

The men tripped and fell in a tangled sprawl. Jian Carlo recovered first, pinned Michael on his back with a forearm against his throat, and pounded Michael in the face.

Adriana screamed.

Michael bumped and jerked, somehow freeing himself from Jian Carlo's hold. For a moment, Adriana thought his greater size and youthful athleticism would win the fight. Then Jian Carlo wrapped Michael's arm in some kind of Jujutsu hold and jolted it with tremendous force. Michael howled in pain as his shoulder popped.

Adriana rushed forward to help. Before she could, Jian Carlo released Michael's arm and pushed it out of the way. He rose on his knees and raised his arms high, ready to strike.

"Stop. Please," she yelled.

But it was too late. Jian Carlo dropped his weight and drove his elbows down into Michael's chest. Bones cracked. He rose again and repeated the strikes. Chest, throat, face. Cracks and thuds. So much blood. Michael used his good arm to cover and deflect, but with one shoulder dislocated, his hips pinned, and his legs locked in place by Jian Carlo's, those elbow strikes kept hitting their targets.

Adriana yanked Jian Carlo's hair, but he kept pounding on Michael. If she didn't find a way to stop him, Jian Carlo would beat him to death.

Rage flooded Adriana's mind and radiated through her body. The emotion was so foreign that it took her a while to recognize it. When she did, it consumed her. She ran to the corner and grabbed one of the wooden canes from Jian Carlo's collection—Brazilian Walnut, one of the hardest woods in the world—and struck the side of his head. The sound cracked like a major league hit, but this wasn't a ball, it was Jian Carlo's skull.

Adriana doubled over, leaned on the cane, and vomited on the floor.

Michael rolled onto his side, moaned and spit blood.

Jian Carlo fell onto his back and clutched his bleeding head.

"You bitch," Serafina screamed.

Adriana stared at the cane in her hand. How could she have hit Jian Carlo with this? She loosened her grip. The cane felt evil. She didn't want it anymore, but it clung to her. Then she heard a sound far more evil than the cane.

Against the wall, Jian Carlo crouched like a wild beast, teeth bared, and glared through bloodshot eyes. He meant to kill her. Michael must have seen it, too, because he cried out and struggled to reach her. He'd never make it in time. But Adriana refused to die. Not with Michael's life still in jeopardy. Not while they still had a chance to live.

As Jian Carlo shoved himself off the wall and lunged toward her, she hefted the cane behind her shoulder. Time slowed. Michael shouted a warning. Jian Carlo roared with blood lust. Serafina screamed. Adriana cracked the cane, with all her might, across Jian Carlo's throat.

# Chapter One Hundred Five

Colors pulsated in time with Francesco's rumbling voice. It was beautiful and hypnotic. Michael wanted to watch it forever, if only Francesco's formerly gentle voice hadn't hardened into a military general commanding him to war.

"On your feet. The barrier is weakening. The sorceress is losing control. This cannot be allowed. The demons want their revenge. If you don't stop them, Serafina won't be the only one who pays."

Michael was too exhausted to care. He wanted to float in the glorious nebula of swirling color, not return to his pulverized body. He tried to focus, but his mind felt soggy.

"I feel bad," he whispered.

"I can help you if you'll just—"

Michael slammed back into his body, ripped from the peaceful nebula. Daggers of pain shot through him. His face throbbed. His shoulder screamed. His ribs exploded in agony with every shallow attempt to breathe. He couldn't see. He wiped the blood from his eyes, took one look at the spinning room, and vomited on the floor.

Francesco had said something about the barrier. Something important. Something Michael had to remember.

He rolled away from the mess and cried out as his dead arm flopped, sending shocks of searing electricity into his shoulder. Dislocated. Had to be. Michael recognized the pain. He vomited again, then braced his dead arm against his waist, and crawled to his feet. This would hurt like a sonofabitch, but it had to be done.

He braced himself against the wall, took a deep breath, and released his arm, crying out as the weight of it pulled on the injured tissue. Nausea hit him again. The room began to spin. Groaning through the pain, he rotated his torso until his back arched and his arm hung behind his hips and gravity stretched the bone from the socket. Gasping through a curse, he straightened his back and pushed through the resistance. The bone popped into the socket.

He slumped against the wall, panted with relief, and surveyed the room.

Jian Carlo lay dead in Serafina's arms. She rocked his corpse and chanted something ominous in Portuguese as the barrier wobbled. The air over the candles pulsated, as if something inside fought to escape.

*The demons want their revenge. If you don't stop them, Serafina won't be the only one who pays.*

Michael was running out of time. And worst of all, Adriana was back on the bed, striking at the air as though fighting off a swooping threat.

*Go now.*

Michael pushed himself away from the wall and headed toward the bed. His torso ached from the broken ribs. His swollen face throbbed. It hurt to breathe. If the barrier repelled him, as it had the first three times without Francesco's protection, he wouldn't survive.

*Doesn't matter.*

He limped away from Serafina and her eerie chant, and stepped across the candles into the anguished wails of a thousand tortured beings. Furies and demons slashed and tore. The innocent suffered. The powerful reveled and the weak were consumed.

A crazed hag flew at Michael, screamed for help as terror contorted a face already marred by boils and rotted teeth. Tufts of stringy hair clung to her patchwork scalp. She clawed at Michael's face, but before her jagged nails reached him, a hideous winged creature with dragon scales and a human face skewered the hag with its talons. She reached for Michael as the demon shoved her into its fetid maw.

Michael screamed.

Francesco's soothing voice cut through the deafening wails. "Nothing can touch you unless you believe."

Michael dropped to his knees. He was well beyond receiving comfort from a spirit. He needed help from a higher power. He bowed his head as his mother had taught him and recited The Lord's Prayer.

"Our Father, who art in Heaven, hallowed be thy name." The words flowed, but his eyelids wouldn't close, forcing him to watch trespasses he could never forgive and would never, *ever* forget.

An abomination with the head and talons of a vulture on the body of a bear charged straight at him.

"Close your eyes, Michael. Close them *now*."

Michael did as he was told and waited for the claws that would rip his throat and split his gut, but the wailing stopped and a blessed silence embraced him. Michael waited, afraid to move yet terrified to remain still.

"These demons cannot hurt you, Michael. Trust in me, and I will guide you through this hell."

Michael nodded. He wanted nothing more than to put his faith and trust in the saintly spirit, but when he opened his mouth to speak, his eyes opened as well. A disturbingly familiar scene took center stage. The girl from his dreams was tied to a stake about to burn.

Colette.

She looked utterly peaceful amid the chaos and gazed at him with such love that he loved her in return.

"You have been touched by God, Philippe." Her soft suede eyes caressed his heart. The melody of her voice sang sweetly through the thunderous noise. "Guard thy gift."

Michael raced to her, and although he felt the wind rush against his face, he did not seem to move. In his place a boy threw himself at her feet.

Philippe.

He sobbed and tore at the knotted rope that bound Colette to the stake, but his small fingers couldn't unravel the knots. He grabbed her calves and climbed up to her knees. "Don't leave me, Colette. Please don't leave."

A farmer yanked Philippe from Colette and tossed him onto the ground.

Michael scrambled to his feet, looking from the pyre to the bed. He had to do something. Colette and Adriana both needed him, but who should he help first?

Révérend Père d'Amboise materialized in front of the pyre, thumped his staff and pointed an accusatory finger at Michael. "You are the one. She dies in your stead."

The wicked priest laughed and hurled his torch onto the pyre, igniting it into flames. Michael shielded his face from the onslaught of heat. When he looked back, it wasn't Colette in the fire, it was Adriana.

He charged forward as a new batch of kindling combusted and sent sparks and flames to block his path. Michael stumbled back and brushed the embers from his sleeves. Laughter mocked his efforts, punctuated by the crack and pop of burning wood. Michael tried to look, but the heat singed his eyes, making them water and blurring his vision.

The blaze wavered making it look less like fire and more like red undulating smoke. From this smoke, a new specter formed, female and formidable, an Amazon with wild black hair and piercing amber eyes.

Serafina.

"Come, Michael." She held out her arms in mock welcome. "We are growing impatient."

Her dark skin and red dress paled into the dingy white flesh and robes of the wicked priest. For a moment, Michael could see both of them together as one, male and female, separated by centuries, united in a common purpose to destroy.

The specter wavered into smoke and revealed Adriana tied to the stake and Philippe clutching her bound waist. Michael felt split in two. Part of him hugged Adriana while the other part watched in horror.

"She burns for us," Philippe cried. "We have to help her."

"No," Michael said. "This isn't real."

As Adriana wept in terror, Michael wasn't so sure.

Despair seeped through his veins like wine through a cloth, spreading everywhere at once and staining him with doubt. He looked up at Adriana tied to the stake, caught in her own personal hell. How many lifetimes of suffering had she endured while waiting for him to do the right thing? How many incarnations had they lived, searching for each other, trying to right this wrong, and failed? How many times had Michael let others pay the price while he ran from the truth?

He was done with this evil. It was time for this nightmare to be put to sleep.

# Chapter One Hundred Six

Serafina reached into the folds of her skirt and removed a piece of chalk, a cigar, a pint of cachaça, and a concave disc of polished bronze that fit neatly in her palm. Moving quickly, she drew a circle around herself and Jian Carlo's body then filled it with smaller circles containing diagrams of intersecting tridents, arrows, crosses, and swords—some straight, some curved, some in the form of waves.

Serafina lit the cigar and blew the smoke around her. She propped the cigar in Jian Carlo's mouth, drank a swig of the cane liquor, sprinkled some to share with the spirits, and tucked the bottle in the crook of Jian Carlo's lifeless arm. The rest of this ritual would have to wait. First, she needed to see what was happening inside the Hell-like prison she had created.

She wiped the bronze disc on her skirt until it gleamed like a mirror and drew a scrying sigil on it with chalk. The surface clouded and swirled like smoke. When it cleared, she saw Michael Cross shielding his face with his arm as hideous creatures clawed and swooped, attacking and devouring one another, not just around Michael but around Serafina, as well.

How was this happening? And why could she hear their screeches and wails?

Scrying spells were only supposed to show images on a disc, but Serafina had appeared inside a flame in the demon prison of her own creation. She was there and here, both places at once.

Michael charged, but the fire around her other self blazed and drove him back. She held out her arms and laughed as they paled and aged into the wrinkled hands and white sleeves of the old French priest.

"Come, Michael. We are growing impatient," her image said inside the fire.

"She burns for us," a boy cried.

Serafina stared into the scrying disc. When she saw Adriana tied to the stake and the peasant boy clinging to her legs, as full of love and fear as he had been for the young French witch, it all came together. Serafina would finally stand on the ashes of those who had vexed her soul for centuries.

She raised her hand to wipe the spell when a new face filled her scrying disc. São Francisco. His church had been her favorite in the Pelourinho District. His sad smile made her feel like a desperate teenager all over again.

"You have strayed far, my sister. Will you not come home?"

Her other self inside the vision laughed. "Home to what? Your church? What did it ever do for me?" She sneered at his shabby robe and bare feet. "What did it do for you? You were once a great warrior, São Francisco. Look at you now."

The spirit sighed, as though greatly disappointed. "Holy wisdom confounds Satan and all his wickedness. You know this, Serafina, yet you close your heart from grace."

Serafina did not like the direction of this conversation nor did she like the saint's feathery touch of peace and hope, the same touch she had felt in her forest terreiro when she was preparing to draw blood for this spell.

"Keep your weakness to yourself, gentle saint, I deal in power, now. Dread and promise wound together, a window of magic to seek, save, and destroy." These were the words that had ridden in on the New Year's Eve tide and landed in Serafina's mind that night on Devil's

Beach. Although she still didn't fully understand them, she knew they were true.

"No, my sister. You will not use this power. It will use you."

Serafina shrugged. Exú had promised her justice and satisfaction in exchange for service and obedience. If his price sometimes grated against her soul, too bad. The power she gained from him justified any suffering she had endured and any suffering she might have to endure in the future.

"Look around you, old man. You're trapped in my work. I am not the pitiful girl who prayed in your church."

She opened her arms to the snarling beasts she had captured not the actual demons from the afterworld but specters of those demons real enough to wound, torture, and kill. All they required was belief, and who could not believe in the face of such terror?

"Adeus, São Francisco. See you on the other side."

# Chapter One Hundred Seven

Michael moaned as the smoke swirled and the dual images of Serafina and the French priest disappeared, leaving Adriana tied to the stake on the burning pyre about to pay for his sins. He couldn't let this happen again.

Francesco blocked his path. "This is not the way."

Michael walked through him.

He reappeared. "You are your own enemy in this, now as before."

Michael walked through him again.

"She made her own decision out of love and devotion, not to condemn you to endless incarnations of guilt."

Colette appeared next to Francesco. "And I'll do it again for as long as it takes, until you're ready to own your gift."

When her image vanished, it felt as if Michael were losing her all over again.

"Hear her," said Francesco.

"I did. She's going to burn, over and over, until I accept my guilt."

"Guilt for what? Being clairvoyant or being a child?"

"Being weak and afraid and—"

Applause and laughter interrupted Michael's confession. Exú had appeared, dressed in his white suit and hat.

"Bravo. Maravilhoso. Keep going, please. I can hardly wait to see how this performance ends." Even the ivory snake, peeking out from under his arm, seemed to laugh.

"This is not entertainment," Michael said. "This is my life."

"Are you sure about that?" Exú brought out his cane and pointed. "Because I thought it was his."

Michael followed the snake's gaze to Philippe as he climbed onto the base of the pyre. Adriana had vanished and Colette was once again tied to the stake. Philippe jabbed at the burning branches, trying to keep them away from her gown, but it was hopeless. Michael knew how this would end. He had seen it in his nightmares. He had lived it in another life.

Francesco placed a comforting hand on Michael's shoulder. "That was her gift."

"Well, it was too damned expensive."

Exú applauded and wiped a tear from his eye. He looked around as if to share his appreciation with another audience member, but not finding any, turned his attention back to Michael. "The acting. The writing. Superb." He dipped his hat in admiration.

Michael advanced toward Exú, ready to kill. But a new visitor appeared in the smoke, golden hair and crystal blue eyes. She slipped her hand into Francesco's. "Be strong, Mikey. Only the courageous may stare into the eyes of guilt and find absolution."

The Lady and The Grandfather, together again—Michael wanted to trust them, but what they asked seemed impossible. Centuries ago, he had spoken the words that had condemned the most important person in his life. Colette had taken the blame and suffered in his place. How could he let her burn again?

"Yes, Michael, how?" Exú asked, reading his mind. He laughed and transformed into the giant war god Michael had glimpsed in the terreiro with his golden scepter and piercing golden eyes.

Michael leaped back in fear. How was he supposed to deal with a demon god?

"No," he shouted to Exú, to Francesco, and even to poor frightened

Philippe, who jumped at the sound and stumbled from the pyre.

At that moment, Michael saw Philippe for who he really was—a child no more capable of betraying Colette than he was of saving her. All he could do was speak what he was compelled to speak, and suffer what he had been forced to suffer.

"Save her. Save her," the boy screeched, as the fire ignited Colette's dress and surged up her body. He turned back to Michael and sobbed, piteously. "You killed her."

It was a horrible sight, but Michael knew it wasn't real. Not this time.

"No," he said. "And neither did you."

As Philippe struggled to understand, his sweet young face contorted through confusion, hurt, and guilt. When he arrived at revelation, the burden in Michael's heart lifted.

"We aren't evil," Michael said, and for the first time, he truly believed it.

The boy's spirit wavered and vanished. Colette and the pyre vanished next, taking with them her shrieks of pain and the pop and roar of burning wood. Wails and snarls filled in the void, accompanied by the thunderous laughter of the demon god.

"You, too." Michael swept his hand for Exú to leave, but the god shed his fearsome image and shrank back into the tiny body of Julius Amodei.

Michael gritted his teeth. He had enough of trickster gods and well meaning spirits. He wanted them gone. He looked from Exú to Francesco, infused his words with two lifetimes of conviction, then yelled, "Get out.

# Chapter One Hundred Eight

Adriana used one end of the bedspread to whip the creatures clawing at her from below and the other as a shield against those swooping from above. Her arms ached. Her heart raced. All she could do was keep fighting and try not to die.

Michael waved at her and yelled. "Jump into my arms."

Had he lost his mind? Couldn't he see the snarling horrors around her? Horrors that for some reason were not harming him.

She swatted another winged monstrosity and dared another glance. Every demon that attacked Michael dissolved into harmless specks of color. Odder still, he hardly seemed to notice.

"Jump."

Talons ripped the bedspread out of her hands and clawed her arm. Blood welled from the wound. Michael held out his arms. She turned away from the attacking demon, crossed her heart, and jumped.

When she landed, he forced her to only look at him. "They're not real. Do you hear me?"

He set her down, waited for her to find her balance on the unseen surface, then grabbed her hand and ran. A goat demon, with daggers where hooves should have been, reared in their path and swiped viciously. Adriana pulled back with a scream.

Michael grabbed her shoulders and pulled her against him. "It's not real." He caught her arms to keep her from fighting both him and the demon. "Trust me."

A dagger stabbed through his throat. Adriana screamed and held out her hands to stop the blood, but there wasn't any. The dagger had passed through without harm and dissolved into specks of color.

"See?"

She nodded, too shocked to speak.

He grabbed her hand. "We have to go. The barrier won't hold."

A wall of fire, larger than the previous one, pulsated as though it might explode at any moment.

She took one step and froze as a grotesque serpent with a woman's face and heaving breasts rose from its coil and poised to strike. Adriana turned away from it and kept her eyes on the goal.

A frail old man threw himself at Michael's feet. "Help me, please."

An enormous wolf-like creature bit into the man's ankles and yanked him between its giant paws. The creature snarled at Michael and spewed thick saliva. When Michael ignored it, the wolf-beast howled in fury and devoured the screaming man.

Michael grabbed Adriana's hand. "We have to hurry."

They picked up speed and raced through lion-vultures, dragon-rats, and badger-vines that whipped and snapped before exploding into dust. The closer they got to the fire barrier, the hotter it became. It felt so real, yet Michael yelled at her to jump.

She landed hard and tumbled onto the wooden floor of Jian Carlo's bedroom. They had survived the inferno but not entirely escaped. The portal remained behind them, pulsating with fire, while in front, Serafina pulled out meters of Jian Carlo's bloody intestines and draped them over her arms and around her neck.

# Chapter One Hundred Nine

Serafina ignored Adriana's scream and focused on her spell.

A blood sacrifice would not be enough, not anymore. Her hold on the demon specters and the mystic prison she had created to contain them grew weaker by the second. She didn't know what the specters would be capable of doing if she failed.

She raised her bloody offering. "Come to me, Exú. Your daughter is in need." When he did not appear, she repeated her cry, again and again, until his magnificent body took form.

Michael shouted. Adriana cried. But Serafina focused only on the Lord of Chaos.

"Help me, Exú."

Instead of helping her to calm the demons and secure the prison, he laughed and changed his form from the stunning warrior she had known into that mocking little man with a white suit and hat. "Why would I help you, little girl? Demons need to eat, and I know how delicious you are."

Serafina shuddered. "But lord—"

He waved his cane. "I know. I promised to help, right?"

She glanced back at the demon specters as they clawed on their side of the portal. How long before they tore their way through it?

Exú chortled, again. "Why so worried? You're about to get exactly what you want. Your mind is just too small to see."

Serafina shook her head and extended her gut-draped arms to point at Adriana and Michael. "Them, you fool. The demons are for them, not me." She gasped. She hadn't meant to belittle him. "Forgive me, Exú, but you promised me justice and satisfaction, not death."

He raised an arched brow and smirked. "One leads to the other, little girl." He tapped the snake cane on his brim and winked. "Adeus, Quimbandeira. See you on the other side."

"No," Serafina screamed, and threw the entrails at Exú's disappearing form.

The demons roared, clawed at the thin veil of the portal, and tore an opening just large enough for the tongue of a serpent-woman to reach through and wrap around Serafina's throat. Serafina dug her fingers into the powerful tongue and pulled with all her might. It cut into her flesh. Other tongues reached through the portal to lap up her blood. Fangs clamped onto Serafina's legs and pulled.

She let go of the garroting tongue and reached out for Adriana or Michael. They watched in horror but did nothing to help her.

She would die as she had lived, as a fighter, as a Quimbandeira, as a woman with courage and power. She would lock her memories of abuse and injustice so deep inside they would travel with her always. No matter how long it took, she would make Adriana and Michael pay.

# Chapter One Hundred Ten

Adriana watched in horror as the demon beasts jumped and snapped at the blood spurting from Serafina's throat. She wanted to stop it—no one deserved this—but her feet were rooted to the floor. The beasts clamped their fangs onto her grandmother's legs and the gruesome tug-of-war began. Beyond the demons, a fireball swirled and grew. Soon, it would reach the portal.

Michael grabbed Adriana's hand. "We have to go."

She followed him through the hall, down the stairs, out the front door, driven by the explosive sounds behind them. The property gates were closed, and while Michael could have climbed over them quickly, Adriana could not. She punched in the gate code, fumbled it, and tried again as the air around them wavered from the heat.

"A little faster, please," Michael said.

She swore, struck the metal box, then punched the numbers again.

The house behind them throbbed from the pressure.

"Adriana…"

"There."

"Go."

He pushed her through the swinging gates as the house detonated. The force propelled him into Adriana, over the street, and into the neighbor's yard where they tumbled across the lawn. Michael covered her body like a shield as pieces of wood and stone rained down on them. A spear of metal stabbed into the ground. The earth shook. The explosion roared. Until it didn't.

The thundering stopped. Projectiles froze in mid-air. Everything hung in suspension.

Adriana stared at the slab of concrete, frozen in the air, meters from slamming into them. "What's happening?"

"No clue."

They scrambled out of the path and stopped as a woeful howl emerged from under the rubble of her house. Growls and crackles added to the sound, growing louder until the noise roared like a thousand vacuum cleaners.

Michael yanked the metal shaft out of the ground and stepped in front of her. Instead of demons charging across the street or the suspended projectiles shooting into them, everything reversed. The cement slab retreated. Bits of wood and stone flew back into the air. The metal shaft yanked out of Michael's hand and, along with everything else, hurled toward the house until every fragment of the estate had been sucked back into the portal. Within seconds, everything was gone.

"Are you alright?" Michael asked, checking Adriana for injury.

All she could do was stare at the scorched land where Jian Carlo's house used to be. The place where she had loved and hoped and longed and suffered. The site of her husband's abuse and her grandmother's twisted revenge. The beautiful prison she had been too afraid to leave.

Gone. As if it had never existed.

# Chapter One Hundred Eleven
## One Week Later

The water felt cool and refreshing on Michael's skin. He could stay here forever, safe and submerged, rolling on the bottom of the Rosario's pool like a lazy seal.

Memories rushed at him—demons, serpents, Carnaval—out of order with flashes of blood, pain, and terror, intermingled with laughter, dancing, and drums. What did it all mean?

The spirits were back, that much he knew. He doubted he would ever get rid of them now that he had seen their true forms. And acceptance? As hard as it had been to accept the powerlessness he had felt as Philippe, it sat easier with him than denial. So many truths had been turned inside out he hardly knew what was real anymore. Maybe he'd figure it out in time.

He and Adriana had entered Serafina's hell on the fourth day of Carnaval and escaped destruction on the first day of Lent, losing an entire day in that demonic place. Sin, penitence, and now peace? How symbolic. What about the centuries in between? Three lives entwined together for lifetimes. Maybe Panchali was right: Some connections were too strong for death to sever.

Michael kicked to the surface, where Adriana's graceful calves dangled in the water, then heaved himself up onto the ledge beside her. "How are you?"

"Good."

"Really?"

She shrugged.

"You're stronger than I am. You know that, right?"

"No," she said. "I don't."

"Well, it's true. I had Francesco to guide me through my emotional crap. You were all alone, getting battered by every hateful accusation Serafina could hurl at you. If that had been me, I would have embraced whatever depravity she wanted to make it stop."

"But I wasn't alone. I had you."

He took her hand and held it to his lips. "And you always will."

"Promise?"

He smiled. "It's been over four hundred years, Adriana. I think you're stuck with me."

# Exú - Epilogue

"Between the beginning and the end there is always the middle."
– Brazilian Proverb

# Epilogue

Exú danced in the night, switching from form to form with every step and reveling in his success. Since his creation, he had pursued his mission with ingenuity and glee as he pushed humanity to the next stage of evolution and self-discovery. Yet even by those standards, Exú felt inordinately pleased.

With Serafina dead, locked across the veil and simmering for revenge, he was almost guaranteed three hundred years of delicious chaos when the Ascending Kali Yuga finally ended and the next epoch in the Cycle of Ages began.

It was Exú's job to spur mankind into its next evolution, but how could he when mankind had stalled so completely from ignorance, hatred, and despair? They needed a common enemy against whom they could rally and unite. Serafina would provide that enemy, once she cracked the veil and set the demons free.

Not the *specters* of demons she had captured in her prison, but *actual* demons.

Exú settled into his trickster form and kissed the head of his ivory snake cane.

He would help her by fueling the flames of resentment, as best he could without crossing into the veil himself, which he was not permitted to do. However, most of his work had already been done when he brought the priest, the witch, and the boy together again.

Exú played a long game and always won.

Hell's endless torment would not shatter the Quimbandeira's mind nor would eternal damnation force her to accept the inevitability of her fate. Serafina Olegario would never succumb, and as much as Michael and Adriana wanted to believe they were safe to live and love, The Lord of Chaos had other plans.

Tender in victory. Vicious in defeat. Everything and everyone was as it should be.

## THE END

# Author's Note

The spark for *Dance Among the Flames* ignited decades ago while writing a screenplay set in Brazil. Being a mixed-race person from multi-cultural Hawaii, I resonated with Brazilian history and spiritualism. I foraged through libraries, dove into the internet, and flew to Rio De Janeiro where the family of my son's Brazilian preschool teacher welcomed me with open arms.

During this time, Yansá and Yemanjá settled into my spirit and infused me with their strength and compassion. Those same qualities were reflected in many of the gods and goddesses I had already connected with in my own Chinese heritage and Japanese ninja studies. Growing up in Hawaii, I also had great respect for our native traditions and spiritual beliefs. This, combined with my parents' Catholic and Lutheran upbringings, made Brazil's blend of East, West, and Indigenous feel natural and empowering.

Long before the Lily Wong mystery-thriller series or my shorter works in horror, fantasy, dystopian, and suspense, I was haunted by the story of a priest, a witch, and a boy reincarnated into a Quimbanda priestess, a California artist, and the granddaughter who bound them together. I saw their visions, heard their voices, and struggled through their quest for empowerment, freedom, redemption, and revenge.

In *Dance Among the Flames*, I strove to illuminate the insidious horror of psychological and physical abuse as well as issues of racial inequity and toxic emotional baggage. I endeavored to explore these issues from a variety of angles to show the light in darkness and the darkness in light.

There were many ways to tell this epic tale, and over the years, I tried them all. In the end, Serafina had her way. She tore at my heart, seduced me with her magic, and stunned me with the depth of her depravity and vengeance. If her journey from good to evil evoked strong emotions, challenged perceptions, and took my readers on a wildly imaginative ride, then I accomplished my goal.

Thank you for reading and for sharing the experience. I'd love to hear from you! Visit my website to send me a message and learn about my Lily Wong mystery-thriller series, the anthologies with my shorter works, and the book club page with discussion questions, recipes, and more. You can also subscribe to my muse-letter for insider news, a free thriller short story, and giveaways. Find it all on my website: ToriEldridge.com.

With thanks and aloha,
Tori

# Acknowledgments

As I mentioned in my note, the spark for *Dance Among the Flames* ignited with my first attempt at screenwriting. Although horrible, I benefited from a painstaking critique by writer/producer Bill La Mond, then took what interested me most about that story and wrote a new screenplay about Quimbanda magic that earned a semi-finalist spot for the Academy Nicholl Fellowship. My deepest thanks to Bill and my sister Vonnie, who begged him to help.

None of this would happened if my husband, Tony, had not encouraged me to write. He's read every manuscript I've ever written and has fostered my career with enthusiasm, patience, and love.

Like Serafina, Michael, and Adriana, *Dance Among the Flames* has lived through many incarnations. In earlier versions, I gained insights and support from my sisters, Christie and Vonnie, my father, my son Stopher (when he grew old enough for the subject matter), Tony, and good friends like Adriana, Dennis, Mary, Kim, and Sheila. Deepest thanks to all.

Later incarnations benefited from the critiques and editorial notes from industry friends like Robert Gleason, Janice Gable Bashman, Thomas F. Monteleone, Tom Colgan, David Morrell, K.J. Howe, and all the agents and editors who offered feedback along the way. You have my ongoing thanks.

I'm blessed with many supportive writing communities and have leaned on and been inspired by hundreds of friends. With *Dance Among the Flames*, I especially want to thank my friends from Horror Writers Association and International Thriller Writers Organization who believed in me and this book throughout its journey. Although I'll kick myself for neglecting important friends, I need to thank Jonathan Maberry, Tim Waggoner, Heather Graham, Sandra Brannan, Cherry Weiner, and Dana Fredsti for championing me and this story over the years.

I'm blessed with a literary agent who values and supports all of my work regardless of the genre, who looks out for my interests, fuels me with her belief, and balances my enthusiasm with wisdom and experience. My deepest mahalo to Nicole Resciniti of The Seymour Agency.

It took a long time to find the perfect way to tell this story and a publishing house through which a magical realism cross-genre book could be shared. I'm so grateful *Dance Among the Flames* found its home with Running Wild Press, a publisher for stories that don't fit neatly in a box. Founder Lisa Kastner fell in love with my dark Brazilian tale and helped me make it the best story it could be.

Last of all, my profound thanks to you, the reader, for joining me on this journey as we *Danced Among the Flames*.

# About the Author

Tori Eldridge the Anthony, Lefty, and Macavity Awards-nominated author of the Lily Wong mystery-thriller series. Her shorter works appear in horror, fantasy, dystopian, and other literary anthologies, including the inaugural reboot of *Weird Tales* magazine. Her screenplay *The Gift* earned a semi-finalist spot for the Academy Nicholl Fellowship. Before writing, Tori performed as an actress, singer, dancer on Broadway, television, and film.

<u>Connect Online</u>

ToriEldridge.com
twitter/ @torieldridge
instagram/ @writer.tori
facebook/ @torieldridgeauthor

# Past Titles

American Cycle by Lawrence Beckett
Whales Swim Naked by Erick Gethers
Running Wild Stories Anthology, Volume 4
Running Wild Novella Anthology, Volume 4

# Upcoming Titles

Running Wild Stories Anthology, Volume 5
Running Wild Novella Anthology, Volume 5
Take Me With You by Vanessa Carlisle
Frontal Matter Two by Suzanne Samples
Blue Woman/Burning Woman by Lale Davidson
Antlers of Bone by Taylor Sowden
The Rerembered by Dwight L. Wilson
Mickey: Surviving Salvation by Robert Shafer

Running Wild Press publishes stories that cross genres with great stories and writing. Our team consists of:

Lisa Diane Kastner, Founder and Executive Editor
Barbara Lockwood, Editor
Peter A. Wright, Editor
Rebecca Dimyan, Editor
Benjamin White, Editor
Andrew DiPrinzio, Editor
Lisa Montagne, Director of Education

Learn more about us and our stories at www.runningwildpress.com

Loved this story and want more? Follow us at www.runningwildpress.com, www.facebook/runningwildpress, on Twitter @lisadkastner @RunWildBooks